**"Come over he** [barcode] **murmured, the** [D0756178] **face pure challe** **sure of what you want."**

He expected the invitation to frighten Chloe off. She could tell from the look on his face. And for a moment it did, freezing all coherent thought. She sucked in a breath, delivered necessary oxygen to her brain. She knew in that moment this was the only opening she was ever going to get with Nico. She either seized it or wondered *what if?* forever.

She shrugged her shoulders and let the towel fall to the chair. Got to her feet and walked over to him.

He didn't resist, but he didn't move to meet the kiss either. She found his lips with hers. Hard, betraying none of that inherent sensuality that was so much a part of him. She thought for a terrifying instant he was going to reject her. Then a soft curse escaped him, his arms clamped around her waist and he lifted her astride him, his hands cupping her bottom in his palms. She had just enough time to take a deep breath before he took her mouth in a hard, demanding kiss that slammed into her senses.

*Demanded everything.*

As if it would make her run. As if he *wanted* her to run.

Instead, it made her skin burn.

# The Powerful Di Fiore Tycoons

*Ruthless in the boardroom
and masters in the bedroom!*

Nico, Lazzero and Santo Di Fiore
saw their lives crumble when their father bankrupted
the family and their mother abandoned them.
Since then these three brothers have worked tirelessly
to rise to the top of their game and become
powerful tycoons envied the world over.

Having lost everything once,
they now have everything they could ever desire…
except the women they can't resist!

Read Nico and Chloe's festive story in

*Christmas at the Tycoon's Command*

Available now

And don't miss Lazzero and Santo's stories

Coming soon!

# CHRISTMAS AT THE TYCOON'S COMMAND

BY
JENNIFER HAYWARD

First Published in Great Britain 2017
By Mills & Boon, an imprint of HarperCollins*Publishers*
1 London Bridge Street, London, SE1 9GF

© 2017 Jennifer Drogell

ISBN: 978-0-263-92550-0

Our policy is to use papers that are natural, renewable and recyclable products and made from wood grown in sustainable forests. The logging and manufacturing processes conform to the legal environmental regulations of the country of origin.

Printed and bound in Spain
by CPI, Barcelona

**Jennifer Hayward** has been a fan of romance since filching her sister's novels to escape her teenage angst. Her career in journalism and PR, including years of working alongside powerful, charismatic CEOs and travelling the world, has provided perfect fodder for the fast-paced, sexy stories she likes to write—always with a touch of humour. A native of Canada's East Coast, Jennifer lives in Toronto with her Viking husband and young Viking-in-training.

Visit the Author Profile page
at millsandboon.co.uk for more titles.

For my editor, Nic.

I couldn't have written this without
your guidance and inspiration.

You are amazing and I look forward to
working on many great books together.

# CHAPTER ONE

SHE WAS NOT losing this one.

Chloe Russo fixed her gaze on the bright yellow taxi that had appeared like an apparition from heaven in the ferociously snarled First Avenue traffic, its lit number her only chance at salvation in the monsoon that had descended over Manhattan.

Shielding her eyes from the driving rain, she stepped a foot deeper into the layers of honking, snarling traffic and jammed her hand high in the air. The driver of a Bentley sounded his horn furiously as he swerved to avoid her, but Chloe, heart pounding, kept her eyes glued to the taxi driver's face, willing him to stop.

The taxi slid to a halt in front of her in a cacophony of screeching horns and spraying water. Heart soaring, she waded through the giant puddle that stood between her and victory, flung the door of the taxi open and slid inside, reeling off Evolution's Fifth Avenue address with a request to step on it that made the cabbie roll his eyes.

"Lady," he muttered caustically, "have you *looked* outside?"

She'd been *standing* in it for half an hour, she wanted to scream. While thirty-five of his coworkers had passed her by—she knew because she'd counted every one of them.

But picking a fight with the last remaining cab driver in Manhattan seemed unwise, given her present situation.

She was late for her first board meeting as the director of Evolution's fragrance division. An inauspicious start.

Her teeth chattered amid a chill that seemed to reach bone-deep. She pushed off the hood of her raincoat and mopped her face with a tissue, thankful for her waterproof mascara. Let out a defeated sigh. She should have left earlier. Had forgotten taxis on a rainy day in Manhattan were akin to spotting a western lowland gorilla in the wild. But in truth, she'd been dreading today and everything about it.

Her cell phone vibrated in her bag. She rooted around to find it as a loud pop song joined the symphony of honking horns. Fingers curling around the sleek metal, she pulled it out and answered it before her grumpy driver deposited her back into the downpour.

"I just landed," her sister, Mireille, announced. "How are you? How was your flight? Did you get settled in okay? It's *so* amazing to have you back in New York."

The verbal torrent pulled a smile from her lips. "Good, good and yes. Although it just took me half an hour to get a taxi. I'm soaked to the bone."

"You've been living in Europe too long." Her sister's voice lowered to a conspiratorial whisper. "Of course, I'm really calling to see how your dinner with Nico went. I've been dying to know. Uncle Giorgio has himself all in a dither with this campaign of his to unseat him."

Chloe bit her lip. Nico Di Fiore, the new CEO of Evolution, her family cosmetic company, was a loaded subject of late. Her late father's godson, Nico had been appointed CEO upon her parents' deaths last spring according to the terms of her father's will, assuming a position that should have been her uncle Giorgio's. He had also been appointed financial regent for Chloe and Mireille until they reached the age of thirty, an unexpected and unacceptable development that had been the last straw for Chloe, because it meant four years of *him* in her life.

"I didn't have dinner with him." Her offhand tone hid the apprehension dampening her palms. "I wanted to keep things professional. I suggested we meet tomorrow instead—on my first day back."

Mireille drew in a breath. "You *blew* Nico off for dinner?"

"It wasn't like that." Except it had been exactly like that.

There was a pregnant pause on the other end of the line. "That really wasn't wise, Chloe."

"He *summoned* me to have dinner with him," she came back defensively. Just like he'd *summoned* her home from Paris, where she'd been perfectly happy. "This is *our* company, not his. Isn't it driving you crazy having him in charge?"

"It was what Father wanted." Mireille sighed. "I know Evolution's your baby—far more than it is mine. That Uncle Giorgio has you all wound up, but you need to face reality. Nico is leading the company. I don't know what's going on between you two, but you're going to have to come to terms with it."

"There's nothing going on between us." Hadn't been since Nico had broken her heart far too many years ago to remember now. And she *had* been attempting to do exactly that—to process this new reality that had seen Nico take over Evolution when her parents had been killed in a car crash in Tuscany six months ago, turning her life upside down in the process. But she couldn't quite seem to get there.

Evolution's stately, soaring, gold-tinted headquarters rose majestically in front of her as the taxi turned onto

Fifth Avenue. A fist formed in her chest, making it hard to breathe.

"I have to go," she murmured. "It's the board meeting tonight."

*"Right."* A wealth of meaning in her sister's tone. "Better you than me." As a junior executive in Evolution's PR department, Chloe's younger sister was not a member of the board. "Promise me you won't fight with him, Chloe."

"That," she said grimly, "is impossible. I love you and I'll see you tomorrow."

She handed the taxi driver the fare as he pulled to a halt in front of the building. Slid out of the car and stepped onto the sidewalk, teeming with its usual wall-to-wall pedestrian traffic huddled under brightly colored umbrellas.

A frozen feeling descended over her as she stood staring up at the giant gold letters that spelled out *Evolution* on the front of the building. Her parents—Martino and Juliette Russo—had spent two decades building Evolution into a legendary cosmetics brand. They had been the heart and soul of the company. *Of her.*

She hadn't been in the building since she'd lost them, buried in work in the Paris lab. The thought of going in there now without them present seemed like the final admission they were gone, and she couldn't quite seem to do it.

The crowd parted like a river around her as she stood there, heart in her mouth, feet glued to the concrete. A woman in a Gucci raincoat finally jolted her out of her suspended state, crankily advising her to "move on." Her fingers clutched tight around her bag, she made her way through the glass doors, presented the security guard with her credentials and rode the elevator to the fiftieth floor, where Evolution's executive offices overlooked Central Park.

A slim, blond-haired woman with trendy glasses pounced on her as she emerged into the elegant cream marble reception area. "Clara Jones, your new PA," the blonde introduced herself, relieving Chloe of her dripping raincoat in the same breath. "You're the last to arrive. Nico is—well, you know..." she said, giving Chloe a meaningful look. "He likes to start on time."

Her heart crawled into her throat. "I couldn't get a cab."

"It *is* awful out there."

Clara led Chloe down the hall toward the large, plush conference room with its expansive view of a wintry, lamplit Central Park. "Nico gave me your presentation. It's ready to go."

Now if only she was. Memories deluged her as she stood surveying the crowded, warmly lit room full of Evolution board members and directors enjoying a glass of wine and hors d'oeuvres before the meeting began. Of her father manning the seat at the head of the table that Nico now would as the chairman of the board. Of her mother swanning around, captivating the executives with her sparkling wit and charm.

Her stomach swam with nerves. She was a *scientist*. Her mother had been a self-made genius with a larger-than-life personality who'd created a multibillion-dollar empire out of a tiny bath products company she'd founded to serve her husband's financial clientele. Chloe was far more comfortable in the lab creating beautiful things than presenting to a stiff-suited board like her mother had been. But this was her job now. A necessary evil.

Any nerves about her presentation, however, faded to the background as Nico spotted her. Clad in a sleek, dark gray Tom Ford suit, the white shirt and silver tie he wore beneath it making the most of his dark good looks and olive skin, he was faultlessly elegant. It was when she lifted her gaze to his that she realized just how much trouble she was in.

His lips set in a flat line, jaw locked, smoky gray gaze full of thunderclouds, he was *furious*. Fingers of ice crept up her spine as he murmured something to the board member he was speaking with, then set his tall, impressive frame into motion, eating up the distance between them. Clara took one look at his face, muttered something about checking the AV equipment and disappeared.

Chloe's heart ricocheted in a hard drumbeat against her ribs as Nico came to a halt in front of her. She tipped her head back to look up at him, refusing to reveal how much he intimidated her. With his leonine dark head, cold, slate blue eyes and cheekbones at forty-five degrees, he couldn't quite be called handsome in the traditional sense because he was far too hard for that.

His wide, full mouth made up for that lack of softness, however—lush and almost pouty when he wanted to seduce a response out of the person in question. Which was not now.

Her heart battered up against her chest in another wave of nerves at the dark fire in his eyes. At the realization that any hope she'd had that she'd developed an immunity to him after seven years in Europe had been utter self-delusion. That the man she'd once thought had been *the one* had hardened into a ruthless, sapphire-edged version of himself she couldn't hope to know.

She might hate him, she *did* hate him for teaching her the cruel lesson he had, but he was still the most potently gorgeous male she'd ever encountered.

"I'm sorry," she murmured, forcing the words past a constricted throat. "I forgot it's impossible to get a cab in Manhattan on a rainy day."

His stormy gaze darkened. "We'll discuss it afterward,"

he said quietly, so quietly it sent her pulse skittering into a dead run. "Take ten minutes to say hello and we'll start."

She nodded. Forced herself through the round of small talk, latching gratefully on to her uncle Giorgio, Evolution's flamboyant director of marketing, before Nico called the meeting to order.

An undeniably compelling speaker, he outlined the big picture as Evolution headed into its first Christmas season without its cofounders. Investor confidence was shaky, he observed candidly—the company's stock price in trouble—with the world worried the loss of Juliette Russo, the creative force of the company, would strike a death knell for Evolution.

Chloe's heart sank as he went on to detail the keys for a successful path forward. It wasn't true that Evolution was a fading star. Her parents had built a company rich with talent. Vivre, the line of fragrances Chloe had spent three years developing with one of the most brilliant French perfumers, *would* be the hit Christmas product the company needed. But, she reminded herself, the world didn't know that yet.

Nico called her up last in the parade of directors presenting their holiday season highlights, after the head of the skincare division had made a big splash with his luxurious, all-natural skincare line. She suspected Nico did it on purpose.

She rose on legs the consistency of jelly, smoothed the pencil skirt of her still-damp suit and moved to the front of the room. Hands clammy, mouth full of sawdust, she clicked the remote to begin the presentation. Focusing on her passion for her work, she began. Too fast and clunky in her delivery at first, she gradually relaxed as she explained her vision for Vivre and the aspirational campaign that would accompany it. It will, she told those assembled, redefine how beauty is framed in a world that badly needs inspiration.

Instead of salivating over her exciting launch plan that featured celebrities who would spread the inspirational message, the board members peppered her with questions.

*"Isn't the perfume market oversaturated?"*

*"Your mother could have sold this, but can you?"*

*"What about all the workplaces that are going scent-free?"*

*"Wouldn't it be better to focus on the all-natural products that are dominating the market?"*

She took a deep breath and answered the questions the best she could. She had been working with her mother in the lab ever since she was a little girl, she told them. She knew where the magic was. She already had her own signature fragrances to back her up. And the celebrity endorsement she had planned for the Vivre campaign would help her create the buzz she needed.

When she ran out of answers and needed big-picture help, she looked to Nico because she didn't have that backup in her head. But instead of coming to her rescue, he sat back in his chair, arms crossed over his chest, and focused that glittering gray gaze of his on her.

Her stomach swooped. He was punishing her. The bastard. She looked at the director of the skincare division, who stared blankly back at her, clearly not about to help either and diminish his own product line. A trickle of perspiration ran down her back.

Finally, her uncle stepped in with a passionate rebuttal, reminding the board of the founding tenants Evolution was built on—luxury perfumes like Vivre that had taken the world by storm. But by then, her credibility was in tatters.

Answering the final question, she sat down red-faced.

\* \* \*

Nico held on to his temper by the threads it had been hanging from all evening as the last board member disappeared toward the elevators and home.

"My office," he murmured in Chloe's ear. *"Now."*

Head tossed back, she stalked out of the room in front of him and down the hall toward his office. It would be difficult, he surmised, eyeing her curvaceous backside, for her to find it when she had no idea where it was.

She came to a sliding halt in front of the sophisticated lounge that was a new addition to the executive floor, her gaze moving over the photos of the company's cofounders gracing the walls.

"What happened to my father's office?" she demanded, spinning on her heel, dark eyes flashing. "Or couldn't you even leave that alone?"

"I didn't think it was appropriate for me to assume it," he murmured, directing her down the hall toward his office with a hand at her back. Something in him hadn't been able to simply wipe his mentor from existence by redecorating a space that had always been quintessentially Martino's. But he didn't feel the need to explain his actions to Chloe at this particular moment. He was barely resisting the urge to strangle her for the ever-present recalcitrance that had pushed him one step too far this time.

He closed the door to his office with a decisive click. Strode to the window and counted to ten because that was what Chloe did to him. Pushed buttons he didn't even know he had. Elicited emotions he had always had to exert the most extreme self-control to silence. Because Chloe was the chink in his armor. The one weakness he couldn't seem to kick. And wanting her had always been a swift trip to hell.

"You were punishing me, weren't you?" Her voice drifted over his shoulder, trembling with rage.

He turned around and leaned against the sill. Studied the fury on her beautiful face. The way her delicate features had settled into an intriguing beauty that was impossible to ignore. The arms she had crossed over her firm, high breasts, the feet defiantly planted apart in her haute couture Parisian suit.

She was a study in rebellion. It was insane the fire that rose up inside him, the desire to crush those lush lips into submission under his own, to shock her out of the self-protective state she'd descended into since her parents' passing. To unearth *some* sign the passionate Chloe he knew still existed.

But having her had never been an option for him. He had conditioned it out of himself a long time ago because he'd had to. Just like he'd eliminated every other undesirable need he'd had in a life that had never had any room for self-indulgence.

He pointed at the chair in front of his desk. "Sit."

She crossed her arms tighter over her chest. "I'd prefer to stand."

*"Bene."* He took a seat on the corner of his desk, eyes on her. "I hung you out to dry in there because you needed to learn a lesson."

"That you are the king of the castle," she challenged, eyes flashing.

"Yes," he said evenly. "I am. And the sooner you realize it, the easier this is going to be on both of us. It was your father's wish, Chloe, that I run this company. And while I don't intend for one minute to deny you your place at the center of it—in fact, my intention is the opposite—you need to get that particular fact straight in your head."

Her mouth curled. "Giorgio should be the head of this company, not you."

"That's why your father made me second in command a year ago?" he rebutted coolly. "Think rationally."

She flicked a wrist at him, ebony eyes snapping with heat. "Because you somehow *brainwashed* him into it. How else would his will have been so *perfectly* in order when he died? Because it was your master plan, of course."

A low curl of heat unfurled inside him. "Watch it," he said softly. "You're starting to sound like your very bitter, very deluded uncle. Martino put me in control of Evolution in the event something happened to him and Juliette because he knew Giorgio would drive the company into the ground with his big spending ways. Your uncle has neither the business brain nor the common sense to run Evolution."

"That's a lie," she breathed. "He is widely reputed to be one of the most brilliant marketers there is. And don't forget," she added, eyes darkening with old wounds, "I have firsthand knowledge of how ambitious you are, Nico. Success is the only thing that matters to you."

"And *that*," he said, emphasizing the word, "is the problem between us, Chloe. I am grieving, too. We are *all* grieving. And yet you are fixated on ancient history when it has no place here. You need to grow up and move on."

Her eyes widened. "I am *not* bringing the personal into this."

"Aren't you?" He slid his gaze over her fire-soaked cheeks. "That's why you've spent the last six months hiding away in Paris instead of taking your place in this company? So I finally had to *order* you back? Because there's nothing personal here?"

A muscle pulled tight at the corner of her mouth. "You have *such* an overinflated ego. Vivre wasn't ready."

"So you said," he responded quietly. "My contacts in the lab say it was ready six months ago. That you have been stalling, perfecting imperfections that don't exist."

He fixed his gaze on hers. "Hide from the world or hide from me, Chloe, both of them are ending now."

She glared at him. "I *hate you*."

"I know." He'd decided a long time ago that was preferable in this relationship of theirs.

She drew a visible breath that rippled through her slim body as she collected her composure. "Have you reviewed my launch plan, then? Since Vivre is so clearly *ready*?"

"Yes," he murmured, picking it up off his desk. "*This* is what I think of it."

Her eyes went as big as saucers as he tossed the sheaf of papers into the wastebasket. "What *are* you doing?"

"Putting it where it belongs." He shook his head, his hands coming to rest on the edge of the desk. "You have no business case in that plan. All you have is fluffy, over-inflated, feel-good market research that relies on your legacy to sell it. A *fifty-million-dollar* launch plan in which the linchpin for success turns on a celebrity endorsement program you don't have a hope in hell of attaining."

Her chin lifted. "That is a *brilliant* launch plan, Nico. I have a *master's* degree, in case you had forgotten. Maybe I should have been more detailed with the numbers—and I *can* be because I was focusing on the big picture—but the consumer testing has been off the charts for Vivre. One of the most important French perfumers in the industry thinks it's inspired—as brilliant as anything my mother has done. *This* is the product that is going to prove Evolution is back this Christmas, not some generic all-natural skincare line you couldn't distinguish from any of its competitors."

He surveyed her flushed, determined face. The passion that had been missing for months. "I am backing Emilio's skincare line for the holiday push. I agree with the board."

Her jaw slackened. "That's *insane*. This company was

built on our signature perfumes. People are looking for an inspirational campaign from us. That's what we do— *we inspire*."

"And you," he pointed out, "delivered the product late. Even if I did approve the campaign, it's the beginning of October. You'd never get it into market in time."

She faltered for the first time. Because he was right and she knew it. He was not, however, oblivious to the fact that Chloe was a genius. That she had her mother's touch. That the success of Evolution rested on her shoulders as Juliette, her mother, had known it would. But sinking fifty million dollars into an impossible-to-execute holiday campaign would be foolhardy when the company desperately needed a Christmas hit.

"Work with the sales and marketing team," he said. "Show me the numbers. Lay the timeline out for me so I know it can work. And," he qualified, "and this is a big *but*, the only way I'd ever green-light a launch plan like this is if you can supply the big-name celebrities you've earmarked up front. Which is very unlikely given the hit the brand has taken. So, consider a plan B."

"There is no plan B," she said flatly. "I chose those celebrities because of their personal history. Because they embody the spirit of the perfumes. I created them with them in mind. If I can talk to them, if they can experience the fragrances, *understand* the message I'm trying to tell, I know I can convince them to do it."

He absorbed the energy that surrounded her. The unshakable belief in what she had created. And wondered if she realized the campaign was about *her*. About the battle she had always fought within herself to shine in the shadow of her charismatic mother and stunning sister.

"Prove me wrong, then," he challenged. "Give me what I'm asking for. But know this, Chloe. Your flashy degree is worth nothing in the real world until you prove you know how to use it. *I* can help you do that. Your father *asked* me to provide that mentorship to you. But I have better things to do than babysit you if you're not willing to learn."

*"Babysit?"* The word dripped with scorn. "You're not satisfied with ruling me financially? Now you need to master me professionally?"

His mouth tightened. "That is exactly the kind of attitude I'm talking about. Every time I try to forge a working relationship between us, you shut me down. You're mysteriously lost in the lab. You're too busy to talk. That ends now."

"I don't do that," she rejected. "I've been extremely busy."

"Unfortunate for you tonight." He rubbed a palm over his jaw. "Here's how it's going to work from here on out. I'll give you the rest of the week to get settled in. To iron out your launch plan. You come back to me with the details and we decide how to move forward.

"Second, we'll start having regular morning meetings beginning next week. I can teach you the business end of things and we can check in with each other as needed. That's what your father did with me. And," he added, pausing for emphasis, "you *will* attempt to listen rather than fight with me at every turn."

A stony look back.

"Finally," he concluded, "we will begin building your profile with the press. The PR department is going to schedule a training session for you."

Her chin dipped. "I'm terrible with the media. I either clam up or say things I shouldn't. Let Giorgio do it."

"Giorgio is not the future of this company. *You* are. You'll learn to do better."

Resistance wrote itself in every line of her delicate

body, her dark eyes shimmering with fire. "Are you done, then? With all your ground rules? Because I'm exhausted and I'd like to go home. The time difference is catching up with me."

"One more," he said softly, eyes on hers. "I am your boss, Chloe. Hate me all you want in private, but in public you *will* show me the respect I'm due."

# CHAPTER TWO

C‍HLOE WAS STILL fuming over her encounter with Nico the next morning as she woke up to brilliant sunshine in her cozy townhouse on the Upper East Side. It was almost as if last night's monsoon had never happened. Everything looking sparkly and brand-new on a crisp fall day that was perfection in Manhattan.

A grimace twisted her mouth. Now if only she could say the same for her combative showdown with Nico.

She slid out of bed, threw on a robe and made herself some coffee in an attempt to regain her equilibrium. Java in hand, she wandered to the French doors that looked out over the street and drank in the sleepy little neighborhood she now called home.

A splendor of gold and rust, the vivid splash of color from the changing leaves of the stately old trees was the perfect contrast to the cream stuccoed townhouses that lined the street. She and Mireille had fallen in love with the neighborhood one Sunday afternoon on a walk through the village. Her father had bought them each a townhouse side by side, Chloe's in anticipation of her return home to New York to take her place at Evolution, Mireille, while she studied public relations at school.

*We know you're too independent to come home and live with us*, her father had teased. *But we want you close.*

A wave of bitter loneliness settled over her. She wrapped her arms around herself, coffee cup cradled against her chest. Usually she managed to keep the hollow emptiness at bay—burying herself in her lab until she crawled into bed at night. But this morning it seemed to throb from the inside out, scraping her raw.

She missed her parents. So desperately much she had no idea how to even verbalize it. How to release the emotion that had been stuck inside her so long lest it swamp her so completely when she did, she would never emerge whole. Because her parents had been her glue, her innocence, the force that had shielded her from the world. And now that they were gone, she didn't know how to restore the status quo. Didn't know how to reset herself. Didn't know how to *feel* anymore.

She was *scared* to feel.

Her mother had been her best friend. A bright, vivid star that bathed you in its warmth—their shared passion bonding them from their earliest days. Her father, the wisest, smartest man she'd ever known, with a heart so big it had seemed limitless. He would be furious if he saw her like this, because Nico was right—she had been hiding, from the world and from herself.

She hugged her arms tighter around her chest as she watched the neighborhood stir to life. She needed to move on. Nico had also been right in that. Paris was no longer her life. New York was now. Assuming the role her mother had groomed her for, even if the thought of doing so without her was one she couldn't even contemplate.

Jagged glass lined her throat. *Baby steps*, she told herself, swallowing hard. She could do this. She just needed to take baby steps. And guard against her feelings for Nico while she did it because her instinctive response to him last night had revealed too much.

She wasn't a teenager anymore in the throes of a wicked crush, overwhelmed by a sexual attraction she'd had no hope of fighting. The connection she and Nico had shared hadn't been special as she'd thought it had been. He'd killed any romantic illusions she'd had about him dead the night he'd slept with another woman and made it clear they were over.

That she still found him compelling was an indication of her weakness when it came to him, one she needed to stamp out dead now that she was back in New York.

Because like it or not, he *was* her boss. The man who could green-light or kill her dream. Either she could keep fighting that fact, fighting *him* as she had been for the past six months, or she could prove him wrong. And since launching Vivre in time for Christmas, preserving her legacy, was all that mattered, her decision was clear.

Her first step was to dust herself off after her disastrous performance last night and make her first day back in New York a success.

A determined fire lighting her blood, she dressed in her most stylish cherry-colored suit, walked to work amid the crisp autumn glory and spent the morning meeting with Giorgio about Vivre.

She was excited to discover the splashy Christmas launch in Times Square she had planned was doable, but the tight deadlines to complete the advertising campaign made her head spin. It meant she would have to have her celebrities secured within the next week, their advertising spots filmed shortly thereafter, which might actually be impossible given how slow those things worked.

But it was doable. She focused on that as she spent the rest of the day nailing down the details Nico had requested so he would have nothing to question when she presented him with the revised plan. Then she took Mireille out for dinner at Tempesta Di Fuoco, Stefan Bianco's hot spot in Chelsea, as she turned her attention to her most pressing issue.

Celebrities were her sister's world. Socially connected in a way Chloe had never been with her sparkling, extroverted personality and undeniable beauty that mirrored their mother's icy blonde looks, there were few people Mireille didn't know in Manhattan.

Her sister refused to talk business until they had exotic martinis sitting in front of them. "All right," she said, sitting back with her drink in hand. "Tell me about the campaign."

Chloe cradled her glass between her fingers. "It's about an authentic beauty, as you know. About expressing your true colors. But we're approaching it from a different point of view with each perfume. One, for example, is about moving past your physical limitations. Another about incorporating a difficult past as part of what makes you unique. *Irreplaceable.*"

"I love it," said Mireille, looking intrigued. "It's brilliant. Give me your list."

Chloe took a deep breath. "Number one. Carrie Taylor." The supermodel had made it big as a plus-size model and was gracing the cover of every magazine on the newsstands.

Mireille cocked a brow. "You aren't reaching high, are you?"

"I told you I was. Second is Lashaunta." A pop singer who had recently had a string of chart-topping records, she had forged a successful career despite a prominent scar on her face. Or perhaps *because* of it, as it gave her such a distinctive look.

"Next?"

"Desdemona Parker." A world-class athlete, she'd made

it to the top of her sport despite the inherited disease that had nearly ended her career. "And finally," Chloe concluded, "Eddie Carello for our men's fragrance."

Mireille blinked. "You're kidding."

"He's a survivor," Chloe said quietly. "He grew up in the projects. He perfectly embodies the spirit of Soar."

Mireille let out a husky laugh. "I can see why Nico cut you down to size. He's not wrong about the brand taking a hit. It isn't going to be an easy sell. Do you have backups?"

Chloe listed them. "But I need my A list. It's Nico's nonnegotiable."

Her sister pursed her lips. "I can help with Lashaunta and Carrie. You're out of luck with Desdemona and Eddie, however. Eddie is near untouchable, he's too hot right now. Desdemona, I have no connections to, and neither does anyone in our PR department. We're not big in sports."

Chloe's face fell.

"Lazzero, however," her sister mused, "might be able to help. I read in the paper this morning Eddie is attending the launch party for Blaze, Lazzero's new running shoe, at Di Fiore's tomorrow night. Desdemona has an endorsement deal with Supersonic. She might be there, too."

Chloe chewed on her lip. Her father had been godfather to all the Di Fiore brothers when his good friend Leone had died, including Nico's middle brother, Lazzero, and youngest, Santo. But only Nico had ended up at Evolution after her father had taken him on as his protégé. Lazzero and Santo had put themselves through school on sports scholarships, going on to found one of the hottest sportswear companies on the planet in Supersonic, with an investment from Martino to help them along.

Chloe's lashes lowered. "I wanted to do this by myself. To prove to Nico I can."

"Lazzero is not cheating. Lazzero is being *resourceful*."

Chloe tapped her fingernails on the table. "Do you think he'd let us attend the party?"

"There's only one way to find out." Mireille picked up her phone and made the call.

"Lazzero, darling," she purred. "I need you."

Whatever was said on the other end of the phone made her laugh. "I do so call you just to chat. But right now, Chloe and I need a favor. We need an invite to your party tomorrow night to chat up Eddie Carello and Desdemona Parker for an influencer deal."

Mireille frowned at Lazzero's response. "Oh, she isn't? That's too bad. Eddie is, though, right?"

Chloe's stomach dropped. *No Desdemona.*

Mireille nodded at whatever Lazzero said in response. "It won't be me, I have plans. It will be Chloe. And I will pass the message on. You are, as usual, a doll."

Chloe eyed her as she signed off. "What did he say?"

"Desdemona is out of town, but he's emailing me and her agent and making the introduction. As for the party, it's a yes. He'll leave your name at the door." A wicked smile curved her sister's lips. "He said to wear a short dress. Eddie likes legs."

And so that was how Chloe found herself the following night passing her credentials to the big lug in a dark suit at the door of Di Fiore's, the upscale bar in midtown Manhattan Lazzero and Santo ran as part of their sports conglomerate.

Clad in the very short, rose-gold dress Mireille had lent her and surrounded by the trendy crowd, Chloe felt hopelessly out of place.

"You can come this way," said the lug, plucking Chloe out of the lineup and ushering her through a side door and into the party that was already in full swing. There he handed her over to a hostess who led her through a crush of people to where Lazzero held court at the bar. He was supremely sophisticated all in black. Chloe had always found his hawk-like profile and dark eyes highly intimidating. Unlike Nico, who had intrigued her from the very beginning with his quiet, serious demeanor—as if the weight of the world had been placed on his shoulders.

Lazzero, however, made an effort to put her at ease, handing her a glass of wine and chatting idly with her about what she and Mireille were up to. Having not had time to eat, Chloe felt the wine go straight to her head, making the crowd seem much less unapproachable.

After a few minutes, Lazzero nodded toward the end of the bar. "Eddie at three o'clock."

Her pulse gave a flutter as she turned to find the famous bad-boy actor lounging his lean, rangy, jean-clad body against the bar while a group of rather exquisite women attempted to capture his attention. Her stomach fell. How was she supposed to compete with that?

She turned back to Lazzero. Ran a self-conscious hand over her hair. She wasn't going to get another opportunity like this. She just had to *do* it. "Do I look okay?"

His dark eyes glittered with amusement. "Affirmative. Ten minutes, Chloe. That's all you've got. I have a rule at my parties—no one hassles you. It makes them want to come back."

She moistened her lips. "Got it."

He eyed her. "Are you sure you want to do this? He's a bit of a piece of work."

"Yes."

He pressed another glass of wine into her hand. "Go."

Chloe took a sip of the wine, sucked in a deep breath and started walking, forcing herself to trace a straight line toward the actor before she chickened out. The girls around him looked down their noses at her as she approached. Used to this treatment when she was with Mireille, Chloe ignored them, walked right up to Eddie and stuck out her hand. "Eddie, I'm Chloe Russo. My family and I own Evolution. I'd like to talk to you about a fragrance I've developed with you in mind."

The actor swept his gaze over her dismissively, before he got to her legs, where he lingered. "Who did you say you are?" he queried absentmindedly.

Chloe repeated her spiel, refusing to give in to the knots tying themselves in her stomach.

Eddie lifted his slumberous dark gaze to hers. Flicked the girl off the stool beside him. "Have a seat."

Nico pointed his car home, a brutally hard day of meetings behind him. A beer and the hot tub at his penthouse beckoned, but so did a phone call with his brothers at the end of the day. Old habits died hard, and checking in with Lazzero and Santo to make sure their world was upright was one of them.

It had been that way ever since their father's company had imploded when Nico was a teenager, his father and his marriage along with it, leaving Nico as the last line of defense between his family and the street when his mother had walked out. When life as you'd known it had dissolved once beneath your feet, you made sure it never happened again.

He punched Lazzero's cell into his hands-free. It rang five times before his brother picked up, the sound of music pulsing in the background.

"Sorry." The music faded as Lazzero moved to a quieter spot. "It's our Blaze launch tonight."

Nico rubbed a palm against his temple. "*Mi dispiace*. I just walked out of my last meeting minutes ago."

"No worries." An amused note flavored his brother's lazy drawl. "You didn't tell me you were sending your little bird my way."

"My little bird?"

"Chloe. She's here chatting up Eddie Carello for some sponsorship deal."

Nico blinked at the bright headlights of an oncoming car. "*Chloe* is there chatting up Eddie Carello?"

"And doing a pretty good job of it I might say. Must be the dress. I told her he likes legs."

Nico brought his back teeth together. "Shut it down, Lazzero. You know better than that. She's no match for him."

More of that patented male amusement in his brother's voice. "She looks like a match for him to me. She has his *undivided* attention at the moment."

"Lazzero," Nico growled. "Shut it down."

"Gotta go," his brother apologized. "A client just arrived. You should drop by."

Nico swore a blue streak, yanked the steering wheel around and did an overtly illegal U-turn. Approaching celebrities was the PR department's job. He was already feeling guilty about the board meeting and the necessarily harsh lesson he'd administered to Chloe. She was so vulnerable despite that sharp mouth of hers. But it had seemed to do the trick of jolting her out of that frozen state she'd been in, and for that, he'd considered it a success.

She did, however, need to be treated with kid gloves at the moment. She was the key to Evolution's success. She had to *believe* she could take her mother's place. But the question mark with Chloe had always been her confidence. Her belief in herself.

It didn't seem to be lacking, however, as Nico strode into Di Fiore's to find Lazzero romancing a tall blonde at the bar and Chloe doing the same with the most notorious womanizer in Hollywood.

Her dark hair shone loose around her lovely face, the champagne-colored dress she wore as she sat perched on the high stool highlighting every dip and curve of her slim, perfect figure. Her legs—and there was a lot of them—were a jaw-dropping, toned work of art. They made his mouth go dry.

And that was before he got to those gorgeous eyes of hers—dark rippling pools framed by the longest, most luxurious lashes he'd ever seen. Eyes that had once made him lose his common sense. He thought maybe she'd put about ten coats of mascara on.

Carello had one hand on his jean-clad thigh, the other around his drink, talking in an animated fashion while Chloe listened, her clear, bright laughter cutting through the din of the crowd. Nico's mouth tightened as the actor slid his arm to the back of her stool and moved in closer.

Resisting the urge to walk over there and pluck her off the stool, he lifted his hand and signaled the bartender instead. The young hipster called out a greeting to him and slid his favorite dark ale across the bar.

"You thought that was a good idea?" he growled as Lazzero lost the blonde and ambled over.

His brother hiked a shoulder. "I'm not her babysitter. You are. How you found yourself in that role is beyond me."

"You know full well how I did. Martino made it impossible to say no."

Lazzero took a sip of his beer. Eyed him. "When are you going to tell her about his cancer? It would make your life easier, you know."

It would. But Martino had made him promise not to tell his girls about the rare form of cancer that would have eventually claimed his life. He'd asked Nico to take care of them instead by taking his place at the helm of the company and ensuring it prospered. Telling Chloe now would only add to the emotional upheaval she was going through. And quite frankly, he needed her head on the job.

He threw back a swig of his beer. Wiped his mouth. "I have no idea why Martino even thought this was a good idea."

"Maybe because you did such a good job with Santo and me," Lazzero goaded. "We are such model citizens."

"I am questioning that right now." Nico slid his attention back to Carello. Watched him put a palm on Chloe's bare thigh. She didn't flinch, throwing her hair back over her shoulder and laughing at whatever he said.

Heat seared his belly. "How much has she had to drink?"

"Enough to boost her confidence." Lazzero leaned a hip against the bar. Slid an assessing gaze over him. "Tough day?"

"Evolution's stock is in the toilet, we desperately need a hit product and Giorgio has been executing an internal smear campaign against me. It's been a joy."

Lazzero's mouth curled. "He is a nuisance. He's not a serious threat."

But he was distracting him at a time he couldn't afford to be distracted. When Evolution was teetering on the edge of a defining moment. And that, he couldn't have.

A tall, lanky male with razed blond hair pushed through the crowd to the bar, leaning over to say something to Eddie. The actor gave Chloe a regretful look, then said something that made her face fall, then brighten as Carello took something out of his wallet and slid it onto the bar.

Nico's fingers tightened around his beer bottle as the actor bent and pressed a kiss to each of Chloe's cheeks, staining her skin with two twin spots of pink. Then he and his entourage headed off through the crowd.

*  *  *

A surge of triumph filled Chloe as she sat holding Eddie Carello's agent's business card, his parting words ringing in her ears. *Call my agent. Give him the details. Tell him I gave this the green light if he's good with it.*

She shook her head bemusedly. Slid off the bar stool, a half-finished glass of champagne in her hand. The world rocked ever so slightly beneath her feet. She'd never had much of a head for alcohol, but Eddie had insisted on that glass of champagne, and OMG, he'd just said yes. Never in her wildest dreams had she imagined he would.

*Untouchable, my foot.*

She turned and headed for Lazzero to thank him. Pulled up short. Nico was standing beside his brother at the bar, the jacket of his dark suit discarded, a drink in his hand.

Her pulse went haywire. Why did that happen every time? And why did he look so good in a shirt and tie? The tie loosened, his hair ruffled, he looked younger, like he had when they'd first met. *Devastating.*

But *that* Nico didn't exist, she reminded herself, heart thumping against her chest like a bass drum. And she'd do well to remember it.

She straightened her shoulders and walked the length of the bar to where the two men stood. Lazzero waved off her thanks and melted into the crowd to greet someone. Nico set that penetrating gray gaze of his on her.

"I told you to *secure* him. Meaning use the PR department. Not take on Hollywood yourself."

She lifted a shoulder. "The PR department didn't have access to him. Mireille said he was untouchable. So we asked Lazzero for help."

He leaned back against the bar, his free hand crossed in the crook of his folded elbow. "What did he say?"

A victorious smile played at the corners of her mouth. It might have been her best moment ever. "He said yes."

His eyes widened. "He did?"

"Yes. But," she qualified, "it's contingent on his agent's approval."

Nico's gaze warmed with a glimmer of something that might have been admiration. "I'm impressed. How did you convince him?"

"I explained the campaign to him. Why he was the inspiration for Soar. He was flattered—said he liked the idea of having a fragrance created for him. It turns out," she concluded thoughtfully, "that men are true to their biology. They like to have their egos stroked. It's their Achilles' heel."

A hint of a smile played at his mouth. "That may be true," he acknowledged. "But Carello is not to be played with. His reputation precedes him. Get his agent to sign off, then leave him the hell alone."

"I *know* that." Irritation burrowed a bumpy red path beneath her skin. "That's why I told him I had a boyfriend. Honestly, Nico, do you think I'm a total neophyte?"

"Sometimes I do, yes."

She made a sound at the back of her throat. "Well, you can go home now. The show's over. Your babysitting duties are officially done for the night."

He nodded toward her glass. "Finish that and I'll drive you home."

*Oh, no.* She was not having him shepherd her home like some stray sheep who'd wandered into the wrong field. She had conquered tonight, and she was leaving under her own steam. Because, truthfully, all she wanted was a hot shower and her bed now that the world had blissfully right-sided itself.

She lifted her chin. "I'm not ready to leave. It was so

nice of Lazzero to invite me. It's a great party. There's dancing and everything. I think I'll stay."

He set his silvery gaze on hers. "Let's go dance, then."

Her heart tripped over itself. She knew how good it felt to be that close to all that muscle and masculinity. How *exciting* it was, because he'd subjected her to its full effects before he'd cast her aside and chosen another.

"I didn't say I wanted to dance right *now*." She held up her half-finished glass of champagne. "I still have this."

"I think you've had enough." He plucked the glass out of her fingers, captured her wrist in his hand and was leading her through the crowd toward the packed dance floor before she could voice an objection. She knew it for the bad idea it was before they'd even gotten there. Eddie had touched her bare thigh and hadn't even caused a ripple. Nico's fingers wrapped around her wrist were like a surge of electricity through her entire body. She felt it right to the tips of her toes.

But then they'd reached the mosaic-tiled dance floor with its elegant chandelier. With a smooth flick of his wrist, Nico tugged her to him. A little more pressure and she was firmly within the circle of his arms, shielded from the other dancers by his height and breadth.

One of her hands in his, the other resting on his waist, it wasn't a close hold. But this was Nico. Every inch of her skin heated as it came into whisper-soft contact with his tall, powerful body. And then the scent of him kicked in, filling her head and electrifying her senses.

Smoky and elusive, it was pure, understated sensuality. Vetiver, the warm Indian grass known for its earthy, hedonistic appeal her mother had highlighted in Voluttuoso, her final fragrance. Chloe had always thought it was sexy. On Nico, with his overt virility and intensely masculine scent, it was knee weakening.

*One dance.* She kept her gaze riveted to the knot of his elegant silver tie. Unfortunately for her, the song was a jazzy, sexy tune, in keeping with the über-cool vibe of the party. A smooth, instinctive dancer, Nico was an excellent lead, guiding her steps easily in the small space they had carved out with a light pressure on her palm.

It should have been simple to exercise the mind control her yoga instructor was always preaching. Instead, her thoughts flew back to that sultry Fourth of July night that changed everything.

Her in Nico's arms…the illicit, forbidden passion that had burst into flames between them…how for the first time in her life, she'd felt truly, completely alive.

She lifted her gaze to his, searched for some indication that everything they'd shared hadn't been the imaginings of her eighteen-year-old mind. That she'd *meant* something to him like she'd thought she had. But his cool gray gaze was focused on her with a calculating intensity that sent that irrational, naive hope plunging to the bottom of her heart.

"We started off on the wrong foot the other night," he murmured. "We need to work as a team, Chloe, *together*, not apart, if we have any hope of preserving what your parents built. Full-out warfare is not going to work."

She arched a brow at him. "Is that an apology?"

"If you like," he said evenly. "Like it or not, we are in this together. We succeed or fail together. You decide which it is."

Her lashes lowered. "I agree we need a better working relationship. But this is my company, Nico. You need to listen to me, too. You can't just run roughshod over me with that insatiable need for control of yours. I *know* what's going to make Evolution a success. There's no doubt in my mind it's Vivre."

"Put the rest of the pieces of the plan in place and I might agree. And," he said, inclining his head, "I promise to listen more. *If* you stop trying to bait me at every turn."

Her mouth twisted. "A truce, then?"

A mocking glint filled his gaze. "A truce. We can celebrate by attending the Palm Beach fund-raiser together. It will present a very public united front."

Her parents' favorite fund-raiser. A glittering, star-studded musical event in Palm Beach every year in support of breast cancer—a disease her mother's best friend had succumbed to. Her stomach did a nervous dip at the thought of attending it with Nico.

She tipped her head back to look up at him. "You mean you don't have one of your hot dates lined up for it?"

Hot in the sense they never lasted with Nico. She wasn't sure she'd ever seen him photographed with the same woman twice.

"I haven't had a hot date in six months," he drawled. "It will have to wait until Evolution isn't in danger of falling through the cracks."

A calculated insult intended to remind her of her irresponsibility and his immutable focus. "However will you survive?" she goaded, skin stinging.

"I will *manage*," he murmured, eyes on hers. "Careful, Chloe, we've barely gotten this cease-fire of ours under way."

She sank her teeth into her lip. At the erotic image that one word inserted into her head. It took very little of her imagination to wonder what he would look like in the shower satisfying that physical need, his beautiful body primed for release.

She closed her eyes. She *hated* him. This was insanity.

The song finished. She stepped hastily out of his arms,

smoothing her dress down over her hips. Nico gave her a pointed look. "Ready to leave?"

The concrete set of his jaw said there was no point arguing. He wasn't leaving her here. He would wait all night if he had to because this was Nico—relentless in everything he did. Patient like the most tenacious predator in achieving what he wanted.

"Yes," she agreed with a helpless sigh.

He placed a palm to her back as they wound their way through the crowd to say good-night to Lazzero. The heat of it fizzled over her skin, warming her layers deep, a real-life chemical reaction she'd never been able to defuse.

It rendered her silent on the trip home, the warm, luxurious interior of the car wrapping her in a sleek, dark cocoon as they slipped through quiet streets. She was so tired as Nico walked her to her door, she stumbled with the key as she tried to push it into the lock.

His fingers brushed against hers as he collected the keys from her hand and unlocked the door. Little pinpricks of heat exploded across her skin, a surge of warmth staining her cheeks as she looked up at him to thank him. Found herself all caught up in his smoky gaze that suddenly seemed to have a charge in it that stalled the breath in her throat.

"Go inside and go to bed, Chloe," he said huskily. "And lock the door."

His intention ever since he'd walked into that bar tonight, she reminded herself, past her spinning head. To prevent her from slipping into Eddie Carello's hands.

She slicked her tongue across suddenly dry lips. Cocked her chin at a defiant angle. "Mission accomplished. I'll be in bed by midnight. But then again, you always get what you want, don't you, Nico?"

His gray gaze was heavy-lidded as it focused on her mouth for an infinitesimal pause. "Not always," he said quietly.

Then he disappeared into the night.

# CHAPTER THREE

It HAD BEEN the champagne talking. Chloe convinced herself of that version of events as she walked to work the next morning. That cryptic comment from Nico on her doorstep, the chemistry that had seemed so palpable between them. Because not once in all the years since their summer flirtation had he ever looked at her like that.

She'd merely been a blip on his radar. A casual diversion he'd regretted when more sophisticated choices had come along. Thinking it had been any more than that would make her a fool where he was concerned and she'd stopped being that a long time ago.

Whatever misguided sense of duty he was displaying toward her, this *power trip* he was on, Nico's ambition was the only thing he cared about, a fact she would do well to remember. She'd agreed to this truce of theirs only for the greater good of the company. Because saving Evolution was all that mattered.

She perfected her spiel for Eddie's agent as she rode the elevator to her office, said good-morning to Clara, whom she'd decided was not only witty but astonishingly efficient, and took the messages her assistant handed her into her office.

Done in antiques, with a Louis XVI writing desk and chairs, ultra-feminine lace-edged, silk curtains and warm lamp lighting, the office that had once been her mother's wrapped itself around her like a whisper-soft memory. But her mind was all business as she picked up the phone and called Eddie's agent. A good thing, too, because when she reached him, he told her he was on his way out of town but could have lunch that day before he left.

Apprehensive Eddie would change his mind if it waited, Chloe jumped on the invitation. Unfortunately, his agent wasn't immediately sold on the endorsement, but in the end he relented, only because Eddie seemed so keen on the project and the actor had a movie coming out at Christmas, just as the massive campaign for Soar would appear.

Chloe floated back to the office and announced her victory to Mireille, who was just as excited as she.

"*I*," she informed Chloe, "have good news and bad news for you. The good news is that Lashaunta is interested. She loves the campaign. It really resonated with her."

Chloe's heart soared. Lashaunta was a megastar. "That's *amazing*."

"The bad news is that Carrie Taylor is a no. She's about to represent a competing fragrance. Desdemona," she concluded, "I'm still working on."

Which meant they needed to secure their plan B supermodel, Estelle Markov, for Nico to give them the green light. He might approve the plan with only three of their four celebrities in place, but any less than that and Chloe knew she'd be out of luck.

While Mireille worked on Estelle, Chloe went off to put the final piece of her buzz campaign into effect, personally delivering samples of the Vivre fragrances to each and every Evolution employee's desk, explaining the story behind the perfumes. A streak of the devil possessing her, she also had Clara courier samples of the fragrances to the board members, making sure she also sent one for their significant other.

She *would* win them over.

Hurricane Chloe had entered the building.

A wry smile tugged at Nico's lips as he waved Chloe into his office late on Friday afternoon and motioned for her to take a seat as he finished up a conference call.

She walked to the window instead, vibrating with the perpetual energy she'd been displaying all week in her very effective campaign to prove him wrong. Her slender body encased in a soft, off-white sweater, dark jeans tucked into knee-high boots and a fawn-colored jacket topping it off, she wore her hair in a high ponytail, her flawless skin bare of makeup.

The hard kick she administered to his solar plexus wasn't unexpected. He'd been fighting his attraction to Chloe ever since the first moment he'd set foot in the Russo household and eyes on Martino and Juliette's eldest daughter.

Twenty to Chloe's sixteen, he'd been hard and bitter from his experiences. But something about the quiet, passionate Chloe had penetrated his close-packed outer shell. Perhaps he had recognized a piece of himself in her—the need they had both had to bury themselves behind their layers to protect themselves against the world. Perhaps it had been how she had sold her subtle beauty short when he'd always found her far more attractive than her stunning sister.

He'd told himself he couldn't have her. That he would never put his position as Martino's protégé in jeopardy— the career that had meant everything to him as he'd finally built a solid footing under his feet. Until unintended and explosive, the attraction between him and Chloe had slipped his reins at the Russo's annual Fourth of July party.

Martino, who'd witnessed the kiss, had brought him up short, asking his intentions when it came to his daughter. Pursue Chloe seriously or leave her alone, he had said, knowing what Nico *was*—a man who would never trust, never commit to a woman because of the scars his early life had left behind.

So he'd walked away. Done it the hard way so it would be a clean break. So he wouldn't be tempted with what he couldn't have. Because Martino had been right—he would have broken Chloe's heart far worse than he had in the end.

Martino might not be alive, he conceded, studying the delicate length of her spine, and Chloe wasn't a teenager anymore, but he had a new responsibility now. To protect her, not bed her. To nurture her as Martino had asked of him. It was a promise he would not break.

His call with the West Coast team over, he pushed out of his chair and walked to where she stood at the window. She turned, her face expectant. "Did you look at the plan?"

"Yes." He glanced at his watch. "I have time to go through it before my dinner plans if you'd like."

When she answered in the affirmative, he strode out to reception, sent his PA, Simone, home, then returned to pour himself a Scotch. When Chloe refused his offer of a drink, he joined her in the lounge, where she stood at the windows, enjoying the view.

Designed to work and entertain with its Italian glass chandeliers, dining room for ten and magnificent vista of a night-lit Central Park, the view was Nico's favorite thing about the space he spent far too much time in.

Chloe turned around. "So what did you think?"

"I think you've made a very persuasive case for Vivre being the Christmas focus. The plan is excellent." A wry smile touched his mouth. "It was also impossible," he conceded drily, "to miss your blitz campaign. Very clever. I couldn't walk the halls without hearing about it. Simone can't stop raving about Be. Jerry Schumacher called me this morning to beg for an early production bottle for his wife."

A tiny smile curved her mouth at the mention of Evolution's most senior board member. "I did say I would win them over. But more important," she added, excitement filling her voice, "the media is raving about Vivre, Nico. The editor of the most influential fashion magazine in America is crazy about Soar. She wants to feature it as her must-have product for Christmas. I think it's going to be a huge hit."

He held up a hand before she got too carried away. "I saw that. I do, however, still have real concerns about the timing. It seems inordinately tight. I want more than Giorgio's rose-colored glasses making this decision."

"It is a tight timeline," she admitted. "I may not sleep. But we can do it. The advertising space is booked, and all four of our celebrities have the time in their schedule to film the spots."

He addressed the one glaring hole in the plan. "I don't see Carrie Taylor in there. What happened to her?"

She sank her teeth into her lip. "She's representing a competing fragrance. But Mireille has a verbal commitment from Estelle Markov, who's making it big in Europe. I think she'll be perfect to target that audience."

"I've never heard of her." He frowned. "She doesn't have Carrie Taylor's cachet, Chloe. Nor is the European market anywhere near the size of the North American one."

"But she's amazing." Her eyes shimmered with fire. "When was the last time you were a twentysomething fashionista with breasts?"

A dry look back. "Point taken."

"Not to mention the fact that Eddie and Lashaunta could carry this campaign on their own if they had to," she plunged on. "Carrie is not a make-or-break for us."

He took a sip of his Scotch. Considered his options. The skincare line he had favored was, in truth, not going to set the world on fire. It would, however, provide very solid profits. Vivre might be that superstar product line Evolution so desperately needed, but was he insane to bet the company on it?

"This is a *fifty-million-dollar* campaign," he said, fixing his gaze on Chloe's. "We've never done anything of this magnitude before. It needs to be executed flawlessly— right down to the last detail. Needs to put Evolution on everyone's lips again. Are you *sure* you can get it into market in time?"

"Yes." Her head bobbed up and down. "Trust me, Nico. I can do this."

He gave her a long look. "Okay," he said finally, pointing his glass at her. "Let's do it, then."

The world tilted beneath Chloe's feet. "Did you just say yes?"

He smiled. *"Si."*

"Why?"

"Because I believe in you," he said quietly. "You're a brilliant scientist, Chloe. Juliette said you have even better instincts than she had at this age. That you have the *magic* in you. I just wasn't sure you or Vivre was ready."

Hot tears prickled beneath her eyelids. A knot she hadn't been conscious of unraveled in her chest. Three years of blood, sweat and tears. Six months of praying she had created something that would do her mother proud. To be so close to watching her dream reach fruition almost undid her.

But there was also *fear*. Her stomach clenched hard at the responsibility that now lay on her shoulders, icy tentacles of apprehension sinking into her skin. What if she failed? What if she'd been overly optimistic and couldn't get the campaign into market in time? What if she was wrong about Vivre? What if it wasn't going to be the smash hit she thought it would be?

She inhaled a deep breath. Steadied herself. She wasn't wrong. She knew it in her heart. She just wished her mother was here to tell her that. To be the second half of her she had always been. Instead, she had to do this herself.

"I know this is the right path for Evolution," she said huskily. "I can feel it in my bones."

Nico nodded. "Then let me give you a few additional thoughts I have."

They sat at the table in the dining room and worked through the plan. Released one by one in limited-edition launches in the weeks leading up to Christmas, the campaign for Vivre was all about buzz building and creating a sense of exclusivity for the perfumes.

Vivre's four celebrity ambassadors would do exclusive appearances at the Times Square pop-up retail location in conjunction with the massive promotional campaign that would blanket the globe, intensifying the buzz.

Nico frowned as he looked at the timeline. "When does Eddie's movie come out?"

"The second week of December." Chloe pointed to the date on the timeline. "That's why we're launching Soar that week."

"What are you doing on his side of things to cross-promote?"

She pursed her lips. "I hadn't gotten that far yet."

"You should do something with the theaters. Hand samples out. Put the fragrance in the gift bags at the premieres. Run the campaign on theater screens."

*So smart.* She tapped her coffee mug against her chin. "I don't know if we have time."

He lifted a brow.

"We'll make it happen," she corrected hastily. "No problem."

He offered a half dozen more brilliant ideas before they were done, Chloe frantically scribbling notes. She had to reluctantly admit by the time they were finished that while she and her uncle had created an inspired plan, Nico had taken it to a whole other level with his innate sense of timing and brilliant business instincts.

Which had never been in question, she brooded as he got up from the table to shrug on an elegant black dinner jacket. Her father would never have taken him on as his protégé if he hadn't possessed Leone Di Fiore's uncanny sense of financial wizardry. What she couldn't forgive was how Nico had taken advantage of the trust her father had placed in him with what Giorgio had described as a systematic campaign to gain power.

She had always believed Nico operated by a rigid code of honor instilled in him by the adversity he'd faced in his younger years. Until he'd slept with Angelique Dubois to seal a deal and she'd seen how far his ambition could drive him.

A painful wound echoed down low. Unfortunately, it didn't diminish her physical awareness of him one bit. He did formal better than any man she'd ever known—the exquisitely cut black dinner jacket accentuating his broad shoulders, the dark pants molding his powerful thighs, the white shirt and black bow tie casting his startling good looks into harsh relief. He was so intensely virile he made her stomach flip.

Clearly he had much more exciting plans than she for tonight. In his life that didn't include hot dates.

"There is," he murmured, returning to lounge against the table, "a condition to my saying yes to the plan."

Her stomach fell. *Not another hoop to jump through.*

She pushed out of the chair and stood to meet him on even ground. "Which is?" she prompted, tipping her head back to look up at him, prepared to do whatever she needed to do to make this happen.

"The company is suffering without a visible creative force. Everyone responsible for the future of the company is looking for a sign the magic is still there—that it didn't disappear along with your mother." He pointed his Scotch at her. "You and I both know it didn't, but that's not good enough."

Her stomach dropped right to the floor this time. "What are you asking me to do?"

"The company needs a face, Chloe. Vivre, with its massive promotional campaign, is the perfect opportunity to position you as the creative force behind the company. The heir apparent. To tell your story. But we can't do that if you're holed up in the lab."

The knot that had begun to unravel twisted itself back into place. "No, Nico. Don't ask me to do this. Not now."

"It has to be now." He lifted a shoulder, a sympathetic gleam in his eyes. "I wanted to put it off. To give you more time to find your feet, but I can't do that if I'm betting the bank on you. On Vivre. It would be irresponsible of me. But I promise you, I will be there by your side every step of the way."

Old demons mixed with the apprehension climbing her throat. With the pressure, too much pressure, that had been heaped on her for months. *Forever.* It rose up inside her, pushing at the edges of the tightly held composure she'd been clinging to for weeks.

"I am not my mother," she said, a raw edge to her voice. "She was larger than life, Nico. She had incredible charisma. I don't have that kind of a story to tell."

"I'm not asking you to be her," he countered. "I'm asking you to be *you*, Chloe. You created your own signature fragrance at *seventeen* that sold like wildfire. How is that not a great story to tell?"

"It's not the same thing."

"How is it different?" He shook his head, mouth flattening into a straight line. "This is your Achilles' heel, I get that. You've never been comfortable in the spotlight. You don't think you can live up to this image you have of your mother and Mireille, so you hide yourself away in the lab, when what you really need to be is comfortable in your own skin."

The oh-so-accurate assessment hit her square in the chest. She *knew* her weaknesses. This, however, was not one she had the bandwidth to deal with right now.

"You would regret it," she told him. "I am a loose cannon with the press. They start firing questions at me and I freeze. Put a camera in front of me and I'm worse. I can't answer a question, let alone articulate a vision."

"You will improve. You'll have the best training available."

She bit her lip. "I can't do it."

"You *won't* do it," he corrected harshly. "This isn't about you anymore, Chloe. It's about a company we're trying to save together."

"No, I can't." She clenched her hands into fists, the band around her chest tightening until she felt like she couldn't breathe. "I know what I'm supposed to be, Nico. I've spent my life trying to live up to that. I have given you Vivre, what I know will be a smash hit. But what you're asking of me now is too much."

"Why?" Harsh, implacable.

Because if she stepped into her mother's shoes, she would have to admit she was gone. She would have to acknowledge a pain so deep it might shatter her into pieces and she might never be able to put herself back together again. Because she was barely hanging on as it was.

Heat lashed the backs of her eyes, swift and unrelenting. She walked unsteadily to the window, where she stood staring out at a glorious amber-and-yellow-painted Central Park.

"Chloe," Nico said huskily, closing his hands around her shoulders. She shrugged, attempted to jerk out of his hold, but he sank his fingers deeper into her flesh and turned her around to face him.

"I know you can do this," he murmured, fixing his gaze on hers. "You just have to *believe* you can do it."

The dark, sensual scent of him wrapped itself around her. An irresistible wall of heat that drew her in a way she didn't want to acknowledge, he was overwhelmingly solid in a world that seemed to have dissolved around the edges. She knew she should look away, put some distance between them, because he was the last man on earth she should be drawn to in that way. But she couldn't seem to do it.

His eyes darkened. Electric currents vibrated the air between them as he lifted a hand to stroke his thumb along the line of her jaw. The tension coiling her insides snaked tighter, caging her breath in her lungs.

*Walk away, Chloe.* It was the smart thing to do. Why, then, would her feet not seem to move?

A discreet cough cut across the charge in the air. Her pulse beat a jagged edge at her throat as she stepped back, inordinately grateful for the distraction. Pivoting, she took in the elegant blonde standing in the doorway.

Nico's date, she assumed. Who was one of the most beautiful women Chloe had ever laid eyes on. Shoulder-length blond hair cut into a sleek bob, curvaceous figure clad in a sapphire-blue beaded dress she wore with sky-high heels, she was undeniably his type.

Turning on that effortless charm of his, Nico asked *Helene* to give them a minute. Chloe turned back to face him as the blonde retreated to reception. "Your *nonhot* date?"

"The president of Germany's largest department store chain," Nico corrected. "She has a thing for Mario Conti. He's doing *Tosca* at the Met tonight."

"And you are solidifying that relationship." She lifted her chin as an ancient hurt lashed her insides. "A specialty of yours."

His gaze narrowed, razor-sharp, as it rested on hers. "The Source Minerale deal was signed a month before my relationship with Angelique began, Chloe. So whatever your list of my faults, you can take sleeping my way to the top off it."

A rush of color stained her cheeks. She tugged her lip between her teeth, caught utterly flat-footed. "It was everywhere in the papers, Nico."

"The announcement was strategically timed to coincide with a key anniversary for Source Minerale. The deal, however, was done way before then." His mouth curved in a mocking smile as he crossed the room to his desk. "Don't lose any sleep over it. I'm sure you'll find at least half a dozen of my other failings to cling to."

Her skin stung from the rebuke. She watched as he dumped a sheaf of papers into his briefcase. Considered this new piece of information. If Nico had not slept with Angelique to seal the Source Minerale deal just days after they had shared that passionate encounter at the Fourth of July party, it could only mean his preference for the beautiful Angelique had dictated his actions.

A low throb pulsed inside her where his betrayal still lived. Clearly what they'd shared had always meant far more to her than it had to him, and she needed, once and for all, to realize that, instead of thinking he was something he wasn't. Instead of imagining *moments* between them like that one just now that weren't real.

Nico snapped his briefcase shut. Set a level gaze on her. "We have a deal, then?"

She lifted her chin. "You're leaving me no choice. But I guess you know that." She scooped up her things and stalked to the door. "Enjoy your evening. Apparently, Mario Conti brings down the house."

Mario Conti did bring down the house in the first half of *Tosca* at the stately, always magnificent Metropolitan Opera House. Puccini's dramatic story of love, lust and murder against a backdrop of the politics of soon-to-be Napoleon's Rome was spectacular, with Conti playing the opera's protagonist, the doomed Angelotti, to perfection.

But Nico's mind was on Chloe instead of the moving performance, and her high emotion as she'd stormed out of his office. Had he pushed her off the edge of the cliff with his demand she be the face of Evolution? Was it too much pressure for her to handle?

He was also, he acknowledged, as Conti took an extended bow, annoyed with her and with himself for letting her goad him into dredging up ancient history in Angelique. Because he'd hurt her again. He'd seen it in her face. And perhaps, in hindsight, ending things like that between them might not have been the right way to go about it. But he'd been young, his emotional IQ not yet fully developed.

His honor, however, he fumed inwardly, had never been in question. And that was what annoyed him most of all. If it hadn't been for his *honor*, he would have taken everything Chloe had been offering that night. Which would have been a disaster for them both.

The standing ovation complete, he escorted Helene to the bar for a drink. While she went to the powder room, he installed himself at the bar. Attempted to right-side his mood. But the bar was jam-packed, which left him cooling his heels with ancient memories of that night with Chloe imprinted in his head.

A kiss in the garden as fireworks had exploded over their heads. Chloe's silky-soft curves beneath his hands. The raging hunger of his youthful hormones as she'd returned the favor with an innocence that had nearly brought him to his knees. He'd put a stop to that soon enough, because that would have been true insanity, but he'd touched her plenty, her short, cherry-colored dress an irresistible temptation, with even softer skin to be found beneath.

His throat went so dry he almost crawled across the bar and poured the drink himself. If he lived to be a hundred, he would never forget the sound of her cries in his ear as he'd brought her untutored body to the peak of pleasure. It had nearly unmanned him.

He threw some bills at the bartender as he arrived with his drink. Took a sustaining gulp of the Scotch, welcoming its smooth, hot burn.

"I didn't figure Puccini as your thing."

A smile touched his mouth as Santo, his youngest brother, slid into place beside him at the bar. Dressed in a sharp black tux, he had their mother's coloring, as light as he and Lazzero were dark. Electing to scruff up his impossibly perfect golden good looks tonight with some dangerous-looking stubble, it did nothing to make him look any less angelic.

"Not so much," Nico commented drily. The arts were Santo's thing. "Who's the lucky female? I'm assuming you brought one."

"Kathleen O'Keefe, a business reporter for one of the dailies." Santo caught the bartender's attention and ordered two glasses of wine before he leaned back against the bar, arms crossed over his pristine Armani. "We're sitting two boxes over from you. I tried to get your attention, but you were someplace else. Who's the hot blonde, by the way? She would have distracted me, too."

"Helene Schmidt, the president of Stil 049."

"Gorgeous and successful," Santo murmured. "Tell me this is ending up horizontal."

"I don't date clients."

Santo fixed him with an assessing look. "*Santo* Nico," he drawled. "Mamma had the names all wrong."

Nico took a pull of his Scotch in response.

"I saw your little bird the other night," Santo said idly. "She looked… *fantastic*. When are you going to admit she is a problem for you, *fratello*? Or should we saint you now and get it over with?"

Nico swirled the amber liquid in his glass. "She isn't my *little bird*. And I took care of that problem a long time ago."

"You think so?" Amusement dripped from his brother's voice. "The first step in addressing a problem is admitting you have one. Chloe is all grown up, Nico. She doesn't need your brand of protection anymore."

She sure as hell did. She'd been as delicate as a wisp of wind in his office tonight. And what had he done? He'd piled more pressure on her.

"Anyway," Santo said with a dramatic sweep of his

palm, "Kathleen gave me a piece of intel last night in bed. I wanted to pass it along."

"Save that for yourself," Nico deadpanned. "I've never had any complaints in that area."

Santo's mouth quirked. "Very funny. Kathleen is a *business* reporter. Her editor had lunch with Giorgio Russo last week. Giorgio spent the whole lunch giving him the background scoop on the 'political unrest' at Evolution. He said he has half the board in his pocket."

Red blazed in his head. His hand tightening around the crystal tumbler he held, he absorbed a burn of pure fury. He'd been content to watch Giorgio spin his wheels with his fruitless internal campaign to discredit him, but taking it public was crossing the line. He wasn't worried about the board being solid behind him because he knew that they were. But if Giorgio was shooting his mouth off to journalists, it could *create* an aura of political instability around Evolution with the very forces that determined its future—the analysts, the market, the shareholders—worried the company would implode from the inside out. And that he couldn't have.

*"Grazie,"* he murmured to Santo. "That is good information to have."

Santo lifted a brow. "What are you going to do?"

"Shut him down."

# CHAPTER FOUR

THERE WERE PRIMA DONNAS and then there was Lashaunta. The pop singer took the concept to a whole other level.

Chloe buried her head in her hands as the diva walked off the set for the fifth time to take a phone call from her boyfriend, with whom she shared some strange kind of bizarre pseudo-addiction. From the high-end champagne she'd demanded for her dressing room to the red roses that needed to cover every surface because they put her in a good "mental place" to the incessant phone calls with Romeo, they hadn't captured even one decent piece of footage all day.

Given the singer went on tour for a month tomorrow, it was a problem. Chloe rubbed her palms against her temples, massaged the dull ache beginning to penetrate her skull. She must have been crazy to think she could do this. The timeline was insanely tight, with absolutely no room for miscues. If she went down in flames with this launch, so did Evolution.

*You are only as good as your supporting team*, Nico had counseled in their morning meetings in which she'd done her best to behave and listen. *Trust them to execute this for you.* Which she did. Now if only her pop sensation would save her torrid romance for the midnight hour so she could wrap this spot up before she and Nico left for

Palm Beach on Friday. Which was key because Lashaunta kicked off the campaign in the middle of November, with Desdemona following her—a one-two punch that would hopefully put her perfumes on everyone's lips.

Lashaunta sauntered back onto the set. Chloe took a deep breath. Walked down onto the set and took the pop singer through the concept for Be. *Again*. Lashaunta stared at her blank-faced. *OMG*.

"Can you think of a moment in your life," Chloe said patiently, "when you realized you had become what you were destined to be? When you let yourself be stripped down, naked, *raw*, to hell with what anyone else thought, because this was *you*, and you couldn't be anything else but what you are?"

The pop singer's exotic eyes brightened. "Sure. When I met Donnie," she said dreamily, "I mean, we are *real* with each other."

Chloe almost cried. "I was hoping for something a little more impactful than that. Not that Donnie isn't that," she hastily backtracked when Lashaunta eyed her, "but you know what I mean."

The diva pressed red-tipped fingers to her wide, passionate mouth. *"Yes,"* she finally said. "When I was standing on the stage at the Billboard Awards last year. I'd just sung 'Butterfly.' It was the craziest moment—the applause went on forever. I just stood there and drank it all in. In wonder, really, because this was just me—the girl from a tiny Caribbean island no one's ever heard of. I knew then," she said huskily, "that finally I'd arrived. It was full-on, girl."

Chloe remembered it. It had held her and the rest of the world transfixed—the moment almost religious in its intensity. "Can you please," she said evenly, "say that on camera?"

"No problem."

Chloe was an hour late for her media training session by the time she flew upstairs to her office. Her headache had, unfortunately, elected to go south, but at least Lashaunta's spot was in the can. Which faded to a pleasant memory as her media trainer, whom she liked to refer to as her military drill instructor, pushed her through two hours of brutal interviews. Which didn't go well because she hadn't had time to read the prep notes and was flying by the seat of her pants.

"Better," said the drill instructor when she'd finished her latest effort. "But can we do it again? I'm not really *feeling* the passion when it comes to what you do."

She gritted her teeth. Felt huge sympathy for Lashaunta. She knew what she was *feeling*, and it was an almost uncontrollable urge to strangle her instructor to a slow and painful death.

Head throbbing, she pulled off her mic. "No," she said, getting to her feet. "I'm done. We can pick this up tomorrow."

The trainer's mouth fell open. "We have two hours left. And you have your big interview on Friday."

"Then we'd better hope I improve by then."

She snatched up her lab coat and stormed out of her office, the crew staring after her. And walked straight into a brick wall in Nico.

It hadn't been that bad, Chloe told herself a couple of hours later as she pulled herself out of the pool in the rooftop executive spa, a perk that put working at Evolution on top of every Manhattanite's dream job list.

Nico *had* been furious with her for ditching the media training session, but thankfully he'd been on his way into a meeting. And she *had* explained what her day had been like to her stony-faced boss.

And who cared, really? She grabbed a thick towel and blotted the water from her skin. She still had work to do in the lab after the break she'd decided was mandatory. She was doing her best, and if he didn't want to see that, well, *tough*.

A glass of cucumber water beckoned, along with the steam room to ease a few of the knots in her shoulders. Slinging the towel over her shoulder, she hummed a tune as she pushed open the glass doors to the luxurious cream marble space. The sight of Nico in low-slung graphite swim trunks lounging on a bench stopped her in her tracks.

*She couldn't be this unlucky.* Her pulse bounded beneath her skin as she took him in. She definitely wasn't staying— that was for sure. But first, she needed to stop drooling over the jaw-dropping washboard abs, which seemed as if they might be a gift from heaven as the sweat poured down them. The muscles that bunched thick in his shoulders. The *thighs* that were so powerful they took her thoughts to places they most definitely shouldn't go.

He was dead to her. He had smashed her heart into little pieces and left her like roadkill by the side of the highway. She kept that thought top of mind as she lifted her gaze to his. Not his normal calm, steely gray, she registered, noting the heated flame that burned there.

A thread of unease tightened around her chest, then unraveled so fast her heart began to whirl. So he hadn't cooled off.

"Enjoy," she murmured, pivoting on her heel. "I've changed my mind. I think I'll shower instead."

He set an even gaze on hers. "Sit down, Chloe. I think we can share the same space without taking each other apart."

She wasn't actually so sure that was true.

* * *

Nico could have cursed Santo. Because all he could think of beyond his extreme aggravation with the woman opposite him was how amazing she looked in that swimsuit.

You couldn't even say it was provocative. There was too much material to the fuchsia-colored bikini for that. Which made it all the more enticing because it left so much of her slim, curvaceous figure unexposed.

Where she'd been all long, slim limbs at eighteen, she had filled out in all the right places since. *Not a teenager anymore.* A beautiful, desirable woman he was sure some man had already discovered. *If* he'd been able to get past her mile-high walls. Why he hated that idea was frankly irrational.

Irritated at his own weakness, he swept a towel across his face. Focused his anger on her instead as she wrapped a towel sarong-style around herself and sat opposite him on the marble bench.

"You cost the company a thousand dollars today. You can't just decide you've had enough and walk out. We made a deal, one you are going to stick to, or I swear I'll pull the plug on your campaign."

She lifted her chin, eyes shimmering, dark pools of light. "I'm only one person, Nico. I'm spreading myself too thin. Something's got to give."

"Stop micromanaging your team, then, and let them do their job."

"We wouldn't have gotten Lashaunta's spot filmed today without me." She shifted on the bench, drawing his eye to a creamy stretch of undeniably luscious thigh.

"I'm terrible at the media stuff," she announced flatly. "I told you I would be. What's the point?"

He tore his gaze away from those delectable thighs. "You would be better at it if you knew your key messages. Have you even looked at them?"

She stared at him, affronted. "Have they been giving you *reports* on me?"

"I asked for one."

Hot color shaded her cheeks. "I fell asleep reading them last night."

"Because you were in the lab until ten o'clock." He shook his head. "You are *banned* from the lab until you master this, Chloe. Not one step past that door."

A slight widening of her big brown eyes was her only reaction. She leaned her head back against the tile and eyed him. "John Chisolm told me this morning my father took a step back last year. That, in essence, you have been running Evolution ever since. What was he talking about?"

Nico kept his face bland. "Your father decided it was time to enjoy life a bit more. He had me, so he could afford to do so."

"My father didn't know the meaning of downtime," Chloe countered. "Evolution was his passion. He always said he'd run it until either his mind or his body gave out."

*Dannazione.* He hated this. "Later life tends to give you perspective," he murmured.

Her gaze sharpened on him. "What is it you aren't telling me?"

"You're reading too much into it," he said flatly. He wiped another rivulet of sweat from his eyes. "What you *might* expend your energy on is convincing your uncle to put a muzzle on himself. All his smear campaign is doing is making him look like a fool while everyone who plays a role in the future of this company worries the internal politics will make us implode."

She was silent for a long moment. "Give me a reason to trust you," she said quietly. "Because right now I feel like I am missing a piece of the puzzle and I don't know what it is. If my father had you running the company, why didn't he tell Giorgio that? Why not make it clear what the succession plan was? Why let it fester like this?"

The thought that he should just *tell* her flashed through his head. Because what did it matter now? Martino was dead. Was keeping Chloe in the dark doing more harm than good? Except, he acknowledged, he'd given Martino his word not to say anything, and his word was his word. As for Giorgio? He'd soon hang himself on his own insurrection.

He set his gaze on Chloe's. "You know you can trust me. Have I ever broken a promise to you?"

"Yes," she whipped back, fire in her eyes. "The one where you promised *to be there* for me and then you weren't."

*Oh, hell.* Chloe bumped her head against the wall as if to knock some sense into herself. She'd sworn she wasn't going there. Had *promised* herself she wasn't going there. And then she had.

Nico closed his eyes. Exhaled. "I have *always* been there for you," he said finally, opening them again. "I started something I shouldn't have that summer with you, Chloe. I was your father's protégé, four years older than you, a *lifetime* at that age. We both knew it wasn't going to end well. It was far too…*complicated* and you were far too vulnerable. You were looking for something I couldn't give."

She blinked. Attempted to take in everything he'd just said. Everything she'd never been privy to because he'd never explained it to her.

"I—I never asked you for anything," she stammered. "I was eighteen, Nico. I just thought we had something good."

"You were infatuated with me," he said matter-of-factly. "For me it was hormones. I wanted you, but I didn't want the entanglements that came with it. You wanted everything—the moonlight, the candles, the romance. I couldn't give you that. Better you go off and find a nice French boyfriend who could."

Instead, he'd kissed her to within an inch of her life, branded her with his touch as he'd made her come apart in his arms and then walked away, leaving that comparison to haunt her every time she'd kissed a man since. Because kissing Nico, experiencing the passion she had felt in his arms, had felt like a revelation.

Her stomach twisted into a tight, hot knot. "So," she said, eyes on his, "you slept with Angelique—why? Because you simply moved on?"

"Because I thought it was the easiest way to drive home the point we were done." He rubbed a palm against the stubble on his jaw. "Perhaps it wasn't the right way to handle it, but I'm not sure anything else would have worked."

Because she'd pursued him afterward. Refused to take no for an answer.

Humiliation flared through her, hot and deep. "You could have just explained it to me, Nico. I would have *gotten it*, I assure you. Because honestly," she said with a shoulder shrug, pride driving her on, "I was simply looking to sample what you offer so freely to other women. That legendary *expertise* you're known for. It would have been an excellent base to work from."

"You think so?" The low rumble in his voice should have been her first clue she'd crossed a line. Some invisible marker that tumbled them straight from a safe, combative place into entirely unknown territory. The incendiary glimmer in his eyes, glowing like the last banked embers of a fire, cemented it. "I think you have no idea what happens when you play with fire. Someone always gets burned, I can assure you. Which is why I walked away ten years ago. Because *this* is never happening between us."

Her heart felt as if it had fallen into a deep, dark pit with no bottom. Swallowing hard, she searched for air. Half of her wanted to know what it was like to walk into the fire—to *get* burned, because she'd never felt as alive as she'd felt in his arms that night. The other half wanted to run for safety—to retreat into the sheltered, familiar world she had always existed in.

She felt shaky, unsure of everything in that moment. *Nothing* felt concrete anymore. Everything seemed to be mired in a gray haze she had no idea how to navigate.

Not messing up this chance to prove herself Nico had given her seemed to be the only coherent thought she had.

"Maybe your lesson in all this," she said, fixing her gaze on his, "is that you don't need to make decisions for me, Nico. I'm perfectly capable of making them myself. In fact," she said quietly, "I wish I had."

She left then. Because it seemed the only rational thing to do.

# CHAPTER FIVE

WHY HAD SHE agreed to this?

Chloe paced her office twenty-four hours after her confrontation with Nico, the key messages she'd been attempting to inhale for her big interview circling her head like puzzle pieces that refused to form themselves into a coherent picture.

The interview was tomorrow morning, looming like her worst nightmare. *D-day*. She *knew* how important it was. The feature piece for the fashion section of the most distinguished paper in the nation was an amazing opportunity to gain profile for Evolution at a time when the company desperately needed it. But if one more person attempted to imprint that fact into her head, she was going to scream.

She collapsed on her mother's Louis XVI sofa and took a deep breath. She was being ridiculous. Of course she could do this. She just needed to get over the block in her head. She thought it might have something to do with the million things she *wasn't* doing at the moment that needed to be done.

Another thing she didn't *need* appeared in the doorway of her office. Dressed in a dark gray suit, a lilac shirt and an eggplant tie that enhanced his swarthy coloring, Nico looked disgustingly energized at seven o'clock in the evening. As if he could take on another full day with one hand tied behind his back. A bit *dazzling*.

She cursed her ever-present awareness of him. She'd been doing so well keeping their relationship on a business footing, but that confrontation in the spa had ignited something between them she couldn't seem to turn off.

"I'm studying," she grumbled, waving the papers in front of her at him. "No need to lecture."

"You look exhausted," he said bluntly. "I heard the session today didn't go great."

"Nope. No surprises there." She sat back against the sofa and exhaled a long sigh. "I have no idea why I'm so blocked. I can't seem to articulate myself the way I want to."

He crossed his arms over his chest. "Then we'll work through it together."

She sat up straight. Eyed him warily. Nico and his overbearing tactics were the *last* thing she needed right now.

"I can handle this myself."

"You could," he conceded. "But I can help. I've done a million of these interviews."

With effortless, supreme confidence, she assumed, watching helplessly as he shrugged off his jacket, slung it over the back of a chair and walked to the bar, where he pulled a bottle of wine from the rack and set out two glasses.

"*That* is not going to help."

He ignored her and opened the wine. "You need to relax. You're so far in your head right now you can't see the forest from the trees."

Likely true. Although she wished she could attain some kind of clarity when it came to *him*. Figure out what he was keeping from her. She'd talked to Mireille about their father's supposed step back. It might have been true, Mireille had conceded, that their father had taken a bit of a foot off the gas over the past year, but he had been sixty-two. Would it really have been so unexpected for him to want to take a break?

No, but why, then, wouldn't he have simply communicated that to Giorgio? She'd spoken to her uncle, who'd insisted his version of events was true. When she'd voiced her apprehension his campaign to discredit Nico would destabilize Evolution, it had been like talking to a brick wall. Which did worry her. She had no idea what he was up to—and that couldn't be good.

Another issue she couldn't tackle right *now*. Nico carried the wine and glasses over to the sofa and sat down beside her. All of a sudden, the delicate piece of furniture seemed so much smaller with him in it. Long legs sprawled in front of him, wineglass in hand, his shirtsleeves rolled up to reveal corded, muscular forearms, he was impossible to ignore.

She'd tried to convince herself that Gerald, the handsome Frenchman she'd dated for a few months, had been just as attractive. But that had been wishful thinking. Nico had a hint of the street in him beneath that outward elegance he'd cultivated. The *rough set of cards life had dealt him*, according to her father. It made him intimidating, fascinating, *dangerous* in a way Gerald could never hope to emulate.

He eyed her. "So what exactly," he asked, pointing his wineglass at her, "is it that you are struggling with?"

"The big-picture questions. My creative vision… I have no idea how to explain it." She waved a hand at him. "Everyone thinks it's this mystical thing that involves divine inspiration, when in reality, it's like a puzzle I have to solve. A painting I need to layer bit by bit. It's different for each individual scent I develop depending on whom I'm creating it for."

He considered that for a moment. "Maybe you need to use some of your mother's techniques."

"Like what?"

"She would use the interviewer as an example, for instance. Pretend she was creating a scent for him or her. It was a brilliant technique—got the journalist very involved in the process. They were fascinated by it."

"Which is fine if you can think on the spot like my mother could." Chloe pursed her lips. "It takes me months, *years*, to come up with a fragrance."

"But you must have some sense when you meet someone what will suit them. What do you do when you design custom fragrances?"

She thought about it for a moment. "I do an interview of sorts, a history taking if you like, to get a sense of who the person is. Their past, present, what they like, dislike. It would give me an initial idea of what kinds of scents they would prefer, but it wouldn't direct me, if you know what I mean. Someone can say to me they like beachy, breezy fragrances, but that might not be what suits them at all. Or what they're really asking for."

He took a sip of his wine. Swirled the ruby-red liquid in his glass. "Try it with me, then. You've never designed a fragrance for me. I would be the perfect test case."

She gave him a wary look. "Right now?"

"Why not?" His eyes held the spark of a challenge. "It would be the perfect test run. I know you can do this, Chloe. Stop censoring yourself and let your instincts take over."

She thought censoring herself was exactly what she should be doing when it came to him. But she had never been one to back down from a challenge.

"Fine," she agreed. "But I need a prop."

\* \* \*

Nico eyed Chloe as she sat down on the sofa with a testing tray in her hands. He was capable of keeping his hands off her, that he knew, but *her* putting her hands on him? That might be a different story. That had been where all their issues had begun in the first place.

He lifted a brow. "Are you planning on putting those on me?"

"No." She observed the skeptical note in his voice. "That would be counterproductive. Everything would blend into one another. I'll put them on scent strips and have you give your impression. It won't be the full test I'd do if I was creating a perfume for someone, but it will give you an idea of the process."

*"Bene."* He settled back against the sofa, wineglass in hand. She plucked the glass from his fingers and set it on the table.

"The red wine will throw your sense of smell off."

"Right." He studied the focus on her intent, serious face. Found it more than a bit sexy. "Do we start with the interview, then?"

"I'm going to skip it because I know you. We'll start with the scent test instead. I can fill the rest in myself."

He opened his hands wide. "I'm all yours."

A flush stained her olive cheeks at the unintended innuendo. He stared at it, fascinated. When was the last time he'd seen a woman do *that*? Chloe had an innocence, a transparency about her that had always amazed him—as if she had been poured straight from the source, uncontaminated by life. Which, he conceded, was pretty much the case.

Was that what had always drawn him to her? Because it was exotic to him, *compelling*? Because it seemed to rub off on everyone who came into contact with her, reminding them of an innocence, a *goodness*, that still existed in the world? Or was it just because he'd always wanted what he couldn't have?

She dabbed two feather-shaped scent strips with a unique essence from the glass bottles. "Think of it as a blind taste test," she instructed, handing them to him. "Except you're smelling instead. This is you picking your favorite scents in a process of elimination that will help me choose the top, middle and base notes of the fragrance."

"So you're not going to tell me what they are?"

"No. Take one in either hand," she directed. "When you smell the one on your left, it's going to be clean and woodsy, with a hint of warmth to it. When you switch to the other, you will smell something deeper, less clean. Tobacco and spice dominate. Now you come back to the initial scent, it's crisp and clean, airy, not as warm as it was before. Then you go back to the second. There's tobacco and spice, a boldness, a complexity to it. A *sensuality*."

He brought the first scent strip to his nose, fascinated to find the experience exactly as she had described—the first light and less complex, the second rich and seductive.

"Close your eyes," Chloe encouraged. "Give yourself over to it. Let yourself be hedonistic, fully aware of your senses. Scent is *intimate*," she murmured. "Intensely personal. React to it. Let *it* tell you where you want to go."

Nico closed his eyes. Listened to her talk him through each pair. Found himself utterly distracted by the passion with which she approached her calling. How sensual an experience it actually was.

On they went, bouncing back and forth. Him choosing his favorite and giving his gut reaction, Chloe making notes.

The slide of her fingertips against his, the sensual lilt to her voice, the accidental brush of the soft curve of her breast against his arm were the most potent aphrodisiacs he'd ever encountered. It turned him hard as stone.

Not his brightest idea.

"And these two?" she prompted.

"The one on the left," he murmured, "reminds me of the cottage we used to go to in Maine as kids. The ocean."

She nodded. "That's called a scent imprint. A memory associated with a scent. We all have them. They're very specific to us personally. Good. And the other?"

"Warmer. Intense, illusive. It smells like—" *Her.* Like the fragrance she'd always worn. Except on Chloe it was exotic and intoxicating, the way it came off the heat of her skin. "Summer," he finished lamely.

She handed him two more strips. "And these?"

"Tropical," he said of the first one. "Sweet. Rich."

"And the next?"

He inhaled. Found himself in the middle of a smoky, earthy scent that was just a little…*dirty*.

"Sex." He opened his eyes and fixed them on hers. "That one is definitely sex."

Her eyes widened. Shimmered with a heat that snagged his insides. Potent and thick, the air around them suddenly seemed dense—layers deep—all his good intentions evaporating as her gaze dropped to his mouth. Stayed there.

She drifted closer, her floral scent melding with his, the hitched sound of her breathing stirring his senses. It took every ounce of his willpower not to close the last few centimeters between them and cover those lush lips with his, because a decade later, he still remembered how sweet they were…how perfect she'd tasted beneath him. How *forbidden*.

"Chloe," he murmured. "Are we almost done? I feel like we should be done now."

"Yes," she breathed, dragging her gaze back up to his.

"You're very good, by the way. That one has lots of indole in it. It comes from—" She sank her teeth into her full bottom lip. "Well…you know."

He didn't know. Didn't *want* to know. Because the only place his mind wanted to go right now started with an *s* and ended with an *x*. And that couldn't happen with this particular woman. Not now. Not ever.

Chloe cleared her throat, her eyes dark, liquid, so brown they were almost black. "There's two more. But we could probably leave those because I'm sure I know which way I'm going to go."

"Good. Let's do that." He reached for his wine and took a gulp. Ruthlessly pulled his libido back under control.

"So," he prompted, "what is your analysis?"

Chloe wasn't sure how her brain was supposed to function after that look Nico had just given her. As if he wanted to consume her whole. As if *she* was what he wanted to get intimate with. Because that hadn't been her imagination talking, she was sure of it.

Her head spun as she made a show of gathering up her materials and stowing them on the tray. Knowing after all this time the attraction between them wasn't one-sided like she'd thought it had been, that it was clear and *present*, was a bit mind-boggling. Also head-scratching was the fact that for a moment there, she'd felt compelled to play with that fire he'd declared off bounds. Which *was* crazy. For so many reasons.

She closed trembling fingers around the stem of her wineglass, lifted it to her mouth and took a sip. Gathered her brain back into some sort of working order because she wasn't done yet.

"You wear my mother's Voluttuoso," she began, setting her gaze on his, "which is a gorgeous fragrance, one of my favorites. And it does reflect the innate...*sensuality* about you. But I would have gone with something different."

"I like that fragrance," he countered. "I think it suits me. Why not it?"

"Because you're more complex than that," she said quietly. "Vetiver, the warm Indian grass that predominates in Voluttuoso, is sexy, but you have a strength, a *toughness* about you that comes from your past. With Voluttuoso, it's only showing one facet of you. If it were me, I would veer toward something darker and more complex."

"Such as?"

"Something with a base note of the tobacco you were drawn to, for instance. I'd have predicted that. It has depth, like you. Some cedar," she continued thoughtfully, "to reinforce the tobacco and to bring in that scent memory you have of your early years at the cottage. Some other warm notes to give it added complexity," she continued, formulas shifting in her head like puzzle pieces. "Amber or nutmeg, perhaps. And jasmine, definitely jasmine, for that sensual edge."

A smile curved her mouth. "Bold, rich and *haunting*."

He lifted a brow. "Haunting?"

She gave a self-conscious shrug. "A turn of phrase. Evocative words sell perfumes."

"And so do you," he murmured. "I was buying everything you were selling, Chloe. Hook, line and sinker. You had me on the edge of my seat." He pointed his wineglass at her. "You didn't *tell* me about the creative process, you *demonstrated* it. Do that tomorrow and you'll be gold."

Or she could blow it completely and let everyone down.

# CHAPTER SIX

ARMED WITH A strong cup of coffee and as much confidence as she could muster, Chloe played host to the hip, young journalist Carrie Mayer from the nation's most respected daily newspaper at 10:00 a.m. the next morning in her office. The reporter spent the first few minutes raving about the decor, which only reminded Chloe of what a big personality her mother had been and cranked up her nerves yet another notch.

How could she possibly *be* that?

But she refused to retreat back into her head, because this was too important. Luckily, she and Carrie clicked and were soon whizzing through the questions. Chloe wasn't perfect in her answers, knew she'd missed some of her key messages along the way she'd probably get her hand slapped for, but she kept things on track, even when Carrie asked about her mother's death and what she had meant to her.

It was, however, when she went through the scent test with Carrie and offered her personal recommendation that the journalist's eyes lit up. "Brilliant," she murmured, madly scribbling notes. "Can I quote all of that, or are there trade secrets in there I can't use?"

Chloe told her to go ahead and use it. Gave the reporter a bottle of her mother's Cygne Blanc, which would suit her perfectly.

Nico, Chloe admitted as she showed Carrie out, was very smart. She might just tell him that. But first, she had a whirlwind shopping trip with Mireille to accomplish in the lunch hour before her and Nico's flight to Palm Beach, because she had absolutely nothing to wear that was in any way suitable for the black-tie charity fund-raiser that evening that attracted the world's elite.

Luckily, Mireille was miraculous with clothes and knew just where to shop. In the space of an hour, they'd found the perfect gown for the Champagne and Diamonds fund-raiser. They'd also acquired a couple of outfits for the warmer Palm Beach weather while they were at it, given Chloe and Nico would spend the weekend at the Di Fiore brothers' luxurious South Beach estate.

Nico had made golf plans with clients tomorrow, which gave Chloe a chance to enjoy a day in the sun. Which was, she acknowledged, another source of nerves. Keeping her attraction to Nico under wraps from a distance was one thing—doing it while they shared the same roof was another.

It was not helpful, then, when she met Nico at the small private airport in New Jersey they would fly out of, to find him dressed in black jeans and a long-sleeved crew-necked sweater in dove gray that matched his eyes. Draped against an unused check-in desk while he tapped away on his phone, he was so stunning every woman in the tiny lounge was making him the preboarding entertainment.

He gave a pointed look at his watch. "We're up next."

"I had to shop. My slave driver of a boss has me toiling all hours."

A curve of his amazing mouth. "How did the interview go?"

"Well, I think. You were right," she conceded with a tip of her head, "the reporter loved the essence test. She said it was brilliant content for the piece." She shrugged a shoulder. "I'm not sure I got every key message across. I was too nervous with the difficult questions. But I did okay."

His smile deepened into one of those rare lazy ones he offered so infrequently, it made her breath catch in her chest. "Then I'm sure it will be great. Now you can relax and enjoy the weekend."

"Yes." She swallowed past the fluttering feeling inside her. "Thank you," she said quietly. "For helping me. You were right. I was so far inside my head, I couldn't seem to get out."

His gray eyes warmed. "I promised you I would be there for you, Chloe, and I will. You are not in this alone."

And why did she feel so reassured by that? She pondered the answer as an official gave them a nod and they were escorted across the tarmac to the sleek ten-person Evolution jet, where the pilot was ready to go. Why was her guard beginning to come down with Nico?

Because she was starting to wonder if she'd been wrong about him, in more than one way? Because everyone she spoke to at Evolution loved working for him—*appreciated* his leadership?

Because he *had* been there for her—exactly as he'd promised? Or had it been that moment in her office where she'd become shockingly aware that the chemistry between her and Nico wasn't one-sided? Was that messing with her head?

She had no idea *what to do* with that particular piece of information. Knew it wasn't wise to pursue it—that Nico had been right about that—but she couldn't seem to get it out of her head.

She was so exhausted, she slept most of the short flight to Miami. Which was helpful, because by the time they arrived and stepped onto the waiting helicopter that would take them to the Di Fiores' South Beach estate, she'd gotten her second wind.

The ultra-modern villa the Di Fiore brothers had built on the ocean was all sleek, square lines, with a spectacular view from its streamlined, wide-open spaces. She felt herself exhaling, the tension seeping out of her bones, as she breathed in the humid, fragrant, warm air.

Boasting double-height ceilings that led to an oversize infinity-edge pool, a custom Italian kitchen and a hand-carved mahogany wine cellar that made her head spin with its extravagant selection, it was Chloe's idea of heaven. Lazzero, who spent the most time at the house, enjoying the party scene for business purposes, had hired a lovely housekeeper, who showed Chloe to a gorgeous, airy bedroom on the second floor, done in dark woods and stark white, with colorful accents thrown in.

Chloe fell in love with the stunning pink-and-orange bougainvillea that seemed to climb into her ethereal bedroom and wished dearly she could take a dip in the ocean before dinner, but since they were due for sunset cocktails at the Buchanans' nearby estate, it would have to wait.

Energized by the heady aroma of tropical flowers and the salty, fresh sea air, Chloe slipped on the gorgeous coffee-colored lace dress she'd bought with Mireille at lunch. Floor length and glamorous, with pretty cap sleeves and a deep plunging back, it was a daring style she never would have chosen on her own.

Catching her hair up in a loose knot, she spritzed on her favorite perfume and declared herself done.

Nico was leaning against the railing, staring at a view of forever, when Chloe joined him on the terrace that overlooked the ocean. A waft of her unmistakable intoxicating perfume hit him just before she did. Then it was his heart going *kaboom* as he turned around and took in the sight of her dressed in a lacy sophisticated number that echoed the creamy color of the silky expanse of skin it revealed.

If he hadn't been fully in lust by the time he'd covered off the delectable curves, he was when he took in her sexy disheveled hairstyle, which left her silky dark curls half up and half down. There was only one thing a man wanted to do when a woman wore her hair like that, and that was to dismantle it completely.

If she was his. Which she wasn't.

He swallowed hard. Santo might be right. He might have a problem. He'd been so far under Chloe's spell during that perfume-testing routine, he'd fled the room moments after it had mercifully ended. Sharing a villa with her wasn't necessarily a great choice either, but with his place ten minutes away from the Buchanans', it would have been silly not to take advantage of it.

What had Santo said? Admitting you had a problem was the first step toward solving it?

Chloe flashed him an uncertain look from beneath those long, amazing lashes of hers. "Am I not dressed appropriately? Mireille thought this would be perfect for tonight. But maybe it's too much?"

"You look gorgeous," he said quietly. "We should go so we aren't late."

She tipped her head back, luminous brown eyes resting on his. "Are you okay? You seem off."

"I'm good." He placed a hand at the small of her back to direct her toward the stairs, his palm nearly spanning her delicate spine. The satiny softness of her skin beneath his fingers unfurled a curl of heat inside him, one he ruthlessly leashed. He might have a problem, but he knew how to deal with it.

They made the quick, ten-minute drive through Palm

Beach's quiet, exclusive streets, behind whose twelve-foot hedges had once resided some of America's oldest families—the Kennedys, Du Ponts, Posts and Fords had all had homes there. The Buchanans' ornate Palm Beach mansion, however, was the king of them all. An eclectic mix of many of the great European architectures—Venetian, Spanish, Portuguese and Moorish—it sat directly on the ocean, more a palace than a mansion, rising majestically among fifteen acres of manicured, glorious gardens.

The statement property mirrored the big personality of its billionaire owners, Josh and Evelyn Buchanan. Josh, a big, bombastic Brit who'd been a close friend of Martino Russo's, had made his money in electronics and now owned an English football team. He'd fallen in love with his American wife, Evelyn, three decades ago and chosen to stay, building Palacio en el Mar, the "Palace on the Sea," for her.

Josh and Evelyn greeted them warmly, introducing them around the poolside soiree where the crème de la crème of the world's elite were gathered to hear the legendary pop star Rodrigo Carrera in a private concert.

It was a magnificent setting—the sun a ball of fire as it sank into the Atlantic, the lazy jazz band that preceded Carrera excellent, the affluent crowd, decked out in their diamonds and black-tie apparel, supremely elegant.

A glass of champagne in his hand, Nico focused on the valuable networking opportunities, rather than the beautiful woman at his side, ensured he and Chloe made that public, political statement of unanimity so necessary for Evolution's stability right now, which was recorded for posterity's sake by the society photographers in attendance.

Chloe tried hard to exercise the same enviable networking skills Nico possessed throughout the cocktail hour and dinner. She found it wasn't so awful as she'd imagined, easier than it had once been for her to complete the endless rounds of socializing with the budding confidence she'd developed and Vivre to talk about.

But it didn't come naturally to her—the ability to make casual small talk, to forge connections out of a throwaway comment someone made. She found herself more susceptible than usual, as a result, to the attentions of the Buchanans' handsome son, Oliver, whose attention over dinner had drawn her out of herself.

Tall and blond, with the most piercing blue eyes she'd ever seen, he was gorgeous. Successful. *Nice.* Exactly the kind of man a woman with a healthy sense of self-preservation should gravitate toward. Unfortunately, that didn't seem to be her. Never had been.

She accepted his offer of another glass of champagne as dinner broke up and the guests mingled on the terrace, waiting for Carrera to begin. Watched as Nico laughed at something the beautiful redhead he'd been sitting next to at dinner had said.

Tall and statuesque, with the perfect bone structure of a runway model, she was stunning. Everything Chloe wasn't. He wasn't looking at *her* as if she had a garbage sack on as he had Chloe earlier. He was looking at her as if she was utterly his type. It hurt in a way she couldn't even begin to articulate. Didn't want to articulate.

Her skin stung, her heart felt sore in her chest. Why had it always been Nico? Why couldn't she just move on? Would it have been different, she wondered, if he'd broken her heart like he surely would have done those years ago? Would she have had closure when it came to him? Because every man since had been a poor substitute—Nico the benchmark by which she had judged them all.

If they could make her feel her emotions right to the

pit of her stomach…if they could make her heart race as he did.

Nico looked up from his conversation with the redhead. Slid his gaze over her. Over the proprietary hand Oliver had placed at her waist. For a single, heart-stopping moment, a flash of heat blazed in his gray gaze. It scorched through her. Singed her right to her toes.

*He wanted her, but he didn't want to want her.* The very visible slip in his daunting self-control rocked her back on her heels. Stole her breath. Then the redhead said something to Nico and he turned away.

Chloe stood there, heart beating a jagged edge. Oliver bent his head to hers. "Let's dance," he murmured. "Carrera is coming on now."

She forced a smile and followed him to the dance floor. She had promised herself she was going to relax and enjoy herself this weekend. Pining after Nico, thinking thoughts that were inherently *unwise* when it came to him, was not accomplishing that. If she were smart, she'd do exactly what Nico was doing—pretend this thing between them didn't exist.

By the time midnight rolled around, however, and Carrera was done with his intimate, fabulous concert, his voice as rich and amazing as it had been in his heyday, Chloe was officially done. She was sure she didn't have one more word of small talk left in her.

"Ready to go?" she asked Nico hopefully.

He nodded. "Let's find Josh and Evelyn and say good-night."

They wound their way through the thick crowd toward their hosts. A feminine voice, with a Southern drawl, cut through the din.

*"Nico."*

Chloe turned to see a beautiful blonde approaching them.

Elegant and undeniably striking with her sparkling blue eyes and chic, sleek bob that angled fashionably to her ear, she moved with a grace and fluidity that captured the eye.

Chloe looked up at Nico, wondering who she was. Found his face frozen solid, not one whisper of emotion visible.

A former lover? She quickly discarded the idea as the woman drew upon them. She had to be in her midfifties. As gorgeous up close as she had been from afar, she must have been outrageously beautiful when she was younger. She still was.

The woman stopped in front of them, her gaze trained on Nico. Nico said nothing, an oddity with his impeccable manners. The woman ignored Chloe completely, waving a fluttering, nervous hand at Nico. "Evelyn just told me you were here. I had no idea. We— I arrived late."

Nico's expression hardened. "I hope you caught some of the concert. It was excellent." He nodded toward Josh and Evelyn, who were seeing guests off. "If you'll excuse us, we were on our way out."

The woman flinched. Chloe drew in a breath. Who was she? And why was Nico being so rude to her?

The blonde shifted her attention to Chloe, as if seeking assistance. "I'm sorry." She held out a perfectly manicured hand. "I'm Joelle Davis. Formerly Di Fiore. Nico's—"

"—mother," Nico finished. "In the biological sense, anyway."

Chloe's stomach dropped. *His mother?* All she'd ever known about Joelle Di Fiore was that she and Nico's father had divorced before his death and Nico never, ever talked about her.

"A pleasure," she murmured, taking Joelle's hand, because it seemed impolite not to.

"As I said," Nico repeated curtly, setting a hand on

Chloe's waist, "we were on our way out. You'll have to excuse us."

*"Nico."* There was no mistaking the appeal in his mother's voice, the raw edge that slid across Chloe's skin. "I hate the way we left things in New York. I don't want it to be this way." She shook her head and fixed her too-bright gaze on her son. "I've recognized my mistake. Can't you at least acknowledge that?"

*"Bene,"* he agreed, his voice utterly devoid of emotion. *Fine.* "I recognize you recognize you made a mistake. Can we go now?"

Chloe gasped. Joelle's blue eyes glistened. "Nico—"

A tall, distinguished silver-haired man separated himself from the crowd and headed toward them. A stony look claimed Nico's face. He pressed his palm to Chloe's back. "If you'll excuse us."

They left Joelle Davis standing in the crowd. Said goodnight to the Buchanans. Nico didn't say a word on the drive home, his face so closed Chloe didn't dare open her mouth. She could feel the tension in him, coiled tight in his big body as he drove, his knuckles white as they clenched the steering wheel. It made her insides twist into a cold, hard knot.

When they arrived at the house, Nico threw his car keys on the entrance table and wished her a good night.

Chloe eyed him. "Do you want to talk about it?"

"No." He flicked her a glance. "Go to bed, Chloe. You look exhausted."

But she couldn't sleep. Her beautiful bedroom with its elegant four-poster bed was heavenly, the book she'd brought with her entertaining, but as exhausted as she was, she was too wired to settle.

She was worried about Nico. About the emotion he always held inside, her head spinning with curiosity about what had happened with his mother to evoke that kind of a reaction. Eventually, she slipped out of bed, put on her new white bikini and a cover-up dress and went downstairs. The house was in darkness, as was Nico's office as she padded across the hardwood floors, but the pool area was lit with recessed lighting, tranquil and inviting under a clear, starry night.

Nico must have gone to bed, she surmised, when she found the terrace deserted, too. It was still warm out, the air just the slightest bit cool on her skin as she took off her dress. A slight shiver moved through her as she descended the steps to the infinity pool with its magnificent view of the ocean. Still warm from the sun, the water was divine.

The heady fragrance of a dozen tropical flowers scenting the air, ideas for a new perfume filled her head. She swam twenty lazy laps with only a cavalcade of stars as her witness. When she had tired herself out, her limbs heavy, body rejuvenated, she climbed out of the pool and reached for a towel on the rack. Stopped dead in her tracks at the sight of Nico sprawled in a lounge chair.

Obscured by the shadows cast by the half wall that divided the pool and lounge area, a glass of what she assumed was whiskey dangling from his fingers, he looked disheveled in a way she'd never seen him before. His jacket and tie gone, the top few buttons of his shirt undone, his hair spiky and ruffled, he looked like he'd been there for a while.

Her gaze shifted to the whiskey bottle beside the chair, a good dent taken out of it. Back up to his stormy gray gaze. He raked it down over her still-dripping body in the brief white bikini, a frank, appraising look so raw and uncensored, it rocked her back on her heels.

Heat, wild heat, unraveled beneath her skin. Stained

her cheeks. She'd always wondered what Nico unleashed looked like. *If* he ever unleashed himself. Now she knew.

She wrapped the towel around herself, tucking it against her chest with trembling fingers. "I didn't see you there."

"I figured." Low, intense, his voice was sandpaper rough. "You couldn't sleep?"

"No."

"I'm sure you will now."

She ignored the unsubtle dismissal and walked over to him on legs that felt like jelly, whether from the swim or the intensity of his stare, she wasn't quite sure. Up close, she could read the lust in his eyes, a stomach-curling need that shimmered through her insides. But there was also darker, angrier emotion. A combustibility, a *volatility* that burned there.

"You're angry with her," she said quietly.

He pointed a finger at her. "*Bingo.* You win the prize."

She swallowed hard. "You need to talk about it, Nico. It's not healthy to hold everything inside." When he simply continued to stare at her as if she hadn't even spoken, she sighed and pushed a stray hair out of her face. "We used to talk. We used to be...*friends*."

His mouth twisted. "Can we just get one thing straight? We are not *friends*, Chloe. We were never friends."

She sank her teeth into her lip, the salty tang of blood staining her mouth. "What were we, then?"

He took a contemplative sip of his whiskey. "I don't think," he said decisively, "that should be a point of discussion tonight."

"Fine," she said calmly, more off balance by this barely censored version of Nico than she cared to admit. She sat down on the lounge chair next to him. "How about we talk about what happened tonight, then?"

He lifted a shoulder. "What's there to talk about?"

"The fact that your mother desperately wants a relationship with you and you threw it in her face."

His eyes flashed. "You have no idea what you're talking about."

"Then tell me. This is clearly eating you up inside."

He rested his head back against the chair. Stared at her with those incendiary gray eyes. "She walked out on us when I was fifteen."

Chloe's stomach contracted. Such a tough age to lose a mother. "Why did she leave?"

An entirely unhumorous smile stretched his mouth. "Do you have all night?"

"Yes." She curled up on the chair and tucked her legs beneath her. He gave her a long look, then turned his head to stare out at the ocean. She thought he would shut her down then, but he started talking instead.

"My mother met my father when he was a young stockbroker on Wall Street. She was a dance instructor from Brooklyn. She'd moved to New York from California to make it on Broadway. Then she got pregnant with me. She was bitter about it, had no interest in being a mother, but my father convinced her to have me. He desperately wanted kids. He started making a lot of money, and then she didn't care so much because she loved to spend it."

"My father was best man at their wedding, wasn't he?" Chloe asked, remembering the photos her father had shown her.

Nico nodded. "Those were the good years. Lazzero and Santo came along. We got a big house, had the fancy cars, everything that came with the Wall Street lifestyle. Then Martino decided to leave and start Evolution. My father thought about it, decided he was wasting his talent on his firm and left to start his own company."

"A stock brokerage?"

"No. One of his clients, a brilliant engineer, had developed a technology to block the effects of wireless fields when cell phones became popular—a tiny chip you could put on the back of your phone. It was revolutionary, had limitless potential, but the client didn't have the money to bring it to market on his own. My father went into business with him—sank every dollar he had into it."

Chloe was completely intrigued. "It *sounds* ingenious."

"It was. Unfortunately, it took more time to take off than they had anticipated. A lot of wooing of big companies that move very slowly. My father started borrowing money to keep things afloat. Then a major company ordered thousands of units and they thought they'd made it. They secured another loan, went into large-scale production, only for the company to have second thoughts and the order fall through."

Her stomach dropped. "Oh, no."

His expression was grim. "It was the end. The death knell. They lost everything. We lost the house because my father had remortgaged it. The cars—all of it. My father started drinking, lapsed into a deep depression he never came out of."

"Why didn't he ask my father for help?" she queried, perplexed. "To start over?"

He rubbed a hand over his jaw. "He and Martino were the closest of friends, but they were also wildly competitive with one another. It was always who could execute the biggest deal, who could land the most beautiful woman. The rivalry continued when they started their own businesses. Except," he allowed, "Martino became massively successful, while my father's business failed."

"And he was too proud to ask for help."

He nodded. "He wouldn't speak to Martino or any of the others when they called. Refused to take handouts. My parents' marriage fell apart, and my mother moved back to California, where she's from."

Chloe gave him a horrified look. "She just *left* you with your father like that?"

His mouth twisted. "She said she hadn't signed on for that kind of a life."

She pressed a hand to her cheek, an ache forming deep in her chest. "How did you survive?"

"I left school and got a job. Went to classes at night. We lived in some pretty seedy places, but we made do."

And somehow, in the midst of it all, while he was taking care of his family, *holding it all together,* he had managed to get himself a scholarship to the university where he'd been completing his business degree when his father had died. Her father had reconnected with the boys at Leone's funeral and taken them under his wing.

She swallowed hard. It all made sense to her now. Nico's intense sense of honor. The laser focus with which he'd conducted his life, the *ruthless ambition* she had accused him of. He'd had no *choice*. He'd had two brothers and a father to take care of.

"I'm sorry," she said quietly. "That must have been so difficult, Nico."

He shrugged, the ice in his glass crackling in the still night air. "My brothers and I have always said it made us who we are. That we wouldn't *be* who we are were if not for what happened. So for that, I'm grateful."

*But at what price?* "Did you have any contact with your mother after she left?"

He shook his head. "She said she wanted to start a new life—that she couldn't do that with the baggage of her past along for the ride. She met and married Richard, the man you saw her with tonight, a year later."

Chloe drew in a breath. "I'm sure she didn't mean that."

"She meant it," he said flatly. "My father went to see her—to plead with her to come back. She sent him away. The next time we heard from her was five years ago in New York. She came to apologize—to make amends for her mistakes. None of us wanted anything to do with her."

Her heart hitched. How could a mother just walk out on her children like that? It was inconceivable to her. But if there was anything she knew from her own experience in life, it was that people didn't always express what was deep inside themselves. They hid their hopes and fears. And maybe Nico's mother had been afraid. Maybe she'd simply been unable to cope with the way her life had disintegrated around her.

She wet her lips. "She seems to want to make amends, Nico. Can't you forgive her?"

"No," he rumbled, making her jump with the force of his response. "She walked out on us, Chloe. She *made* her decisions. It is ancient history, and I'm at peace with it."

He looked anything but. There was so much emotion on his face it hurt to look at him. He'd just worked his way through a good portion of a bottle of Scotch—Nico, whom she'd never seen have more than a couple of drinks. And now she knew why.

"Anger is not being at peace with it," she pursued. "Maybe you need to listen to her. To find forgiveness to find that peace in yourself."

He lapsed into silence. Made it clear the conversation was over as he drained his glass. "Go to bed," he said, without looking at her. "You've heard the whole sordid story now. No more to tell here."

"I'm not leaving you like this."

"I don't want to talk, Chloe."

She leaned back on the chair, palms planted in the cushion. "Fine, we won't talk."

He moved his gaze back to her. Hot, *deliberate*, it singed the curves of her breasts where the towel had fallen loose. "I don't want company either. Not when we both know what a bad idea that is."

Her stomach tipped upside down, a tremor moving through her. "Why?" she queried huskily. "We're consenting adults. You wanted to kiss me that night in my office during the perfume testing. I know you did."

He went still. "Which I didn't," he said harshly, eyes on hers, "because I knew the insanity that it was. Which it *is*, Chloe."

She knew he was right. Knew she should keep up her guard when it came to him. But the severe, taut lines of his face held her spellbound. The redoubtable control he prized so greatly. Everything about him that did it for her like no other man ever had.

Did he still kiss the same way? As if he could do it all night? Would he make her turn to flame if he touched her again? Could she bear it if he never did?

She hugged her arms tight around herself. Felt a chill move through her that had nothing to do with the cool night air. She'd been cold for so long, *frozen* for such an eternity, she didn't remember what it felt like to be alive. To live in the moment. And suddenly she knew she couldn't do it one second longer. She wasn't going to leave him alone.

She lifted her chin. Trained her gaze on his. "Maybe I know it's crazy. Maybe I know I'm going to get burned. Maybe I haven't felt alive in so long I don't care."

A muscle jumped in his jaw. "You *should* care. I am not in the right headspace for this, Chloe."

But the heat in his smoky stare said otherwise. She was mesmerized by it as it melted her insides. By the chemical reaction that popped and fizzled between them. When she was in the lab, she manufactured reactions like this. With

Nico, they were *real*. Out of her control. It made her pulse stutter, like she'd ingested some kind of dangerous drug.

"Come over here, then," he murmured, the hard lines of his face pure challenge. "If you're so sure of what you want."

He expected the invitation to frighten her off. She could tell from the look on his face. And for a moment it did, freezing all coherent thought. She sucked in a breath, delivered necessary oxygen to her brain. Knew in that moment this was the only opening she was ever going to get with Nico. She either seized it or wondered "what if" forever.

She shrugged her shoulders and let the towel fall to the chair. Got to her feet and walked over to him. He rested his head against the back of the chair and drank her in. Teeth buried in her lip, heart beating a jagged edge, she sat down on the inch of lounger beside him that was free. He was so gorgeous, so formidable in his disarray, sleeves rolled up to reveal corded, powerful forearms, heavy dark stubble dusting his jaw, her stomach went to dust.

His formidable control held even as his eyes turned to flame. He wasn't going to be the one to cross the line. It was going to be up to her to do it. And so she did, leaning forward and wrapping her fingers around his nape, absorbing the shift of tensile muscle and tendon beneath her fingertips as she brought her mouth down to his.

He didn't resist, but he didn't move to meet the kiss either. She found his lips with hers. Hard, betraying none of that inherent sensuality that was so much a part of him, she thought for a terrifying instant he was going to reject her. Then a soft curse escaped him, his arms clamped around her waist and he lifted her astride him, his hands cupping her bottom in his palms. She had just enough time to take a deep breath before he took her mouth in a hard, demanding kiss that slammed into her senses. *Demanded everything.*

As if it would make her run. As if he *wanted* her to run.

Instead, it made her skin burn. Her insides dissolve into liquid honey. The strong muscles in his neck flexed beneath her fingers as he angled his head to deepen the kiss. *Took*, until he seemed to be everywhere inside her, the taste of him dark and dangerous.

A groan tore itself from his throat. He shifted his hands to cup her jaw and slicked his tongue over the seam of her lips to gain entry. She opened for him, helpless to resist his sensual onslaught. Gasped as he stroked and licked his way inside her mouth, his hands at her jaw holding her in place for his delectation. As if he wanted to taste every centimeter of her. *Devour* her.

As intimate as the sexual act itself, *more*, the kiss made her stomach curl. She spread her palms against his chest, absorbing the latent strength that rested in every honed muscle. He tugged the clip from her hair and sent the heavy weight of it tumbling around her shoulders. Threaded his fingers through it and slowed the kiss down to a hot, languid seduction. The kind she remembered. The kind that went on forever.

His mouth left hers. Chloe murmured a protest, but then his lips were busy on her jaw, and then her neck, inducing those same brain-melting sensations. She shivered as he slid his hands from her hair down to cup her breasts. Tested their weight. Stroked his thumbs over the hard peaks, pushed taut by the night air. The shockingly pleasurable caress through the thin material of her swimsuit sent a wave of heat to her core.

"*Nico,*" she breathed.

The tie of her bikini top gave way to the sharp tug of his fingers, and then there was only the delicious sensation of those strong, provocative hands on her bare flesh. The roll of her nipples between his fingers that made her moan deep in her throat. The heat of his ravenous gaze as he drank her in.

"You're beautiful," he said huskily. *Reverently.* "God, I've wanted to see you like this."

The look in his beautiful eyes made her fall apart inside. The heady male scent of him, the unmistakable musky smell of his desire, the iron-hard strength of his thighs beneath her were like seeing, *feeling*, the world in Technicolor again. She didn't think she could ever get enough of it.

She moved closer, seeking, *needing* more. Encountered hot, aroused male, burning her thighs through the material of his pants.

*Oh. He was phenomenal.* As into this as she was.

She melted into him, liquid with longing. Emboldened by the power she held over him. Whispered his name against his mouth.

"Chloe," he murmured, even as he took more of her weight in the hands he slid to her hips, rocking her against that most impressive part of him. "This is madness."

She bent her head and tugged his sensual bottom lip between her teeth. "I don't care."

His hand at her hips rocked her more firmly against him. Deeper, higher, the inferno raged until she was a slave to it. Until nothing existed except what he was making her feel. She whispered how much she wanted him in his ear. He told her how much he loved to hear her talk to him like that. How passionate, how honest her response had always been.

She gasped as he gripped her bottom tighter and raked her against the hard, aroused length of him, the wet, thin fabric of her swimsuit a delicious friction against the intoxicating steel beneath his pants.

Fire seared through her. She whimpered, moved against him, desperate, *hungry* for him to assuage the sweet ache between her thighs. For him to make her feel the things only he had ever been able to make her feel.

He angled her more intimately against him, giving her what she asked for. Ground himself against the aching center of her again and again until she sobbed her release in his ear.

"God, that is sexy," he murmured, a hand at her buttock holding her there, rotating his body against her until he'd wrung every last bit of pleasure out of her. "Give it all to me, sweetheart," he rasped. "All of it."

She collapsed against him, gasping for air. Shattered by the force of her release, incoherent with pleasure, rocked by the experience they had just shared. He had taken her apart, *dismantled* her. She felt exposed, *bare*, in a way she'd never experienced before.

She laid her head on his chest, listening to the pounding of his heart as he held her. Soothed her. Brought her back down to earth with the smooth stroke of his hand across the bare skin of her back.

Nico wasn't actually sure when he'd lost his mind. It might have been the sight of Chloe climbing out of the pool, dripping wet in the sexy white bikini, all of that flawless, creamy skin on display. Or maybe it had been that first sweet touch of her mouth against his. The palpable vulnerability that clung to her like a second skin. But he hadn't been able to resist her. Or maybe it was himself he hadn't been able to refuse.

His breath a jagged blade in his chest, he clawed back control. Every male urge he had said to finish it, to take what he had always craved. To burn them both to oblivion in what followed, because surely it would be amazing. And completely, utterly *insane*.

He rubbed a palm against his temple, head hazy. What

the hell was he doing? Was he really that weak that one kiss had been enough to dismantle the promises he'd made? To forget he was her boss…in a position of authority over her?

Or maybe it had been the whiskey, something he never should have started on. Another lapse in judgment.

He pulled in a breath, fury at his mother for starting this, disgust with himself, mixing in a potent brew. There was still time to assume control. He hadn't let things go *that* far.

Chloe pulled back to look at him, those devastating brown eyes of hers wide and shell-shocked, luminous with desire. "Nico," she murmured, reading the regret on his face. "Don't. I—"

He pulled her bikini top back into place, his hands fumbling over the ties as he redid them. Stood up, with her in his arms, and carried her inside. He didn't trust himself to talk with her half-dressed, and he sure as hell wasn't continuing what they'd started.

Taking the stairs to the second floor, he strode down the lamp-lit hallway and set her down outside her bedroom door. Leaning a hand against the wall, he pulled in a breath. Searched for something to say. But his lack of control when it came to her was such a lapse of judgment, any coherent thought dissolved in a red tide of fury directed solely at himself.

"That," he said harshly, "should not have happened."

She lifted her chin. "I wanted it to happen," she said evenly. "We have something, Nico. Ignoring it is only making it worse."

He gave her a withering look. "You are too vulnerable to have any idea what you're saying, and I'm too much of a son of a bitch not to have walked away. So *find* a way to get it out of your head, Chloe. For both our sakes."

# CHAPTER SEVEN

NICO WOKE WITH a pounding headache. His alarm clock sounded like a fire engine, the sunshine pouring through the windows threatened to blind him, amplifying every throbbing beat of his head. Swiping at the clock with his hand, he silenced it. Sagged back against the pillows.

The events of the night before infiltrated his head. His mother showing up...that red-hot scene beside the pool with Chloe... *Merda.*

He hauled himself out of bed, showered and drank a gallon of the black coffee his housekeeper brewed for him, apparently not unused to the aftereffects of the whiskey phenomenon with Lazzero's hard-partying nights. The idea of walking for hours in the bright sunshine seemed an abhorrent idea, but as his golf game was with the president of the largest beauty retail chain in America, canceling was not an option.

He left the house with a thermos of coffee tucked under his arm and a prayer of silent thanks Chloe was still in bed, because he could definitely wait until dinner to address *that* giant misstep.

Sliding into Lazzero's Porsche, he gunned the powerful car to life and followed Ocean Boulevard to his destination, a pristine stretch of blue ocean flanking his right.

*You're angry, Nico... Perhaps you need to find forgiveness to find peace.*

Chloe's words from the night before echoed through his head. He tightened his fingers around the steering wheel. Damned right he was angry. His mother had been a selfish, bitter creature who'd beguiled his father with her undeniable beauty, then made him pay every day of his life for getting her pregnant with him, even though, by all accounts, she'd been a dancer of mediocre talent who'd resorted to teaching to pay the bills.

Money had been the currency his mother had been willing to trade in. His father had sold what was left of his soul to give it to her. And when he'd eventually folded under the pressure, his mother had made him pay for failing to provide by walking out on New Year's Day.

*Forgive her?* He took a sip of his coffee. Wiped an infuriated palm across his jaw. *Never.* He was the one who'd had to pick up the pieces after the flashy-suited banker had left the Di Fiorcs' Greenwich Village home after delivering his instructions to repossess the house and everything in it. He was the one who'd taken one look at his father's grief-stricken face, his father who was *no longer there*, and assured his brothers that everything was going to be okay, when, in actual fact, he wasn't sure it would be at all.

He jammed his foot on the brake as a car cut in front of him. Hell yes, he was angry. *Furious* with his mother for approaching him like that when he'd made it clear he wanted nothing to do with her. He was also, he conceded, furious with himself for his own lack of control. For drowning himself in whiskey, pouring out the whole sordid story to Chloe and allowing himself to fall under the spell of a woman he'd vowed to keep his hands off.

A wave of bitter self-recrimination washed over him. He

should have walked away. Instead, he'd put his hands on her, on everything he'd wanted from the first moment he'd seen her in that dress last night, and crossed the line. Had been so caught up in her uninhibited, innocent responses to his caresses, in the heat they'd generated together, he hadn't *thought*—he'd just taken.

Clearly he needed to find a better solution to his problem than the one he currently had. Luckily, he observed grimly, as he pulled into the perfectly manicured front entrance of one of Palm Beach's most prestigious golf clubs, he had eighteen holes to find it.

*Find a way to get it out of your head.*

Unfortunately, all Chloe *could* think about was last night with Nico as she brooded over a pot of coffee on the terrace in the morning sun. Hot, *erotic*, what they'd shared was indelibly burned into her head, never to be forgotten.

The way he'd *looked* at her…the things he'd said. It had been even more intense, more amazing, than her eighteen-year-old self had remembered.

Her skin burned, a flush spreading from her chest up to her cheeks, singeing them with a fiery heat. Nico had been as caught up in the moment as she had been. As if he'd been giving in to his feelings, too. As if he hadn't been able to help himself. It validated everything she'd thought about them all those years ago. As if that had been the truth of them.

To know she could affect him like that, that she could make him lose control, shook her to her toes.

And then he'd walked away. *Again.*

She sank her teeth into her lip. Stared out at the sparkling, azure sea. She had seduced Nico into kissing her. Pushed him over the edge. With the hopes that what? He would take her to bed? That he would say to hell with the consequences, of which there were many, admit that what they had was special and be so lost in the moment he wouldn't be able to resist her?

Her stomach turned over on a low, antagonized pull. He had *confided* in her. That meant something, because Nico never talked to anyone. Now she knew the experiences that had shaped him—why he never formed lasting attachments with women. Because he didn't *trust* them.

Which should be a giant, blinking yellow caution sign. One she should heed for her own self-preservation. Instead, she felt exhilarated. *Invigorated.* Alive. She'd put herself out there, gone after what she'd wanted for the first time in her life, and it had been *amazing.* And that was where her thought processes began and ended.

She spent the day on the beach, until the sun slanted lower in the sky, Nico's return from his golf game imminent. Then she peeled herself off the lounger and headed up to the house to shower and change for dinner.

Sliding on a short, baby-doll-style dress in moss green silk that hinted at her curves in the subtlest of ways, she caught her hair up in a simple high ponytail, applied a light dusting of makeup, then made her way downstairs, her stomach tight with nerves.

Nico was waiting for her on the terrace. His skin tanned an even darker brown from the day in the sun, muscular body clad in faded jeans that clung to his powerful thighs and a black T-shirt that did the same for his amazing abs, aviator sunglasses on his face, he was drool worthy in a way that stopped her heart in its tracks.

Also vastly intimidating.

"How was your day?" he asked evenly, clearly back in full Nico control.

"Lovely." She could play this game, too. "Yours?"

"It was a good networking day." He tipped his head to the side. "I thought we might have a drink before dinner."

*A good idea.* They could have a mature, honest conversation about last night so her stomach would stop crawling with nerves.

He poured her the glass of white wine she requested. Fixed himself a sparkling water with lime and leaned back against the bar, cradling it between his fingers. Chloe sank her teeth into her lip.

Was he going to take the sunglasses off or was she going to have to guess at what he was feeling?

As if he'd read her mind, he reached up and slid the glasses off. His cool gray gaze met hers. "I think we should talk about last night."

"Agreed." She took a sip of her wine with a hand that trembled ever so slightly. Eyed him.

"It can't happen again." Flat. Definitive.

"Why?"

His gaze narrowed. "Would you like me to list the reasons? Because I am your boss. Because you are my responsibility, Chloe. Because it would be a big, giant mess."

She shook her head. "That's an excuse, and you know it. Yes, we have to work together, but our current situation is already complicating that. As for you being my boss," she said, shrugging, "that's semantics really. I *own* Evolution, Nico. It's my company. So there is no power imbalance between us. Which only," she concluded, "leaves us with the real issue here—that you keep walking away and why."

"I don't sleep with the people I work with," he said matter-of-factly, "regardless of any power imbalance. It's a policy of mine. And you *are* my responsibility, that's a fact. I am your regent."

"And last night?" she prompted, lifting a brow. "What

was that? Because I would say we well and truly crossed the line."

A muscle twitched in his jaw. "It was a...*slip* on my part."

Humiliation fired her cheeks, the clear regret in his voice activating that deep-rooted insecurity she did so well. "Because I threw myself at you again?" she suggested huskily. "A *pity* kiss to get me off your back?"

His lashes lowered in a hooded gaze. "You know that's not true."

"Then what *was* it?" She shook her head, frustration stinging her skin. "I'm going a little crazy here, Nico. I think I'm imagining things one minute, then I'm sure I'm not the next. You're hot, then you're cold. Which is it?"

A flicker of antagonism marred his deadly gray cool. "What would you have me say?" he bit out. "That I wanted to make love to you last night? That I was one step short of carrying you to my bed and taking everything you were offering? Because we both know that I was. And where would that have gotten us?"

Her insides dissolved, the sensory impact behind his words slamming into her brain with visceral effect. How *close* to the edge he'd been with that iron-clad control of his.

"To a place of honesty," she murmured, wrapping her arms around herself. "What you said to me the night of the board meeting. About me hiding from you. Hiding from myself. You were right, Nico. I have been. Because you make me feel things I've never felt with anyone else. Things I want to explore—things I'm *terrified* to explore. But by far, my worse crime has been hiding from myself. Denying what I want and need in life because I'm too afraid to go after it. So last night I did."

His eyes widened imperceptibly, before he schooled his

expression back into one of those inscrutable looks. "You don't want me, Chloe. The relationships I have with women are short and transactional. A few enjoyable nights spent together, a dinner or two thrown in and then I walk away. There are *rules* to it."

"That's right," she murmured, voice dripping with sarcasm. "Your *rules*. Those personal *entanglements* you avoid like the plague. Funny, when I've never asked for that from you. Maybe you should ask yourself what *you* are hiding from."

His jaw hardened. "*Chloe.* Stop pushing."

"Why? Because we might finally get at the truth here?"

He muttered an oath. Strode to the edge of the railing to stand looking out at the ocean, a long silence passing between them. "I made a promise to your father to take care of you. I won't break it."

She blinked. Followed him to the railing. "What promise?"

He turned to face her. "Last spring, your father developed a cough. He thought nothing of it, but when it persisted for a few weeks, he went to see his doctor. He was diagnosed with incurable lung cancer. Told he had two years to live."

Her breath whooshed from her lungs. "*Lung cancer?* He didn't smoke."

"He did back in his Wall Street days. He said it was a bad habit that had finally caught up with him."

Her brain struggled to process what he was telling her. That step back her father had taken...his pristine will and succession planning. It all made sense now. *He had known he was going to die.* That he would not be around to guide Evolution.

"I don't understand," she said numbly. "Why didn't he tell us?"

His gaze softened. "He didn't want to worry you. He told your mother, of course. Me—because he wanted to get the succession of the company in order—to ensure Juliette and you girls were taken care of before he made the news public. Which he wasn't going to do until he had to because he felt the rumor and speculation would be harmful to the company."

Hot emotion bubbled up inside her, threatening to spill over her carefully contained edges. "You should have told me," she rasped. "I could have come home from Paris. I could have spent that time with them. Time I will never get back."

"Your father didn't want that," he said evenly. "He wanted you to live your life. He wanted to see you fly. It was his *wish*. I couldn't just circumvent it."

*"Yes, you could have."* She threw the words at him, hands tightening into fists by her sides. "How many openings have I given you to tell me this, Nico? I *knew* a piece of the puzzle was missing, I *asked* you, and still you didn't tell me. Where is that trust you were demanding? I'm not seeing it."

He pushed away from the railing. Reached for her. She stepped back, eyes on his.

"I was trying to protect you," he said quietly. "You've had enough blows. I needed you focused on saving Evolution with me."

"And you didn't think I could have *handled* it?" She threw him an infuriated look. "Why does everyone think I need my decisions made for me? Do you think I'm that delicate that I can't handle the truth?" She waved a hand at him. "I'm a grown woman, Nico. You keep telling me to have confidence in who I am—to *believe* in who I am—but you won't trust me enough to make my own decisions."

He regarded her silently for a moment. "You're grieving, Chloe. It makes you vulnerable."

*Vulnerable.* That word she was beginning to hate. "What about my uncle? Does he know?"

He shook his head. "Your father knew how badly Giorgio wanted to run Evolution. That it was going to be a blow that he hadn't chosen him. He was going to tell him at the right time. Position it the right way."

"Instead, he died, leaving Giorgio furious with you and confused about why my father did what he did. A *rogue element.*"

"Yes."

And he, because he was rock-solid Nico, impenetrable in a storm, had taken everything she and Giorgio had thrown at him because he was uncompromising when it came to his sense of honor to those he was indebted to. And he was indebted to her father. He had given Nico a second lease on life, and he would never forget it. Nor would he break his promises when it came to her.

Once again, her choices were being taken away from her.

She pressed her palms to her temples, her brain too full to think. Except for the one thing in her head that *was* crystal clear. "Can we just establish one point?" she murmured, echoing his words from the night before. "I am not too *vulnerable* to handle what happened between us last night. And I don't need you taking care of me, so you can absolve yourself of that responsibility, too, along with your propensity to make decisions for me. I no longer require it."

"Chloe—"

Numb, furious, she turned and headed for the stairs to the beach.

"Where are you going?" he fired after her.

"For a walk. I'm too angry with you right now to be in your presence."

She flew down the stairs. Kicked off her shoes and started walking, the sand still warm beneath her feet, the sun a kaleidoscope of shattered gold on the horizon.

Anger flared inside her, hot and wild, as she walked, toes sinking into the sand. At her father for keeping the truth from her. For taking away her chance to spend that time with him and her mother. For taking away any chance she might have had with Nico. At Nico for not telling her the truth.

Hot tears filled her eyes, blurred her vision. She sank down on the concrete break wall and covered her face with her hands. She wasn't ever going to get a chance to say goodbye…to tell her parents how much they'd meant to her. That phone call in Paris on her way home from work, the one that had seemed far too surreal, far too unfair, far too *sudden*, had been it.

A tear slipped down her cheek. Then another, until they were a steady stream of hot warmth, the salt staining her lips. And once started, she couldn't stop, all of the emotion she'd had locked up inside her escaping on a wave of despair, until her sobs robbed her of her breath, shattered her from the inside out, the pain in her chest nothing compared with the one in her heart.

Nico told himself to leave Chloe alone. That this had been a long time coming. That the wise, *rational* course of action would be for him to give her the space she'd asked for—to allow her to get it all out without complicating things further with an even deeper emotional attachment to a woman he couldn't have. But he couldn't seem to do it, her raw sobs squeezing tight fingers around his heart.

He took a seat beside her on the wall, picked her up and

pulled her onto his lap, cradling her against his chest. She stiffened, as if she might resist, then another sob racked through her and she melted into him, her tears soaking his T-shirt.

He smoothed a hand down her back and murmured words of comfort against her silky hair. Long minutes passed, until finally her sobs turned into hiccuping big breaths and she went quiet against him.

The rhythmic sound of the rolling surf stretched between them, the sun a fiery, yellow ball as it sank into the sea.

"I want them back," she murmured against his chest. "I miss them every day."

A strange ache unearthed itself behind his rib cage. "I know," he said softly, tucking a stray strand of her hair behind her ear. "I do, too. But you have to let them go. And when you do," he promised, pressing a hand against her chest, "you'll find they're *here*."

She looked up at him, eyes twin glimmering mahogany pools. "Is your father there? For you?"

He nodded. "The man he was. Not the man he became."

Her gaze darkened. "I'm glad." She exhaled a long breath. Swiped the tears from her cheeks. "I guess it's just frightening, you know? They were always there for me when life got bumpy. A phone call away. *My safety net.*"

"You don't need it," he said softly, eyes on hers. "You've got this, Chloe. You're proving it."

She caught her bottom lip between her teeth. Something unfurled beneath his skin. A need to comfort, to soothe, to *touch*. To protect her as had always been his urge. To take her amazing mouth with his and make everything better. But a stronger part of him knew it for the mistake it would be. That one more taste of her would be his undoing.

He wasn't *hiding* from his feelings for her—he simply knew his capabilities. He didn't have the capacity to take on another person's happiness, had had enough of that for a lifetime.

"Nico—" She reached up and smoothed her fingers over his jaw, her brown eyes luminous.

He caught her fingers in his. "Dinner's ready," he murmured. "I think we should go up."

Her mouth firmed, eyes cooling. Sliding off his lap, she brushed the sand from her dress. Set off up the stairs to the house, without looking back at him, her spine ramrod straight.

*Bene.* They were back to her hating him. Him knowing it was the better way. At least it was a status quo he knew and understood.

# CHAPTER EIGHT

CHLOE SPENT THE week back at work doing her best to focus on the frantic preparations for the Vivre launch rather than her roller-coaster weekend in Palm Beach with Nico. But she found it almost impossible to do so.

Knowing why her father had done what he had done had made everything seem more confusing rather than less, because that meant Nico *was* the honorable man she'd always thought him to be. It meant she'd been wrong about everything when it came to him, not helpful when he'd taken any chance of *them* happening off the table.

She couldn't change the fact that she'd been wrong about so many things, nor could she do anything about Nico's overinflated sense of honor she loved and hated at the same time. About the fact that he had distanced himself from her ever since Palm Beach. What she could do was make sure Vivre took the world by storm, to *fly* as her father had wanted her to do.

With her campaign set to go live in just a couple of weeks on November 15, everything was falling into dizzying place. She'd travel to Europe to meet with the regional teams next week to put the final pieces in place for the launches in London and Paris. Then she'd come back to New York to launch the campaign at the Evolution Christmas party, with Be on sale to the public the day after, in a splashy launch with Lashaunta.

They were operating on the razor's edge, but they were pulling it off.

She gave her phone a cursory glance as she waited in line for her midmorning latte. Almost dropped her purse at the photo that came up in her news feed.

Juggling her bag and phone in one hand, she scrambled for money with the other, found some dollar bills and shoved them at the barista. Stepping to the side to wait, she scanned the cutline of the photo of Eddie Carello and his current girlfriend emblazoned across the front page of a popular gossip site.

*Eddie Carello Enjoys*
*Wild Night in the Bahamas!*

*Things got a bit out of hand on the weekend at a luxury hotel in Nassau, where Hollywood heart-throb Eddie Carello was enjoying a wild post-concert party.*

*A hotel suite was allegedly trashed during the incident, which apparently caught Carello in flagrante delicto amid a supposed ménage à trois with girl-friend Camille Hayes and a waitress from the hotel.*

*The ruckus began when guests complained about the noise levels in the hotel and staff were dispersed to handle the complaint.*

*When asked about the incident, Carello's spokes-person replied that "the whole thing has been over-blown and people shouldn't believe everything they hear."*

*Meanwhile, Hollywood's hottest star seems to*

*have upped his outrageous antics in advance of his*
*new movie,* Score, *giving everyone something to talk*
*about around the water cooler this morning.*

*Nooo.*

Chloe clutched her phone in one hand, latte in the other
and hoofed it back to work. She was out of breath by the
time she reached Mireille's office. Her sister, who was on
the phone, gestured her into the seat opposite her. Chloe
threw her phone on Mireille's desk and collapsed into the
chair, attempting not to panic.

Her sister finished the call. Picked up Chloe's phone
and scanned the story. Started to laugh. "Well, you knew,"
she drawled, "he wasn't lily-white. But that was the attraction, right? He's a rebel—the new James Dean. A perfect
fit for Soar."

"Yes, but—" Chloe gestured at the phone "—isn't this
*bad* PR?"

"PR is rarely bad." Mireille sat back in her chair and
crossed one elegant leg over the other. "If anything, this
is going to make him a hotter property. I wouldn't be surprised if they manufactured this for the buzz. Although,"
she conceded, "he doesn't need it."

"I don't *want* him doing things like this," Chloe said
worriedly. "He was fine the way he was."

Mireille lifted a shoulder. "Not much you can do about
it. If you had a major sponsorship that he was riding on,
you might have something to say about it. But in your
case, he's doing you a favor. Sit tight," she advised, "let
it burn itself out. The news will be on to something else
by the weekend."

Since Mireille was the expert, and she knew nothing
about these things, Chloe took a deep breath and sat back
in her chair. "Okay."

Mireille fixed her with a speculative look. "Any reason Nico bit your head off in the meeting this morning?"

Chloe, who'd planned on keeping her mouth shut about the whole thing, found her cheeks heating. "I kissed him."

Mireille sat up in her chair, eyes wide. "I'm sorry. Can you repeat that?"

She bit her lip. "I kissed Nico…in Palm Beach."

Her sister stared at her. "Forgive me. I'm still stuck at the part where you just said you kissed your boss."

Chloe scowled. "You are not being helpful."

Mireille smiled. "Oh, come on, Chloe, it's about time. In fact, I'm not sure how it hasn't happened sooner. You two have had a thing for each other as long as I can remember. Santo and I always joke about it."

Chloe gave her a horrified look. "You and Santo joke about it?"

Mireille waved a hand at her. "Why the long face, then? What happened?"

Her lashes lowered. "He told me it was a mistake. That it never should have happened."

"Because you are his responsibility. Because he's Nico." Her sister shrugged. "Nico was never going to be a forever kind of guy, you knew that. He's a night-to-remember guy. If you're suicidal enough to want that after everything he did to you, seduce him again and do it right this time. Or find someone else to get over him with."

She didn't want anyone else. That was her problem. She never had.

The passion she and Nico had shared that night flickered through her head—an intoxicating, irresistible memory that refused to be extinguished. A surge of determination coursed through her. Maybe she was done letting everyone else make her decisions for her. Maybe it was time for her to convince Nico this *was* her decision to make.

\* \* \*

Nico waited until he and Jerry Schumacher, the most senior member of Evolution's board, had finished an excellent dinner at Jerry's favorite Manhattan steakhouse, including a superior bottle of amarone, before he broached the subject of the current thorn in his side.

"Giorgio Russo," he said bluntly. "How big of a problem is he?"

Jerry sat back in his leather chair and swirled the dark red wine in his glass. "There are a few board members who have always been sympathetic to him. Maybe he's picked up another couple of late with his campaign. But your support is solid, Nico. Deliver a good Christmas and you'll silence him."

He slid a file across the table to Nico. "The names you asked for."

Nico slid the folder into his briefcase. "*Grazie.* I owe you one." He took a deep sip of his wine. Contemplated Jerry as he set the glass down. "Christmas will be good. We are going big with Vivre—a fifty-million-dollar launch with the A-list celebrities Chloe presented at the meeting. It's going to put Evolution back on the map."

A smile twisted Jerry's mouth. "You never were the faint-hearted type, were you? A chip off the old block."

Nico inclined his head. Refused to reveal how the comparison burrowed under his skin. Jerry had known his father during his Wall Street days when Leone Di Fiore had been known for his big, risky deals—suicidal, some had liked to call them. But he'd always pulled them off. Until he hadn't with the most important one of them all—the one he'd gambled his life savings on.

"The signature fragrances are what the company was built around," Nico pointed out. "They're what's going to bring the company back to life."

A rueful look painted itself across Jerry's face. "My wife sure as hell is a zealot. She's mad about that damn perfume. What is it… Live?"

"Be," Nico corrected.

"Be, right." Jerry frowned, his bushy, white brows drawing together. "Wasn't one of Chloe's celebrities that Eddie character? The Hollywood guy?"

Nico's lips curved. "Yes. He has a big movie coming out in December. Perfect for the launch."

Jerry reached down and scavenged around in his briefcase. Pulled out a newspaper. A tabloid, Nico noted as Jerry handed it to him.

"You buy this stuff?"

The retired CEO gave him a sheepish look. "My wife. She made me promise to bring it home. Apparently, it was all over the radio this morning."

Nico scanned the story on Eddie Carello and his wild threesome in Nassau. He would have been amused by the actor's exploits if he wasn't the cornerstone of his fifty-million-dollar Vivre ad campaign. It was a sensational piece, no doubt about it. Who knew how much of it was true? But he'd seen enough Hollywood stars implode under their own egos that it worried him.

"It will sell lots of perfume," he said to Jerry.

He headed back to the office after he'd dropped Jerry at home. Sought out Giorgio, who was still working. The older man greeted him with his usual lazily satisfied attitude until Nico flipped open the file Jerry had given him and listed off the names of the board members Giorgio had been courting. When Giorgio sputtered and attempted to defend himself, Nico closed the folder and slid it back into his briefcase.

"Food for thought," he told the arrogant, egocentric fool, "while you consider your future within the company.

Because one more errant move on your part and you'll be out of a job."

Leaving him to scramble in a web of his own making, Nico sought out his second, perhaps bigger problem.

Chloe wasn't in the lab when he checked there, the one other person who was telling him she was up in the lounge, screening her promotional spots.

He found her curled up on the sofa in the lounge, watching Eddie's commercial, a pizza box and an assortment of soda cans in front of her. Dressed in black leggings and a figure-hugging sweater, the high boots she'd been wearing kicked off, her hair loose around her shoulders, she looked sexy and takeable.

His inability to forget that hot encounter by the pool appeared to be his third problem.

She eyed him. Sat up straight, picked up the remote control and put the video on pause.

"I just informed your uncle I will fire him if he doesn't cease his smear campaign."

Her eyes widened. "You can't *fire* him. He owns part of the company."

"Your father gave me the green light to do so."

She was silent for a moment, eyes on his. "He loves Evolution, Nico. Tell him the truth."

"He'll find another reason to perpetuate his antics. He has a choice. He can make it." He threw the tabloid he'd purchased on the coffee table. "That discussion is closed. *This* one, however, is a problem."

She glanced at the tabloid. Back at him. "I talked to Mireille. She says there's no reason to panic. That, if anything, this will amplify the buzz around Eddie. Make him even more popular."

"Maybe so," he agreed. "But this is a fifty-million-dollar ad campaign, Chloe. We have staked the future of the company on it. Eddie Carello is a loose cannon...a wild card. What if his behavior amplifies instead of de-escalates?"

"It *will* die down," she insisted. "Mireille thinks it's even possible his handlers manufactured this as movie publicity."

"Not something I want to gamble the Evolution brand on." He blew out a breath. Shoved his hands in his pockets. "I think we should cut him. The other three can carry the campaign."

Chloe gaped at him. Rolled to her feet and came to stand in front of him. "We can't throw Eddie away. He's the anchor of the campaign, Nico—marketing gold. He is going to make the Evolution brand *relevant* again."

"He's too much of a risk," he countered flatly. "Remember when I said not one thing can go wrong with this campaign? I meant *not one thing*, Chloe. This is asking for trouble."

She crossed her arms over her chest. "You're overreacting."

"I am not overreacting. There are no second chances with this. This campaign goes south, so does the company. It's that simple."

"I *know* that." Fire flared in her eyes. "I had the same reaction as you when I walked in today. Then Mireille set me straight. *You* are the one who has been telling me I need to listen to the experts. To lean on my team when I need to. To *learn* from them. Well, I have, and Mireille is telling me it's fine, so it's fine."

He closed his eyes. She pressed the advantage. "The others can't carry Soar. It's a men's fragrance. Eddie needs to. He *is* Soar."

He bit back the response that came to his lips. To *order* her to cut Eddie, because that was what he would have done. He *had* counseled her to consult the experts. Which she had, and Mireille, whom he trusted, had weighed in. So how could he turn around and veto them both?

Perhaps he *was* overreacting. And maybe he didn't know what the hell he was doing anymore. He only knew his head wasn't entirely clear when it came to her.

He had removed a piece of her clothing in Palm Beach. Had been imagining doing it again ever since. Except *all of it* this time.

His mouth thinned, a throb unearthing itself at his temples. He was starting to think *he* had been the naive one to think he could separate the personal from the professional when it came to Chloe because he didn't seem to be doing a very good job of it either.

He brought his back teeth together. Followed his own advice and went with the experts. "Call Eddie's agent. Tell him to tone it down."

She blinked. Nodded. "I will. Thank you."

He gestured toward the TV. "Are you almost finished here? It's late. I can drive you home."

"No, I have more to do. I—" She jammed her teeth into her lip and stared at him.

"What?"

"You're avoiding me and you're snapping at me in meetings."

Caught utterly off guard, he kept his face impassive. "I am not avoiding you."

"You canceled three of our meetings this week, Nico."

"I am busy running the company, in case you hadn't noticed."

She pursed her lips, long dark lashes fanning down over her cheeks. "That's what you said to me about me hiding in Paris. I think you're doing the same with us."

She was right. Absolutely right. He *had* been avoiding her, because his lust was a problem. But he wasn't about to admit it.

"You're imagining it," he said blithely.

"Am I?" Her gaze remained unwavering on his. "Are you punishing me for what happened in Palm Beach?"

*"Yes,"* he agreed, voice heavy with sarcasm, "I am punishing you, Chloe. As we make fifty-million-dollar decisions together."

Her gaze dropped to her stocking-clad feet for a moment before she looked back up at him. "I can't get what happened that night at the pool out of my head. The way it was between us. I don't think either of us can. I think we need to address it."

His gaze narrowed. "*What* exactly are you suggesting?"

"I want to explore what we have. I want to know what that kind of passion feels like. No strings attached."

His jaw dropped. "You're suggesting we have an affair?"

"Yes."

His head pounded, like a grenade ready to go off. Was she really standing there, calmly suggesting they have an affair? The no-strings-attached type he specialized in? She was *insane*.

Except was it really that insane? A part of him knew it hadn't been the whiskey that had made him cross the line that night in Palm Beach. That he'd crossed it because he'd wanted to. Because he wanted *her*. Because it had been a long time in the making. But that didn't mean Chloe's was a sane solution.

"We can't maintain the status quo," she murmured, pressing forward in the silence.

"Perhaps not," he rasped. "But I can assure you that *now* is not the right time for this discussion."

"When do you think might be?"

*"Not now."* He stooped and picked up his briefcase. "Go to Paris, Chloe. Make this launch happen. And keep that damn actor of yours on a leash."

# CHAPTER NINE

PARIS WAS A BLUR.

Nico's warning to execute the launch without a hitch echoing in her head, Chloe threw herself into the final preparations with the regional teams in Europe, visiting Paris first to ensure the pop-up store on the Champs-Élysées was gleaming and ready to go. She stayed at her apartment she'd kept in the sixth arrondissement while she was there, and had dinner with the team and Estelle at one of her favorite cafés to run through the launch event logistics.

Funnily enough, she didn't feel homesick for her adopted home like she'd been sure she would. She found herself at peace instead. She was doing what she was destined to do, there was no longer any question in her mind. And she *knew* she could do it now.

Her meetings with the London team went off seamlessly, as well. She flew back to New York just in time for the Evolution Christmas party. Always scheduled during mid-November, it served as the official kickoff to the holiday season—the most important sales season for Evolution. After the party for the company's employees, customers and partners that evening, Be would be launched to the public the next day with an appearance by Lashaunta in Times Square.

Chloe was running on an adrenaline-induced high by

the time she arrived at her town house to dress for the party with Mireille, a Christmas tradition. It was only when Mireille waved Carrie Mayer's newspaper feature at her that her stomach sank.

What if it was awful? Mireille's deadpan expression wasn't giving anything away.

Heart pounding in her chest, Chloe sank down in an armchair with the paper and took a deep breath.

*Scent of a Woman*
*by Carrie Mayer*

*When I sat down with Chloe Russo, daughter of legendary American perfumer Juliette Russo, I wasn't sure what to expect. A teenage phenomenon who launched her own fragrance at seventeen, she has remained out of the public eye for much of her life.*

*I wondered if she would have her mother's intense charisma...or perhaps she would be the opposite, languishing under the weight of the expectations placed upon her to fill the shoes of a woman who burned as one of the industry's brightest stars.*

*Instead, I found a bit of an enigma. A warm, engaging woman who entranced me from the moment I sat down. Who captivated me with her passion for her calling. A woman whose talent clearly stands on its own.*

*There is, however, clearly a message behind her new perfume line, Vivre, that perhaps echoes the struggle she has waged to forge that identity. And that, according to Russo, is to simply "be." To let your spirit define you. To know the only limitations in life are the ones you place on yourself.*

A tear slipped down her cheek as she read the rest. Then another. They were a steady stream by the time she put down the paper and her sister pulled her to her feet for a hug.

"You've done it, sweetie. Mamma would be so proud. This is your night to shine."

"Oh, no." Chloe pulled out of her arms. "I forgot to buy a dress in all this insanity."

"That's what you have me for." Her sister threw her a satisfied smile as she plucked one off the back of a chair. *"I knew you would. Voilà."*

Chloe tried on the black dress her sister presented. Halter-style, it had straps that crisscrossed around her neck, leaving her shoulders and much of her back bare. Body hugging, it fit her like a glove, highlighting every dip and curve.

It was sophisticated, *daring.* Chloe pursed her lips. "I'm not sure I can pull it off."

"You're the only one who *could* pull it off." Mireille waved a dismissive hand at her. "You wear all those French creations I could never hope to fit into. It's going to make Nico's eyes bug out of his head."

Butterflies swooped low in her stomach. Was that what she wanted? She'd been so busy since she'd left for Europe, she and Nico hadn't broached the subject of *them.* She wondered if she was crazy to have even proposed it. But she knew in her heart it *was* what she wanted, this chance to be with him. So she was letting the chips fall where they may.

Except where were they going to fall? It was almost painful, the waiting.

She slipped on decadently high black heels and the ornate triangular onyx earrings Mireille had given her for Christmas last year, while her sister dressed in a fire-engine-red gown that fit her vibrant personality. And then they were ready for Evolution's big night.

Restored to its original glory in 2008, The Grand Ballroom of the Plaza, which had once played host to Truman Capote's famous Black and White Ball, had retained its glorious neoclassical decor with its grand arches and stunning massive antique chandeliers.

Tonight, as the setting for Evolution's annual Christmas party, the ballroom echoed that classic black-and-white theme, with the invitations, catering and decor all reflecting the elegant color scheme, because it had been Juliette Russo's favorite.

High black vases brimming with white lilies graced the tables scattered around the room, champagne with blackberries as its adornment was the opening cocktail and the massive Christmas tree in the center of the room glittered in cream and ebony.

With the Vivre campaign playing on screens placed discreetly around the room, the stunning, evocative creative adding the perfect touch of Hollywood glamour to the evening, it was simply *magical*. And with Eddie and Lashaunta in attendance tonight, it was also Manhattan's hottest ticket in town.

Chloe and Mireille had arrived before the guests to make sure everything was perfect, as their mother had always done. But the events team had outdone themselves, every festive piece in place. Relaxing with the hotel manager, they chatted about some of the legendary parties that had taken place in the ballroom as they waited for the guests to arrive.

Chloe wasn't exactly sure when she sensed Nico's presence in the room. It was instinctive with her, this awareness of him that seemed to reach soul deep. But when she turned around, he still took her breath away.

Dressed in an elegant black tux, his dark hair slicked back from his face, his fabulous, severe bone structure cast into harsh relief, he looked sleek, lithe and outrageously good. *Dangerous* in a way that sent a convulsive shiver up her spine. Because two weeks away hadn't lessened her attraction to him. It had only intensified it.

Greeting both her and Mireille, he pressed a kiss to Mireille's cheeks first. When her sister discreetly faded away to "check on a piece of missing decor," Nico set his gaze on Chloe. The not-so-subtle heat singed her skin as he moved it down over her body. Lingered at the bare sweep of her shoulders, the length of leg, before he brought his perusal back up to her face.

"You look stunning," he murmured, his husky voice sending another shiver through her as he bent his head and brushed his lips to both of her cheeks. She sucked in a breath at the electric contact, any air she'd managed to consume lodged somewhere in her chest as he straightened and set a silvery gaze on her.

"Did Mireille show you Carrie's piece?"

"Yes." Her chest tightened, as if a fist had wrapped itself around it. He'd been there for her all along. Not just now, but during the hardest months of her life when her parents had died, managing things in the background. *Always there.* She just hadn't seen it.

She wasn't sure she could articulate how much it meant to her. But she tried. "Thank you," she said, eyes on his. "For believing in me. For supporting me. It means everything."

His eyes darkened to a gunmetal gray. "You did it, Chloe, not me. I simply kept you on track."

"But you put your faith in me. It was what I needed."

"I put my faith in your *talent*." A smile flitted across his mouth. "Now we just need to sell some perfume."

And wasn't that the fifty-million-dollar question? "We will," she said, more confidently than she felt.

His smile deepened. "Let's go greet the guests, then. They're starting to arrive."

Santo rested a hand against one of the pillars flanking the ballroom, his eyes on the elegant black-and-white-clad, bejeweled crowd.

"Quite a party," he murmured. "Lashaunta and Eddie Carello in attendance…the mayor, even. This must put even *you* in a festive mood."

Nico ignored the gibe. He hated Christmas. Had ever since their mother had walked out on New Year's Day. It had been all he could do to make it through the elaborate Christmases at the Russos' house in Great Neck without climbing out the window.

"It's a good party," he acknowledged, with a tip of his head. "Your ex was at the bar earlier with her jet-set crew."

"I saw her. She did your print campaign this year, didn't she?"

Nico nodded. Santo's ex—a model scaling the heights of superstardom—was still crazy about his brother. He couldn't figure their relationship out. Neither could his brother, it seemed, the way it went back and forth like a Ping-Pong match.

Nico cocked a brow. "What did she think of you and your reporter date?"

Santo lifted a shoulder. "Not so thrilled. But a relationship can't just be about lust. I'm looking for a soul mate."

Nico's mouth twisted. "Do you actually *believe* the things you say?"

*"Si."* Santo gave him an unconcerned look. "I believe love exists. I simply think it's hard to find."

Santo, Nico mused, was an eternal optimist. How he managed that particular attribute after watching their parents' bitter wreck of a marriage disintegrate was beyond him. At least Lazzero, currently off on business in Brazil, had no interest in Santo's concept of eternal love. Lazzero was even more cynical than he.

"Speaking of beautiful women," Santo said, nodding his head toward Chloe, who was dancing with Eddie in the center of the room, "this is certainly her night. All the big stars repping her perfumes…she must be on top of the world."

"She is." There was a curious tightness in his chest, a pride, he told himself, in everything Chloe had accomplished. She'd become the strong, confident woman he'd always known she could be, taking on her demons with courage and slaying them one at a time. Had demonstrated a core of steel as she'd made an impossible campaign timeline work, refusing to let any setbacks faze her.

He'd be a liar if he said she didn't affect him, because she did. She always had. And perhaps Santo was right. Perhaps she didn't need his brand of protection anymore. Perhaps she was capable of knowing what she wanted when it came to them. Perhaps burning this thing out between them *was* the right answer. But could she handle an affair with him? Or would it make even more of a mess of the situation than it already was?

Eddie bent his head and said something in Chloe's ear that made her laugh. Her bright, vibrant smile kicked Nico right in the chest. He'd missed her these past couple of weeks she'd been in Europe—her quick wit, that razor-sharp brain, the way she challenged him at every turn.

If he were being honest, he'd admit he was fighting a losing battle over something he'd wanted for far too long.

Chloe's head was spinning from all the dancing and conquering she'd done. More than one journalist had pulled her aside to tell her how much they loved her perfumes. Jerry Schumacher's wife had gushed to her about Be and how much she adored it, and the silent auction of her yet-to-become-available complete set of Vivre perfumes was going for thousands.

Eddie and Lashaunta had been a huge hit, Eddie, thankfully, on his best behavior tonight. It couldn't have gone any better. Except, of course, if Nico had danced with her. Which he hadn't. Once again, he'd danced with everyone *but* her.

"It's almost midnight," Mireille murmured. "You need to put the star on the tree."

Chloe's stomach knotted. Putting the star on the Christmas tree had always been her mother's job—the symbolic kickoff to the most exciting, important time of the year for Evolution. She knew it was her job now, she just wasn't sure she could do it.

But Nico, true to his usual, impeccably punctual self, appeared then. The knot in Chloe's stomach grew as they walked toward the center of the room. "I'm not sure I can do this," she murmured.

"Yes, you can," he countered firmly. "I thank everyone for their contributions this year and you stick the star on the tree. Nothing to it."

Except when they got to the center of the room and Nico had quieted the crowd to give his remarks, her heart was beating so loudly it echoed in her ears and her knees felt like jelly.

However was she going to climb that ladder? She could

feel five hundred sets of eyes on her as she toed off her shoes and stepped onto the first rung, Nico spotting her as she went. Climbing to the top, she affixed the beautiful white star to the tree with trembling fingers. Felt something in her heart break. She thought she might have finally said goodbye.

Nico caught her hand in his as she got to the bottom of the ladder. "Put on your shoes," he said. "I haven't danced with you yet."

If she'd thought her heart had been beating fast before, it felt like it might career right out of her chest now at the look of intent on his face. She took a deep breath, slid her feet into her shoes and took the hand he offered.

The band started playing a slow, lazy tune in deference to the late hour. Catching her fingers in his, Nico pulled her to him. One hand laced through his, the other resting on his shoulder, she moved into his arms. Shivered as he slid an arm around her waist and pulled her into an utterly respectable hold that somehow didn't feel so innocent with the undercurrents running between them.

His palm at her back burned like a brand against her bare skin. When she tipped her head back, there was a sexy, smoky heat in his eyes that turned her insides to mush.

"Are you sure you can handle this?" he murmured. "I don't do relationships, Chloe. If we do this, it's to burn this thing between us out. We both walk into it on the same page. Nobody gets hurt."

Her core melted into a pool of fire.

She pulled in a deep breath. Gathered her courage. "I know what I want," she said firmly. "I've always known what I want. If this past year has taught me anything, it's that life is short. You have to seize the moment. And I don't want to spend tonight alone. I want to spend it with you."

He fixed her with an unreadable gaze. Her chest felt tight, hot, as if she could hardly breathe. Finally, after an interminably long moment that seemed to stretch forever, he bent his head to her ear. "You have security access to my penthouse from the night you dropped those papers off. Finish up here and meet me there. I'll leave after you do."

# CHAPTER TEN

NICO'S PENTHOUSE ON Fifth Avenue was dark and masculine, with a stunning cityscape view through floor-to-ceiling windows that left the entire space encased in glass.

Chloe kicked off her shoes in the foyer and walked into the open-concept living room with its jaw-dropping panorama of Manhattan. Oyster suede sofas and tan leather chairs were scattered around the space, gleaming birch floors a perfect foil for the dark architecture of the room. But she was too nervous to sit still, Mireille's analysis of Nico burned into her brain.

*Nico isn't a forever kind of guy. He's a night-to-remember guy.*

Her stomach swooped, like a book dropping off a high shelf. Was she crazy to think she could handle this? What if she couldn't? What if she was a disaster in bed with him—too nervous to enjoy any of it? She'd slept with only one man in her entire life, and that hadn't been a momentous experience.

She stood there, stomach crawling with nerves, until she heard the swish of the elevator arriving. The sound of Nico depositing his keys on the front table. She didn't turn around when he walked into the living room because she was too apprehensive to. The thud of his jacket hitting the sofa made her jump. Sent goose bumps to every inch of her skin as the sound of jazzy, sexy music filled the room.

*Part of his practiced seduction routine?* She almost jumped out of her skin when his hands settled around her waist and he pulled her back against him, his delicious dark, sensual scent wrapping itself around her.

"Maybe we should have a drink," she breathed. "I seem to be a bit jumpy."

"We don't need a drink," he said huskily. "I think we should dance instead. I didn't get a chance to do that with you. Not the way I wanted to."

She sucked in badly needed air. Closed her eyes as he bit down ever so gently on her earlobe, the sensual caress ricocheting through her. "How would that be?" she managed to croak.

He didn't answer. Turned her around and took her in his arms instead. The fingers of one hand laced through hers, he splayed the other across her hip. Possessive, intimate, it made her pulse pound.

His forehead resting against hers, they danced to the sultry tune. Their bodies in perfect sync, as if they'd been molded to fit together, it was, quite simply, the most heart-stoppingly romantic moment of her life.

"Nico," she murmured. And then his mouth was on hers, his thumb stroking her cheek, the slow, leisurely slide of their lips against each other like the magical prelude to a passionate symphony that would only build and grow.

She stood on tiptoe. Curved her fingers around his neck. Moved deeper into the kiss until she wasn't sure where she began and he ended. His fingers at her jaw, he angled her head to position her the way he wanted her. She opened her mouth to his command, was rewarded by the lazy, sensual slide of his tongue against hers. Deeper, *hotter* the kiss went until every limb in her body melted, utterly supine against his.

He moved the hand he had at her hip down over her bottom. Cupped her in his palm and brought her closer until she felt the thick, hard evidence of his erection against her. Her knees went weak, threatened to give way, but his hand at her buttock held her easily. Kept her pressed against his impressive arousal, his physical strength vastly exciting to her.

So *this* was the kind of dance he'd been talking about. Her blood thundered in her veins, her heart battered up against her ribs, every inch of her skin pulsed to life. It was like she'd spent her entire adult existence waiting for him to touch her like this. She wanted to memorize every second for future reference.

"Tell me what you like," he rasped in her ear. "How you like it. How you *want* it."

"Like that," she gasped as he rotated his hips against her in a sultry movement that turned her insides to molten honey. "You feel so good, Nico."

He took her mouth in a hungry kiss that held no restraint. Raw, erotic, he made love to her mouth with the hot slide of his tongue until she whimpered and pressed closer. He angled her more intimately against him and let her feel every centimeter of the steely length that pressed against his trousers. Gave her more of that pleasure that had driven her crazy that night at the pool.

"Don't stop," she whispered, on a broken plea. But he did, bending to slide his arm beneath her knees to pick her up and carry her to the bedroom. Setting her down beside the bed in the minimalistic airy room with a spectacular view as its only decor, he moved behind her, set his fingers to the zipper of her dress and drew it down. His hands settling around her hips, he pushed the dress up and over her head, cool air caressing her skin as he tossed it in a pool of silk on the floor.

A wave of self-consciousness settled over her as he sat down on the bed and drew her to him. His fingers dealt with the clasp of her bra with an experience and dexterity that made her pulse pound. Off it went into the pile. And then she was naked in front of him except for the black lace panties that clung to her hips.

Standing in front of him, his gaze level with her bare, aching breasts, she took in the hunger in his stormy gray eyes. "You are so gorgeous," he said roughly. "So perfect. I need to have you, Chloe."

Her insides fell apart. He tugged her the last step forward. Cupped her breasts in his hands. Kneaded them, weighed them. Brushed his thumbs over the straining, tender tips until she moaned and pushed closer, his caresses melting her limbs.

With a muttered imprecation, he dropped to his knees in front of her, his hands cupping her buttocks to bring her close. "Nico," she murmured, heart racing as she read his intention. "You can't do that." No man had ever touched her like that.

He looked up at her, eyes hot. "I've waited forever to have you like this. I want to kiss you. Touch you. *Let me.*"

His words took her apart. Annihilated the last of her defenses, what she'd said to Lashaunta that day filling her head.

*When you let yourself be stripped down, naked, raw, because this was you and you couldn't be anything else but who you are.*

It had always been like that with Nico. He had seen every part of her. This would be no different.

She relaxed beneath his hands. Let him part her thighs. He pressed his lips to the trembling skin of her abdomen in a hot, openmouthed kiss. Her muscles tightened as he moved his mouth down to the band of her panties. *Lower.* And then he was caressing her through the damp lace with his mouth, his tongue, his hands at her bottom holding her in place for his delectation.

She dug her fingers into his coarse dark hair. Whispered mindless words of pleasure, her knees jelly beneath her. Begged for more. He sank his fingers into her hips, turned her around and pushed her back on the bed. Sliding his fingers beneath her panties, he stripped them off.

Her heart nearly burst through her chest as he pulled her to the edge of the bed and spread her thighs wide with his big palms. Drank her in. And then he parted her most delicate flesh with his fingers, his gaze reverential.

"You're beautiful here, too," he murmured. "So pink. Wet. *Perfect.*"

She closed her eyes. Curled her fingers in the bedspread. He set his mouth to her, hot and knowing, doing the same wicked things he'd done to her before, only this time there was nothing between her and the searing caress of his mouth, and it was so earth-shatteringly delicious she was lost.

He fluttered his tongue over the tight bundle of nerves at the heart of her. Told her how good she tasted in raw, uncensored words that inflamed her. She begged for more. Holding her hips tighter, he laved her, flicked at her with his tongue, the powerful lash of his caress almost too much to bear.

Her back arched off the bed. "Nico—*please.*"

He slid a palm beneath her hips and lifted her up. Slid a thick, masculine finger inside her in a slow, controlled movement that made her crazy. Gently, insistently, he caressed her with firm, even strokes. It felt so good, so *amaz-*

*ing*, she bit down hard on the inside of her cheek to prevent the cry that rose in her throat.

"You like that?" he murmured huskily, eyes on hers. "It makes you crazy, doesn't it?"

She nodded in helpless surrender. Moved into the sexy, sensual caresses he was administering with a tilt of her hips, because she knew how he could make her come apart with those skillful, amazing hands of his.

The pleasure built. She dug her nails into the bedding, gasping her pleasure, because she couldn't hold it in anymore.

"That's it, sweetheart," he said throatily. "Talk to me. That's so damn sexy."

He filled her with two fingers. Worked them in and out until she was arched like a bow, sobbing for release. Then he pressed a palm to her abdomen, wrapped his lips around the peak of her sex and tugged at her until he sent her flying into a sweet, hot release that radiated from the heart of her outward, until every inch of her was in flames.

Nico felt like someone had drugged him as he pushed to his feet, eyes on Chloe as she lay sprawled across his bed. Exactly as he'd imagined her. But oh, so much more jaw dropping in the flesh.

She was perfection with her taut, high breasts…the slim curve of her waist that flared out to hips that were deliciously feminine…the long legs, toned and magnificent, that he wanted wrapped around him while he took her long and slow and hard.

He swiped a hand over his jaw, heart pounding. He could still taste her in his mouth, how sweet she was. Could still feel how perfect she'd felt beneath his hands—like silk. He craved her so much, his lust so thick in his throat, he wasn't even sure how he wanted to take her. He only knew that now that he'd given in to the insanity, he was going to drown himself in it.

She opened her eyes. Set her shimmering brown gaze on his. He started unbuttoning his shirt. Yanked it off, buttons flying, when it didn't happen quickly enough. Her eyes darkened as he undid his pants, slid the zipper down and pushed them off his hips, his boxers following close behind. The heat of her gaze turned him hard as a rock.

He lifted a brow. "You didn't answer my question."

"About?" Her voice was lazy. Sated.

"How you want it?"

That woke her up. She levered herself up on her elbows. Worried her lip with her teeth. "I don't know."

"What?" he gibed. "There's finally something you would like to defer to me on?"

"Yes." She sank her teeth deeper into the soft flesh he wanted to taste again. It tipped him over the edge.

"You on top," he said evenly. *"Now."*

Her eyes widened. He found a condom in the bedside table. Stretched himself out on the bed and beckoned to her. She crawled over to him, uncertainty and desire glittering in her beautiful eyes.

"You took on the world tonight," he murmured. "Surely you can handle me."

The uncertainty morphed into a look of pure challenge. She straddled him, her gorgeous body a feast for the eye. It was such a turn-on, this confident, spectacular creature she'd turned into, he was transfixed. High color streaking her cheeks, her hair a tumble of silk around her face, she bent to kiss him.

"You were saying?" she murmured, lips parting sweetly against his. He reached up, cupped the back of her head and brought her closer, his mouth melding with warm, honeyed temptation. She tasted exquisite, the subtle stroke of her tongue against his as she kissed him deeply, intimately, offering him all of her in that way she had that made him completely lose his head.

Her hands found his hard length pulsing against his thigh. She caressed him, her smooth, even strokes unpracticed and so much more hot because of it. He cursed as she pushed him close to the edge. "Baby," he murmured, clamping a hand around hers. "Either you do this or I take control."

Her eyes flashed. She didn't like that idea. He handed her the condom. Her hands stumbled over the task. He settled his fingers over hers and rolled it on, the intimate act thickening the air between them to unbearable levels.

Blood pounded his temples as she positioned herself over top of him. Brought the thick crest of his arousal to her slick velvet heat. Cradled against her, he rubbed the length of her. Relished her low groan.

*"Nico."*

It was his turn to groan as she took him just barely inside her. "Slowly," he bit out. *"Dio.* You are so tight."

Her eyes locked on his as she took him deeper, the erotic connection between them so hot it fried his brain. He set his palm low on her belly. Found her center with the pad of his thumb and massaged her in slow, sensual circles. She closed her eyes, full mouth slackening. Her body softened, took him deeper inside, slowly, excruciatingly slowly, until finally she had sheathed him with her hot, silky flesh.

She opened her eyes. Fixed them on his. "I didn't know it could be like this," she breathed. "You feel so good, Nico."

Blood roared in his head. He could have told her it wasn't like this. Not usually. That sex could be good, but it wasn't always this mind-blowing. But that would be admitting things he chose to ignore. That she had always touched a piece of him no one else ever had.

He grasped her hips in his hands. Moved her against him in a slow circle. She was plush, tight, so damn good, he almost lost it right then and there. Gritting his teeth, he counted from ten back to one. Which proved ineffectual when, eyes trained on his, she picked up his rhythm. Drove him insane with the sexy, circular movements of her voluptuous hips.

He curved a hand around her nape. Brought her mouth down to his. Mated his tongue with hers as he possessed her hot, sweet body with insistent, powerful thrusts that made her gasp with every drive. She begged, panted into his mouth. Hands at her hips, he positioned her so she came down at the right angle for him to hit that tender spot inside her.

"Like that," she gasped. "Oh, Nico. Like that."

"Let go," he bit out, fighting a deep, primal need to take. To mark her as his as he'd always wanted to. Then lost the battle as her body contracted around his in a tight fist and she cried out, nails digging into his shoulders. His hands grasping her hips, he thrust up inside her, yanking her down to meet his punishing lunges.

Harder and thicker he swelled inside her, taking his pleasure, until she splintered him apart in a deep, shuddering release and he came harder than he ever had in his life.

The rasp of their breathing the only sound in the room, he held her, sprawled across his chest, stroking a hand over the silky, soft skin of her back until she fell into an exhausted sleep curled against him.

An insidious tendril of unease wound its way through him alongside the powerful, more potent emotions swamping him in the aftermath of the intimacy they'd shared.

It was just good sex, he told himself. Perhaps the best

he'd ever had. He and Chloe shared an intense physical attraction—one he'd been fighting for far too long. What man wouldn't react that way when a woman was so sweet and willing in his arms? So sexy and vulnerable all at the same time?

Curving Chloe's soft, warm body against his, he let sleep take him. They were going to need some *rules*. But tomorrow would be soon enough to have those awkward, line-reinforcing kinds of conversations they needed to have.

# CHAPTER ELEVEN

CHLOE WOKE TO the first, soft yellow light of day making its way into the sky, shrouding the tall skyscrapers in an almost otherworldly glow. It was such a magnificent view, she simply drank it in for a moment.

Her sensory perception expanded beyond the jaw-dropping panorama to the heavy, solid weight draped around her middle. The hot, hard male body pressed against the length of hers. The very *naked* hot, hard male body pressed against hers.

She was in Nico's bed. She'd spent the night with Nico. *OMG*.

Her heart thumped wildly in her chest. She pressed a palm to the hard, staccato beat in an attempt to steady its racing rhythm, but nothing seemed to help. Everything felt utterly off-kilter—like it would never be the same again. Not after *that*.

She sucked in a deep breath. Blew it out slowly. Last night had been indescribable. Romantic. Sensual. *Soul consuming*. Everything she'd dreamed about and more.

She'd always known Nico would be an amazing lover. That unparalleled control of his, the intensity he wore like a glove, the sensuality that was so much a part of him. But nothing could have prepared her for the depth of intimacy they had shared. It made her toes curl to even think about it.

It seemed impossible to imagine that what they had shared was an ordinary connection. It felt *extraordinary*. Nico had taken her apart, exposed every part of her. Made her feel so alive it was *terrifying*. And she could have sworn he'd felt it, too. That it could be the start of something amazing if he let down his walls.

*And maybe that was highly naive, unwise thinking.* She had no experience with a man like Nico. With that kind of passion. Maybe what they'd shared was simply powerful chemistry. The only thing she *was* sure of was that she was completely and utterly out of her depth.

She sank her teeth into her lip. Twisted to face him. His arm fell away to rest above his head, his severe features relaxed, long dark lashes shading his cheeks. He was so gorgeous it made her melt. But it wasn't just the stunning outer packaging that drew her to him. It was the man *inside* the gorgeous facade. Who he was at the heart of him— impregnable in a storm, unyielding in his sense of honor, solid in a way she'd never encountered.

Finding out he was the man she'd always believed him to be had only underscored the feelings she'd always had for him. Made them more inevitable. If she was smart, she knew, she'd guard her heart. Keep her head.

She turned back to look at the bedside clock. *Six thirty. Thank goodness.* Some internal alarm must have woken her. She needed to be downtown at the Times Square store by 8:00 a.m. to prep for Lashaunta's appearance. Given she had no clothes, only the dress she'd worn the night before, that was a problem she needed to rectify. *Fast.*

She slid out of bed. Went searching for her underwear. Another wash of heat claimed her cheeks as she found it scattered around the room. Snatching up her bra and panties, she slid them and her dress on. Pursed her lips as she considered a sleeping Nico. Was she supposed to wake him up and say goodbye? What *was* the proper procedure?

In the end, she let him sleep. Maybe it was the coward in her, because she wasn't sure how to handle this right now. But it seemed the easier way.

Facing Nico's elegant, perfectly pressed doorman while clad in her sparkly dress and high heels wasn't so easy. What did Mireille call it? The *walk of shame*? It certainly felt like it. The doorman, however, greeted her smoothly and whistled for a taxi, as if seeing off women dressed for the night before was all part of a day's work. A good reminder that she was simply *one* of those women for Nico.

She showered and changed at home, then jetted downtown. The crowds outside the store stretched for blocks, Lashaunta every bit the draw she'd hoped she would be. Practically jumping up and down with excitement, Chloe watched as the pop singer sang four songs from her new album for the crowd and the shelves began to empty of the limited-edition Be. Her problem, she soon realized, was going to be keeping up with the demand, because the same thing was happening worldwide.

She was practically floating on air by the time she arrived back at the office. She had just enough time to check in with Clara before she sailed into a meeting. Which was a budget meeting that happened to include Nico. The nerves came back like a fast-moving tornado.

Sitting across from her at the large boardroom table full of executives, he looked ridiculously handsome in a dark, pin-striped suit and a crisp white shirt. Her heart tripped over itself as she took a sip of the coffee Clara had thankfully provided. He had one of those inscrutable looks on his face. All business.

She told herself to play it cool. Wrapped her nerves in a reservoir of calm she wasn't close to feeling. But she couldn't concentrate on the meeting for the life of her. She kept wondering where she and Nico stood after last night.

After an hour of attempting to pretend he didn't exist, she weakened near the end of the meeting and allowed herself a glance at him. Found him staring at her, a flash of something in his gray eyes that made her breath catch in her throat.

"Nico?" the CFO prompted. "You on board with that?"

Nico nodded.

"Chloe?"

She stared blindly at the balding executive. "Ah—yes. Definitely."

"Good. Let's move on."

Nico was in a bit of a mood. He had never, in his life, had a woman walk out on him after a night spent together. There was an etiquette to it—an acknowledgment of how good it had been—a mutual expression of *appreciation* to be communicated.

Instead, he'd woken to an empty bed. Not a text, not a note. He'd known Chloe had her event today, had planned to drive her home *after* he'd had her again this morning. And perhaps that was the problem. He'd woken up hard and hungry for her with a need that hadn't abated, and that was never a good way to start the morning.

He sat back in his chair. Took a slug of his coffee. Considered her across the table. Just to be clear, it *had* been mind-bendingly good sex. *Emotional* sex, even. The most intensely involved experience of his life, if he were to be honest. They had been crazy for each other. So where was the clinginess every woman seemed to display the morning after? It didn't seem to be coming. Instead, Chloe looked cool and aloof. Distant. *Did she regret last night?*

The meeting drew to a close. Chloe headed for the door.

Nico moved fast, stepping into the hallway at the same time she did.

"A minute," he said softly.

Simone, who'd left the room behind them, stopped to ask him something. Her gaze shifted from Nico to Chloe and back again. Registered the charge in the air. She murmured something about asking him the question later and moved off in the direction of his office.

Nico looked at Chloe. "How did the launch go?"

She leaned back against the wall, eyes on his, her lip caught between her teeth. "It went great. We sold out. Had to restock."

"Congratulations." He leaned a palm on the door frame beside her, catching a whiff of her elusive, sexy perfume. "Do you have any idea what budget you just agreed to in there?"

She shook her head. "None."

"You don't think that's a bit irresponsible?"

"I do." A slow nod. "Forgive me. My mind was elsewhere."

"*Where*, exactly?"

"The regions," she murmured. "I have a call with Europe in minutes."

A curl of heat unleashed itself inside him. He didn't believe her for a minute. But he had a meeting, too. "We can talk later, then."

"Of course."

It wasn't until seven o'clock that evening, however, that he had a chance to seek Chloe out, a brutal day of meetings behind him. She was in her office sitting behind her desk, frowning over a report of some kind. Her suit jacket discarded on the back of her chair, she looked gorgeous in a sheer cream silk blouse and a gray pencil skirt that showed off her fabulous legs.

He wanted to unbutton her and consume her whole. But first, he wanted to find out what was wrong with her.

Wary, so wary, were the big brown eyes that landed on his as he shut the door behind him. But there was also a shimmering, dark glitter in her gaze, a sensual awareness that heated his skin.

He walked over to lean against her desk. "What's going on? And don't tell me it's Vivre, because I'm not buying it for a second. I've seen the sales reports. They're astounding."

She put down her pen. "Nothing's going on. What do you mean?"

Frustration fizzled up his spine. "Okay," he murmured, "let's talk about last night, then. How are you feeling about it? Usually women like to talk about it. I thought you might want to, since you walked out this morning without a word."

A guarded look crossed her face. "I had to get to my event. I didn't want to wake you."

"I was going to *drive* you there, had you woken me up. You took a damn taxi home, Chloe. That is not all right."

Her lashes lowered, sweeping her cheeks like miniature black fans. "Last night was amazing, Nico. More than I ever could have imagined. I don't regret a thing, if that's what you're wondering."

Straightforward, matter-of-fact. *Honest.* But then again, this was Chloe, and she didn't play games like other women. She wasn't *like* any other woman he'd ever met. Hadn't he always known that? Wasn't that what had scared him away in the first place? Everything he wanted to know was right there on her face. In those ebony eyes, which looked terribly uncertain at the moment.

"If that's the case," he said quietly, "then why do you look like that?"

"Like what?"

"Like you regret it."

"I don't regret it."

*"Chloe,"* he growled.

She closed her eyes. Was silent for a long moment before she opened them again. "I am out of my depth," she said softly. "You took me apart last night, Nico. Split me wide-open. It *affected* me. *You* affect me. I was trying to get my equilibrium back."

The muscles around his heart contracted. He'd known this was going to happen. Known it was going to be a mess. Chloe had never been able to separate her emotions from her head. But neither could he lie to himself and pretend last night had been just about sex, because it hadn't. What he felt for her had always been more complex than that.

"You don't think I feel something for you?" he rasped, eyes on the naked vulnerability written across her face. "You don't think I was *affected* by last night? You don't think I'm crazy for you, Chloe? Examine my behavior over the past few weeks and it might give you a clue."

She stared at him. The muscles in her throat convulsed. "I want to kiss you again," she whispered. "So badly, I can't stop thinking about it."

His blood fired. Pushing her chair back with a foot, he sank his hands into her waist and lifted her onto the desk in a single, fluid movement that pulled a gasp from her throat. "You should get on that," he said softly, planting his hands on the wood on each side of her thighs. "Although," he murmured, lowering his head to hers so their breath mingled in a warm, intimate caress, "I'm not sure just a kiss is what I'm looking for."

Her breath hitched. He waited, until she curved her fingers around his nape and brought him the rest of the way. It was all he needed to take her mouth in a hot, greedy kiss that blew his brains out. Cupping his jaw in her palms, she kissed him back, opening her mouth for him as he stroked inside with his tongue. Arched her neck back to take him deep.

He abandoned her mouth to explore the delicate line of her jaw. Traced the throbbing line of her pulse with his tongue. His hands dealt with the pearl buttons on her blouse with ruthless efficiency. Exposed her beautiful, rose-tipped breasts cupped in cream lace.

"Nico," she murmured huskily. "We are in the office."

"Everyone's gone home. I checked."

One hand on her hip, the other closed around her breast, he bent and licked the tip of one tightly furled nipple. Absorbed the low moan that raked through her. Played her, teased her, until she pushed into his hand and demanded more. Cupping her firmly, he took her deep into the heat of his mouth. Rolled the straining, taut nub over his tongue. Between his teeth. She was so lush and perfect, so responsive to his touch, she lit his blood on fire.

He transferred his attention to her other nipple. Swirled his tongue around the hard peak as he plumped her other breast in his palm. "I need to have you," he whispered against her ear.

Dragging her closer with the hand he held at her hip, he pushed her skirt up her thighs until he exposed her cream lace panties. They were so sexy against her coffee-colored skin, the blood thundered in his veins.

"Nico," she breathed. "We can't do this here."

"Yes, we can." He stepped between her thighs. Cupped her knee. Gentled her mouth with his. "Let me touch you, please you," he murmured against her mouth. "I need to have you."

Her knees fell apart. She watched him with big, hot eyes as he cupped her damp warmth with his palm. Inhaled the musky smell of her desire. "*Dio*, what you do to me," he breathed. "You make me lose my mind."

Pulling her panties aside, he ran a finger down her desire-swollen folds. Caressed her with leisurely strokes. Her eyes darkened to twin ebony pools.

"Nico," she breathed.

He circled his finger at the slick entrance to her body. Pushed in gentle demand. She was silky and exquisitely tight. He eased inside her, waited while she adjusted to his touch.

"*Please.*" She fixed her gaze on his.

He moved his finger in and out of her in a slow, sweet rhythm that had her moving to meet him with greedy movements of her hips. Pressing a kiss to the ultra-sensitive skin below her ear, he filled her again and again. Felt the tiny tremors that moved through her.

"Nico." She pressed against him in a sinuous movement.

He set his lips to her temple. "You want to come for me, baby?"

"*Please.*"

He rubbed his thumb against her while he filled her with two fingers. Parted them inside her to caress her intimately. To ready her for his possession because he was like steel beneath his pants and she was small and delicate and he wanted her with a craving he'd never felt before—a voracious need that threatened to consume him.

"Nico," she begged, sinking her fingernails into his shoulders.

Wild for her, utterly unhinged, he reached for the button of his trousers, undid it and pushed his zipper down. Pulling her to the edge of the desk, he slid one hand beneath her hip, palmed his hard, hot flesh with the other and slotted himself against her velvet heat. The sensation of her silken flesh cradling him was indescribable.

He let out an oath. Chloe pulled back to look at him.

"A condom," he gritted out.

"I'm protected," she murmured. "It's fine."

He pushed inside, her tissues like liquid fire around him—squeezing him, stroking his length. His mouth at her ear, he told her how much she affected him, how much he wanted her, how much he'd *always* wanted her. She arched her hips, took him deep, until he was buried to the hilt. Seated inside her, sharing the ultimate intimacy, he held her gaze as he withdrew completely, then pushed back in, a mind-blowing, staggering penetration that made his heart beat like a drum.

"Nico." Her passion-filled gaze rested on his, dark, luminous, *irresistible*.

"You make me break all my rules," he rasped. "Every damn one."

He took her mouth in a hot, hungry kiss. Knew in that moment that one more taste of her had been his undoing. That now that he'd let himself have her, he wouldn't be able to stop. But he was too far gone to care.

Grasping her hips tighter, he thrust inside her with a power that made her gasp, until they came together in a release that shook him to his core.

# CHAPTER TWELVE

CHLOE WAS SO EXCITED, she could hardly contain herself.

Checking her appearance in the mirror for what might have been the fifth time, she convinced herself her short fiery-red dress, made of some rich, satiny material that showed a different depth of color every time she moved, was not, in fact, too short, her makeup—subtle but smoky—was unsmudged and the sleek hairstyle she'd chosen to match the sophisticated dress still in place.

She looked the same as she had five minutes ago. But maybe the dress *was* too short.

*Oh, for heaven's sake.* She spun away from the mirror with a disgusted sound and rummaged for her evening bag in the drawer. Perhaps it was the leftover adrenaline from the Soar launch with Eddie today that was making her jumpy. It had been amazing, frenetic, every TV camera in town out for it. Or maybe, she conceded, stomach clenching with nerves, it was the fact that Nico was back from Europe tonight, she hadn't seen him for a week and he was escorting her to Eddie's *Score* movie premiere.

She shoved a lip gloss and her phone into her bag, along with her keys. It could also have been the very sexy phone conversation she and Nico had shared last night when he'd gotten back to his hotel room that had left her skin crawling with anticipation. Or the way they'd gorged on each other for the two weeks before he'd left, Nico seeking her out in the lab or in her office each night, as if he couldn't resist the pull between them any more than she could.

She was falling for him—truly, madly, deeply—an unchecked spiral she knew wasn't wise. If she were *smart*, she acknowledged, pulling high black heels from her closet, she would be keeping her emotions out of this. Sticking to the deal she'd made with Nico, with *herself,* of a no-strings-attached fling. But she was sure he felt something more for her, too. Something deeper. Felt it every time he touched her. She thought he was hiding behind his walls—that it was going to take him time to trust how he felt.

And maybe, she conceded, sliding the heels on, that was simply the rosy view she chose to paint for herself. Maybe it had nothing to do with reality.

And maybe, she concluded, stomach sliding out from beneath her, she needed to get her head together. That appeared to be a top priority.

Snatching up her bag, she went downstairs and pulled a warm wrap from the closet. Was digging through her bag to make sure she'd thrown in the right lip gloss to match the vibrant dress when the doorbell rang.

Her heart beat a jagged rhythm. Setting the bag on the entryway table, she rubbed damp palms against her thighs and pulled in a steadying breath. Attempted to manage some sort of composure as she undid the two dead bolts her father had installed on the door.

All of it, unfortunately, flew out of her head as she swung the door open to find Nico leaning against the brick wall of the entrance in black jeans, a white shirt and a blazer.

God, she loved him in jeans. There wasn't a man on the planet who looked better in denim, all long legs, lean hips and raw masculinity. And then there were the muscles bulging beneath the hip tailored jacket—those powerful, corded arms she'd learned he needed only one of which to hold her in extremely creative positions.

*Good heavens, Chloe.* She dragged her gaze up to his. Registered the amusement glittering in his gray eyes.

"Hold that thought," he murmured. "Unless you'd like to skip the movie. I'm more than up for that."

Her stomach did a flip at that very tempting idea. But she shook her head with a smile. "Not a chance."

She'd never attended a premiere before, and this one was slated to be extremely glamorous with Hollywood's biggest stars set to shine. Not to mention the fact that Soar was going to be everywhere: in the Evolution refreshing stations at the after-party, in the gift bags for attendees, not to mention the fact that Eddie would be wearing it. She didn't plan on missing a minute.

*"Bene."* He walked past her into the hallway and shut the door. She turned to face him, heart thumping like a drum. Snaking an arm around her waist, he tugged her to him, one hand landing on her hip, the other at her jaw. Nudging her up on tiptoes with the hand he held at her bottom, he brought his head down to hers.

"I *like* this," he murmured, sliding a hand over her silk-covered bottom. "It's very sexy. I'm going to enjoy taking it off you."

She couldn't answer because she was pretty much panting for him to kiss her, the brush of his lips against hers igniting a thousand tiny lightning strikes in her blood. Then he did, claiming her mouth in a deep, slow kiss that melted her bones, a sensual tasting that seemed to last a lifetime. Powerless to resist, she wound her arms around his neck and surrendered.

She felt his smile against her mouth as he ended the kiss oh-so-languidly and let her feet slide to the ground.

When she might have slithered right to the floor, he held her up with the hand he had at her bottom.

"That was wholly unfair," she whispered, eyes on his.

"Say the word and we stay in."

She pressed a kiss to the hard line of his mouth. "Hold that thought."

He gave her a look that said he'd rather not. Chloe's mouth curved in a smile as he escorted her to his car and spirited them the short distance to the Museum of Modern Art in midtown Manhattan, where the premiere was being held.

The red carpet shimmered in the spotlight as they arrived at the entrance to the impressive modern building, its entire exterior facade a wall of gleaming glass. The crowd that had gathered to watch the arrival of the stars was dozens deep.

They wouldn't walk the carpet, only the stars would, but Chloe wanted to watch, so they joined Santo and his date in a viewing area for guests off to the side, the atmosphere in the crowd electric. Santo didn't blink an eye at the protective hand Nico had placed at her back, introducing his date instead, a lovely reporter for one of the New York dailies. And then the stars were arriving in long black limousines.

Near the end of the parade of Hollywood glamour came Eddie and his sultry, stunning girlfriend, actress Camille Hayes. Tall and sleek in a plunging silver-and-gold gown, Camille was outrageously beautiful, the perfect dark foil for Eddie's blond good looks. His hand at her back, he escorted her down the red carpet to the appreciative roars of the crowd.

Chloe was so thrilled, she could hardly stand it. Eddie had a megawatt star power that glittered like no other with his saucy smile and entertaining wit as he talked to the press. And with her Soar ad playing on a screen just to the right of the logo-emblazoned step and repeat banner where the stars stopped for photographs, Evolution was front and center tonight.

If she could get any higher, Chloe thought, as they moved inside to watch the action-packed adventure movie *Score*, she wasn't sure how. It was the most exciting night of her life.

The after-party for *Score* was held in a trendy, swish bar close to the museum. A New York institution, the establishment was legendary for its elaborate Christmas decorations, draped in fifty thousand dollars' worth of glitz tonight, according to Santo, who kept track of such useless trivia.

Nico immediately felt his skin tighten at the overabundance of shiny balls, icicles and endless lights hung from every available surface. He would have turned around and walked out the door if it had been any other occasion. But Chloe was having fun, and far be it for him to steal her joy when she'd worked so hard for her achievements. When Evolution was shining tonight and Eddie Carello had taken it upon himself to introduce her around as the creator of his signature fragrance, his massive ego out in full force.

Ignoring the whole unavoidable ambience, he caught up with his brothers at the bar, while Chloe took Mireille and Santo's date off to visit the Vivre refreshment bar, where patrons could touch up their makeup and perfume.

"No date?" Nico observed as Lazzero did his usual aloof, unattainable routine leaning against the bar, which only made half the women in the room turn and stare.

Lazzero lifted a shoulder, his eyes trained on a group of people near the windows. "I felt like flying solo."

Nico followed his brother's perusal to a beautiful brunette who stood at the edge of the group. "Who is she?"

"Who?" His brother took a sip of his bourbon.

"The woman you keep staring at."

"No one important." Lazzero dismissed the subject, clearly unwilling to discuss the fact that she was *something*, because he'd undoubtedly had about twenty women lined up to accompany him this evening and he'd chosen to come alone. But Nico had learned a long time ago Lazzero confided when and how he wanted to.

Santo pointed his glass of bourbon at Nico, clearly coming to the same conclusion. "I see *you're* keeping better company these days."

Nico kept his tone nonchalant. "Chloe and I have agreed on a casual thing."

Santo took a sip of his bourbon. Rolled it around his mouth as he considered him. "You don't just casually see a woman like Chloe. You do it with intent or you don't do it at all."

Nico, who'd been ignoring that very fact for weeks, inclined his head. "And your point is?"

"Nothing," Santo said innocently. "I was just making an observation."

An observation that once in Nico's head, refused to budge as a friend of Santo's came up to greet them and Lazzero set off in the direction of the brunette. His head half in the conversation and half out, he considered Chloe in the very sexy red dress as she chatted up an A-list actress at the perfume bar.

She was glowing, in her glory tonight. It did something strange to his insides to see her like this, rearranged them in a foreign pattern he didn't recognize. She was smart, beautiful, passionate and empathetic. *Transparent*. Everything he'd convinced himself didn't exist in a woman.

He *had* missed her while he'd been in Europe, and not just in a physical sense. He'd missed her *presence*. How alive she made him feel. How she filled him up in places he hadn't even known he'd been empty.

He was crazy about her, if the truth be told.

The admission, after weeks of denial, rocked him back on his heels. But then again, he conceded, taking a sip of his bourbon, hadn't he subconsciously known it was true? He'd broken every one of his rules for her. Was *still* breaking them. And it felt right in a way he couldn't articulate.

"Can you believe it?" Chloe said, bubbling over with excitement as she rejoined him, champagne glass in hand, and they walked outside to the patio to get some fresh air. "Sasha Pierce wants me to design a custom perfume for her. *Sasha Pierce*, Nico. She's *legendary*."

He smiled, drawing her back against his chest as they stood at the railing and enjoyed a view of a light-emblazoned Manhattan. "Of course she wants you to design a perfume for her. Be is the number three fragrance in the world right now. Soar is going to be a huge hit. You're the talk of the town."

She wrinkled her nose. "Not quite."

She was silent for a moment, as if taking it all in, the silence of the high balcony wrapping itself around them. The balcony was deserted, the heaters not quite able to keep up with the chill in the air. And for that Nico was glad because it gave him a chance to clear his head.

Chloe swiveled to look up at him. "Are you having fun, though? You seem quiet."

He shrugged. "It isn't really my thing. But you're having fun—that's what matters."

Something in Nico's voice, a quiet, distant note, made Chloe lean back against the railing to look up at him. Study his face in the diffused, soft lighting the lamps cast across them. "What's wrong?" she murmured. "You've been off since we arrived."

Another of those uncommunicative shrugs. "It's nothing. Jet lag."

"Nico," she said softly, trailing a finger down his cheek. "I know you well enough now to know something's wrong."

"My mother walked out on New Year's Day," he said flatly. "A week later our house was repossessed by the bank. This time of year doesn't hold very good memories for me."

Her throat locked, her skin stretching painfully tight across her body. "I'm so sorry. I didn't know. You never said anything."

"It wasn't exactly dinner-table conversation at the house in Great Neck."

She considered the hard, impenetrable lines of his face. "That must have been awful."

"It was surreal." A shadow whispered across the clarity of his gaze. "My father lost it that day. I mean actually *lost* it. He had been sinking into a depression for some time, but when she walked out, it was the end of him."

A knot formed in her throat. Grew until it was hard to swallow. He'd been only *fifteen*.

"What did you do? Where did you go?"

He balanced his glass on the railing. "I called my basketball coach. He was a mentor to me and my brothers. He knew a guy who owned a corner store in the neighborhood. I went to work for him, and he let us live in the apartment above the store in exchange for the work."

While he'd gone to school at night, refusing to give up on his own future. Her heart gave a painful lurch. "Lazzero and Santo were so young," she murmured. "They must have been devastated."

His mouth flattened. "They were in shock. Lazzero retreated into himself, refused to talk. Typical him. Santo started to cry because he wasn't sure which bike to take with him."

The ache inside her deepened until it hurt to breathe. She bit the inside of her mouth, the salt tang of blood staining her senses. "I think," she said huskily, reaching up to smooth her fingers over the hard line of his jaw, "that you are extraordinary, Nico Di Fiore. That you had the composure and presence of mind to take charge at that age."

He lifted a shoulder. "Who else was going to do it? It wasn't easy—no. I was bitter. Angry at the responsibility I hadn't asked for. Angry at my *life* and the loss of my freedom. But you do what you have to do."

Worse, she imagined, was what it would have been like to watch the man he'd so clearly admired in his father suffer from such a debilitating disease. To become a shadow of himself.

She tipped her head to the side. "You said in Palm Beach you think of your father as the man he was, not the man he became. What was he like—in the early days?"

"Complex." He took a sip of the bourbon. Swirled it around the glass. "He was never home when we were young. The life of an investment banker—always on, always working, always socializing with clients. It made my mother crazy. But to me," he acknowledged with a faint smile, "he was larger than life. He loved us, loved being a father. Whenever he did have time to spend with us, it was the best. He would take us to baseball games, up to the cottage, out fishing. That's when he was his true self. Away from all the pressure."

She frowned. "I remember my father saying he was *the guy* on Wall Street. That everybody wanted to be him. That he was fueled by this ambition that seemed to consume him." She pressed the rim of her glass to her chin. "Where did that come from, do you think?"

He considered the question for a moment before replying. "The estrangement from his own father was a part of it. His father was abusive to his mother. He tried so many times to intercede—to persuade his mother to leave—but she wouldn't. So he left when he couldn't handle it anymore and came to New York to start a life for himself. He had nothing. No money, no one to fall back on. *He* was it.

"It fueled his ambition on Wall Street. He was imminently successful because of it—a risky, brilliant deal maker. But his ambition was also his Achilles' heel. Once he got caught up in the rush, he couldn't turn it off. He constantly needed *more*. The money, the power—it all went to his head. He had affairs, began living on the razor's edge."

Chloe frowned. "So your mother had reasons for being unhappy, other than the loss of her career?"

Antagonism darkened his gaze. "She *drove* him to it. She was never happy, not from the beginning. The affairs weren't right, clearly, but I can see why it happened."

And she could see the whole story was far more complex than it seemed on the surface, even if she understood why Nico wanted to blame his mother for all of it. "There are always two sides to a story," she said, treading carefully. "Perhaps you don't know the whole truth."

His jaw hardened. "Perhaps I don't want to know. Perhaps I don't care. Maybe it's a fact that two people always mess up a relationship one way or another."

"That's not true," she countered quietly. "Look at my parents. How in love they were. What a great team they were. They were *stronger* together."

"What Martino and Juliette had is a rarity, I promise you."

"Perhaps," she agreed. "But it does exist."

"Anything's possible." He shook his head at her. "Don't start spinning romantic illusions around me, Chloe. I've never been a believer in fairy tales. My experiences have taught me differently."

She took a sip of her champagne. Studied the cynicism on his face. He made so much sense to her now—why he was the way he was. He had the same driving ambition his father had had, for exactly the same reasons. Because his once-safe, if tumultuous life had splintered apart and he would never let the same thing happen to him. Would never make the same mistakes his father had.

Instead, he had made himself into a rock in the middle of the storm for his brothers. For *her*. He had given Santo and Lazzero the faith that life could be trusted, people could be trusted, because he had *been there* for them like his parents hadn't been for him.

A hand fisted her insides. She wanted to be that for him. The one who taught Nico he could trust. That he could *believe* in what they had. Because she couldn't lie to herself any longer and say she didn't want all of him, because she did. She always had. And maybe, just maybe, she had enough faith for both of them.

Or perhaps, she acknowledged, her stomach hollowing out, she was setting herself up for a fall.

A dark fire lit his gaze. "Hey," he murmured, his arm sliding around her waist to pull her close. "That's ancient history. We are not letting it kill the mood. And I am in the *mood*. It's been a week since I've had you."

Heat shimmered through her insides. She let him remove her champagne glass from her hand. Framed his face with her hands as she kissed him long and deep. Refused to let fear rule her, that instinctive need to retreat that had always directed her actions, because she was through doing that. She was seeing this thing with Nico through to the end, just like she'd promised herself, because she thought he was worth it. She thought *they* were worth it.

"Are you ready to go?" he murmured, when they came up for air. "I'm done with *holding that thought*."

Her blood on fire for him, she nodded. They said their goodbyes to Mireille and his brothers, collected the car from the valet and made the drive back to Nico's penthouse in an expectant silence that had every nerve in her body tense with anticipation.

Nico tossed his keys on the entrance table when they walked into the penthouse, shrugged out of his jacket and threw it on a chair in the living room. Sinking his fingers into the knot of his tie, he set his gaze on Chloe as he stripped it off, his body hard and hungry after a week without her.

Lowering himself onto the sofa, he reached for her, pulled her onto his lap.

When her lush lips parted in invitation, her dark eyes full of passion, he didn't hesitate, didn't even try to resist her. Cupping her cheeks with his palms, he settled his mouth over hers in a hot, hungry kiss.

She sighed. He took full advantage, sliding his tongue inside her mouth to tangle with hers, tilting her jaw up to provide him with better access. The taste of her exploded through him, sweet from the champagne she'd consumed. Uniquely her.

He slid his hands beneath the slippery, shimmery material of her dress that had been inflaming him all evening. Found the warmth between her thighs and stroked her through the silky material of her panties with leisurely, teasing caresses. She moaned low in her throat, her soft, breathy sighs making him crazy. But when he would have lifted her to straddle him, desperate to have her, she swept her delicate hand along the hard ridge of him instead, erasing any coherent thought.

"Chloe," he murmured. "I am more than ready."

She ignored him, sliding her fingers up to the button of his jeans to undo it. Every muscle in his body tensed as she lowered his zipper, the rasp of metal against teeth amplifying the pounding of the blood in his head. And then her hands were on him, uncovering him, pulling him out of his boxers.

His heart thundered in his chest as she slid to the floor in front of him. She had been too shy to do that to him up until now, and he hadn't been into pushing her because he'd known with the passion they shared it would happen. He just wasn't sure he could handle it tonight. Didn't know if he had that in him with the need driving him.

He watched, transfixed, as she slid her mouth over the velvet length of him, used her lips and tongue to make him wild for her. Blood pulsing through his body, he arched into her touch, spellbound by her unpracticed seduction.

"Like this," he instructed hoarsely, sliding his hands over hers, showing her how he liked to be touched. How hard. How fast. How to drive him higher.

When he couldn't take it anymore, when he knew he'd finish it that way if he didn't put a stop to it, he reached for her, picked her up and laid her on the sofa like a feast for his consumption.

Red silk dress askew, plunging open to reveal her taut, creamy flesh, her long legs a tangle of olive skin, he had never known such lust. Such need. She was sweetness and innocence, brilliance and fire, an intoxication to his senses he couldn't seem to fight.

He pushed the dress up to her waist. The tiny panties that clung to her hips did little to hide the shadow of her femininity, firing his blood to a fever pitch. He spread his palm over her abdomen, absorbing the shiver that went through her. Trailed his fingers down to the tantalizing piece of silk that covered her. Eyes a deep, dark espresso, she watched him strip it from her.

He got rid of his pants and boxers in one swift move. Came back over her, caging her in with his arms braced on each side of her. "You burn me up," he whispered against her mouth, "until I can't think for wanting you."

She pulled his head down to hers, her fingers sliding into his hair. He slicked his tongue over her lips and gained entry to her sweet mouth. Every stroke, every lick, sensual and earthy, bound him to her in a way he'd never experienced before.

Sliding his palm over her thigh, he found the hollow at the back of her knee. Curved her elegant leg around his waist so that she was open to him. His to take. Settling himself against her moist, welcome heat, he held her gaze as he stroked inside her with a single hard thrust. Claimed her tight, silken flesh with a possession that made her internal muscles spasm in erotic response.

"Fast or slow," he murmured. "Your choice."

"Slow," she breathed, eyes locked on his. "As slow as you can make it."

He regretted asking because he wasn't sure how slow he could take it. His breath coming hard and fast, he possessed her with smooth rhythmic strokes, corralling the fire raging through him as her silken body clenched around his pulsing flesh. Her eyes were liquid fire, the perfection they created together written across them as she curved her leg tighter around his waist and met him thrust for thrust.

It was too intense, *too much*. Burying his mouth in her neck, he tasted her salty skin as he drove harder into her amazing body until they came together in a rush of violent heat that blanked his head.

Emerging from a sex-induced haze what felt like hours later, he took her to bed and made love to her again. When he couldn't sleep, his internal clock messed up from the travel, or perhaps from the intensity of the emotion chasing through him, he left Chloe curled up in bed, went into the living room and poured himself a glass of water.

He carried it into the living room. Sat staring at an always-on Manhattan spread out before him.

He'd told himself he was walking into this thing with Chloe to burn out the attraction between them, when in reality what he'd really wanted was *her*. A no-strings-attached affair had been a convenient excuse to avoid admitting how he really felt about her. That she'd always made him want more. Made him want to *be* more, and he wasn't sure he could be that.

He cared about Chloe—deeply if he were to be honest. But even if he'd always suspected she might be *the one*, offering her the love she needed wasn't a place he was ever going to let himself go. He'd severed that piece of himself the day his life as he'd known it had imploded. Had told himself he needed no one because he'd had to—it was the only way he'd known how to exist.

He took a sip of the water. Tipped his head back as the cool liquid slid down his throat. What would happen when Chloe began to hate him for what he couldn't give her? Because it *would* happen eventually. People changed, emotions changed, and that was when it all fell apart. He knew it as surely as the sun would rise tomorrow.

Martino's voice from that Fourth of July night floated through his head, his raspy Italian lilt as clear as if it had been yesterday.

*You need to make a choice, Nico. Decide whether you can give her what she needs or walk away.*

Hearing the words now, filtered through a decade's

worth of perspective, gave them a different cast. He had assumed Martino had been telling him to walk away, when what he realized now he'd been telling him was that he had a choice—he could decide he could be more, or he could remain the closed-off, hardened man he'd become.

Life was about choices.

How would he even know if he was capable of being what Chloe needed if he didn't try? Would he forgive himself if he didn't and let her go, only for some other man to offer her what he couldn't? He didn't think he would. Not now.

He sat there for a long time, his head too full to think. The only thing he was sure of was that Santo had been right. Either he committed to Chloe or he walked away. There was no in between.

Bright sunlight filtering through a crack in the blinds woke Chloe. She was alone in bed, the sound of water running in the en suite bathroom indicating Nico had risen before her. The man didn't sleep, she marveled, sinking back into the pillows to recall the utterly perfect evening of the night before.

She'd had so much fun showing off Vivre to Hollywood. *A custom perfume for an A-list actress.* It was a coup worthy of her mother. Topped off by an utterly unforgettable, passionate night with Nico.

Her good mood persisted as she slid out of bed, intent on joining him in the shower because that was the way she liked best to wake up. She was almost across the room when her phone rang. *Mireille*, from the distinctive ringtone she reserved exclusively for her sister.

She frowned. Mireille was decidedly *not* a morning person. Maybe she'd seen all the social media coverage from last night and had called to congratulate her on a successful evening. Backtracking, she plucked the phone off the nightstand and took the call. "You're up early."

"Chloe." Her sister's voice was eerily calm. "You and Nico need to meet my team at the office as soon as you can get in."

Her fingers tightened around the phone. "Why?"

"Eddie got into a fight with Camille last night. A big blowup at Gianni's. Club security had to intervene. Also," her sister added, a grim note to her voice, "he said some very derogatory things about women someone caught on video. It's all over the internet."

*Nooo.* Cold fingers clamped down on her spine. The entire Vivre campaign was built around the empowerment of women.

"How bad is it?"

"Bad, Chloe. You need to get in here."

She sucked in air, her breath a sharp blade in her chest. Exhaled. Panic was not going to help. "We'll be there in thirty minutes."

Nico walked out of the bathroom, his brow furrowed. "What was that?"

She pushed a chunk of hair out of her face. Took another deep breath, but it seemed impossible to get the words out of her mouth. Because Nico had warned her about Eddie. He had wanted to cut him. And now, a week before Christmas, the most important sales week of the year, they had a disaster on their hands.

Nico tossed the shirt he was carrying on the bed, walked over to her and tipped her chin up with his fingers. "What's going on?"

She swallowed past the tightness constricting her throat. "It's Eddie. He went off the rails again last night. There was a fight with Camille at Gianni's...club security had to intervene. He also," she added, her gaze falling away from his, "said some awful things about women someone caught on video. It's all over the internet."

Nico uttered a filthy word she'd never heard him use before, his hands falling away from her face. Heart slamming against her ribs, she risked a look up at him, but he wasn't looking at her. He was in full damage-control mode.

"Get dressed," he said curtly. "Was that Mireille on the phone?"

"Yes." Her voice steadied in the face of his fury. "They're waiting for us at the office."

"Good." He ripped the towel off his hips and started to dress. She stood there, frozen.

"Nico, I'm sorry. This is— This *was* my fault."

He spared her a quick glance. "It doesn't matter whose fault it is. We need to fix it."

Mireille and the PR team were waiting in Nico's office when he and Chloe arrived thirty minutes later.

Mireille, always cool and composed, was ashen-faced. "I'm sorry. This was my call."

Nico waved the apology off. "It was a collective decision. I could have cut him." Pouring himself a cup of coffee, he took a seat at the conference table, a move Chloe mimicked. "What's the game plan?"

Cara Cioni, Mireille's boss, who had two decades of experience managing crises for a major auto manufacturer, got up and went to the whiteboard. "First," she said, "we cut Eddie loose. Void the contract using the morality clause. But," she added, a frown pulling at her brow, "we have to be very careful with this. He's the most powerful man in Hollywood. It needs to be finessed."

*"Bene,"* said Nico. "How do we communicate this?"

"A short statement to the press within the next twenty-four hours announcing the split. Reinforcing Evolution's historic commitment to women. I would say today, ideally, for the statement, but that may be unrealistic. Legal will want to go through it with a fine-toothed comb. Tomorrow morning, latest."

Nico nodded. "What about the ad campaign? We're going to need to pull it."

Giorgio, who looked remarkably unruffled, spoke up. "Online is no problem—we can cut it immediately. TV is the issue. It will take forty-eight hours to get the ad off the air."

During which time Evolution and Eddie would be inextricably linked in consumers' minds. Tension knotted Nico's stomach as he realized this wasn't going to be as simple as distancing the company from the actor with a quick statement. It was going to be far messier than that.

"Give me the names of the presidents of the networks if you have to," he bit out, fixing the older man with a stare. "I'll call them myself. I want that ad off the air, Giorgio. *Now.*"

"That will distance us from Eddie," Chloe broke in, "which we clearly want to do because the entire Vivre campaign is all about empowerment, and since three of our spokespeople are women, it's more about female empowerment than anything."

"Yes," said Cara. "Exactly. Soar might be in trouble, but we want to protect the other three fragrances and the investment we've made in them. The *brand.*"

A look of dismay crossed Chloe's face. Nico knew what she was thinking. Soar was her baby. Yet it was now synonymous with Eddie because she'd said publicly the actor had been the inspiration for it, a strategy that might cost her the fragrance.

He pushed on because sacrifices would have to be made. "What about Evolution's reputation when it comes to women?" he asked Cara. "How do we reinforce that?"

"We need to make a gesture of some sort. Underscore the commitment we've always had. But it can't be self-serving—it has to be genuine."

Nico raked a hand through his hair. "What about a philanthropic program for women? I'd been thinking we should build something off Vivre—use Lashaunta or Desdemona to kick it off."

"That's a great idea," Cara acknowledged, "if they aren't poised to drop us. It's a real possibility they could. Which is our next point of consideration," she said, eyeing Chloe and Mireille. "We need to get on the phone to them now. Reinforce everything we stand for. Make sure they don't jump ship."

They both nodded. "We can run the philanthropic idea past them while we do it," said Chloe.

Cara turned to Nico. "This would not be cheap. We're talking millions. Are you prepared to invest in a program like this on a yearly basis?"

Nico looked grim. "We've staked the future of the company on Vivre. There's no turning back now."

Nico spent the day doing damage control with the PR team to prevent Evolution from being caught up in the public outcry that ensued over Eddie's vitriolic outburst about women that had been carried to every home in America via the amateur video it had been taken on.

Not only had the actor labeled his girlfriend, Camille, *a pointless piece of trash*, he'd dubbed women in general *an inferior species that are more trouble than they're worth*. Not to mention the punch he had allegedly thrown at his girlfriend, which, thankfully, in his drunken state, had missed.

With Evolution's public statement about the incident in legal review for distribution to the press first thing the next morning, Nico inhaled the key messages the PR team had developed for him in preparation for the press interviews that would come. But by early evening, a Boycott Evolution hashtag had appeared on Twitter, social media was ablaze with ironic amateur videos of Eddie's commercial spot edited to include his inflammatory comments about women and Nico was fighting the biggest crisis of his career.

By the time he made it back to the office after a dinner he'd been scheduled to attend, he was annihilated. Throwing his jacket over the back of a chair, he went to the bar to pour himself a drink. Froze with his fingers on the cap of the bottle of Scotch. Alcohol, thank goodness, had never been a problem for him like it had been for his father. But that had been before he'd drunk a good portion of a bottle of whiskey and given in to his craving for Chloe and put this disaster into motion. Because wasn't that exactly what had happened?

Pulling a bottle of spring water out of the fridge, he grimly poured himself a glass. He had *known* he should cut Eddie. But he had bet the bank on Chloe and her Vivre launch—on a suicidally risky campaign that would either revive the company or sink it, and he'd needed Eddie as the cornerstone of it.

The problem was, he wasn't impartial to Chloe. Never had been. While he'd been making fifty-million-dollar decisions that affected the fate of the company, he'd been imagining what it would be like to bed her. Last night, when all hell had been breaking loose, he'd been buried *inside* her—putting the promises he'd made—Evolution itself—in jeopardy. Because his head hadn't been in the game, it had been on *her*.

He swore under his breath. Braced his palms on the bar. Clearly he *was* his father's son after all, because it was apparent he couldn't juggle his personal and professional life any better than his father had. Over what? Over a relationship he had a questionable ability to fulfill?

He'd seen the look in Chloe's eyes last night. She was in love with him. He had chosen to ignore it because as strongly as he felt about her, he wasn't *there*. He might never be there.

A cold knot tightened in his gut, the pressure that had been building in his head all day throbbing at his temples until he felt as if his head might explode. Had he not watched his father unravel himself over a woman, putting all he'd built into jeopardy? What the hell was he doing playing at something with Chloe he could never follow through on?

A part of him wanted to be that man. To be everything for her. But in reality, he knew how to do only one thing, and that was how to keep the boat afloat. To make this company prosper. And right now, he wasn't even doing a good job of that.

How the hell was he supposed to pull this out of the fire?

Chloe stood in the doorway of Nico's office, her stomach churning. It had been that way ever since she'd gotten the phone call from Mireille, but now it was worse because Nico had been freezing her out every time she'd been in the same room with him, and now she had to deliver more damaging news.

She took a deep breath and crossed to the window where he stood. He turned, as if sensing her presence, the look on his face as remote as it had ever been.

"I have an update on our celebrities."

He inclined his head for her to go on.

"Lashaunta," she said, "thankfully, seems unfazed. Which is a huge relief, because she can carry this for us.

And she loves the philanthropy program. She's in, if it fits with her recording schedule.

"Desdemona," she continued, "worries me. She was very edgy on the phone, but when I explained the women's initiative to her, she said she'd consider it if we get the Eddie situation under control."

"That's positive."

"Yes." She bit her lip. Forced herself to deliver the bad news. "Estelle is out. Her agent wants nothing to do with it."

He looked remarkably calm. "If one jumps ship," he observed, "another could follow suit when they get wind of it. We need to work fast, ensure that doesn't happen."

"I told Lashaunta and Desdemona we'd get them details on the philanthropy program by the end of the week."

He nodded. "You and Cara can spearhead it together. Let me know what I need to know."

She inclined her head. "How was your dinner? Did you get any questions?"

"A few, but Cara had me prepped." His gaze slid over her face. "Have you eaten anything today? You look pale."

"No—I'm not hungry." Needing his reassurance, his *comfort* right now, she lifted a hand to brush her fingers across his jaw. "I know you're angry with me and I understand why, but you can't freeze me out like this."

He caught her hand in his and brought it down to her side. "I'm not angry, Chloe. I'm focused. Go home, get some sleep. I'm going to stay here tonight and monitor things with the team."

Hurt lanced her insides, confusion enveloping her. "Nico, what's going on? Why do you look like that?"

That utterly inscrutable look remained painted across his face. "I don't think now is the right time for us to be having this discussion."

Her stomach turned to stone. "Why not?"

"Because we are in the middle of a *crisis*, Chloe. We need to be focused on fixing it."

That lit a fire inside her. "I *am* focused on fixing it," she bit out. "I've been killing myself all day to that end. We are going to fix this *together*, Nico, because your idea for the philanthropy program is brilliant. Because that's what a partnership is all about. But right *now*, I want to know what's going on with you. Why you're being like this."

"Don't push me," he said quietly. "You know better."

"Why not?" she demanded, ignoring the warning glint in his eyes, because her insecurities were ruling her now.

"Because instead of having my head on my shoulders," he bit out, "I've had it buried between your legs for weeks, that's why. Because I can't *think* when you are in my head, Chloe."

Her jaw dropped. "You cannot possibly be blaming this on us."

"No," he said evenly, "I'm saying it was a mistake. *We* are a mistake. I need to be focused on running this company."

She recoiled as if he'd struck her. "You're *ending* this?"

Not a flicker of emotion in those remote gray eyes. "I'm saying we need to cool it off."

Her heart contracted. He *was* ending it. He didn't have to say it. She could see it in his eyes. "Be honest, Nico."

He shrugged. "I told you from the beginning what my capabilities are. We were both clear on what this is."

Her heart kicked against her ribs. She'd thought it had been *love*. She'd thought he had been falling in love with her. Had been so sure of it, she'd let down every last barrier for him so all he'd had to do was just admit it. Walk right into it. But seeing the impassive expression on his face, how easily he'd delivered that cutting blow, she realized he'd never really given them a chance. That she'd been the one who had been hopelessly deluded—at least when it came to his ability to evolve.

Because hadn't he done this to her *twice*? How many times did she need him to slap her in the face before she got it?

Except she knew where this was coming from. Knew his personal history was at play here. She knew *him* now.

"This is about your need for control," she said quietly. "You aren't in control of this situation. You aren't in control of *us*, so you'd rather choose to walk away than confront what we have. You'd rather use *this* as the perfect excuse to end it, when, in actual fact, we did exactly as you counseled, Nico. We made sound decisions. We listened to the experts, and they made the call. No one," she said, waving a hand at him, "could have predicted Eddie was going to go off the deep end. We all thought it was movie publicity."

"I did," he countered flatly. "And I should have listened to my instincts."

She had no response for that because he was right. He had.

He raked a hand through his hair. Eyed her. "It was always going to end with us, Chloe. It was just a matter of time. You know it and I know it. I am incapable of giving you what you need."

The way he so easily discarded what they had infuriated her. "I think you'd rather *believe* yourself incapable of love than expose yourself to it, Nico. Because then you'd have to allow yourself to *feel* something. Well, I'm not buying it for a minute. I've seen you with your brothers. I know your capabilities. They are miles deep. *Unconditional.* But they aren't on offer to me."

"They aren't on offer to anyone," he said evenly. "We

have a good thing, Chloe. But what's going to happen when you want a man who can love you? Who can give you more? When you start to hate me because I can never give you that?"

It was a fair point. Because the way he was tearing her apart inside right now, she wondered if she was a bit on the masochistic side.

"I love you," she said quietly, before she closed herself off completely. "I have always loved you, Nico, you know that. You are the strongest, most admirable man I know. But if you walk away now, it's the last time, because you're right, not even I'm that much of a glutton for punishment."

His gray eyes glimmered with an emotion she couldn't read. "Better it happen now. Go home, Chloe. Get some sleep."

# CHAPTER THIRTEEN

CHLOE WALKED HOME on a frozen Manhattan night, feeling as numb as the sheet of ice beneath her feet.

She shouldn't have pushed him like that. But if she hadn't, she never would have found out the truth. That, in his mind, Nico had never seen a future for them. That while she'd been spinning those romantic fantasies he'd warned her about, while she'd been offering him everything, he had been preserving those cast-iron walls he had perfected, never intending to let her in.

Letting herself in her front door, she shrugged off her coat and threw it on the bench in the hall. The cozy space felt unfamiliar, *foreign*, because she'd spent the better part of the past couple of weeks at Nico's place, caught up in the fantasy she'd spun for herself. It felt so empty it made her hurt inside.

She couldn't go curl up at Mireille's because she was still at the office working with the team on the statement that would go out in the morning. Numb, utterly unsure of what to do with herself, she made some hot cocoa. Allowed herself a brief look at Twitter, which was a huge mistake. The Boycott Evolution hashtag had caught fire. There were thousands using it.

Her heart crawled into her throat, a feeling of dread twisting her insides. If they didn't contain this tomorrow, if their plan to announce the philanthropy program next week didn't turn the tide, Evolution and everything she'd worked so hard for would be in jeopardy. Everything her parents had entrusted to her.

She raked trembling fingers through her hair. It was all too easy to second-guess everything. Her overly ambitious launch plan, how closely she'd tied her fragrances to the personalities that represented them, how she'd ignored Nico's advice, when if she had listened, they wouldn't be in this situation.

It all ran through her head as she curled up and tried to fall asleep in her four-poster bed. *Alone.*

Hot tears stung her eyes, but there was also anger in that potent brew. Fury that Nico had been such a bastard to her. Fury that he would hide from himself like this, because she knew how he felt. Fury because she needed him now more than ever, his ability to right-side her world something she'd always depended on.

Blinking back the tears, she refused to cry. Refused to let *this* be the thing that felled her. She'd come too far for that. She'd become too much of a fighter. Nico was a *coward*, that was what he was. She would not be that.

She woke at an insanely early hour, just as dawn was creeping into the sky. A determination filled her, steely in its foundation. The massive sales, the overwhelmingly positive response to Vivre could not be wrong. She had not been wrong in her decisions. She could not abandon her vision now or it would all be for naught.

She might have been wrong about Eddie. She *had* been wrong about Eddie. So now she had to fix it. Unfortunately, she had a feeling this was going to get a lot worse before it got better.

It did get worse. By 9:00 a.m., Evolution's already fragile share price had dropped 20 percent and Nico was fielding calls from worried board members in between a seemingly endless number of press interviews, the media's thirst for Hollywood's latest scandal seemingly unquenchable.

Chloe took it upon herself to check in with her uncle to see if he'd made any progress on pulling the television ads before Nico flipped his lid. When Giorgio's PA announced he was on a call, she leaned against the doorway to his office and waited for him to finish. His back to her, his feet on the windowsill, she gathered it was Keith Taylor, one of the Evolution board members, on the other end of the line.

She frowned. Why was Giorgio talking to Keith? She didn't even think they knew each other. The gist of the conversation soon set her spine ramrod straight. *He was pressing his case with Keith as the man who should be running Evolution in the middle of a crisis that could bring the company down.*

Fury singed her blood. She was livid by the time Giorgio set the phone down and swung his chair around. His gaze sliding over Chloe, he had the audacity to wave her into a seat for a coffee with a lazy, self-satisfied expression on his face.

Chloe set her hands on her hips and raked a look over her uncle, the resemblance to her father so strong it hurt sometimes. "You are *courting* the board in the middle of a crisis?" she breathed. "At Nico's expense?"

Her uncle shrugged. "It's the right time to get rid of him. You weren't so happy about him becoming CEO before you started sleeping with him."

She curled her hands into fists by her sides. He was out of control. Utterly out of line. How had she not seen it before? Had she been so deluded about *everything*?

"You're fired," she bit out. "Effective immediately."

Giorgio stared at her, astonished. "You can't do that."

"Father gave Nico the power to do it." She lifted her chin. "And I'm backing him up. This is unacceptable, Giorgio."

She marched out of his office. Absorbed the look of shock on his PA's face. "I will reassign you," she muttered, before she stalked into the hallway.

Her heart broken at her uncle's betrayal, she marched up to Nico's office, told her boss what Giorgio had done and that she'd fired him, then burned a path to her own office, where she focused on the nascent philanthropy program she and the team were creating, keeping in touch with Lashaunta and Desdemona to update them on things and ensure they didn't jump ship. By the end of the week, she and the team had a platform they could brief the two stars on.

Lashaunta and Desdemona both loved the program, which would allocate millions over the next few years to women's causes, and both of them signed on. Helped in part by the fact that things on social media had gradually begun to calm down with Evolution's clear assurance the company had cut ties with Carello.

Lashaunta, with whom Chloe had developed a close relationship over the past few weeks, even agreed to fly to New York for the unveiling of the program, given she was already in America on tour.

By the time Chloe and Nico unveiled the program to hundreds of journalists at a press conference at Evolution, Lashaunta and Desdemona at their sides, Chloe was so exhausted she could barely put one foot in front of the other, investing everything she had left into the emotional remarks she made about why the program was so important to her—how everything she and her mother had ever done had been to empower women with their own particular kind of beauty.

When it was over, she knew she'd done everything she could. Now it was up to the world to decide Evolution's fate. What she could not seem to repair was her broken heart. It was still raw and bruised as Nico and she stepped off the podium and removed their mics.

"You were incredible up there," he said quietly, a warmth in his smoky gray eyes that had been missing for days.

She wrapped a layer of Teflon around her heart. Lifted her chin. "Because I knew we could do this together. Because we are a great team, Nico. That we can weather any storm together. It's you that didn't believe."

Nico stood looking out at a Christmas light extravaganza that was New York in December, nursing a Scotch as he surveyed the view from the floor-to-ceiling windows of his penthouse.

He thought Evolution might finally have turned the corner today. Its stock price had rebounded after its disastrous drop and sales had done the same, with Be flying high again. The one price to pay from all of this might be Soar, of which sales had plummeted. But if that was the only casualty of this mess, he'd take it.

Ads for Be had been everywhere on his way home, plastered across the city, a big flashing reminder of the woman who had shown her steel spine today in that press conference with Lashaunta and Desdemona, passionately and fearlessly handling interviews with the major daily newspapers.

She was light-years from the woman he'd dragged home from Paris—a warrior. *Something to behold.* It cast his own inability to grow in far too harsh a light.

He'd spent the past couple of months forcing her out of her shell—insisting she evolve into what he knew she could be—even when it had meant stretching her to the very limits of her capabilities. Forcing her to acknowledge her innermost fears and expose them for the fraud they were. And what had he done? Reverted to old patterns—to a knee-jerk reaction to end things between them instead of taking a good look at himself. Instead of facing his own fears.

Chloe had been right. If he didn't allow himself to care about another person, if he didn't allow himself to *feel*, no one could destroy him like that ever again. Burying himself in his work, *providing* had been the only way he'd known how to survive. It was the way he'd operated since he was fifteen years old.

Which had been fine until Chloe had battered through his defenses with her courage and fire. Until she'd made him question his limitations. Made him want *more*. Until she'd made him want to *be* more. And that had scared the hell out of him.

He lifted the Scotch to his lips, welcoming its low, fiery burn. He missed her. He'd told himself his knee-jerk reaction to end them had been the right one, because dragging this affair out any longer was only going to hurt her more. Had buried himself in his work with twenty-hour days, expecting its usual anesthetic effects to function as it always did. But it hadn't.

Instead, her absence in his bed at night had only illuminated how lacking his life was in the spirit and warmth she brought to it. How being programmed as a machine to do only one thing wasn't enough anymore.

The problem was, he thought, staring out at a cavalcade of lights, he might have killed the one chance he'd had of having more because of a past that had owned him for far too long.

Christmas Eve had always been the most magical night of the year for Chloe. Right from the very beginning, when her father had read her and Mireille *The Night Be-*

*fore Christmas* in full theatrical voice while they sat on his lap at the house in Great Neck and drank big mugs of cocoa laced with her mother's candy cane syrup.

Later, when they'd gotten older, and Evolution had been founded, the magic had come from her father's big heart. He couldn't stand the idea of any of his employees spending Christmas alone, so he'd rounded them up like stray kittens and invited them to dinner, which had sometimes meant forty or fifty people at the table, her mother holding her head and muttering *numbers* the whole while.

But her mother had loved those boisterous, chaotic celebrations as much as Chloe and Mireille had. It was like the whole word had come to their big, warm, happy house on the hill.

And then there'd been the year the Di Fiore boys had shown up, looking shell-shocked in the middle of the crowd. Chloe thought she might have taken one look at Nico as he'd sat through her father's traditional end-of-year philosophical rant, so serious as he'd soaked it all up as if it was the most profound thing he'd ever heard, and fallen in love with him that instant.

But, she reminded herself as an ache surfaced deep inside her, she wasn't thinking about *him* right now. She and Mireille were going ice skating at Rockefeller Center, before they had wine and fondue at home. A new tradition. And she wasn't going to cry about that either, because Be was under half of Manhattan's Christmas trees, she knew her mother would be so proud of her and she was going to hold her memories close to her heart, exactly as Nico had said.

*Damn him. He was everywhere.*

Hat planted on her head, mittens at the ready, she tapped her foot impatiently on the hardwood floor. She had just glanced at her watch for the third time when a knock sounded on the door.

"You're late," she said impatiently, swinging the door wide. "Why is it I'm—" She stopped dead in her tracks at the sight of Nico standing on the doorstep, the memory of that kiss, that *show-stopping* kiss, flashing through her head.

Oh, no. She was not doing this tonight.

"Go away," she said firmly, refusing to acknowledge how beautiful he looked in jeans and a dark turtleneck sweater. "Mireille and I are going ice skating."

"Mireille isn't coming until later."

Her eyes widened. "Why not?"

"Because we need to talk." He gestured toward the door. "Can I come in?"

"No."

He sank his hands into her waist, picked her up and moved her aside. She gasped and gave him a furious look as he closed the door. "I don't want to talk to you. Nor do I want to kiss you until I lose my head. I want to go ice skating."

"Chloe," he said quietly, eyes on hers, "I need to talk to you. Hear me out and I promise I'll go away if that's what you want."

He looked serious, so serious she relented, toeing off her boots and leading the way into the living room. Perching herself on the sofa, she eyed him warily as he sat down beside her.

He raked a hand through his hair in an uncharacteristically fidgety move. "You were right," he began, "about why I pushed you away. This time and *every* time. Because I have always felt too much for you. Because you make me *feel* too much."

Her heart lodged in her mouth. "My father *was* a workaholic," he continued. "He was addicted to the buzz, but he was also addicted to keeping my mother happy. She messed with his head, she played him for all he was worth. If he'd *had* his head fully in the game, I'm not sure he would have made the mistakes he did, taken the risks he did, and maybe the outcome would have been very different."

She shook her head. "You can't say that. It may simply be that he had an addictive personality, a disease. To blame it on your mother is unfair."

His mouth compressed. "I'm not so sure. I went to see my mother, Chloe. That's how much you've turned my head upside down. I thought maybe you were right—that it would help me to understand better. Reframe things in my head."

Shock rendered her speechless. "What did she say?" she finally managed.

"That she was to blame for most of it. That she resented losing her career. She felt unequipped to be a mother, and she took it out on my father." He lifted a shoulder. "She also said she felt a great deal of sorrow about the decisions she's made."

"And did you believe her?"

"She seemed genuine about it." He rubbed a palm over the thick stubble on his jaw. "She said my father had the affairs to hurt her. To strike back. It became a vicious circle between them."

"Relationships are rarely simple," she murmured. "Even my parents, as in love as they were, had fights that would take down the rafters. They were passionate people. But the point is, they worked through it. They loved each other enough to make it work."

"Yes," he agreed. "They did." He dropped his head in his hands. Was silent for a moment. When he looked up, she saw the glitter of an emotion she couldn't read in his eyes. "I told myself I would never go on that kind of an emotional roller-coaster ride with a woman. I made *sure*

I never did. But with you, I didn't have a choice. It just *was*. And when things fell apart with Eddie, it raised all my red flags and I mentally disengaged. A force of habit."

She shook her head. "We're better together, Nico. We are more *powerful* together. That's what held it all together. You and me."

"Yes," he acknowledged, "I know that now. But all of my baggage came into play. I started to question what I could be. Something Martino said to me." He rubbed a hand against his temple. "He saw us on the Fourth of July, Chloe."

Her jaw dropped, disbelief filtering through her. "He never said."

"He talked to me about it afterward. He told me to date you seriously or walk away."

She sank her teeth into her lip. "I can't believe he did that. It was *my* life."

"You were eighteen, Chloe. A baby. I was a hardened twenty-two. And he was right," he conceded. "I couldn't offer you what you needed. You needed to grow up and learn what life was all about. I already knew *too much* about life."

If she thought she'd been furious with her father before, she was livid with him now. Because what would she and Nico have become if he hadn't interfered? What *could* they have become?

"So why are you here now?" she tossed at him, her insides hollow and empty, as if they'd been scraped out with something sharp. "If you're so sure you can never be what I'm looking for?"

His gaze locked with hers. "Because you've always been the best thing in my life. Because I was a fool to walk away from you again, and if you give me one more chance, I promise I won't mess it up."

"How do I know?" she whispered, hurt throbbing from the inside out. "I can't go through that again, Nico. Not one more time."

"Because I love you," he said, without missing a beat. As if they weren't the most earth-shattering words he'd ever uttered to her. "Because I've been in love with you a long time and I'm tired of fighting it."

Her heart skipped a beat. Hope bloomed inside her, so powerful, potent, it would have knocked her off her feet had she been standing. But there was also fear—fear he would do this to her again.

Clearly realizing how badly he'd screwed up, he reached into his pocket and pulled out a brightly wrapped box. The blood in her veins pumped, jagged, erratic, as he sank down on one knee in front of her.

*"Nico,"* she gasped, "what are you doing?"

"Proposing." He gave her an annoyed look. "I took Santo jewelry shopping, for God's sake. Let me get there."

Her stomach fell off a shelf and crashed to the floor. Oh, no, he wasn't doing this to her on Christmas Eve. The night fairy tales were made of.

"Marry me," he murmured, eyes on hers as he held up the most brilliant sparkling diamond she'd ever seen.

"Don't you think this is a bit extreme?" she breathed, eyes glued to the ring. "I forgive you. There, I've said it."

He shook his head. "It's always been you, Chloe. Always you."

That was it. She was done for. Forever and always.

She held out a trembling hand. Watched as he slid the brilliant diamond on her finger. It was like watching her most secret, most unobtainable fantasy come true. She couldn't speak, could only fling her arms around his neck as he gathered her up and sat down with her in his lap.

"I love you," she murmured against his amazing mouth.

"So much. I've been so miserable, I think Mireille was dreading spending the evening with me."

"She's coming back. She's bringing Lazzero and Santo with her."

She pulled back. "You were that sure of me?"

He shook his head. "Willing to crash and burn."

Her heart contracted on a low pull. "I'll have one of those rather earth-shattering kisses now, thank you. You've earned it."

He gave her exactly that. When they finally came up for air, he pulled another box from his pocket. "One more."

She slid the box open to find a stunning Murano glass star nestled inside.

"So we can start our own traditions," he explained quietly. "Make new memories."

Her heart shattered. Turned to dust. But it was a good thing because with that last barrier smashed, she knew they would put each other back together again. Stronger. *Better.* Because that was what they'd always been about.

Nico stood with her in his arms. Boosted her up to set the star on top of the tree. She wrapped her arms around his neck as she stared up at it, glittering like the most gorgeous jewel in the sky.

"When did you say the others are coming back?"

He carried her toward the stairs. "*Later.* There's a tradition I'd like to start right now."

Her thoughts exactly.

\* \* \* \* \*

## Rio's hands lifted to Tilly's shoulders. His expression was dark.

Without make-up, her skin glowing from the shower, her hair pulled up into another messy bun, and with a tiny towel barely covering her, she was the most desirable woman he had ever seen. Rio glided his hands over her upper arms, but he wanted more. His hand moved to the back of her towel, pushing her towards him. She connected with his body—by design this time. She was soft and small, her curves fitting perfectly to him, as though they'd been designed for one another.

Her lashes were too dark—feathered fans against her flushed cheeks. And the small moan she made sent his pulse into overdrive. Would she moan when they made love? Would her pillowy lips part, breathing those sweet sounds into the air?

His need was a tsunami inside him, crashing inexorably towards land. She was the shore, she was the anchor, and he was powerless to fight the pull of her tide. Rio had never considered himself powerless before. But he didn't care.

He lifted his hand to her face, cupping her cheek and sweeping the ball of his thumb over her lower lip. Her eyes flew open, pinning him with the same tsunami of need that was ravaging his defences.

'We shouldn't do this,' she said quietly, but her hips pushed forward, moving from side to side in ancient silent invitation.

His fingers plaited through her hair, pulling it from the bun, running through the ends. 'We shouldn't,' he agreed darkly.

**Clare Connelly** was raised in small-town Australia among a family of avid readers. She spent much of her childhood up a tree, Mills & Boon book in hand. Clare is married to her own real-life hero and they live in a bungalow near the sea with their two children. She is frequently found staring into space—a surefire sign she is in the world of her characters. She has a penchant for French food and ice-cold champagne, and Mills & Boon novels continue to be her favourite ever books. Writing for Modern Romance is a long-held dream. Clare can be contacted via clareconnelly.com or at her Facebook page.

### Books by Clare Connelly

### Mills & Boon Modern Romance

*Bought for the Billionaire's Revenge*

Visit the Author Profile page
at millsandboon.co.uk for more titles.

# INNOCENT IN THE BILLIONAIRE'S BED

BY
CLARE CONNELLY

First Published in Great Britain 2017
By Mills & Boon, an imprint of HarperCollins*Publishers*
1 London Bridge Street, London, SE1 9GF

© 2017 Clare Connelly

ISBN: 978-0-263-92550-0

Printed and bound in Spain
by CPI, Barcelona

# INNOCENT IN THE BILLIONAIRE'S BED

Amy Andrews—
It was friendship at first sight.

# PROLOGUE

IT WAS STRANGE that here, on an island where she'd spent only a few weeks of her life, Rio should feel so close to his mother. It was almost as if her presence roamed the walls of the shack, or drifted in off the salted waves that were rolling towards him. He didn't see her here as she'd been at the end, so weakened and ill. Here he imagined her free, running across the sand, her laugh tumbling out of her of its own volition.

He cradled his Scotch, swirling it slightly so the ice chipped against the glass. The sound was swallowed by the surrounds of the island. The beach, the birds, the rustling of the trees. Even the stars seemed to be whispering to one another—and there were so many stars visible from this island in the middle of the sea, far from civilisation.

Rosa had loved it here.

He didn't smile as he thought of his mother.

Her life had been shaped by loss and hardship, right to the end. And now he sat on the island of the man who could have alleviated so much of that pain, if only he'd bothered or cared.

No.

The island was no longer Piero's.

It was Rio's.

A too-little-too-late offering that Rio sure as hell didn't want.

Even now, a month after his father's death, Rio knew he'd been right to reject him. To reject any overtures at reconciliation.

He wanted nothing to do with the powerful Italian tycoon—never had, never would. And as soon as he'd offloaded this damned island he'd never think of the man again.

# CHAPTER ONE

'CRESSIDA WYNDHAM?'

This was the time to correct the lie. To be honest. If she wanted to back out of this whole damned mess, then she should just say so here.

*No, I'm Matilda Morgan. I work for Art Wyndham.*

But her back was well and truly against the wall this time. What had started out as an occasional favour for the high-maintenance heiress had turned into an obligation she couldn't really escape. Especially not having accepted thirty thousand pounds for this particular 'favour'. She'd been bought and paid for, and the consequences would be dire if she didn't go through with the plan.

Besides, it was only for a week. What could go wrong in seven sunny days?

'Yes...' she heard herself murmur, before recalling that she was supposed to be acting the part of an heiress to a billion-pound fortune. Mumbling into her cleavage wasn't really going to cut it.

She lifted her head, forcing herself to meet the man's eyes with a bright smile. It froze on her face as recognition dawned.

'You're Rio Mastrangelo.'

His expression gave nothing away. That wasn't surprising, though. Illario Mastrangelo was somewhat renowned for his ruthless dynamism. He was reputed to have a heart of ice and stone—he walked away from any deal unless he could get it on his terms. Or so the stories went.

'Yes.'

The speedboat was rocking rhythmically beneath her. Was that why she felt all lurching and odd? She looked to the driver of the boat—a short man with a gappy smile and weathered skin—but he was engrossed in his newspaper. No help there.

'I had expected to meet with an estate agent,' she said, because the silence was thick and she needed to break it.

'No. No agent.' He stepped into the shallow water—uncaring, apparently, that his jeans got wet to just below his knees.

*No agent. Great.*

Cressida had been explicit that there would be.

*'It's going to be you, some man from an estate agency, and whatever servants come with the island. Just tell them all that you want to spend time on your own to really get a sense of the place and then relax! You'll get to chill all day, get fed gourmet meals—perfect holiday. Right? It's no big deal.'*

No big deal.

Only, looking at Rio Mastrangelo, Tilly thought the exact opposite was true. He was both a big deal and a big deal-*maker*, and she was hopelessly out of her depth even in the crystal-clear shallows that lapped against the side of the beautiful boat.

'Have you got a bag?'

'Oh, right…' She nodded, reaching for the Louis Vuitton duffle Cressida had insisted on Tilly bringing.

Rio took it and lifted his eyes to her, a look of glinting curiosity in his expression.

Her stomach rolled in time with the waves. He was far more handsome in person. Or maybe she'd never really paid proper attention.

She knew bits and pieces about him. He was a self-made real estate tycoon. He'd been on the news about a year earlier, interviewed because he had bought a large parcel of land in the south of London to develop. She remembered because she'd been glad; there was a beautiful old pub there—one of the oldest in London, with wonky floors and leaning walls—and she'd worked there for a summer after she'd left school. The idea of it being knocked down had saddened her, and Rio had said in the interview that he intended to rejuvenate it.

'You travel light,' he remarked.

Tilly nodded. She'd thrown a few bikinis into the bag, along with a pair of flip-flops, a few books, and some of her go-to summer dresses. Perfect for a week alone on a tropical island.

He slung the bag over his shoulder and then lifted a hand towards her. She stared at it as though he'd turned into a frog.

'I can manage,' she said stiffly, wincing inwardly at the prim intonation of her words.

Cressida was definitely not prim. A snob of the first order, yes, but prim...?

*Please.* Cressida's antics generally made a trip to Ibiza look like a visit to a retirement village. Cressida's father—Tilly's boss—had been thrilled that Cressida had shown a little interest in the business finally, and agreed to visit this island and scout it as a potential hotel site.

Rio Mastrangelo wasn't Hollywood handsome, Tilly mused as she moved towards the dark stairs that dipped into the back of the boat. Not in that boy-next-door, blond, blue-eyed way that she usually found impossible to resist. Nor was he corporate and conventional, as she would have expected. He was...wild. Untamed.

The words came to her out of nowhere, but as she risked a sidelong glance at him she knew instantly that she was right.

His skin was a dark brown all over, and his lower face was covered in a thick stubble that spoke of having not shaved for days, rather than an attempt to cultivate a fashionable facial hair situation. His eyes were wide-set and a dark grey that would match the ocean at its deepest point. They were rimmed with thick charcoal lashes, long and spiked in curling clumps. His hair was jet-black and it turned outwards at the ends, where it brushed the collar of his shirt.

He had the kind of physique that spoke of an easy athleticism. He was tall, broad-shouldered and leanly muscled. His forearms flexed even as he held her bag.

It was those eyes, though, she thought, turning her attention back to the twin masterpieces in his face.

She felt as though she'd been slapped. They locked to hers: grey warring with green. The boat lurched again. She reached down to the polished timber rail to steady herself, her manicured fingers running over it for strength.

She'd chosen a simple dress for the flight to Italy. It was a designer brand, but she'd picked it up in a charity shop a long time ago—before this crazy plan had even been hatched. It was turquoise—her favourite colour. It complemented her eyes and set off the auburn highlights in her long cherry-red hair. And her skin, though nowhere near as deep a tan as Rio's, looked golden all over. She'd chosen the dress because it looked good on her and she'd wanted to look good. But not for Rio.

She'd chosen it for the photographers who might snap her passing through Rome's airport, or travelling on the ferry to Capri. For the tourists with cell phones who would recognise Cressida Wyndham, her doppelgänger, en route to a luxurious Mediterranean holiday. She'd kept her head bent, as though she really was an heiress avoiding attention, but she'd courted it at the same time.

She'd chosen to wear the dress for those reasons.

For Rio, she suspected, she would be safer wearing a nun's habit.

Anything to discourage his eyes from drifting over her in that slow, curious way they had.

She understood the speculation in them; she'd met enough men in her twenty-four years to know what interest looked like. Cursed, in many ways, with the kind of curves most women would kill for, Tilly had long ago come to despise her generous cleavage, neat waist and rounded bottom. There was something about her figure that seemed to signal to men that she wanted to strip naked and jump into their bed.

The boat shifted again, as a wave rolled beneath it, and she paused, reaching for the rail once more. The driver had backed it as close as possible to the shore but even so it wouldn't be possible to disembark from the boat without getting her feet wet. She slipped her shoes off and hooked them with her finger, self-consciously aware that Rio was watching her from the shallows of the ocean.

She stepped down, and at the bottom moved to disembark from the luxury craft. But she mistimed it—badly. Another wave rolled and she lost her footing, stumbling almost completely into the water.

Rio caught her, of course. With Cressida's bag hoisted safely over one shoulder, and taking only a single, long step in Tilly's direction, he swept his arm around her back at just the moment she would have gone completely underwater.

He pulled her upright, his eyes crinkled with mocking amusement.

He was even more devastatingly handsome up close, where she could see the freckles that danced on his aquiline nose and appreciate the depths of his eyes, which weren't just grey. They had flecks of black and green in there too, swirling together in a combination of shapes and colours that she could stare at all day.

'I thought you could manage?' he prompted.

Tilly was stricken. What a fool she was! Cressida would *never* have fumbled such a basic manoeuvre as exiting a speedboat. No, Cressida would have taken his damned hand when he'd offered it and run her fingernails over his palm, encouraging him to stare at her all he wanted. Inviting him to do much more than that.

Matilda Morgan, though, was a Grade A klutz. Falling off a speedboat was just the kind of thing her twin brother Jack would have laughed about, and she would have joined him. Tilly never missed a chance to be amused by her own lack of finesse.

She heard the amusement escape from her mouth as a giggle at first, and then finally a full-blown laugh, though she lifted a hand to cover it.

'I'm sorry.' She smiled up at Rio, lifted a hand around his neck in an automatic response. 'I'm perhaps the clumsiest person you'll ever meet.'

Her laugh, and the admission of a lack of coordination hot on its heels, caught him unawares.

When Art Wyndham had said he'd be sending his daughter Cressida to complete an inspection of Prim'amore Rio had felt mixed emotions.

On the one hand, the beautiful heiress was known to be vapid and uninterested—he suspected he'd have her desperate to buy the island in a day or two at the most. And on the other, from what he'd heard of the mogul's daughter, Cressida Wyndham was the kind of woman he had only ever found good for one thing. She was all beauty, no substance, and she was the last person he'd willingly spend time with—except, possibly, in his bed.

But he had to admit her laugh was lovely. Like music and sunshine.

Still smiling, she pushed away from him, standing on her own two feet. 'I'm fine,' she assured him. 'Just a little wet.'

He made a guttural noise of agreement and then released her abruptly. 'You can dry off inside.'

He nodded towards the shoreline and for the first time her attention moved to the island. It was lush and green, right in front of them, but a little way further down she could see dark red cliffs that were bare of greenery. High above them there was more red, like ochre, and then in the distance the hint of trees—cypress, olive and citrus, she guessed. Back down on the coastline the sand was crisp white in both directions. Only one building broke up the expanse of beach.

A boathouse of sorts, it was of simple construction, a cross between a cabin and a hut. It was whitewashed stone, and the window frames had been painted a bright blue at one time—though a lot of the paint looked to have chipped off now. There was a small deck at the front, with two cane armchairs propped on either side of a small card table. A jaunty pot plant that had clearly been tormented by the wind stood sentinel at the door, though it had grown heavily in one direction, casting a diagonal shadow. To the side of the cabin a motorbike was propped, and beside it a speedboat on a trolley, smaller than the one she'd just stepped off— or rather leaped off into the ocean.

It was on the tip of Tilly's tongue to ask Rio what the building was, but he was already moving towards it. Sand clung to his bare feet as he strode easily across the beach. She didn't rush to catch up. Not because Cressida wouldn't rush, though she wouldn't. Tilly was captivated by the beauty of this place and she wanted to savour this, her first opportunity to drink it in.

Halfway between the shoreline and the cabin she stopped walking altogether. A light breeze trembled past her, but it was a hot day and it brought welcome relief to her through her wet clothes. She stared up at the sky, her eyes noting the colour—a glistening cerulean blue.

'It's beautiful,' she said to herself.

But Rio caught the words and turned. Her dress was saturated all the way to the top. Did she have any idea that she might as well have been standing on the beach completely

naked, for all the fabric did to hide her body? Her red hair
was trapped in a messy bun on top of her head but he was
pretty sure it wanted to be free, to fly down her back as
it might have done on Boudica or one of Titian's models.

He turned back to the cabin, his jaw clenched.

Of *course* she knew how alluring she looked. Cressida
Wyndham had made flirtation an art form. He didn't really know anything about her, and nor did he read the gossip magazines, but he did know that her name couldn't be
mentioned without the implication that she was an entitled,
spoiled tramp with little morality.

And for some reason that angered him now.

He paused at the steps that led to the deck. They were
timber, built from one of the trees that covered the island.

'What's this?' she asked, her green eyes, almond in
shape, moving across the frame of the hut.

'Where we'll be staying.'

*Where we'll be staying?* Her heart skidded against her
breastbone. Surely he'd meant *Where* you'll *be staying*?
Though he spoke English fluently, his voice was accented.
It wasn't inconceivable that he'd made a mistake.

Because this place was definitely not going to accom-
modate the two of them.

He moved ahead of her and she followed.

'It was built around fifty years ago,' he said as he shoul-
dered the door inwards. It groaned a little. It was just wire
pressed against an ornate wrought-iron pattern. There was
no actual door.

The heat of the day hadn't managed to penetrate the
thick walls. It was cool and dark. A hallway—quite wide,
given the size of the building—went all the way to the back
of the home, though at the rear, she glimpsed a sofa. There
was more light there, too.

'Your bedroom.' He nodded towards a room as they
swept past. She had only a brief impression of a narrow

single bed and a bookshelf. He nodded to another door. 'My bedroom.'

Her heart thumped harder.

'Bathroom.'

She peered in as they walked past. It was simple, but clean. It smelled of him. She caught the masculine scent as they walked past and her stomach squeezed.

'And the kitchen.'

It was also simple, but charmingly so, with a thick timber bench, a window that overlooked the beach, a small fridge and a stove. There was a table with four chairs, and across the room a sofa and an armchair. Another larger window framed a different perspective of the beach.

'Your...your bedroom is...opposite mine?' The words were almost a whisper and she shivered.

'Surely you didn't think we'd be sharing?' he prompted, enjoying the blush that spread across her face and the way her nipples stretched visibly against the wet fabric of her skin-tight dress.

'Of course not,' Tilly snapped, before remembering that she was Cressida, and Cressida would never have taken offence at such a suggestion. She would have purred right back that he shouldn't rule anything out... 'I just didn't re-alise we'd be staying in the same house.'

His smile was laced with sardonic amusement. 'It's the only house on the island,' he said. 'Didn't your father tell you?'

She shook her head, but questions were floating through her mind...suspicions. Shortly after Cressida had said there'd be servants she'd said that Tilly would be left to her own devices. She'd made it sound like a glamorous beach retreat awaited.

Had she known that Rio Mastrangelo would be literally shacking up with her? Had she wisely decided to keep that titbit to herself, knowing that Matilda would have found it impossible to go along with such an elaborate deception in close quarters with a man like him?

'He must have,' Tilly said with a shrug, as though it didn't matter, but inside she was fuming.

If she hadn't desperately needed that thirty thousand pounds, how she would have loved to tell Cressida to go to hell!

Only she wouldn't have. She couldn't have. For, as much as the heiress drove her absolutely crazy, Tilly felt sorry for her. And the longer Tilly worked for Art and felt the warmth of his affection, the more she saw him disapprove of Cressida and ruminate on her lack of intelligence, skills and focus, and the more guilt Tilly felt—and more pressure too.

This was the first time Cressida had ever asked Tilly for more than an easy favour, though. And certainly the first time she'd outright lied to her! This wasn't going to a film premiere dressed to the nines, or slipping out of a top-notch restaurant early to divert the paparazzi's focus. This was a whole week in close quarters with a gorgeous stranger.

'And you forgot?' he responded with a droll inflection.

'There were a lot of instructions.' She forced herself back to the present, pushing aside the sticky question of just what Cressida had kept to herself to get Tilly on board with this deception. Were there any more surprises in store for her?

'Such as?'

'Such as don't fall out of boats.' The snappy response was watered down by a spontaneous smile. 'Mind if I get changed?'

*Yes*, he wanted to say. He liked watching her in this dress. Seeing the way it clung to her was flooding his body with desire—desire he wouldn't indulge with *her*, of course.

Yet he hadn't been himself since hearing of his father's death. His libido—something he liked to give free rein to, often—had taken a hit in recent times. Feeling his body stir to life was good. It was nice. He revelled in the sensation of anticipation, knowing that relief would be worth the wait.

He wouldn't give in to temptation with Cressida—that would be foolish. But once he left the island he'd call Anita or Sophie, or one of the other women always happy to join him in bed and rediscover some very pleasurable habits.

'Make yourself at home,' he said, with a shrug that was the personification of nonchalance.

She nodded, her eyes not meeting his. He was still holding her bag and he made no attempt to hand it over. She crossed the tiled floor until she was within arm's reach. At this distance she could see the flecks of black that marked his grey eyes, and she caught more of that enticingly masculine fragrance.

'I'll need some dry clothes,' she prompted, a smile tickling her full lips as she nodded towards the duffle.

He unhooked the bag from his shoulder and passed it to her. She reached for it without looking downwards and her fingers curved over his.

It was like being bitten by a snake.

She immediately released her grip on the bag and he did likewise, so that it dropped with a thump to the floor.

'Sorry,' she said breathlessly, as though it had somehow been *her* fault rather than an involuntary reaction to the spark of electric shock that had travelled through her fingertips and flooded her entire body.

'What for?' he murmured, reaching down for the bag.

Her frown was spontaneous. Neither Tilly nor Cressida were prone to inane, babbling apologies. 'I don't know.'

His laugh tickled her overstretched nerve-endings; it was a deep, throaty sound and she imagined his voice would be husky like that when he was driven by other emotions. A charge of awareness surprised her and she felt her nipples strain hard against the fabric of her bra.

His eyes dropped to them and his lips flickered in a droll

smile of sardonic appreciation. 'Go and get changed, Cressida,' he said, dismissing her.

It was on the tip of her tongue to challenge him, *Or what?* when he replied, 'Before it's too late.'

Too late? A frisson of awareness pulsed through her, teasing her spine and making her shiver.

She took the bag from him and moved quickly down the hallway towards the bedroom he'd marked as hers.

Too late for what?

Her mind pushed away the most obvious reading of the statement—that there was some inevitability that they were running from. It was a silly interpretation, no doubt fuelled by her propensity to read far too many romance novels.

She kept her head ducked until she reached the door he'd indicated would lead to her own accommodation.

Her first assessment had been right.

There was a small bed, a bookshelf, and a hat rack near a high, small window that had geraniums in a window box, creeping halfway up the glass in an enthusiastic display of clustered red.

There was a mirror too, and she caught her reflection and moaned audibly. She looked... She might as well be naked. The fabric of her dress had turned a dark green and it hugged her tightly, moulding her breasts, her stomach, her bottom, and clinging in a V to her womanhood.

Her fingers shook as she went to remove it quickly, stripping it off her shoulders and pushing it from her body. The sight of her bra and G-string wasn't any better. Angrily she discarded them, until she was naked, still wet, but not caring.

Her phone was in the side pocket of her bag and she lifted it out. The picture of her and Jack smiled at her when she activated it, and for a moment she felt her stomach swoop in relief. He would be okay. She'd made sure of it.

This week was a small price to pay for his safety. What the hell had he been thinking?

She swiped her phone to life and flicked up the emails.

An error message appeared. With a frown, she realised there was no internet. No signal whatsoever, in fact.

A grim sense of being completely and utterly alone with Rio Mastrangelo sent a shiver down her spine.

How could Cressida do this to her? The more Tilly thought about it, the more convinced she was that Cressida had lied. But why? What could be so important that she'd orchestrate this deception? She obviously hadn't wanted to risk Tilly saying no—which she would have, had she known about this tiny shack and the drop-dead gorgeous billionaire only a wall away. Damn her!

Well, this would be the end of it. Once she got back to London she'd tell Cressida that their arrangement was at an end.

She ripped at the zip of the bag, pulling it roughly and lifting out another dress. But it was low at the front, and she didn't want to wear anything that might feed into the idea Rio had of her.

Cressida Wyndham, with her fake breasts, ready smile and casual attitude to life in general and sex specifically, would have been working out how to seduce the ruthless tycoon... But Tilly wanted no part of the man.

Did she?

# CHAPTER TWO

'ARE YOU HUNGRY?'

He didn't look up as she entered; Tilly hadn't even re-alised he'd heard her.

'Not really.'

She paused inside the doorframe, studying him surrep-titiously from behind hooded eyes. She caught the mo-ment he lifted his head, saw his eyes running over her figure, his face giving nothing away. She'd have loved to pull on a baggy shirt and jeans, but she'd only packed frothy dresses and bikinis. She'd chosen the most conservative of the dresses—a dark blue linen that fell to her knees.

Wary of distracting him when he was in the middle of working, she gnawed on her lip for a moment. Then, 'My phone doesn't work here.'

That caught his attention. He flicked a brief glance at her. 'No. There's no cell tower. No infrastructure of any nature.'

She nodded, but one side of her mouth quirked down-wards at the corner. 'What do you do in an emergency?'

'What kind of emergency?' he prompted curiously.

'Um…any kind. A band of marauding pirates storming the beach, or any angry flock of seagulls pecking their way across the sand…'

His smile was unexpected—and so was its effect. Her tummy filled with frantic butterflies; her skin dotted with goosebumps.

'You don't think I could defend you against a band of pirates?'

She arched a brow. 'I think you have an inflated sense of your physical abilities.'

He arched a brow. 'A theory I'm willing to disprove at any time,' he promised darkly.

And now the butterflies went into overdrive, fluttering down to her knees and making them wobbly.

'I'm serious,' she said, the words stiffened by disapproval. 'What if there's a fire, or you break your leg or something?'

'I have a satellite phone.' He shrugged.

'But what about emails?'

'I can connect to it for internet access,' he said. 'It's slow as hell, but it gets the job done.'

'Electricity? Water?'

'Generator. Tank.'

Her mind was busy processing that. 'Whoever built this *really* wanted to be off the grid.'

'Not a lot of options on a deserted island,' he pointed out, with a pragmatism that annoyed her.

'I don't know... It seems like a post-apocalyptic bolt-hole.'

Or the perfect love-nest for a cheat and liar, Rio amended silently. How many women had Piero brought here over the years? Whispering sweet nothings about Prim'amore, promising a future he had no intention of providing.

'Do you need to use the phone?' he asked belatedly, drawing his attention back to her original query.

Fantasies of calling Cressida and unloading on her were clouds Tilly would never catch. Of course she could do no such thing. Besides, Cressida had said she was 'going to ground' until the wedding—that she didn't want to be seen or heard by anyone for the week, and that included turning her cell phone off.

Tilly shook her head, a distracted smile flickering across her lips. 'I thought I'd go exploring.'

He stood, and ran a hand through his hair. His shirt

lifted, revealing an inch of tanned flat abdomen. She looked away as though she'd been burned.

'You know I only have a week, and Art is... Daddy is,' she corrected quickly, 'keen to hear what I think of the place.'

'Your wish is my command.' His voice was low and husky and her body reacted instantly, her nipples straining against the fabric of her dress, her eyes widening. And he saw. She just *knew* he was aware of the effect he was having.

'I'm fine.' She shook her head with an attempt at professional detachment. 'I can find my own way.'

His face wore a slow, sardonic grin. 'Just like you were fine to get off the boat?'

She huffed. 'That's not very gentlemanly of you.'

'What gave you the impression I'm a gentleman?' he queried softly, moving closer so that she found thoughts difficult to string together.

'Nothing,' she muttered. 'But I really will be fine. I'm just going to walk along the beach today. If I get lost, I'll turn back. Even *I* should be able to navigate my way around an island without coming to grief.'

'Still,' he said, wondering in the back of his mind why he was arguing with her. 'I'm here to show you around.'

She nodded, lifting her gaze to his face thoughtfully. She caught a flicker of emotion in his eyes that she didn't understand. 'Why?'

He shrugged. 'Because it's a big island and you could get lost.'

'No, I mean why *you*? You must have people who could sell an island for you.'

'Yes.' His mouth was a grim slash in his face.

'So? Aren't you too busy to act as tour guide?'

Rio thought of the paperwork cluttering his desk in Rome and shook his head. Contracts for the high-rise in

Manhattan. The lease for the Canadian mall. The purchase offer he'd made on a mine in Australia.

It could wait. Keeping the invasive tabloid press away from his private life was priority number one. He'd spent the last five years making sure his parentage wasn't revealed, and he wasn't going to let the truth come out now. Involving more people than necessary in this deal was a sure-fire way to invite public attention.

'Yes.'

Why had he decided that distraction was the best way to get her off the scent and stop her questions? He couldn't have said, but he moved closer, noting with interest the way her pupils darkened.

'But I don't really like the idea of you drowning in my ocean. Or tumbling off a cliff on my land.'

'*Your* ocean? *Your* land? Someone's got a bit of a God complex, haven't they?'

His laugh was deep; it resonated right through her.

'Until your father signs on the dotted line, that is the truth of the matter.'

She tilted her head to one side, lost in thought. 'I don't know if I believe *anyone* truly owns an island like this.'

'I have a piece of paper that would beg to differ.'

She waved her hand through the air distractedly. 'Yes, yes—*legally*. But don't you think...?' She left the sentence unfinished as she realised what she'd been about to say. Discussing her personal philosophies wasn't part of the job. And, essentially, she was on Prim'amore to work.

She'd been paid—and paid a small fortune. Now she had to uphold her end of the bargain.

'Yes?' he prompted, but Tilly had zipped away from their conversation.

'Well,' she said, injecting her voice with the same sense of entitlement she'd personally been on the receiving end of any time Cressida had called and asked for a favour, 'if you really want to waste your time playing sales agent, then let's go.'

He arched a brow, but if he was surprised by her pronouncement he didn't otherwise show it.

Tilly did a pretty good Cressida huff as she strode down the corridor and pushed the door to the cottage open. But the moment she stepped on to the small deck she froze, a gasp escaping her mouth.

He followed, almost bumping into her. 'Problem?'

She shook her head, her eyes wide as they took in the sheer beauty of the spot. He watched her, and understood the wonderment in her face. Hadn't he felt a similar sense of incredulity when he'd first arrived?

*It is heaven on earth, mi amore.'*

His mother had been confused at the end. She'd slipped in and out of her past just as a dolphin rippled over the surface of the ocean, and most of her memories had revolved around *him*. Piero. The bastard who'd broken her heart and left her pregnant and destitute.

*'It is as if God left a small piece of heaven just for us to find and enjoy.'*

His expression was grim as he studied the horizon, seeing it as Cressida was. The ocean was immaculate. A deep turquoise colour disturbed only by the gentle cresting of waves. The sky was a blanket of deep blue, the sun an orb of white, high in the sky.

'I feel like we're the only ones on earth,' she said with a shake of her head. 'I hadn't expected the island to be so...'

He waited, curious as to how she would choose to describe it.

'It's not just beautiful,' she said, searching for words. 'It's...magical.'

'Magical?' he repeated derisively, ignoring how close the description was to his mother's first impression.

The amusement in his tone was enough to drag her back

to the present. 'Yes.' She forced a cynical smile to her face. 'At least that's what Daddy will be hoping hordes of tourists think.'

He nodded, dismissing the sense that she was hiding something from him. 'The island's perfect for a holiday resort. Close enough to Capri to provide entertainment, but totally isolated at the same time. It's easy to imagine how special any resort would be here.'

She nodded, but there was sadness in her heart. Having been on the island less than an hour, she already knew she hated the idea of buildings and roads cutting across it. Of people bobbing in the ocean, boats churning across its smooth surface, voices shouting through the serenity.

'Yes,' she said, her frown carrying into the simple word.

'What would you like to see, Cressida?' he asked, and the use of the socialite's name reminded Tilly forcefully of just what her duties were.

'I was just going to walk along the beach,' she murmured, nodding in one direction.

'Fine. We'll walk.'

He moved towards the stairs and she followed, though his presence was knotting her tummy again.

'You really don't have to come with me,' she said softly, pressing her teeth into her lower lip as she tried to calm the butterflies that were having a party inside her.

'I really *do* have to come with you,' he corrected quietly. 'For as long as you are on Prim'amore you are my responsibility.'

A frisson of anticipation danced along her spine. She moved quickly down the stairs, her feet sinking into the sand once she reached the level shore.

'Prim'amore... First love.' She glanced at him. 'It's a romantic name. Any idea of the history of it?'

'No,' he lied.

Secrets, secrets. So many secrets. Hell. *He'd* been a se-

cret most of his life. Only in recent years had his father
lifted the ban on his identity being known, and by then the
exposure had outlived any usefulness or appeal.

'Why are you selling it?'

She was at least a foot shorter than he was. He adjusted
his stride to match hers, shoving his hands in his pockets
as they moved towards the water.

'I do not want it.'

She frowned. 'You don't want a pristine, untouched island off the coast of Italy?'

'No.'

Her laugh was carried by the breeze. He turned to chase
it, wishing it was louder.

'Why ever not?'

He met her eyes, his smile feeling heavy somehow. 'I
already have an island. A bigger one.' He thought of Arketà, with its state-of-the-art home and pier, the helicopter
pad and three swimming pools. 'Two seems excessive.'

'And here I was thinking you to be a man who thrived
on the excessive,' she heard herself tease.

At the edge of the water she paused, kicking her shoes
off and bending to retrieve them. She moved closer to the
ocean, flexing her toes as she reached the water's line, then
stepping beyond it so that the waves caressed her ankles.

'So why buy it if only to sell? Or was it an investment?'

He looked at her for a moment, wondering at the in-
stinct throbbing through him to speak honestly to her. To
admit that he hadn't bought the island so much as inherited it. That in the month he'd possessed Prim'amore it had
sat heavily on his shoulders like a weight he didn't wish to
bear. That the gift was unwelcome and that selling it was
his primary desire.

'Not exactly.' His smile gave little away. 'I do not need
it. Your father has been shopping for a resort site in the
Mediterranean for years. The match is too good to ignore.'

She nodded, but he could practically see the cogs turning. 'You said your island is called Arketà?'

'Yes.'

'I like the sound of that.'

He nodded. 'It means pretty in Greek.'

She arched a brow, her grin contagious.

'I inherited the name when I purchased it. The previous owner christened it so for his daughter.'

'I see.' Tilly nodded, but her smile didn't drop.

'That and I'm a hopeless romantic,' he responded with an attempt at sarcasm.

Tilly shook her head. 'Nope. I would bet my life that "romantic" is not a word ever associated with you.'

'Oh? And how *would* you describe me?' He prompted, curiosity leading him down a conversational path that his brain was urging him to reconsider.

She slowed for a moment, her eyes skimming across his face as her full lips pouted. She was a study in concentration and it almost made him laugh.

'I think it's better that I don't say,' she said finally, turning her gaze back to the beach. 'Do you spend much time there?'

It took him a few seconds to realise she was back on the subject of Arketà. He shook his head. 'I thought I would when I bought it.'

'But?' she prompted.

His shrug lifted his broad shoulders. She tried not to notice the strength in those shoulders, but she was only human.

'Work.'

'Ah. Yes.' She knew the demands of Art Wyndham's schedule intimately, and could only imagine how much more hectic Rio's was. 'So you're in Rome most of the time?'

'*Si.*'

Tilly could imagine that. He had an effortless chicness about him that was completely ingrained. It wasn't an affectation. He didn't have to try. He was both masculine, wild, untamed and…handsome. Nothing about him screamed ostentation, yet he exuded power and wealth.

'And you?' he surprised her by asking.

Tilly almost lost her footing, but she righted herself before he felt the need to intervene. 'What about me?'

Out of nowhere she thought of Cressida. Cressida who was so visibly similar to her that Tilly had thought she was looking into a mirror the first time they'd met. Their red hair was long, their eyes green, their skin a similar colour—though Tilly's tanned more easily. They were both of medium height, and though Tilly was naturally more curvaceous, Cressida had bought breast and rear enhancements two years earlier, making their figures almost matching.

'I gather you've made an art form out of living fast and loose?'

Tilly frowned. As always, a whip of sorrow for the billion-dollar heiress flayed her. True, Cressida's lifestyle was a masterpiece in modern-day debauchery, but Tilly somehow just understood her. And there was a lot more to the glamorous fashionista than partying. If only she'd let anyone see it.

'Not really,' she heard herself say. 'The papers don't always give me a fair shake.'

Now it was Rio's turn to slow. He angled his face to study her profile. 'Papers make up stories, but photos never lie.'

Her heart thumped hard against her chest. Had he seen photos of *her*? Could he tell the difference? For, as much as she and Cressida were uncannily similar, they were not the same person, and it was easy to see the differences when you set your mind to looking.

Though Tilly had an answer ready for that. She wasn't

wearing more than the bare minimum of make-up, and Cressida was never papped without a full face. Even her morning coffee run was completed in full glamour style. It was completely plausible to explain away the slight differences in their appearance by claiming a lack of cosmetic help. At least to a man, surely?

'I think people look at photos of celebrities and see what they're looking for,' she said softly. 'I could leave a nightclub at three in the morning, stone-cold sober, arm in arm with a guy I've been friends with for years, and the next thing you know I'm drunk and three months pregnant with his baby.'

She rolled her eyes, her outrage at such misreporting genuine. She'd personally placed enough calls to Art's solicitor, lodging complaints and libel suits, to know how frequently Cressida was photographed and lambasted for something that was perfectly innocent.

'Am I to feel sorry for you now?'

She lifted her face to his, her expression showing mutiny. 'I don't want sympathy.'

'I can see that.'

She stepped over a jellyfish, marooned elegantly against the sand, its transparent body no longer capable of bobbing in the depths of the ocean.

'So you are *not* a wild, irresponsible party girl, then?' he asked, his voice rich with disbelief.

Tilly shook her head, thinking of Cressida. She was everything Rio accused her of, and yet Tilly couldn't stomach the idea of him looking at her and seeing Cressida.

'I'm not *just* a party girl,' she said after a beat had passed. 'Honestly, I'm more comfortable somewhere like this. Somewhere away from the cameras and press. Somewhere I can just be by myself and read.'

*Read?* Hardly Cressida's favourite pastime, but no matter. He wasn't ever going to discover that fact for himself, was he?

'It is hard for you to be alone when you're in London?'

'Yes,' she said. But impersonating Cressida was wearing thin. 'When did you buy this island?'

His eyes bobbed out to sea, chasing something invisible and transient on the horizon.

'I recently acquired it,' he said silkily, tweaking his response slightly to fit the facts.

'And now you're selling it?'

He nodded. 'We've covered this.'

Her lips pulled downwards. 'It just doesn't make sense.'

'On the contrary—it makes perfect sense. I own an island I do not need or want. Your father desperately wants an island of this size, within easy boat distance of the mainland, and he is prepared to pay the price I have stipulated. Provided you do not go back and report that the volcano is about to explode, I will no longer own Prim'amore in a matter of weeks.'

There was more to it. Tilly could almost feel the words he wasn't saying; they were throbbing beneath her fingertips. But she needed patience to massage them to the surface.

'Volcano?' She moved the conversation to less critical ground. 'You're not serious?'

'Absolutely. It is extinct now—a relic. The lava no longer flows in its belly.'

She shuddered. 'How can you be sure?'

His laugh was warm honey on her sensitised muscles. 'Because a team of geologists have told me so.' He stopped walking and angled his whole body to face her. 'Would you like to see it?'

Her breath hitched in her throat. Staring down the chasm of a volcano would be the most dangerous thing she'd ever done. Well, almost. The more time she spent with Rio the more she was coming to realise she'd taken a step into the terrifying unknown by agreeing to pose as Cressida.

'Yes,' she heard herself agree. 'I would.'

'We'll go tomorrow.'

He nodded with the kind of confidence that had surely been born out of his success in the boardroom. Or given rise to it. She blinked up at him and wondered if anyone ever told him no.

'Not often.'

She frowned, her confusion apparent.

'I am not often told no.'

'Oh!' Evidently her mouth had run away with her—and without her permission too. She felt heat warm her cheeks and began to move again, along the shoreline, kicking the water as she went, enjoying the feeling as it splashed against her shins.

'I expect it has always been the same for you?'

Tilly thought of her family. Her parents who had worked hard all their lives, who adored her and would have found a way to give her the moon if she'd asked it of them.

'Why do you say that?' She returned his question with a question.

'Because I have known women like you before,' he said simply, shrugging his broad shoulders.

'And what's *that* supposed to mean?'

His smile was derisive, and yet her heart flipped as though he was offering her a bunch of flowers. She turned away, frustrated at the schoolgirl crush she seemed to be developing.

'That you grew up with more money than most people see in a lifetime. And that in my experience women like you tend to be...'

'Yes?' she prompted, her hackles rising despite the fact he was making assumptions about her doppelgänger, not her true self.

What had he wanted to say? Did it matter that the spoiled rich girls he'd bedded in the past were all boring, entitled, selfish and dull? Why were they talking about this?

His frown deepened. He was supposed to be showing her the island; that was all. It was the kind of thing he'd never have deigned to do under normal circumstances. God knew he had more important things to focus on. Still, he couldn't—*wouldn't*—let the press get wind of his ties to Prim'amore. Rio, and Rio alone, would handle all the contracts associated with the sale.

But it should have taken days. Not a week. Art had been strangely insistent, though. Cressida wanted a week 'to really get a feel for the place', and Art had expressed his relief that his wayward daughter was showing such good business sense.

But he didn't need to spend the whole time taking beach strolls with the admittedly beautiful heiress. And certainly not sharing his innermost thoughts.

'Never mind,' he said, his voice a dark contradiction of the light banter they'd been sharing. 'This beach stretches for another two miles before the cove curves inwards and we'll need to climb the cliff. I suggest we leave that for another day.'

He was being deliberately unpleasant.

No, not unpleasant.

Just a big, gorgeous roadblock to any conversation she tried to make.

He'd been like it as they'd walked on the beach. As though he'd flicked a switch and she no longer held any interest for him. He'd pointed out details of the island, suggested positions that might be suitable for a hotel, but he had made it clear that he felt obliged to provide her with business information and that was the end of it.

So why did it bother her?

She'd come to the island expecting to meet with a dull estate agent. She'd brought books and bathing costumes, anticipating a delicious week on her own, soaking in the sunshine and relaxing.

But now her nerves were stretched on tenterhooks.

She flicked the page of her book, even though she had no concept of what she'd read, and briefly lifted her eyes to where he sat. There was only one living space in the house and he'd taken up position on the small table. It held his laptop, and thick files spread in each direction. His head was bent, he had a pen in his hand, and as he read one of the files he occasionally scratched a note angrily in the margin.

Unexpectedly he flashed his eyes in her direction and she looked away, stumbling her focus back to reading. His eyes continued to burn her skin, though.

He stood abruptly, scraping his chair noisily against the tiles. She kept her head bent as he moved into the kitchen and she heard the fridge open and shut.

She turned the page—again with no concept of where she was in the story.

The sound of butter simmering in a frying pan finally captured her interest, and she risked a glance towards him.

Her heart stuttered. Rio Mastrangelo was a seriously gorgeous man at any time. But with his shirtsleeves pushed up to the elbows, his head bent as he chopped tomato and fennel…he was the poster boy for sexiest man alive.

'What are you doing?' she asked, wishing she hadn't when his eyes lanced her and she felt her stomach swoop.

'Stringing a fishing line,' he replied, with a sarcasm that he softened by smiling.

He had a dimple in one cheek. Deep enough to dip her finger into. She looked back at her book.

'I presume you eat normal food?' he asked, with a challenge she didn't understand in his question.

'It depends what you call "normal."' She gave up on the book, folding down the corner at the top of a page and placing it on the sofa.

She stood and padded towards the kitchen, curious as he added basil leaves to the chopping board. He reached for the fridge once more and returned with fish, adding each fillet one by one to the sizzling frying pan. He sliced a lemon down the middle and squeezed it over the top, then ground salt.

'That smells delicious,' she said seriously. 'You like to cook?'

He shrugged. 'I like to eat, so...'

Her smile was involuntary, and her attention was momentarily distracted by the sizzling fish, so she didn't realise that his eyes had dropped to her mouth and were staring at it with an intensity that would have boiled her blood.

'I would have thought you'd have a chef. No—a *team* of chefs. All ready to obey your every whim.' She lifted her brows as she turned her attention back to his face.

'No.'

More of the stonewalling she'd faced that afternoon.

'No? Why not?'

'Because, Principessa, not everyone grew up in the hyper-indulged, rarefied way you did. I learned to cook almost as soon as I could walk. Just because I can *afford* to employ chefs it doesn't mean it's necessary.'

The hostility of his statement hurt far more than it should have. He was judging her—no, he was judging *Cressida*, she reminded herself forcibly—and she didn't like it. Not one bit.

Her throat ached. With mortification, Tilly realised his harsh rebuke had brought her to the brink of tears. She took a steadying breath and looked away.

He expelled an angry breath and reached for the fish,

flicking it deftly. 'I'm sorry,' he said after a moment. 'That was rude of me.'

If his judgemental bitterness had surprised her, the apology had even more so.

She lifted her eyes to him slowly. 'You think I'm spoiled.'

His smile was brief. A flicker across his face that she thought she must have imagined. He reached for two plates and scooped the tomato and fennel mixture into the middle, then added several fish fillets and half a lemon. It had the kind of presentation a five-year-old would have been proud of, but it smelled incredible. Her stomach groaned in agreement with that thought and she cleared her throat in an attempt to cover it.

'I believe you drink champagne?'

Tilly frowned, and was on the brink of pointing out that she really didn't drink much at all before remembering that Cressida was practically fuelled by the stuff. She found it perfectly acceptable to start her day with a glass of bubbles. And, despite the fact she could knock off a bottle on her own in no time, she never seemed affected by it. Which showed she had an incredible tolerance for the stuff. Unlike Tilly.

Yet she nodded, knowing it would lead to questions if she disavowed something so intrinsic about the heiress.

He reached into the fridge and pulled out a bottle—Bollinger, she saw as he unfurled the top.

'The cabin is not exactly well appointed,' he explained, pulling out a single tumbler and half filling it with champagne. He handed her the glass, then scooped up their plates and cutlery.

'You're not joining me?'

'No.'

He moved down the corridor, pushing the door to the balcony open with his shoulder and holding it for her to move past. It surprised her; she'd assumed they'd sit inside at the table.

But when she looked up she let out a sound of astonishment.

Somewhere between their walk on the beach and the pages she hadn't read, the sky had caught fire. Red, orange, pink and purple exploded in every direction, backlit by warmth and turning the ocean a vibrant hue of purple.

'Wow!'

He set the plates on the small table, his eyes following hers.

*'Remember when we swam as the sun dipped down and the sky was orange? And you told me I was a mermaid who'd come from the sea?'*

His mother's voice had been crackly and faint. The last of her cancer treatments had left her disorientated and confused.

*'Prim'amore—my love, my first love. For ever.'*

When death had been at her doorstep, she'd thought only of *him*. Piero. A man who hadn't even come to the funeral—who hadn't so much as acknowledged her passing.

Rio compressed his lips, his appetite diminished.

Not so Tilly's.

She sat opposite him and attacked her fish with impressive gusto, pausing occasionally to turn back to the view, before remembering that she was starving, apparently, and pushing another piece of her dinner into her mouth.

A beautiful mouth. Full and naturally pouting, with a perfect cupid's bow that out of nowhere he imagined tracing with his tongue.

His body stirred at the idea. The sooner he got off this island the better. Any number of women would make more suitable, less complicated lovers than Cressida Wyndham.

'You didn't answer my question.'

He leaned back in his chair, his eyes roaming her face.

'Yes.' His nod was concise. 'I think you're spoiled.' His eyes dropped to her lips once more—lips that were parted now with indignation. 'But it is not your fault.'

'Oh, geez. *Thanks*.' She reached for her champagne and sipped it, pulling a face when the water she wanted to taste turned out to be bubbly and astringent. Still, it slid down her throat, soothing her parched mouth and calming her nerves.

His laugh sent her pulse skittering.

'I mean only that anyone raised as you were would be spoiled. You have been indulged from the first day of your life. Adored. Cherished. All your dreams made a reality, I imagine.'

Tilly couldn't have said where the need to defend Cressida came from, but it was like a sledgehammer in her side. Sisterhood? Girl power? Her own childhood had been idyllic. *She*, Tilly, was the one who had been spoiled. Not with material possessions—money had always been tight in the Morgan household—but with time and love.

'Yes, well, that may be true, but there's more to life than physical possessions, and far better ways to show affection than by giving gifts.'

Curious, he leaned forward. 'Poor little rich girl?' he prompted, and when she kept her face averted, her chin set at a defiant angle, he felt a surge of adrenalin kick in his gut. 'Have I hurt your feelings, Principessa?'

She reached for her champagne once more and held it in one hand, her eyes roaming the ocean before lifting to his face. 'You haven't hurt my feelings.'

She spoke with a calm control he hadn't expected.

'You've made me curious about yours. You haven't even known me a day and yet you speak of me with derision and contempt. That can't possibly be based on who I am, seeing as you barely know me. It must be because of who *you* are. And *your* hang ups. You think less of me because I come from money.'

* * *

She had surprised him and he hadn't liked it. *At all.*

Her insight had been rapier-sharp. He'd judged her because of what he'd presumed her to be, and that was hardly fair. He'd have never made his mark in business if he'd carried such assumptions alongside him.

He swirled his Scotch, his eyes resting on the now dark sky.

Was she asleep? She'd finished her dinner abruptly after her incisive comment and scuttled inside. He'd listened to the sound of the sink being filled and dishes being washed, all the while pondering the mystery of Cressida Wyndham.

When Art had said his daughter was coming to inspect the island Rio had instantly formed preconceptions. He knew enough about Cressida to know what to expect. But since she'd arrived she'd defied each of the ideas he'd held. She'd fallen into the water…and *laughed.* She'd accepted the humble accommodation without complaint. She'd read her book, and she'd thanked him for cooking. Hell, she'd done the dishes.

None of that fitted into the way he'd envisaged someone like Cressida behaving.

She'd been right. He didn't like her. He didn't like women *like* her.

How could someone like Rio, who'd been raised in abject poverty, feel anything but resentment for the kind of indulged lifestyle that had been made available to the Cressidas of the world?

His thoughts wandered distractedly to Marina. The heiress he'd thought himself in love with many years ago. She'd been beautiful, too, and she'd seemed interesting and genuine. But she'd taught him an important lesson: never trust a beautiful woman who cared only for herself.

He leaned back on the deck, his eyes lingering on the silver streak of the moon reflected in the water. His mother had tried to provide for him. Had she not become ill, undoubtedly their lives would have been comfortable. His expression was grim as he remembered that sensation of hunger and worry. Even as a young boy he had been sent to school in uniforms that were a little too small, shorts that didn't quite fit, shoes that were second-hand and badly scuffed.

All the while his wealthy father had refused to intervene. And now he'd given him this! A parting shot. A last insult. An island that intrinsically reminded him of Piero and all the ways he'd failed Rio and Rosa.

# CHAPTER THREE

SHE WAS IN AGONY.

Being tortured alive with every bump.

The bike was old, yet powerful, and the man drove it with expert ease. Still, there wasn't a road so much as a track, and she had to keep her arms wrapped tight around his waist, her legs squeezed against his. She could feel his heart racing beneath her hands, smell his intoxicating masculinity, and her stomach was in knots.

Every hitch in the road brought her womanhood closer to him, bouncing her on the seat. Needs long ago suppressed were being pushed to the front of her mind. Heat flamed through her and it had nothing to do with the morning sun that was beating down on her back.

Tilly had never been into cars or bikes. She liked nice, smart, kind men. Men who had blond hair and white teeth and clear blue eyes. Who called her mum 'ma'am' and liked to watch the football with her dad and Jack.

*Nice* guys.

There was nothing 'nice' about Rio Mastrangelo, but her body was sparking with a desire she'd never felt before.

She angled her head, focussing on the view of the island as the bike climbed higher, around the track, but it was no use. Her eyes saw the glistening ocean, and the spectacular greenery between them and it, but in her mind she was imagining making love to Rio on top of this very bike. Straddling him and taking him against the leather seat.

She was ashamed of herself!

Then again, she'd woken up in a state of confusion and arousal because she'd dreamed about him. Dreams that had made her body sensitive. And that sensitivity was not being helped now, by the bumping of the bike along the road. Nor by the feeling of his powerful legs moving inside hers. The broadness of his chest and the rise and fall of his back.

She was in trouble.

Cressida might have no trouble getting into bed with strangers, but Tilly didn't do the whole casual sex thing. She wasn't a prude, but she'd never really wanted any guy enough to ignore common sense. She wanted the fairy tale. She wanted to meet a man who swept her off her feet and offered love and happily-ever-after.

Rio would never be that.

What he would be was a sensational lover.

She groaned under her breath at the very idea. Her hands, curved around his chest, wanted to drop lower. To find the hem of his shirt and push it up so that her fingertips could connect with bare flesh.

This was a nightmare.

No way could she act on these feelings! Apart from anything, she'd feel as if she was letting herself down. Where could this go? She was lying to him—pretending to be someone she wasn't. A secret she absolutely had to keep!

It wasn't just the money Cressida had paid, though that was a huge part of it. Cressida had *begged* her to play along, and not for the first time in Tilly's life she'd felt sorry for the glamorous heiress.

*'I have a wedding to go to. Mum and Dad would never approve. It's really important, Tilly, or I wouldn't have asked.'*

Matilda suspected that Art and Gloria would indeed have disapproved, but that wouldn't have stopped Cressida from going. It just would have led to yet another loud shouting match, resulting in Cressida storming out and Art fretting for days over how he could handle his wayward daughter more effectively.

Having worked for Art for four years, Tilly had seen

enough of those confrontations to know they were best avoided. Art wasn't in great health, and every time he lost his temper with Cressida, Tilly worried.

No, she'd saved everyone a whole heap of trouble by coming to Prim'amore in Cressida's place. After all, it was only a week. Cressida would attend the wedding, Tilly would stay on the island, and then they'd get back to their normal lives with no one ever knowing they'd performed a switcheroo.

She ignored the niggle of disquiet over that—and the inevitable conclusion that after this week she would never see Rio Mastrangelo again.

He turned the bike around a corner, leaning into it, and she leaned with him, holding on tight as the bike seemed to dip close to the grass on one side. He straightened, but she kept on holding him tight. Finally he brought the bike to a stop, pressing one powerful leg down to kick the stand.

'This is where the path stops.' His words were accented.

Belatedly, Tilly realised she was still gripping his waist and that there was no reason to do so. She jerked her arms away and fumbled her way off the back of the bike, scratching her calf in the process.

He had no such difficulty. He lifted himself off as though he'd been riding bikes all his life.

'You're a natural at that,' she said, the words thick.

He lifted his helmet off and placed it on the seat, the turned to unclip hers. 'It's not rocket science.'

'Still...' She held her breath as his fingers brushed against the soft flesh under her chin.

He reached for the clasp and pressed it; the helmet loosened and she reached up to dislodge it at the same time he did. Their fingers tangled but he didn't pull away, and nor did she. His eyes held hers for a beat longer than normal, and her stomach swooped up and then down.

She cleared her throat, pulling her hands away and smiling awkwardly. *Yeah, great.* Just what Cressida would have done, she thought with an inward groan of mortification.

He didn't seem to realise. He pressed the helmet onto the seat and then reached back towards her.

His hand in her hair was like the start of her dream coming true. She watched, mesmerised, as he studied the red lengths, pulling his fingers through it, a slight frown on his face. Her breath hitched in her throat and anxiety began to perforate that strange mood.

Had he recognised who she was? Or rather who she *wasn't*?

'Do you dye this?'

She pulled a face, not comprehending why he'd ask such a question. 'No!'

'I didn't think so.' His frown deepened. 'It's like copper and gold.'

'Yes.' She nodded, stepping backwards and almost tripping on a rock that jutted out of the ground. His hand on her elbow steadied her, then dropped away again. 'I hated it, growing up. I used to get teased mercilessly.'

'I find that hard to believe.'

Strangely, it was something that Cressida and Tilly had in common. They'd discussed the dislike they'd felt as children, for having such unique colouring.

'Yes, well—says you, who's probably always looked like a mini-Greek god.'

The words were out before she could stop them.

'I'm Italian,' he pointed out, his grin doing strange things to her blood pressure. 'And there is nothing miniature about me.'

'You know what I mean.' Her cheeks flushed bright red. She might as well have blurted out that she couldn't stop thinking about how gorgeous he was.

He nodded, apparently taking pity on her because he

didn't pursue it. 'I wouldn't have teased you for your hair. Or anything.'

Her heart thumped. 'Is this the volcano?' She nodded at the jagged mountaintop that was still a little way above them.

He grinned, his eyes lifting to the peak. 'Yeah. The track stops here.'

'So we'll walk?'

'Sure.' He lifted the seat of the bike and pulled out a black rucksack, hooking it over his shoulder. 'Let's go.'

She'd packed flip-flops and dresses, neither of which were especially suited to scaling a Mediterranean volcano. But she wasn't going to complain.

'The volcano would make an excellent tourist attraction. I know the previous owner of the island had plans drawn up to run a cable car across the top.'

'That's a great idea,' she murmured.

The climb was steep and her breath was burning, despite the fact she was generally in good shape.

'Just say if you require a break,' he murmured.

*Not bloody likely*, she thought to herself, sending him a sidelong glance. 'I'll be—'

'Fine,' he responded. 'The thing is, you usually say that before you fall over, so perhaps we should pause.'

'That happened *once*,' she said with a laugh, reaching across and pushing at his arm playfully.

He grinned back, but it was no longer playful. The atmosphere was electric.

She swallowed, forcing the conversation to something less incendiary. Something safe. 'Was the previous owner looking at developing the island for tourists?'

Rio's step slowed. *'Si.'*

'I wonder why he didn't,' she murmured.

'He died. Unexpectedly.'

'Oh! What a shame. That's awful.'

He stopped walking and turned to face her. 'Look, Cressida.'

He nodded behind her and she spun.

An enormous smile broke across her face. 'I'm on top of the world!' she said, shaking her head.

The ocean spread like a big blue picnic blanket in every direction, but from this height she could make out ships in the distance, and another island dotted with bright homes.

'Capri,' he explained. 'It is only twenty minutes away by boat.'

'So close. And I thought we were all alone in the middle of the sea...'

She smiled up at him, but the look of speculation in his eyes stole her breath. There was no way this awareness was one-sided. He felt it too. Didn't he?

She jerked her eyes back to the view, her mind spinning, her blood rushing.

'I was wrong last night. And you were right to point that out.'

His admission had come out of nowhere. She looked up at him, then turned away again. It was like staring at the sun.

'So what is it with you and money? You have a fortune, right? Why do you have a chip on your shoulder about people like...like me,' she finished, a small pause punctuating her question as she forced herself to remember just who she was supposed to be.

'I told you. I have known a lot of women like you.'

He shook his head, clearing the image of Marina once more. The two women were nothing alike, apart from their beauty and the fortunes they'd grown up knowing to be at their fingertips.

'And yet they were not like you. They were women of the same background. I expected you to be the same. And yet you are...'

'Yes?' A breathy question, a plea for him to continue.

'Unique.' He grinned, breaking the mood that was swirling around them.

'Thanks.'

She turned her back on the view. They were close to the top now.

'You didn't have money, growing up?'

His expression darkened and she understood that he was wrestling with whether or not to answer the question.

'No,' he said after a moment, taking a step towards the precipice of the volcano.

She fell into step just behind him. 'Your parents?' she prompted, curious about this man.

There'd be information on the internet, if she looked him up, but that wasn't possible for the next week. Her phone had no reception on the island.

'My father wasn't in the picture,' he said, and the words were clipped, as though they were being dragged from him. 'My mother worked hard to make ends meet. But she got sick and wasn't always able to hold down jobs.'

'I'm sorry,' Tilly murmured, her heart squeezing. 'Is she...okay now?'

'She died. A long time ago.'

'Oh, Rio.'

She reached out and curled her fingers around his forearm, forcing him to stop. He was much taller than she was, but a step ahead of her the difference was even more pronounced.

She stared up at him, saw the sun golden behind his head. 'How old were you?'

A muscle jerked in his jaw. Her eyes dropped to it, and she understood his anguish and pain.

'Seventeen.'

She shook her head slowly from side to side. 'What happened?'

Again, it seemed he wasn't going to answer. She watched him weigh up his words and finally he turned around, resuming his course up the hill and breaking their contact.

'Cancer,' he said under his breath, just loud enough for her to catch it.

She nodded, but her heart was breaking for the young man he must have been. On the cusp of adulthood, alone in the world.

'What did you do?'

His laugh was a brittle sound. 'What did I *do, cara*?'

The term of endearment came without warning but she didn't question it. She infinitely preferred it to his use of Cressida's name.

'I finished school and then I worked.'

She nodded. 'And your father wasn't able to…?'

'He wasn't in the picture,' he repeated.

He stopped walking abruptly, and before she could bump into him and tumble backwards he turned and hooked an arm around her waist. The gesture was intimate; it set little flames burning beneath her flesh.

'Look.'

He nodded straight ahead and, curious, she moved in that direction.

'Don't fall in,' he said softly, from right behind her.

The drop from the top of the volcano was several hundred feet, and there was a lot of stone along the way.

She threw him a withering look over her shoulder—and then missed her footing altogether, stumbling on the rocky path and pitching forward dangerously.

With an oath, he reached for her and pulled her backwards, holding her against his chest. Her breathing was forced, her heart pounding—though from adrenalin or the proximity to Rio, Tilly couldn't have said.

'You are *unbelievably* clumsy,' he snapped, but his eyes were on her lips, and his hands, firm against her back at first, were soft now, moving slightly, caressing her through the flimsy fabric of her dress.

His body was firm and hard; he smelled like sunshine and sweat. A pulse between her legs was firing wildly and her dream was playing out right before her eyes. She wanted him to kiss her. No, she wanted to kiss *him*.

Cressida would have. She would have wrapped her arms around his neck and pulled his head down, leaving him in little doubt of just what she wanted.

But, though they looked like twins, Tilly was nothing like Cressida.

'I lost my footing,' she said, not breaking their contact. 'I wasn't going to tumble to my death.'

*'Mio Dio,'* he said darkly, his eyes caressing her face where she wanted his fingers, his mouth to touch. 'That is exactly what you would have done if you'd been a foot closer.'

'But I wasn't,' she murmured, not sure what they were arguing about any more. 'Rio...?'

Her eyes moved to his lips and she darted her tongue out, moistening the outline of her mouth, staring at his, needing him to kiss her.

His chest was moving rapidly, but he wasn't out of shape. It was something else that was causing his breath to explode from him.

'I feel as though I need to shadow you from now on,' he said with a shake of his head, his eyes glued to her face. 'To keep you out of danger.'

Her smile lacked humour. 'I think there's danger here, too.'

His eyes flickered with recognition. She was right. He was about two mad moments away from plundering her mouth, from tearing at her dress and laying her on the ground. Her, Cressida Wyndham, a woman he barely knew, a woman who was on the island as his guest.

He dropped his arms and stepped backwards, moving his attention back to the volcano. 'Can you be trusted to look without falling?'

He'd flicked a switch and was back to normal. As though his hands *hadn't* just been stroking her back, his legs straddling hers, his face an inch away and aching to kiss her.

Tilly found it harder to return her mind to its scheduled programming. She jerked her head in agreement, but as she stepped closer to the edge of the mountain he stayed close. Close enough to grab her.

The temptation to fake another fall was strong, but she resisted it.

'I have never seen anything like this,' she said honestly.

She hadn't been sure what to expect, but not this. It looked as though the earth had been dug out, hollowed, and right at the bottom of the valley there was a lagoon so blue she ached to swim in it.

'I had no idea. Is this what happens to volcanoes when they die?'

'I believe each one is different,' he said.

'Can you go down there?'

He laughed. 'No. Not *you*. I think that would be a disaster.'

She sent him a look of muted impatience. 'I'm really not that bad. You must have a rope or something?'

Realising she was serious, he sobered. '*Dio, cara*, you're going to give me a heart attack. Are you seriously suggesting scaling this volcano?'

'Look at that water,' she said plaintively. 'It's divine.'

He eyed her thoughtfully for a moment. 'It does look nice. But there is nicer.'

'Yeah? Where?'

'Come. I'll show you.' He unhooked his rucksack and pulled out a water bottle. 'Thirsty?'

She shook her head. She might have been before, but other needs had subsumed everything else.

'Hungry?'

She shook her head again, but her tummy did a little squeeze.

'Well, I am.'

His smile was rueful. Beautiful. She was lost.

He reached into the rucksack and pulled out an apple.

She arched a brow. 'Really?'

He nodded. 'What's wrong with fruit?'

'Forbidden fruit,' she muttered under her breath, but his grin showed that he'd heard.

'Want a bite?'

He held it out to her and she eyed it warily before shaking her head, more firmly this time.

'Suit yourself.' He shrugged, making short work of the apple before tossing the core into the undergrowth. 'Let's go.'

Another twenty minutes on the bike did little to calm her overstretched nerves, and by the time he pulled it to a stop in the middle of what seemed to be a forest of thick cypress trees, she was almost ready to burst.

He removed his helmet and stood, but before he could reach for hers she unclipped it hurriedly, adding it to his on the seat in front of her.

His smile was droll and she had the distinct impression he was laughing at her.

'Well?' she asked, with an impatience born of embarrassment. 'What are you showing me?'

'You wanted to see some spectacular water,' he reminded her, his expression carefully blank of emotion.

She climbed off the bike, wishing she'd thought to pack some shorts and jeans. There was no neat way to dismount, and she stood pushing her dress down, only to look up and find his eyes arrested on her legs.

Heat flared inside her.

'Which way?' she asked, the question a husk in the middle of the forest.

He jerked his head slightly to the left but then his eyes met hers and Tilly felt it.

Inevitability.

She was fighting it, and so was he, but they might as well try to stave off night's fall.

This thing between them—whatever it was—was going to happen.

# CHAPTER FOUR

'WELL?' HE PROMPTED, looking not at the water but at the beautiful British heiress.

Her eyes, so green they matched the ocean, sparkled. Her lashes fanned her cheeks as she blinked rapidly, looking from the trees that nestled right up to the edge of the white cliff face to the water that was a pristine turquoise.

'Oh, yes…' She nodded, crouching down and peeking over the edge. She looked away from the cliff, following the water to the point where the island separated and admitted the ocean. 'This is perfect.'

Her voice was soft and full of emotion.

Curious, he crouched beside her. 'You are upset?'

'No!' She smiled, but her eyes were sparkling with unshed tears. 'I'm…overwhelmed. Overcome. This is impossibly beautiful.'

His life had been a tribute to the pursuit of beauty; rather to preserving it. He had never met another person who felt that as strongly as he.

'That probably seems really stupid,' she mumbled, turning back to the water.

'Not to me.' His smile was reassuring. 'Well?'

She stood, sucking in a deep breath. It tasted like Italy. Salty, sweet, with the hint of cypress and fresh air.

'Well what?' she queried, placing her hands on her hips.

'Care to join me for a swim?'

She eyed the water thoughtfully. It was damned tempting. The heat of the day, not to mention the fire raging between them, had left her with a distinctly raised temperature. A dip in the crystal-clear water would feel wonderful.

'What's the matter?' he asked teasingly. 'Don't you want me to see your underwear?'

She gasped, her eyes enormous in her face. 'I'll have you know I'm wearing a bikini,' she responded archly, but her pulse was firing again, her cheeks pink.

'So?'

He grinned, and before she knew what he was doing his fingers had reached for the bottom of his shirt and lifted it over his head. She had a second to take in perfect abdominals ridged into a broad, tanned chest, a line of dark hair that ran down the middle, disappearing into his waistband.

He tossed the shirt to the ground, then began to unzip his jeans.

She fluttered her eyes closed as desire ran rampant through her.

'You confuse me,' he said thoughtfully, a moment later.

She blinked, flicking her eyes to his nether regions and expelling a sigh of relief to see that he wasn't completely in the buff. A pair of dark boxers covered his masculinity. But there was plenty of him on display. Legs that were strong and muscular, tanned and hair-roughened.

Legs that she was imagining curling around her waist.

Oh, heck. She was in serious trouble.

'Do I?'

'*Si*. Why would you be shy about swimming?'

'I'm not shy,' she promised—but, oh, she was. Shy and exhilarated.

'I didn't think so. You were, after all, photographed skinny-dipping with about three hundred festival-goers in Germany earlier this year.'

She stared at him, not sure what to say to that. She was tempted to point out that the photographers had only *guessed* that Cressida had been naked—she hadn't been. Or to query his knowledge of gossip pieces. But that story hadn't been restricted just to the scandal rags. It had gone into the mainstream news. Even the broadsheet papers had covered it because of the timing—Art Wyndham had been meeting the President of the United States of America that same day.

'There are no photographers here. Just you and me. And I promise we will keep some clothes on.'

She sent him a withering look, but her pulse was racing. Slowly she reached up, her fingers unsteady as she hooked them into the straps of her dress and slid them down her arms. He followed their progress with his eyes and she could have sworn he was holding his breath.

The bikini she'd chosen was no less and no more revealing than her others, but when she stood before him wearing only the flimsy scraps of white fabric she desperately wished she'd put up with the heat and stayed clothed.

'Wow...' he muttered, his eyes taking their time as they trailed over her body.

'Is something the matter?' she snapped, resisting the impulse to cross her arms over her chest.

'No.' He grinned, flashed his eyes to her and then returned to his inspection of her body. 'I am just...overwhelmed.'

She opened her mouth to say something, but when he made a copycat sniffling sound she laughed and ran towards him, pushing at his chest. 'I'll make you pay for that.'

'Yes?' He grabbed her wrists and held them by her sides, so that only her harsh breath sounds punctuated the stillness. 'How do you suggest you'll do that?'

She bit down on her lip, her mind completely bereft of responses.

When he reached down and lifted her up, cradling her against his chest, she made a small sound low in her throat.

It all happened so fast.

One minute she was processing just how good it felt to

be close to him, and the next he'd leaped off the edge of the white cliff. They were flying through the air.

His laugh was the last thing she heard before they hit the water.

*Splash!*

There was noise, then complete immersion in the water, and finally his letting her go, so that she could splutter her way to the surface.

Her red hair was straggling over her face, and she spun around, trying to pinpoint him.

'You…you…' she spluttered when he lifted out of the water, a grin crossing from ear to ear over his handsome face. 'How dare you?'

He tilted his head to one side, his eyes darkened by an emotion she couldn't comprehend. 'We have a problem, *cara*.'

'Yeah?' She could think of about a hundred! 'What's that?'

His smile lifted as he pulled one hand out of the water, something white clutched in his fingers. It took several seconds before she realised it was her bikini top.

With a squawk, she lowered herself in the water, treading water as he made his way to her.

'Give that to me,' she demanded indignantly.

'I intend to.'

He was right in front of her and she turned her back on him, embarrassment and coyness making her want to shield herself from him.

'Here.' It was a gravelled husk. A word that invited her to turn around and stare at him.

She fumbled with the bikini in the water—no easy task when she had to simultaneously kick her legs to stay afloat.

'Would you like help?'

If she'd been in a generous mood, she might have appreciated that without help she was unlikely to succeed. But Tilly's mood was all over the place.

'No. I'm fine.'

His laugh teased her, and she felt her own lips lifting in response.

'Don't laugh at me,' she responded, attempting to sound angry when actually she was being flooded by a confusing degree of happiness.

'Don't make me laugh, then,' he said simply. 'Here.'

He swam to her back and reached for the clasp of her bikini. He had every opportunity to milk their close contact, but he didn't. His fingers moved with professional detachment, clipping both the halter neck and the back without lingering.

And how she'd wanted them to linger!

'I truly didn't realise jumping into the water would lead to you getting almost naked,' he said, but something about his face made her wonder if that was a lie.

'Yes, well… No harm done.'

Such a prim expression! She winced, and for the hundredth time since arriving couldn't help but imagine how Cressida would have reacted in such a situation.

'This cove is incredible.' She changed the subject desperately, gliding through the water.

'It is quite unusual, isn't it?' He caught up with her easily. 'There are caves through there. I have only swum in a couple of them, but I understand the network is elaborate.'

'Really?' She moved towards the entrance he'd indicated, curiosity thumping inside her. 'I'd love to see them.'

'Not today,' he said quietly.

'Oh?' She turned in the water. 'Why not?'

'I have to go through some contracts this afternoon. My secretary is waiting to hear from me.'

She blinked at him, remembering that he was a property mogul first and foremost, not really a tour guide at her beck and call.

Disappointment was a hole in her gut.

'You can go back. I'm sure I'll find my way.'

He shook his head. 'It's five miles. Swim now and I will bring you back another time.'

*Another time.* This was the second day of her week. It was still early. But the idea of losing an afternoon because he had to work sucked the happiness out of her mood.

'Fine.' She shrugged, duck-diving under the water and kicking away from him.

She went towards the ocean, surfacing when her lungs were burning and begging for more air to be drawn into them. He was where she'd left him, treading water.

'What are the contracts for?' she called across the water, spreading her arms wide and kicking at the ocean to stay afloat.

He moved through the water easily, his stroke that of someone who swam often. He pulled up a little distance from her. Water droplets ran over his smooth shoulders.

'A high-rise I'm buying in Manhattan.'

She tilted her head to the side, her smile spontaneous. 'Seriously?'

He flicked some water at her, smiling as she flinched away. 'Why not?'

'You already have two islands. A high-rise in Manhattan seems excessive.'

He arched a brow, and beneath the water waved his hands perilously close to her sides. She felt the tremble of water but didn't move away. Deep down, she knew she wanted him to touch her.

It was illicit. Forbidden.

Inevitable.

Hadn't she already realised that?

'I have another high-rise in Manhattan, too. And one

in Hong Kong. Dubai. A mall in Canada. Is that excessive enough?'

She rolled her eyes. 'Now you're just trying to impress me.'

'I would think those assets far too pedestrian for someone like you to be deemed impressive.'

She sucked in a breath and flicked a gaze at the water. It was rippled by their movement. If only he knew that her parents lived in a small, pebbledash semi-detached bungalow in Harlesden.

'What I find impressive is that you did all this yourself,' she said with truth. 'You say your mother struggled? And she passed away when you were still a teenager? Yet by the time you were twenty you were a force to be reckoned with.'

Emotions flicked across his face, none of which she could interpret. 'You have been researching me?' he asked quietly at last, when her nerves felt as if they were about to snap.

She leaned closer, her expression conspiratorial, her nose wrinkled. 'Nope. Not even a bit. I hate to be the one to break it to you, but...'

'But?' he murmured, his eyes resting on the tip of her nose before lifting to hers.

'You're kind of famous.'

His laugh resonated around the cove. 'Is that so?'

'Well...well-known.' She grinned, her head bobbing in agreement.

Art had mentioned Rio several times. She'd listened. She'd learned. Though she had never imagined herself coming face to face with the man.

'What's the building?'

He frowned.

'In New York?' she supplied.

'It's a turn-of-the-century masterpiece,' he said with

a grin. 'Art Deco, with original fittings on almost all the floors. It's on the edge of Harlem, and for a long time it was ignored, but now the area has begun to gentrify.'

'And you want to be in on that?'

His eyes were dark in his face. 'I want to stop it being knocked down to make way for yet another steel monolith.'

She nodded thoughtfully. 'You have a habit of doing that. Of buying old buildings.'

Again, she thought of the pub in London he'd saved.

'It's good business,' he said with a shrug. 'To see value in what other people disdain. It's served me well.'

She tilted her head to one side. 'I think it's more than that.'

His laugh was a rumble. Desire skittered along her spine. 'Do you? Why?'

Because she looked at him and saw something she didn't understand. Because she'd known him a day and felt as if she'd seen into his soul. Because he was a confusing mix of machismo and compassion. Because she just did.

'You bought a pub in London.'

His eyes honed in on her, waiting for her to continue.

'It's really beautiful. Old. Dilapidated. And you saved it. I think you buy these old buildings because you want to save them.'

'That's a by-product of what I do,' he agreed.

'Why don't you admit it?'

He laughed. 'There is nothing to admit.' He flicked his fingers along the water's surface. 'The first building I bought was something no one wanted. It was very cheap. I couldn't save it.'

'What did you do with it?'

He grinned. 'I thought you knew everything about me?'

'What did you *do* with it?' she repeated, too curious to exchange teasing jokes with him.

He sobered, leaning back in the water a little and staring at the canopy of trees overhead. 'I arranged to demolish it but I salvaged everything. My first business was a brokerage of historic building parts. Tiles, bricks, marble, mirrors, light fittings—even carpets.'

'How did you know that would even work? That people would be interested in buying the parts alone? I would have ended up with only a run-down old building to my name.'

'There is value in beauty,' he said finally. 'Always.'

She bit down on her lower lip, focussing her attention on the cliff face. His words had set her pulse racing, but it wasn't just him and his words. It was the island. The whispering trees. The warmth of the sun and the saltiness of the water.

'What's there now?'

'A steel monolith,' he responded with wry humour.

'Ah.' She flicked her eyes to his face to find him staring at her. Her heart skipped.

'The building in Harlem isn't just a collection of bricks. It marks a time in the city's history when man was mastering the skills of constructing homes in the sky. It is a snapshot of time, a testament to what *was*. To the strength and resilience and the wonderment of what could be. It speaks of history and hope. If we demolish all of these old buildings there will be nothing left to show what used to be.'

Her pulse fired. His words sparked passion in her blood; their cadence was a call to arms she was quick to hear.

'I agree.' She smiled at him, her enthusiasm radiating from every pore. 'London is an ever-changing city. So many of the buildings in my area have been knocked down to make way for new developments and every time I go past them I feel sad at what we're losing. Homes that survived wars don't have value any more.'

He lifted his fingers from the water. She watched, mesmerised. They were beautiful fingers. Lovely hands. Strong. Confident. Tanned. She blinked and looked away, before she did something stupid like reach out and wrap her fingers around his.

'Where did the previous owner of the island want to build the hotel?' she asked, bringing the conversation neatly back to business, desperately looking to stifle the desire that was wrapping around her.

'Not far from the cabin.' His words were spiced with an unknown emotion. 'It is an ideal spot.'

'I think you'd be hard-pressed to find anywhere here that *isn't* ideal.'

He shrugged. 'Perhaps.'

He rubbed his fingers over his shoulder, scratching at something she couldn't see.

She swallowed and looked away.

But the trees whispered above her.

*Inevitable.*

*Don't fight it.*

*It's going to happen.*

She sent them an angry look and swam closer to the rocks.

What did trees know, anyway?

He was right behind her, but at the same time he kept his distance. A distance that allowed her to breathe.

'I'd be interested to pick your brain on that. You've spent more time on the island than I have. Even in a week, I'm sure I won't have really got to grips with the place.'

'There are plans you can look at—plans the previous owner commissioned many years ago for a potential hotel,' he suggested, without realising what he was saying.

He caught at the offer a moment too late; there was no way to pull the words back. Rio was not a man who made mistakes. *Ever.* Yet offering up his mother's drawings was like giving her the key to his longest held secrets.

'That would be great.' She was nodding, her mind skipping several steps ahead. 'I want to put together as much information as possible for Ar— Daddy.'

That was a little bonus she'd decided on for Cressida. Thirty thousand pounds had bought Cressida a week off the radar, celebrating a wedding with her friends. But Tilly was going to throw in the kind of report that would make Art think Cressida had turned over a new leaf.

'Fine.'

Was he angry? Tilly studied him from beneath her lashes. His dark face was tilted away from her, his cheekbones slashed with colour. She wanted to reach over and trace his jawline, dip her finger into the cleft of his chin and the dimple in his cheek. She wanted to feel his stubble tickle her cheek as she ran her face close to his.

She wanted so much.

'Ready to go back?' His words were thick.

She turned to him and nodded. 'I'm ready.'

And, come what may, she really, really was.


She dreamed of Jack that night. Jack, pale and shaking. Jack, crying, his eyes dark and his cheeks stained by tears. Jack, afraid. Jack, in danger.

She saw him vividly—not through a veil of sleep and memory, but as he'd really been. As he'd been only six weeks earlier, when he'd turned up on her doorstep and told her everything.

*'I made a bad bet, Tilly. A really bad bet. I didn't realise it at the time but...but the guy...the bookie...'*

She'd waited, impatient and also annoyed that he'd had the nerve to rock up on her doorstep at three in the morning when she had a big meeting to attend at work the following day.

*'His name's Anton Meravic. I didn't know he was hooked up, Tilly. I swear.'*

'"Hooked up"?' she'd asked, not exactly sure what that

meant. It had been late, after all. Her mind had been fogged by sleep.

*'To the mob! The Russian mob. He's in with Walter Karkov and I owe him twenty-five thousand pounds! They're going to kill me.'*

She dreamed of Jack, pale and shaking.

She dreamed of Jack, her twin.

Her brother.

Her other half.

And she woke with a start.

Her heart was racing, blood was pounding through her body, and her mind, her brain, were slamming with fear and adrenalin. The crashing of the waves echoed through her as bit by bit she remembered where she was.

Jack was safe. She'd done what she needed to pay off his debts. Thanks to Cressida, and the payment for this week's 'job', she'd been able to fix it for him.

Nothing mattered more than keeping Jack safe. *Nothing.*

Not even the strange feeling that Rio was beginning to wrap his hands around her heart and squeeze it tight.

# CHAPTER FIVE

IN THE MORNING she woke early, and was still tired.

Her eyes were scratchy, her mind exhausted.

*Jack.*

Her sigh perforated the silence, slitting her stomach with worry and doubt.

Some people were easy to worry about. They had problems that could be understood and therefore reliably navigated. With Jack it was like a dark cloud of uncertainty all the time. Wrong turns abounded. Since they were children he'd been that way. Not a naughty child, and certainly not unkind. Just worrisome and vulnerable. He'd made poor decisions, bad friends, worse choices.

And now, at twenty-four, he was still making those bad choices.

Only the stakes were much, much higher.

She shook her head, tilting her head towards the window and staring out at the sea. The day was breaking, the sun's yolk spreading across the sky in a fog of orange and peach.

He'd be okay. She'd make sure of it.

Having paid off his debts to whoever the hell this mobster was, she wanted to believe Jack was out of trouble for good. But that wasn't guaranteed.

She stood slowly, planting her feet against the tiled floor, her eyes not leaving the view.

What time was it?

She crept closer and then pushed the window open slowly, carefully, not wanting to wake Rio. A hint of the night's cool brushed her cheeks, kissing them pink. She breathed in deeply, catching the tang of salt and smiling despite her nightmares.

It was early and the house was silent.

She lifted her shoes off the floor and padded barefoot from her bedroom, then tiptoed down the hallway. The front door to the cabin was unlocked. She pushed it outwards and her smile widened as she emerged onto the deck. The steps were covered in sand; it felt ice-cold beneath her bare feet. She paused to slip her shoes on and then thought better of it, tossing them to the ground and walking away from the house.

The wind was decidedly brisk. She wrapped her arms around her waist as she walked, her eyes focussed on the dawning day.

The island was stunning. It almost beggared belief to find such a piece of untouched paradise in this day and age.

It wouldn't be untouched for long, though. Her lips shifted, a small frown dragging down her mouth at one side. Would the island still resonate with magic and mystery when buildings crowded it? When a cable ran across the volcano, allowing tourists to spy into the cavernous top and see its secrets?

Her frown deepened. And how could Rio care so little about what happened to this place? Why had he bought it? And why was he selling it so quickly? He was a businessman, and he'd made a career out of preserving beautiful buildings that were in jeopardy. Surely he felt the same about nature.

Was it possible that he really didn't care what happened to Prim'amore?

She stopped walking and stared out to sea as the breeze pushed past her, lifting her dark red hair and whipping it into the air behind her. She wanted answers. Not because it would change a damned thing. Art would still buy the island and do what he wanted; and Rio would sell. She didn't think she had a chance to change their minds. But that didn't mean she couldn't ask questions. Curiosity was alive inside her, begging for release.

Her hair was a flame. It shifted with the wind, creating contrast with her pale skin. He stared out at her, transfixed. The morning sun was bathing her with its buttery light and she looked soft and sweet.

*Sweet.*

Hardly a word he'd thought would ever apply to Cressida Wyndham.

He watched as she swooped down and lifted some sand into her fingers, then spread them wide to let it sprinkle on the ground like billions of pieces of confetti. Even at this distance he could see her smile and the way it shone across her face.

Her eyes shifted, moving towards the cottage, and despite the fact he was looking through a window, he moved away. The impulse to hide made him laugh.

Rio Mastrangelo didn't run from anyone.

With a guttural sound of impatience he stalked out of his bedroom and into the kitchen, pressing a pod into the coffee machine and watching the thick, dark liquid pool into a mug. He paused it mid-flow, needing just a hit of caffeine and the taste of something other than desire to warm his gut.

So she was beautiful. Stunning. Sexy. That he had expected. But, knowing what he did about her lifestyle, he'd thought her charms would hold little appeal.

That belief had been scuppered by a hard-on he'd been grappling with since they'd swum together yesterday. Since she'd turned her back and waited for him to clip her bikini in place. Her skin had been so smooth beneath his hands. How he'd wanted to reach around and cup her breasts, to stroke her nipples and ease her backwards against him so that he could trace kisses along her neck.

It had been too long since he'd been laid. That was all. For a man used to indulging his virile libido whenever he wanted—a man who had any number of women lining up to join him in his bed—a month of abstinence had been a spectacular feat. Being in close proximity to a woman like Cressida, with her body men would go to war for, was like pouring gasoline into a room and leaving a packet of matches by the door.

He just had to move the matches.

'Oh! You're up.'

She smiled as she breezed into the kitchen, smelling like sand and sunshine, and looking like a water nymph who'd risen from the depths of the sea, her long hair tangling down her back as he'd imagined it the first time they'd met.

He reached for his coffee and sipped it without dropping his eyes from her face. 'It's almost nine,' he pointed out.

'Right.' Her cheeks were pink, as though she'd been running. 'I've been exploring.'

It was such a conspiratorial confession that he almost laughed. The urge to chastise her for going on her own, without him to save her from plummeting off cliff faces, died in the face of her obvious joy.

'Have you? And what have you found?'

'Just the most beautiful island,' she said, with a smile that was lit from inside.

The gasoline dripped closer to the matches.

'I can't believe how lovely it is here.' She eyed his coffee thoughtfully and then walked, barefoot, into the kitchen. She left little drifts of sand in her wake. 'Mind if I make a coffee?'

He shook his head. 'Of course not.'

'Would you like another one?'

Surprise at the simple courtesy flared. 'No. Thank you.'

The machine made its tell-tale groaning noise as she

brought it to life and waited for coffee to fill the cup she'd selected.

'Do you have those plans? I'd love to take a look at what the architect came up with.'

His expression gave little away. 'They are somewhere here.'

Mischief danced in her eyes. 'Is that like a clue? Am I to hunt them out, *à la The Secret Seven* or *The Famous Five*?'

He stared at her blankly and she rolled her eyes.

'Please tell me you've read them?'

'Read what?' He was lost.

'The books! Enid Blyton mysteries.'

He shook his head, dragging a hand through his hair. 'No.'

'How deprived your childhood must have been!' She laughed, and then sobered as she recalled his claim that he'd had nothing growing up. 'I didn't mean… I meant… Oh, crap.'

She clamped a hand over her mouth and speared him with a look of such bewilderment that he burst out laughing.

'You think you have hurt my feelings? That I am crying inside?'

She dropped her hand and looked away, back to the coffee. How ridiculous she was being! Talking to him as though they were old friends, teasing him about not having read Enid Blyton books and reacting as though she, Tilly Morgan, had the power to hurt him! Rio Mastrangelo! The man who was renowned for his ruthless cold temperament.

With effort, she shoved her enthusiasm and delight deep inside her and assumed her best mask of casual arrogance—just as she'd seen Cressida do a thousand times.

'I'm serious about those plans.' She cradled the warm mug in her hands.

He stared at her for long enough that the air began to crackle around them. Time stood still, but her emotions did not. They were a fever in her blood. Uncertainty, lust, confusion, danger.

She bit down on her lip, and then stopped when his gaze lowered, his eyes knitting together as he traced the outline of her pout with heavy eyes.

*Uh-oh.*

Her heart was pounding hard and fast.

'I am going to Capri later today. Would you like to come and see it?'

The question came to her from a long way away. Her mind was jelly. She swallowed, but her pulse was throbbing so loudly that she wasn't even sure she'd heard him properly.

'Capri?' she murmured, shaking her head slightly from side to side.

Rio stood and prowled towards her. There was no other word for it. He was like a powerful animal stalking its prey, his eyes hooded as he gained ground, closing in on her. He hooked his mug beneath the coffee machine, his body only inches from hers. So close she could feel his warmth. A shiver danced along her spine.

'I'm sure it's not like your usual haunts. Only a few nightclubs. No couture boutiques that I know of…'

Her cheeks flushed and her eyes met his beseechingly. He was determined to think the worst of Cressida. It shouldn't have bothered her. So why did she find herself wanting to plead the other woman's case to him?

'No, thanks.'

His eyes narrowed speculatively, as though he'd been expecting her to jump at the chance to get off the island. She gathered it hadn't entered his head that she might prefer to stay where she was.

'I'd prefer you to come.' The words were a gravelly command.

She arched a brow, her eyes jolting away from his. 'As

much as I'm here to fall in with your every wish, I want to stay on the island. And look at the plans.' Her tone was unwittingly belligerent, but it was a pretty good impersonation of Cressida's.

He reached for his coffee, his forearm brushing against her in the process. She started, flames of need dancing through her.

Her nerves stretched, pulling tighter. 'Have fun, though.'

He scowled. 'You don't think you should appraise the island for yourself?'

'That's what I'm doing,' she pointed out, her heart hammering. Pride kept her where she was, but her sanity was urging her to step away. Far away.

'Capri, I mean,' he corrected. 'Its proximity to Prim'amore is a point of interest. I imagine your father would want to hear your thoughts on it and the crossing.'

Her eyes were wide in her face. Damn it. He had a point.

'Come on,' he murmured, as a snake charmer might. The words were enticing, seductive, impossible to ignore. 'It will be a quick trip, and afterwards I will find the plans.'

She ground her teeth together. 'Are you blackmailing me?'

He grinned. The butterflies were back—a whole kaleidoscope of them.

'Yes.'

'Why do you want me to come with you?' She asked, dropping her eyes to the ground between them.

The silence was a thick, knotted ball. When he spoke, the words seemed almost dragged from him.

'That is a good question. And I'm not sure I have an answer to it.'

Her heart turned over. Agony and pleasure warred in her heart. 'Okay.' She nodded, her voice hoarse. 'I'll just need a few minutes to get ready.'

He lifted his coffee cup between them, relaxed now that she'd acquiesced. 'Take your time. I'm going to have this.'

She didn't need long, though. Unlike Cressida, Tilly generally threw on what she had to hand and finger-combed her hair to make it slightly less wild. The most she ever dressed up was on the occasions when she was pretending to be Cressida Wyndham.

She showered, scrubbing her skin until it was pink, then wrapped a towel around her body. She peeked down the hallway, making sure he wasn't nearby, before stepping out of the bathroom. She moved quickly to her room, but just at the second she reached the door he stepped out of his, and his powerful frame connected with hers—hard.

She had the brief impression of his head having been bent, his mind distracted—enough to convince her that it was an accident.

'Ow!' she snapped, forgetting momentarily that beneath the towel she was naked and wet. 'Watch where you're going!'

But he *was* watching. In that moment he was watching every single movement on Tilly's face, seeing so much more than she was aware she was showing. The way her eyes clouded, turning a darker green when they met his. The way her pupils dilated under his watch, spinning into big black orbs. And the way her lips parted, revealing a moist tongue that nervously traced her lower lip.

Rio lifted his hands to her shoulders, his expression dark.

Her breath was rasping and fast. She stared at him, and all thoughts of being strong and keeping him at arm's length fled her mind. Only desire was left.

His eyes probed hers and his fingers on her wet flesh were gently insistent as they stroked. She moaned, low in her throat, and swept her eyes closed.

Without make-up, her skin glowing from the shower, her hair pulled up into a messy bun, and with a tiny towel barely covering her, she was the most desirable woman he had ever seen.

Rio glided his hands over her upper arms, but he wanted more. His hand moved to the back of her towel, pushing her towards him. She connected with his body—by design this time. She was soft and small, her curves fitting perfectly to him, as though they'd been designed for one another.

Her lashes were dark, feathered fans against her flushed cheeks. And the small moan she made sent his pulse into overdrive. Would she moan when they made love? Would her pillowy lips part, breathing those sweet sounds into the air?

His need was a tsunami inside him, crashing inexorably towards land. She was the shore...she was the anchor... and he was powerless to fight the pull of her tide. Rio had never considered himself powerless before. But he didn't care. What did power matter when there was the delight of Cressida Wyndham to be had?

He lifted his hand to her face, cupping her cheek and sweeping the ball of his thumb over her lower lip. Her eyes flew open, pinning him with a look that held the same tsunami of need that was ravaging his defences.

'We shouldn't do this,' she said quietly, but her hips pushed forward, moving from side to side in an ancient silent invitation.

His fingers moved through her hair, pulling it from the bun, running through the ends. 'We shouldn't,' he agreed darkly.

'I don't...just sleep with guys,' she whispered, closing her eyes on the confession.

And it *was* a confession, he realised. There was guilt and shame in it—as though she had been keeping it a secret. It confused the hell out of him, because he would have put money on Cressida sleeping with pretty much anyone she found attractive.

Curiosity flared and challenge lay before him. Not to sleep with her so much as to find out more about her before he gave in to temptation.

'Do you kiss them?' he asked.

She smiled, but before she could answer his mouth was crushing down on hers. It was a kiss driven by a passion that had burst out of their control; it was its own force, enormous and undeniable. His tongue was fierce in her mouth, and she surrendered to him willingly. She melted against him, her whole body catching fire.

Her hands pushed into his hair. His body was a weight against hers. He moved her easily, pushing her back against the wall. The pressure of his frame kept her standing, his strong legs pinning her on either side, his mouth making her forget anything except this. This moment, this need.

The world seemed to stop. His hands reached lower and it wasn't until they curved over hers that Tilly realised she'd been about to unhook her towel, wanting to lower it, to be naked *for* him and *with* him. His hands held it still, though, and he broke the kiss just enough to look down at her.

'No.' He shook his head, and his expression was so serious that she wondered for a terrifying moment, if she'd mistaken his interest in her. But he'd kissed her? Hadn't he? Or had she kissed him?

Doubt and worry replaced desire, dousing it quickly. 'Oh, I thought...'

'You don't just sleep with men, remember?' he prompted, his breath strained, his chest moving quickly.

Her eyes clouded, almost changing colour as she reached through the strands of memory to recall what he was talking about. 'Oh, right,' she muttered, wishing she could eat those words.

'And if you take this towel off I don't think either of us

will be able to stop what was about to happen from happening.'

She nodded, but embarrassment was making it difficult to accept his explanation. Because Tilly didn't want to stop. She wanted to give in to this—them—here and now.

'I am only human, *cara*,' he said gently. 'And already I find I cannot get you out of my mind.'

She drew in a deep breath at the admission. 'Really?'

His laugh came from deep in his throat. 'Really.'

'I thought maybe I was the only one fighting this.'

He shook his head and moved forward again, pinning her with his body so that she could be in no doubt as to how he felt.

'I have been like this since we swam, yesterday.'

Her cheeks suffused with colour. 'Oh…'

He grinned. 'Yes. Oh.'

She bit down on her lip and forced herself to meet his gaze. 'So…?'

'I am not often surprised,' he said, and it was a thick admission. 'But you surprise me. I like that.'

It did little to clear up her feelings, but she nodded. 'I… I guess I'll get dressed, then.'

If Tilly had thought her nerves stretched tight before, they were now at breaking point. A bumpy boat ride to Capri hadn't helped. Nor had the sight of Rio at the helm, his shirtsleeves pushed up to his elbows, exposing tanned forearms and capable hands, his strong body braced as they crested the waves.

By the time they arrived she was parched, and just about ready to beg him to relent, to find some place where they could be together and see if that cured her desperate state of longing.

He pulled the boat directly into a cove, bringing it to a stop beside a wooden jetty. He stood up and tossed out a thick rope, catching a hook which he used to bring the boat in closer. He jumped up, in an impressive display of athleticism, looping the rope several times and then putting a hand down to her.

Tilly eyed it suspiciously, but his smile made her laugh. 'Yeah, okay. I've learned my lesson.'

Still, she was tentative as she reached up and placed her fingers in his palm.

It was like being electrocuted. Her whole body was quivering with it. Her eyes met his helplessly. She was lost.

From what she could tell, Rio was focussed only on getting her out of the boat safely. She climbed up, knowing that she must look ridiculous as she scrambled onto the jetty. She went to thank him and pull away, but he shifted his fingers, lacing them through hers, holding on to her hand.

Emotion caught at her throat.

It was just about the sweetest gesture she'd ever known. A simple touch, an innocent closeness, and yet it filled her with pleasure.

The shore of Capri was dotted with colourful homes built right into the sheer cliff face. Shops and restaurants dotted the shoreline, and in the small bay bright boats bobbed gently on the water.

'What do you need?' she asked, her eyes taking in the picturesque scene.

'Apart from the obvious?' He grinned. 'I have to pick up a few things.'

'That's cryptic,' she teased.

'Uh-huh. That is me. International man of mystery.'

She laughed. 'Okay, mystery man. Where to first?'

The marina at which Rio had moored the boat was small, but a short stroll away there was a market.

It turned out that grocery items seemed to be the sum total of what was required. He paused to pick up a baguette, some tomatoes, olives, oil and cheese. While Rio shopped, Tilly followed, pausing to admire the stalls that caught her attention, wondering at the artful displays and delicious-looking treats.

He paused to speak to a man selling grapes and she spied a little shop across the cobbled path. 'I'm just going to have a look in there,' she murmured, moving away before he could speak.

She slipped inside and breathed in the familiar scent of second-hand books. Dust and imagination swirled around her.

'*Buongiorno.*' the woman behind the counter smiled, her wiry frame shifting forward a little in acknowledgement of Tilly's arrival.

'*Ciao.*'

Tilly disappeared into the shelves, picking up a few titles that interested her before settling near the children's books. The titles were difficult to translate, but the names of the authors were obvious.

At the very bottom, hidden behind a wall of Harry Potter translations, she saw a familiar binding. 'Aha!' She slipped it out. *Il Castello Sulla Scogliera* stared back at her. She had read all the *Famous Five* books as a child. She flicked the pages and ran her finger over the words. A foreign language couldn't diminish the promise of the book.

She moved to the cash register and placed her trophy down, hoping her smile would compensate for the fact that she didn't speak more than a few words of Italian.

The woman nodded, as if understanding, and pointed to the price on the cover. Tilly fumbled into her handbag, bypassing her phone on her way to her wallet. Her phone! She hadn't even realised that here in Capri she must have reception.

She placed a ten euro note on the counter and waited for change. The woman slid the book into a brown paper bag, her smile dismissive.

'*Grazie*,' Tilly murmured, nestling the book into her bag as she lifted her phone. She switched it on and waited for it to load up.

A few text messages came in—one from Jack, thanking her again for saving his life, one from her mother, asking if she was coming for dinner at the weekend, and one from Art asking where a file had been saved on her computer.

She tapped out a quick reply to Art, and then went into her emails. There was nothing from Cressida.

She lifted her gaze, scanning the market, and located Rio instantly. Though he was surrounded by other shoppers, she could have spotted him from five times the distance.

As if sensing her inspection, he looked up, his eyes clashing with hers. The zing of lust was strong enough to make her slow to a stop. It was overwhelming.

He made up for her lack of movement, cutting through the shoppers easily until he was right before her.

'Lunch?' he prompted, his eyes dropping to her lips in a way that made her want to lift her mouth and kiss him.

Wordlessly, she nodded.

Lunch first. And whatever else he wanted after that

# CHAPTER SIX

THE RESTAURANT OVERLOOKED the whole bay. It was up at least a hundred narrow steps, but as Tilly stared over the sweeping ocean, seeing the colourful boats and the golden sun, she admitted to herself that the climb had absolutely been worth it.

Lavender framed the terrace, exploding from terracotta pots, spiking the air with darts of mauve. She reached forward and clipped one of the leaves, lifting it to her nose. The tell-tale scent came to her quickly, but there was something else. She craned forward and beneath the pot plant saw a tiny jasmine vine scrambling up the wall, reaching towards her.

'Do not even *think* about falling,' a dark voice murmured from just behind her.

She straightened, casting a look over her shoulder and rolling her eyes.

But her heart slammed against her ribcage when she saw Rio holding a bottle of wine and two glasses. Her eyes stuck to him, as though glued.

'I have ordered lunch,' he murmured, nodding towards the table directly beside them.

She nodded—a tiny movement.

He poured two glasses of wine; it was ice-cold and a buttery yellow colour. He lifted one and handed it to her, his eyes holding hers.

'Cheers,' she said as she took it, and he lifted his glass, clinking it against the side of hers lightly. 'Have you been here before?'

'To Capri?'

'No. To this restaurant.'

'Ah. Once, when I first visited Prim'amore.'

Her curiosity over his decision to buy it flared back to life. 'Did you inspect the island like I am?'

'No.' He forced a smile to his face. 'It was a sudden visit.'

'Why?' She sipped her wine automatically and found it to be delicious. Fruity without being cloying, and refreshing.

He angled his face to hers. 'There wasn't time to explore.'

'Are you being deliberately evasive?'

He sipped his wine, his eyes locked to hers over the rim. 'No.'

'So...?'

He expelled a sigh. 'I have spent a lifetime not discussing this.'

Her interest doubled. She waited, holding her breath, for him to continue.

'There is something about you...' He shook his head slowly. 'I inherited the island,' he said after a moment's pause. 'A little over a month ago.'

'Oh.' Sympathy clouded her expression. 'I'm sorry.'

'What for?'

'Well, if someone left you a whole island, you must have meant a lot to them.'

His smile was brief: a flicker of disagreement disguised as a polite acknowledgement. 'I don't want it.'

She mulled over that for a moment. 'Because of Arketà?'

'Because it reminds me of things I would rather forget,' he corrected.

A sound alerted them to someone's approach. Rio straightened, and his air of confiding drifted away.

The waiter placed two plates on their table. One held an assortment of seafood—calamari, prawns, *vongole* and oysters. The other had slices of tomato, white spheres of cheese and marinated artichoke hearts.

Her stomach gave an anticipatory lurch. She was impatient to taste the flavours. But her mind was even more impatient. She wanted to know everything about him.

Apparently she was not alone in her curiosity.

'I misjudged you completely,' he said slowly, thoughtfully, leaning back in his chair and waving a hand over the plates, indicating that she should help herself. 'I thought you would be selfish and boring. Vapid and vain.'

'Gee, thanks,' she snapped, fluttering her lashes to look down at the food. She reached for some calamari and a few pieces of tomato, simply to disguise the guilt on her face.

'I have apologised for this,' he said seriously, his voice deep. 'I meant it. You are not the woman I thought. So who *are* you?'

She swallowed. Despair was a chasm beneath her, trying its hardest to suck her in. What could she tell him? Not a lot. At least not without breaking the promise she'd made to Cressida.

She met his gaze, but her eyes were hesitant. 'What do you want to know?'

He was thoughtful, as though she'd suggested he write a blank cheque and he was appraising how much to make it out for. 'I was under the impression that you were…how should I put this? *Liberal* with your affections?'

She smothered a laugh of indignation. 'Is that a euphemism for being easy to get into bed?'

He shook his head, a rueful smile on his lips. 'I make no judgements. I enjoy sex as much as anyone. I do not care how many partners my lovers have had before me.'

She squeezed her eyes shut. Just the idea of being grouped in with his lovers made her blood simmer painfully inside her. 'How enlightened of you.'

'It is this that fascinates me. This coy embarrassment, your prudish disapproval. As though you have never slept with a man.'

Her lips formed an 'oh' of surprise. 'Just because this morning I said I wasn't in the habit of having sex with random men?'

'Partly.' He sipped his wine, his eyes still appraising her. 'But it is more than that. It is the way you tremble when I touch you—even lightly.'

As if to prove his point, he reached across the table and lifted her hand, pressing a kiss against the sensitive flesh of her inner wrist. To her chagrin, a shiver of awareness flew over her, coating her flesh in goosebumps and warming her core.

The widening of his eyes showed he had seen the effect he had on her. 'Nothing about you adds up.'

Fear stilled her. She was failing. She was letting her own selfish needs get in the way of what she was supposed to be doing. What she'd been paid handsomely to do.

Cressida was counting on her and Tilly had given her word.

She had no right to be jeopardising everything just because she was…falling in love?

Her mouth parted in surprise. Was that what she was doing? It felt so alien to her.

Her heart rocketed in her chest and her mind ran away with her. *Love?* She'd never been in love. Not once. She'd dated some nice guys, and she'd even slept with two of her boyfriends—the ones she'd thought might eventually become serious prospects for Happily Ever After. And there'd been one ill-advised one-night stand that had taught her she didn't go in for casual sex.

But she'd never felt anything remotely like this.

'I'm not an equation,' she mumbled, pulling her hand away and reaching for her wine. 'I'm not something to make sense of.'

'On the contrary, you are a riddle I want to solve.'

She swallowed, her throat knotting visibly as she tried

to refresh her parched throat. When that didn't work she lifted her wine to her lips and gulped it gratefully.

She toyed with the collar of her dress. 'Speaking of solving riddles,' she said, in a heavy-handed attempt at changing the subject, 'I have something for you.'

He was quiet, but she sensed his impatience with the roadblock she'd erected. She reached into her handbag and pulled out the book, passing it to him with a shy smile.

He unfolded it, and when he saw the title his confusion grew. 'This is the book you told me of?'

'It's not just a book,' she corrected. 'It's a series. This is one of them. The only one I could find at that little shop.'

She sipped her wine again, surprised to realise the glass was almost empty.

'Thank you,' he murmured, flipping the pages and giving them a cursory inspection before putting it aside. 'Did you read a lot when you were growing up?'

She wasn't fooled for a moment. He seemed to be making casual conversation, but it was all part of his same quest to solve the riddle of who she was—a riddle she'd never be able to answer.

Desolation washed over her. Was there any way she could be honest with him? The idea gnawed at her mind.

She reached for her wine, the idea taking purchase inside her. If she told him the truth, then what? Would he go along with her ruse? Would he still look at her as though he wanted to peel the clothes from her body and make her his? Or would he judge her for engaging in this kind of subterfuge? For taking payment for a lie?

Or what if she could speak to Cressida? What if she confessed the truth to the other woman and asked her to release Tilly from their agreement? She'd have to pay the money back but, given time, she could do that.

Suddenly keeping this secret for the heiress felt all kinds of wrong.

'That does not seem like a complex question,' he prompted.

Her eyes were enormous in her face. 'Huh?'

'Did you read much when you were growing up?'

She pulled a face, doing her best to hide her embarrassment and refocus her attention on their conversation. 'Yes.'

She had lived in the pages of books. Jack, less so.

'And these were your favourites?'

'Amongst my favourites,' she agreed. 'I adored any mystery books. I must have read the same ones a thousand times.'

He reached for the bottle of wine, topping her glass up as he settled back in his chair.

'And you?'

'No, I didn't read.'

'Not at all?' she murmured, finding that almost impossible to comprehend. 'That's so sad.'

He laughed. 'I had other pastimes that I enjoyed very much.'

'Such as?'

'Exploring.' His face flashed with an expression similar to what she imagined he might have worn as a young boy. 'My mother and I would walk—at least we would when she was well enough.'

He stared out at the ocean, a smile crinkling the corners of his eyes as he thought back to those brief windows of happiness in his childhood.

'She didn't have a lot of money, as I have said, so she would pack a bag with apples and water, and a little *cioccolata* for me. We lived above the *marcato*, and every now and again she would surprise me with a fresh-baked pastry or some deli meat. We would leave early in the morning and not return until nightfall. All day we would walk through the winding streets of Rome, studying the ancient buildings, learning about the city.'

He turned his attention back to Tilly.

'I do not consider I missed any advantage because I wasn't an avid fan of books.'

She dipped her head forward and a wisp of red hair brushed against her pale complexion. Tilly had read in order to have exactly the same adventures.

'Those walks sound beautiful,' she said softly. 'Was she sick often?'

His eyes met Tilly's, and again she had the sense that he was waging an internal war. Perhaps it was easy for her to recognise because she was fighting a similar battle. What to show and what to hide.

'Yes.'

It was impossible to flatten the sorrow in her expressive eyes. She reached across the table and curled her hand over his. He stared at their fingers, as did she. Was he noticing the way they fitted together so well? Even the contrast between his deep tan and her cream complexion created a striking image.

'When I started school, I remember her telling me that things would be different. I didn't realise at the time why—only that she seemed buoyed up by the prospect of something on the horizon. With hindsight, I understand. Finally I would be cared for during the week, which would allow her to work. She saw an opportunity to get her life back on track.'

'Do you think her life *wasn't* on track, Rio?' Tilly asked thoughtfully.

He swirled his wine in the glass without drinking it. Having not spoken to a soul about his childhood, he found the combination of sunshine, wine and the beautiful woman opposite like a magical key to the doorway of his past.

'She was twenty-four when I was born,' he murmured, his eyes lifting to Tilly's face. 'Your age.'

She ran her thumb over his hand. 'What did she do? For work, I mean?'

His smile was perfunctory. 'She was an architect.'

Pieces of the jigsaw slipped into place, building a framework as to who he was.

'She taught you to love old buildings,' Tilly murmured thoughtfully.

'Yes. Though it wasn't so much teaching as opening my eyes. Whenever we walked past demolition sites we'd marvel at what might have been done if only someone had intervened. She loved history. The past. She wanted to preserve it.'

'She sounds like a wonderful person.' And a lot like her son, she added silently.

'*Si.*'

He wondered at the way he was opening up to this woman he barely knew—a woman he had thought he would despise. But the more he got to know her, the more he understood Cressida's differences from the Marinas of the world. Cressida didn't have it in her to lie.

'And when did she first get sick?'

His eyes were as hard as flint; they showed no emotion, but Tilly could feel it vibrating from him in waves.

'A month after I started school. She thought it was a cold, but it wouldn't go away. Then there was stomach pain.'

He closed his eyes for a moment, and when he looked at her once more it was as though he was piercing her with his pain. Tilly felt his trauma as if it was her own.

'She was too sick to work. She lost her job. Money became tighter…she became increasingly ill.'

'Oh, Rio,' Tilly murmured, shaking her head as she contemplated his life. 'What about her parents? Your father?'

'Her parents didn't speak to her from the moment they discovered she was pregnant.'

'Not even when you were born?' Tilly demanded, aghast and outraged in equal measure.

His expression was sardonic. 'Not when I was born. Not when she got sick. Not even when she died—though they are both alive to this day.'

'And do you speak to them?'

He shot her a look of impatience. 'Would *you*?'

Her heart flipped painfully.

She searched for something to say—something that might alleviate his suffering—but he continued, 'I do not believe in second chances, Cressida. We have one opportunity in life to make the right choice. They did not. Nor did my father. Forgiving them would be a sign of stupidity—a weakness I will never allow myself to possess.'

The words were spoken with such passion that she couldn't help but comprehend the depths of his commitment. But the philosophy itself…? It spread panic over her—and not just because she feared her deceit was something else he would not forgive.

'But what if they regret what they did? What if—?'

*'No.'*

He slashed his free hand through the air and her nerves quivered.

'No,' he softened it, bringing that same hand to rest on hers, sandwiching it between his palms. 'If you can imagine the way she lived her life—the shame she felt at our poverty, the worry she felt when I complained that I was hungry…'

His eyes met Tilly's and the strength of burning emotion made her want to say or do something—anything to erase his pain.

'I was always hungry.' He gave a short, sharp laugh.

'You were a growing boy.'

'And she was a dying woman,' he said softly. 'She stayed

alive until I was almost finished at high school, and I believe that was through determination alone.'

He pulled his hands away, reaching for his fork and spearing a sphere of *bocconcini*.

She didn't see him eat it. She was imagining this proud, strong man as he'd been back then. 'What about your father?'

He forked a piece of calamari. 'What about him?'

'You said he's not in the picture,' she prompted. 'But surely when she got sick…?'

'No.'

Her brows knitted together. 'Did he know?'

He flicked her a look of subdued amusement. *'Si, cara.'*

'Perhaps he wasn't in a position to help,' she suggested, finding it impossible to reconcile the idea of a man turning his back on the dying mother of his child.

Rio's eyes narrowed and he was a businessman again. One capable of eviscerating his foes without breaking a sweat. 'Why are you so determined to see the best in people?'

She sipped her wine nervously. 'I don't know. I didn't know that was something I do.'

He nodded curtly. 'You do. And I would think you've had enough experience with people and their selfish proclivities to adopt a more cautious attitude.'

'No.' She shook her head. 'Not yet.'

He lifted one dark, thick brow. 'I hope you do not change,' he said quietly. 'Your optimism is refreshing.'

'But misplaced?' she suggested.

'Yes—in this instance. My father was a very wealthy man. He could have bought my mother an apartment, given her an allowance and ensured I went to excellent schools. It would have been barely small change to him.'

'Surely he did *something* to help?'

His laugh was a dark sound. 'He offered to pay for the termination.'

Tilly's gasp was loud. There was one other couple in their corner of the terrace and they turned towards them, apparently curious at what was going on.

With an effort at discretion, she said more quietly, 'Are you sure? Are you absolutely sure?'

Though she didn't want to suggest it of the woman he obviously viewed as a saint, it wasn't inconceivable that his mother had lied at some stage, to sour Rio against the father he'd never met.

As if he'd read her mind, he said, 'My mother never told me. At least, she didn't mean to. But there were times when her pain was so severe that her doctors put her on huge quantities of morphine. It made her…communicative.'

Tilly grimaced. 'That's rough on your mother. To have kept a brave face through so much adversity, raising you without badmouthing your father, no matter how sorely she was tempted, only to find the confession escaping without her control. How invasive.'

His eyes showed surprise at her perception. 'That is exactly how I feel. I would never have confronted her with what she'd said. Seeing her experience guilt for telling me would have been mortifying. Worse, if she'd tried to apologise. In any event, I was glad to have answers. I had always wondered about him. I was relieved to discover that I could hate him. That I was right to feel that. It had been in me for a long time, but we are taught not to hate our parents, no? I felt vindicated.'

She nodded, but knew there was nothing she could say to relieve his pain. It must be a pain akin to death.

'Is he still alive?'

'No.'

She reached for her wine and lifted it towards her lips without drinking. 'I don't know what to say.'

A muscle jerked in his square jaw. 'You are the only person I have ever spoken to about this. It is enough that you have listened.'

Was it wrong to feel such delight in a moment of sadness? Tilly did. Her heart soared. He had confided in her—and confided something that he had never shared with another soul.

'I imagine your mother would be very proud of you.' To Tilly's mortification, she found herself choked by the words.

He shrugged. 'She always was.'

His eyes met hers, and she couldn't have looked away for a million pounds. She was trapped in his gaze and there was nowhere else she wanted to be.

'Even my smallest feats attracted an improbable amount of praise.' He was amused—or perhaps aiming to lighten the tone.

'My mother is like that,' Tilly said, thinking of Belinda Morgan with an indulgent smile. 'If I won a spelling competition at school it was like an Olympic Gold to her.'

His expression was watchful. Almost calculating. Tilly didn't realise why at first, but a moment later it dawned on her. Cressida's mother was nothing like Belinda, and she had certainly never been proud of her daughter.

'I see.'

Tilly panicked for a moment, wondering if he really did. She needed to regroup urgently. She needed to speak to Cressida.

'Would you excuse me a moment?'

He nodded and she stood, scooping up her bag as she made her way across the terrace and back into the restaurant. She pushed inside the restroom and lifted her phone out of her bag, dialled Cressida's number.

It went straight to voicemail.

She tried again—without success.

Tilly stared at herself in the mirror for a moment, studying her face, bracing her hands on the counter.

She'd promised Cressida she'd help, and generally she wouldn't even think of letting someone down. But she'd never known a man like Rio before, and the sense that she would stuff everything up if she kept lying to him was like a snake tightening around her chest.

She tapped out a quick message to Cressida.

We need to talk. I have limited email access. Please get in touch.

She made her way back to the table, her mind overflowing with erratic, confused thoughts as she eased herself back into the seat.

'You said you've known lots of women like me?'

It was out of left field, but he caught her drift immediately. 'And then I said you are unique.'

The hair on the back of her neck stood on end. Pleasure was dancing through her.

'You have an active social life?' she asked, moving back to her original subject.

He seemed to allow the shift, and she was utterly relieved. She reached for her wine and drank thirstily. But when she placed the glass back on the table she felt woozy. She had barely eaten, she chastised herself inwardly, reaching for a piece of cheese and popping it in her mouth.

He was watching her. More specifically, he was watching her lips. Her mouth.

He picked another piece of cheese off the plate and lifted it to her lips, brushing it across them, waiting, watching. She parted her mouth just enough and he pushed it inside. His thumb stayed at the corner of her lip and she chewed, but her heart was like thunder in her breast.

'Yes.'

Confusion swirled inside her. 'Yes, what?'

'Yes, I have an active social life. I presume that's a coy way of referring to my sex life?'

More wine. No. More food. Her wine glass was empty anyway. She needed water. She looked around, searching for a waiter. There were none nearby.

She nodded. It was a confession she might never have made if it hadn't been for the two decent-sized glasses of Pinot Grigio she'd just consumed in rapid succession and on an empty stomach.

'Have you ever been serious about anyone?' she asked, the question escaping as if blurted out by accident.

His eyes shimmered with an emotion she didn't comprehend. *'Si.'*

Jealousy fired in her soul.

'Really?'

He nodded. 'A long time ago.'

'What happened?'

His laugh was light-hearted enough. 'She broke my heart.'

'Really?'

'No, *cara*. Not really. At the time she betrayed me I was angry. I thought I might be falling in love with her.' He shook his head, his smile natural. 'I wasn't. I couldn't have been. Everything she was turned out to be a lie.'

Acid was bubbling down Tilly's spine. She stared at him with a sense of deep panic.

*Everything she was turned out to be a lie.*

'A lie how?'

He shook his head. 'It doesn't matter.'

'You're still upset? Too upset to talk about it?'

'No, it just serves no purpose,' he said with a shrug. 'I have learned again and again that people who lie don't get second chances.'

'How did she lie to you?' Tilly pushed, her heart hammering painfully in her chest, guilt at her own deception becoming a maze she needed to find her way out of.

'You really want to know?'

Tilly nodded, but panic was weighing her down.

'We had been seeing each other for nearly a year. I was busy. My business was taking off and, while I liked her, and even thought myself on the way to being in love with her, I had no real plans for her to be a serious or permanent part of my life.'

He looked towards the ocean, catching the glistening sun as it bounced off the sea.

'Marina perhaps began to sense this and, concerned, took matters into her own hands.'

'How?'

His smile was grim. 'By faking a pregnancy.'

Tilly froze, the look on her face pure shock. 'She did what?'

'Mmm…' he agreed. 'Very poor form, no?'

'Absolutely.'

'She knew I would propose. And I would have. But too much didn't add up and eventually she confessed. She was very apologetic—and I understood, to some extent. Marina grew up with everything she ever wanted landing in her lap. She wanted *me*, and my reluctance to commit was not something she was willing to accept.'

'But to lie about being pregnant…' Tilly said angrily.

'*Si.* It was very foolish. I ended our relationship the day I found out and I have not spoken to her since.' His look was loaded with dark emotion. 'I do not invite betrayal twice.'

A shiver ran down her spine and her own predicament swirled through her like a raging tsunami. The imperative to get through to Cressida was growing by the moment, suffocating her with urgency. She had to fix this somehow.

'I don't like to think about you with other women,' she

said, but the words were difficult to find in her brain and they came out sounding forced and strange.

She didn't miss the look of intense speculation on his face. 'Jealous?'

Tilly was more than jealous. She was...*devastated*.

She needed time and space to process this. She sipped the wine he'd topped up automatically, desperate to blot the pain from her mind.

'It's not like *my* social life is quiet.'

'And, again, when you say "social life" you mean sex life?' he clarified.

She was Cressida—in that moment, at least.

'Sure. Yeah. You know—sex is sex,' she said, with an attempt at a blasé flick of her wrist. 'Speaking of which...' She leaned forward, placing her hand over his. 'Can we go back to the island now?'

His eyes lanced her. But when he stood and took her hand it was with pure, sensual determination.

This was happening.

# CHAPTER SEVEN

'This isn't going to happen.'

Tilly stared at him, her mind foggy. The afternoon sun was bright overhead. In fact it was sultry, and the air was thick. The boat lurched as he pulled it towards Prim'amore, slowing to meet the shore.

'What?'

He stared pointedly at her hand. Without her permission, it had landed on his thigh. No—half on his thigh and embarrassingly close to his arousal.

Wine had made her slow; her mind lagged. 'I...'

'You're drunk,' he said darkly, and with such arrogant disbelief that she was spurred into denying the accusation.

'I am absolutely not,' she snapped, standing up to prove the point.

The boat rocked and, just like the first day they'd met, she began to topple forward. With a muttered curse he caught her, holding her tight around the arms.

'And you are trouble,' he said, without a hint of the affection that had warmed her over lunch.

'*You* are,' she retorted childishly.

'Sit.'

'"Sit",' she mimicked, but she did as he'd said, planting herself back on the seat.

He returned his concentration to the boat, driving it close to the sand and then jumping easily over the front. He used his hands to guide it to the shore and she leaned over the edge, watching him and studying the water at the same time. A school of fish swam beneath them.

The boat thudded as he rolled the tip of it onto the sand

before coming around to her side. He held a hand up to Tilly but she stared at it mutinously.

'I can manage.'

He made a derisive noise. 'I've heard that before. Take my hand.'

'No way. Not until you apologise for calling me drunk.' Her demand was somewhat ruined by the hiccough that sliced the sentence in half.

'You had *two* glasses of wine. How can you possibly be intoxicated?' he asked in exasperation.

'I don't...' *Don't drink very often.* The admission died on her lips. 'I don't know,' she finished lamely. 'And I'm fine, thank you very much.'

'Like hell you are,' he snapped. 'Let me help you.'

'You think I'm going to drown in two inches of water?'

'If anyone's capable of it...'

She poked her tongue out and moved to the other side of the boat. He was quick, but she had the advantage, for Rio had water to wade through before he could reach her. She stepped out, nailing the landing.

It was the pirouette that she made in order to gloat that undid her.

She knocked her hip on the edge of the boat and it jolted her backwards—into the water. A brief recognition of his angry expression was the last thing she saw before landing in the water.

Again.

She spluttered, pushing up onto her elbows, but Rio was there, lifting her out of the ocean and hoisting her over his shoulder.

'Put me down!' she said crossly, but she didn't try to wriggle out of his grip. Not when her hands were dangling over his curved rear. Curiously, she let her fingers move towards his waistband, separating it from his shirt until she found skin.

'And let you fall into a hole or be eaten by a crab? No, Cressida. I think you need to be chained to a bed for a while.'

The image was startling. She froze and he let out a noise from deep in his throat. 'Or a chair. Anywhere out of harm's way.'

'I like the bed idea…'

He mounted the steps and kicked the door open, carrying her through the hallway and depositing her unceremoniously so that she was sitting at the kitchen bench.

'Do not even *think* about moving,' he said, with such determination that she was pretty sure the smart thing to do was what he said.

As soon as the front door slammed shut again she wriggled off the bench. Stars flashed in her eyes and she steadied herself by pressing against the fridge. Water. She needed water.

But she was already wet.

She needed to not be wet.

She swore angrily, mentally shaking herself.

*Get changed, then drink something.*

She nodded.

It was an excellent plan.

Only Rio wasn't gone long, and her fingers were fumbling too much to perform anything efficiently.

When he walked back into the cottage and found the kitchen deserted, he checked her room.

The door was wide open, and standing by the window was Tilly, in the process of pulling a dry dress on. He saw a glimpse of her naked back, her curved bottom and pale hips. Enough to fuel his fantasies for years to come, he thought grimly.

'*Dio*…' he groaned.

She spun around, and had he been looking at her face he would have seen how unexpected his intrusion was. But his eyes were trained on the body that he'd just caught a tantalising glimpse of, and he possessed her with his gaze when he didn't dare touch her.

Her fingers dropped to the hem of her dress, lifting it, her eyes trained on his, her meaning clear. If he didn't act quickly she was going to be naked again, and he sure as hell wouldn't make any promises about how he'd respond to that.

'I told you,' he said with grim determination. 'This is not going to happen.'

It didn't make sense. He felt it too; she knew he did. He wanted her. 'But I…'

'You can barely stand up, Cressida. Do you think I am the kind of man who would take advantage of a woman so inebriated?'

Alcohol had apparently robbed her of any inhibitions. She walked towards him, her curves hypnotising him as she moved.

'How about letting an inebriated woman take advantage of you?' she suggested quietly, wrapping her arms around his neck, lifting her body higher, pressing her soft round breasts to his torso. 'I want this to happen. Sober or not, I want this.'

He closed his eyes for a moment and then stepped backwards. 'Well, I do not. Especially not like this.'

His words cut her to the quick. Even alcohol couldn't dull the throb of pain.

'Oh.'

He expelled a long, slow sigh, as if taming himself while subduing her. 'Lie down,' he commanded in a dictatorial tone that was softened by a small smile. 'You'll feel like hell in a few hours.'

'I need water,' she said belligerently.

'I'll bring it.'

She didn't thank him, even though she knew she ought

to. She practically stomped to the bed and lay down, not bothering to pull the covers back.

She was asleep when he returned a minute later, glass of water in hand. He placed it quietly on the bedside table then left her in peace—before his will-power finally deserted him.

He deserved a bloody medal of valour for that act of self-torture.

After a month of celibacy a gorgeous woman offered her beautiful, perfect self on a platter and he walked away? Hell, it was two glasses of wine—not even half a bottle. How many times had he slept with a woman who'd drunk champagne at a party?

But she hadn't just had two glasses of wine. Or rather, she *had*, but they'd had the effect he would have expected two *bottles* to have. She'd been completely addled. Cressida Wyndham, he had been led to believe, was a sophisticated woman who moved in socially elite circles. A couple of glasses of wine over lunch should not have affected her like that. And yet undeniably they had.

The moment they'd stood up from the table he'd realised that she was no longer herself. It had become more apparent as they'd made their way through the marina and he'd practically had to carry her past the shops. Then there had been the boat ride. The way she'd stroked his thigh the whole way. He'd been tempted to throw the thing into neutral and make love to her then and there.

Had she *any* idea how much stamina it had taken to turn her down?

And what had happened to make her so utterly affected by the wine?

He added that question to the pile of things that simply didn't make sense.

Cressida Wyndham was a mystery. And he was going to solve her.

* * *

He'd been right.

She felt awful when she woke. Not least of all because of the sense of temporal disorientation that had made her jerk awake. It was dark, but it didn't feel like the middle of the night. She reached for her phone, pressing the button so that she could see the time.

It was just after nine o'clock.

Why was she asleep so early?

And what was that furry feeling in her mouth?

And just like that it all came flooding back to her.

'Oh, God.' She squeezed her eyes shut.

Embarrassment curdled her blood. She screwed her eyes up tight, but that only made it worse. With her eyes closed, the whole day played out like a movie reel. She'd fallen in the water. Again! And... Her skin burned. She'd practically begged him to make love to her. And he'd told her he wasn't interested!

Tilly jerked her head around, her eyes landing on the glass of water. She lifted it up and drank from it quickly.

The only problem was that then she needed to use the restroom.

And that meant leaving her bedroom and possibly facing him.

She could hold it.

Or not.

She stood up and tiptoed towards the door. The handle was an old Bakelite one and she turned it slowly, so slowly, wincing as it creaked a little. She kept her eyes shut as she pulled the door inwards and then poked her head out quickly.

Left, right—he was nowhere in sight.

*Phew.*

She practically ran to the bathroom. She felt as fresh as

a ten-year-old toothbrush, and a cursory inspection in the mirror showed she looked little better.

She ran her fingers through her hair and splashed water on her face, pinching her cheeks before brushing her teeth and rubbing in face cream. Her skin was warm, perhaps from the sun…or embarrassment. With a grimace, she pulled the door inwards, forgetting to be quiet.

It wouldn't have mattered anyway. Rio was lounging against the wall opposite, his lips twisted in the hint of a knowing smile.

'Don't,' she said quietly, her eyes dropping to the floor. 'Don't lecture me.'

His voice was thick when he spoke. 'I have no intention of it,' he promised. 'How do you feel?'

'How do you think?' she whispered.

He reached out for her hand but she stepped backwards. 'Please, don't,' she said softly. 'I…' What? What could she say? 'I just want to forget today ever happened.'

'I'm sorry to say that is not possible. At least, not for me.'

She groaned, mortification chewing through her.

'Come and eat something.'

'No, thank you.'

'You will feel better in the morning if you go to bed with food in your stomach.'

'Please,' she said sharply. 'It was two glasses of wine. I'm hardly hungover. I just need privacy.'

His eyes narrowed. 'Eat something and I will leave you alone.'

'Are you bribing me with food?'

He shrugged. 'It is your choice.'

Her stomach twisted. She *was* actually hungry. 'Okay,' she said ungratefully. 'Fine.'

He turned on his heel and walked towards the front of the cabin, holding the door open for her.

The night was as balmy as it was beautiful. A thick blanket of stars danced overhead, and the sky was as dark as an inkpot. Streaks of cloud ran like frail fingers towards the moon.

'Here.' He handed her a plate and she looked at it with an unimpressed frown.

'Crackers?'

'Just something light.'

She wrinkled her nose but, truth be told, she wasn't sure she could stomach anything else. She sat down and curled her knees under her chin, biting into a biscuit while her eyes roamed the ocean.

She ate, and silence surrounded them but for the occasional sound of a night bird and the throbbing of the ocean. Once the plate was emptied, she stood again.

'I'm going to bed. Unless you have any objections?'

'Not a one,' he replied. 'Sweet dreams, *cara*.'

The words followed her all the way down the hallway, mocking her.

She'd have sweet dreams, all right, and they both knew who'd be starring in them.

The air smelled different when she woke.

The light had changed too.

Her room felt thick and damp. She turned over in bed, angling her body towards the window. It had blown open during the night and mist had burst in, wrapping around her.

'Lightning,' she said to herself, sitting up and rubbing her eyes.

It was raining heavily, the sound of it falling on the roof adding to the depth of the ocean's thunder. A tremor of emotion built inside of her. Thunderstorms had always stirred strong feelings in her, even as a girl.

She pushed the sheets off and stood, pacing across to the window and standing on tiptoe to see out. The geraniums were in disarray, their blooms drooping indignantly, covered in water. She reached out and flicked at one reassuringly, sending droplets of water scurrying.

The beach looked entirely different. The sand was grey, not white, and the waves were leaden, topped with angry white curls of temper as they hammered against the beach. The sky was steel-like, brightened only by the brief flash of lightning, and then a roll of thunder rattled past her.

Even in her sleep she'd been dreading facing the music with Rio. The weather was heightening the drama of that confrontation. She checked herself in the mirror, pinching her cheeks for colour and brushing her hair so that it was slightly less wild, then skimmed her eyes over her phone to check the time.

It was still early.

Perhaps he wouldn't yet be awake?

The thought of a strong black coffee before she had to see him was cause for optimism.

What would she say?

Memories of how she'd behaved almost made her groan aloud. She'd been rude, provocative, flirtatious, demanding...*drunk*.

Embarrassment made her skin crawl. Sucking in a deep breath of storm-soaked air, she made her way quietly to the kitchen.

'*Buongiorno,*' he said quietly, his eyes appraising her from where he stood, looking impossibly virile and unforgivably *not* hungover.

He had a coffee cup in one hand, and was wearing only a pair of shorts. A swirl of desire almost drove the mortification from her mind.

'Hi.' She cleared her throat, eyeing the coffee machine and realising she'd have to perform penance first. 'I'm... sorry. About yesterday.'

He arched a brow, and she couldn't tell from his expression if he was still angry. Out of nowhere she saw his face as it had been when she'd fallen in the water. He'd been furious with her.

Tilly dropped her eyes, staring at her brightly painted toenails with earnest concentration.

'I think it was because I hadn't eaten breakfast,' she said quietly. 'And it was hot…and I was thirsty. I just drank too fast,' she finished weakly.

He made a noise of agreement. 'Do you do that often?'

Her eyes were wide. Torn between playing Cressida and defending Tilly, she couldn't say what she wanted. Cressida was practically a professional drinker—and goodness knew what else she indulged in when the party spirit took her.

Tilly shook her head. 'I'm sorry,' she said again, shrugging her shoulders, deciding to stick as close to the truth as possible. 'I'm so embarrassed.'

He strode across the kitchen, putting a hand briefly under her chin so that her face was lifted towards his. 'I do not care that you enjoyed too much wine. I care that you made yourself vulnerable. I care that you exposed yourself to danger. I care that you probably do that often and that any number of men would have revelled in what you offered. You *begged* me to sleep with you, Cressida. How many times have you done that? How many men have taken advantage of you in that state?'

He swore angrily and moved away again, towards the coffee machine. He slid a pod into it and pressed the button, watching as it burst into life.

Tilly couldn't look at him. She stared straight ahead. 'I can take care of myself,' she said quietly.

'I don't believe that.'

He pulled the cup out and handed it to her. She caught its aroma with a stomach-flip of relief. Coffee. Essential. She sipped it quickly, enjoying the pain when it scalded her throat.

'Thank you for last night,' she said softly, changing the subject. 'For not…not…'

His eyes were mocking as they trailed over her body, but he said nothing.

The silence stretched between them, punctuated by the sharp crack of lightning and the rattling of the windows. She curled her fingers more tightly around her coffee cup.

'As tempting as I found you,' he said, and the words were a thick admission, 'I would not have forgiven myself.'

She sipped her coffee, tasting the sweet balm with relief. She should have been grateful for his chivalry, but she felt empty inside. Her longing was enormous and it had been ignored.

'We will be stuck in the house today,' he said. 'The storm is setting in.'

'It's pretty intense,' she agreed, moving towards the windows at the back of the house and peering out, pretending she wasn't still awash with mortification at the scene she'd made the night before. 'Are storms like this common?'

'No. Very rare,' he responded, propping his hip against the kitchen bench.

'You think it'll be like this all day?' She turned to face him and her heart gave a little lurch.

'*Si*. At least.' He crossed the room, pausing beside her, following her gaze. 'We just have to wait it out.'

Just what she needed. To be locked in a tiny house with the man she'd begged to make love to her the night before.

Her smile was weak. 'Great.'

# CHAPTER EIGHT

TILLY WAS GOING to burst.

Besides the lashing of the rain and the bursting of thunder the house was silent, and had been all morning. He'd worked, and she'd read—or pretended to read. All she'd been able to do was replay the mortifying moments of the previous day, cringing inwardly as she remembered each little bit of information.

Had she actually been *stroking* him when they were on their way back?

Her cheeks flushed pink. She would never forgive herself. And she'd sure as hell never touch wine again.

She shifted on the couch, curling her legs beneath her and flicking a page.

He had been the perfect gentleman. Was that surprising? No.

It wasn't.

It was Rio.

Well, so far as impersonating Cressida went she'd nailed it. At least that was some consolation.

He hadn't said a word. And nor had she—though curiosity over what he was doing had begun to fill her, distracting her from the book.

Finally she set it in her lap, her eyes lifting to him.

'Yes?' he murmured, without looking up.

Embarrassment flushed through her once more. She felt like a naughty child caught snacking from the cookie jar. 'Nothing.' She bit down on her lip. 'What are you working on?'

He turned to face her now, his eyes like granite in his handsome face. 'Evaluations.'

'For insurance?'

'No. For purchase.' He pushed back from the table a little, stretching his arms above his head.

Tilly nodded, but she wasn't really thinking about his work. Before she could find another topic a sharp, bright burst of lightning cracked overhead, and was followed immediately by the rumbling of angry thunder so loud that the windows shook. And then the lights began to flicker, before going off completely, plunging them into an eerie semi-darkness.

Though it was the middle of the day, the island was wrapped in grey, the sky thick and unyielding, the sun nowhere to be seen. The cabin almost glowed.

'What happened?' she murmured, standing up instinctively.

He frowned. 'My guess is the generator blew a fuse.'

She blinked. 'Something you can fix?'

'Sure.' He scraped his chair back and moved to the window, peering around the corner of the cabin. 'I'll take a look.'

He'd pulled on a shirt at some point, and now he slipped his shoes on and pushed out through the front door. Curious, she followed—though she stopped on the deck and moved to the side, so she could see him without getting wet.

The generator was apparently round at the side of the house. She peeked around the wall, and more specifically at him. Rain was lashing against him; he was saturated. His clothes were plastered to his body, his hair a dark pelt against his head. He moved confidently, his fingers testing the switches in a box.

He shook his head, his eyes scanning the house before resting on her. 'It's the generator.'

She nodded. Wasn't that what he'd said he'd fix?

He moved closer, standing just beneath her and shouting so she could hear him above the aggressive storm. 'The

generator is over there.' He nodded towards a small structure she hadn't noticed before. 'There's a key in the kitchen.
Would you get it?'

'Yes. Where?'

'In the drawer with the cutlery.'

She nodded, already moving back into the house. She
located it easily and jogged back to the deck. But instead of
handing it to him she skipped down the steps. The rain hit
her like a wall. Within seconds she was as saturated as he.

He swore under his breath. 'What are you *doing*?'

'Helping.' She handed him the key and he took it with
a small shake of his head.

'Go inside! I don't need help.'

She compressed her lips and turned her back on him.
She didn't go inside, though. She picked her way over the
muddy ground, towards the timber construction he'd indicated.

She waited for him, so wet that she barely felt the rain
now. But it was still hammering into her, enormous drops
falling thick and fast.

'Fine.' He spoke loudly, but she still had to lean forward
to catch his words. 'Seeing as you're here, hold the door
open for me.'

He crouched down and unlocked a padlock, then pushed
at the slatted door. She hooked her fingers over the top and
pulled it wide, holding it even as the wind grew and tried
to pull it away from her.

He leaned further into the box, his hands pushing at
various things, and Tilly wondered how the heck he knew
what he was doing. Or maybe he didn't, and he was going
to break the generator and they'd have to leave the island.

The idea pulled at her in a strange way. She hadn't
wanted to come away for a week, and yet now, four days
in, she couldn't bear the thought of leaving. Was that all it
took? Four days? Four days to become so hooked on some-

one that the idea of waking up without knowing you were going to see them filled you with despair?

He stood up again, pulling the door out of her grip and slamming it shut. He locked it and then nodded towards the house.

He didn't speak until they were on the deck, drenched and dripping. The rain was just as loud there, though, the roof doing little to block out the sound.

'Something's fried it. Could have been the lightning. Could have been an animal running scared. I've rebooted it, so with any luck it will be on again in a few hours.'

A shiver ran down her spine. 'And if it's not?'

'We're stuck here until the storm passes. We will just have to make do.'

Stuck here. In a dark cabin. With Rio. All she needed was candles and music and she'd be about ready to step straight into fantasy.

'There are some candles in the bathroom,' he said, thinking aloud, his eyes scanning her face. 'You need to get dry.'

'So do you,' she pointed out belligerently.

'You are shivering.'

'I know.' She nodded, her teeth chattering together.

'Go. Get dry.'

'What are you going to do?' she asked.

'Check the perimeter,' he shouted, as another flash of lightning slammed through the air around them. 'Make sure the roof is secure.'

'Then I'm coming with you.'

'*Dio!* For once can you just *not* argue with me?'

She crossed her arms. 'Which way?'

'No!' He reached for the door of the cabin and held it open, waiting for her to go inside.

But Tilly was stubborn—especially when she was right. And even more so when she was in love.

'I will work quicker if I am not making sure you don't fall over or bang your head. Go inside.'

She stared at him, her temper spiking. Sure, she was accident-prone, but he didn't need to be so unkind about it!

The memory of the day before—the way she'd crashed out of the boat and into the water—was at the top of her mind.

'I want to help,' she said loudly, but the words were uncertain.

'Then go inside. I will be five minutes.'

She glared at him angrily, her chin tilted defiantly. 'Unless you physically push me inside, then I'm going to follow you.'

He muttered something under his breath—something she didn't quite catch.

'What?'

'I said, don't tempt me!'

Thunder crashed, breathing urgency into the situation. Apparently thinking better of arguing with her, he shook his head and stormed off down the steps. She followed, bracing herself for the rain a micro-second before it began to hammer against her head.

Rio was so fit—so strong. She marvelled at the way he reached up and pushed at the windows, then overturned an old crate and stood on it, pushing a thick piece of wood into the gutter and freeing clogged leaves. He moved around the back of the cabin then, still checking windows.

When they'd almost looped back to the front, he sent her a look that was fulminating with anger. Tilly didn't understand it—though that was perhaps because she hadn't realised that her skin was white and her teeth were shaking in her mouth as she shivered unstoppably.

He stood abruptly and moved towards her, putting a hand in the small of her back and propelling her towards the deck. She turned to face him, but one look at his profile kept her silent.

At least it did until they were on the deck, with the rain lashing in sideways.

'What is it?' she shouted. 'Why do you seem so angry with me?'

'Angry with you?' He pulled the door to the cabin inwards. 'You think I'm *angry* with you?'

'You're shouting at me!' she yelled back. 'Why?'

He shook his head; water droplets fanned out, splashing against the walls. 'Because!'

'That's not an answer. What *is* it? I've already... I said I was sorry about yesterday.'

He closed his eyes for a second, and when he opened them she felt as if he was trying to get a grip on his temper. His eyes were a storm that raged as intensely as the one outside. He swore sharply—a sound that tore through the house as he moved towards her quickly, crushing her body with his far bigger one, pushing her back until she connected with the wall.

His kiss had the strength of an ocean. His tongue drove into her mouth, clashing with hers, his hands pushed at her shoulders and his legs kept her pinned to the wall.

'I am not angry with you, *cara*,' he muttered into her mouth.

The words came to her from a long way away. Her senses weren't capable of absorbing anything but this—this feeling that was tearing her body apart with a need she had never known possible.

Her fingers pushed at his wet clothes; they stuck to his body stubbornly and she groaned into his mouth, pushing her body forward, needing closeness, wanting more. So badly wanting more.

He had far more success—tearing the dress over her head, breaking the kiss for the smallest moment possible in order to shift the fabric over her face. Her mouth chased him, seeking him, needing him, hating his absence. Her pulse was louder even than the thunderstorm.

His hands ran over her sides and she shivered.

'You're cold,' he said, lifting his head.

She shook her head. 'No.'

'You are covered in goosebumps,' he pointed out thickly, the words dragged from him.

'Not cold.' She shook her head and pulled at his shirt, bringing him back to her.

His kiss was everything that had been building up inside her since she'd arrived on Prim'amore. It was all the longing and wanting, the needing and watching. It swirled around them both, churning them, changing everything.

Her fingers tangled in his hair and he groaned into her mouth—a guttural sound that perfectly expressed what she wanted. He pushed at her, guiding her, pulling her, until she was through the door to her bedroom. But he didn't stop. His body kept pushing at hers until she fell backwards onto the bed, a tangle of limbs and desire.

His mouth on hers was demanding; she gave him everything. But then he moved, dragged his stubbled jaw down her body, pushing at her bra so that he could take a nipple in his mouth.

His tongue flicked at it relentlessly, and the pleasure was so intense it was almost too much. She cried out, her hands needing to touch him, to feel him. She pushed at his shirt and finally he paused, so that he could remove it for her. She drove her nails along his back, feeling his supple skin as he turned his attention to her other breast, his fingers picking up where his mouth had left off. She arched her back as pleasure throbbed hard in her abdomen.

'I am not angry with you,' he said again, though she was no longer worried he was.

She nodded, words failing her. He brought his mouth

to hers and his kiss was gentle. Slow. Deep. As if he could taste her soul and wanted to cherish her.

It was the most erotic thing she'd ever felt.

'Rio…' she whispered, her skin flushed, her heart thumping.

Rain lashed at the window and lightning struck, but it was mute to them. Only the thundering of their own need registered. He kicked at his trousers; they didn't move easily. He stood, his eyes pinning her, his hands pushing at his clothes so that finally he was naked.

And spectacular.

Tilly stared at him, her eyes hungry for his nakedness, her body needing him. And he understood that need for it was eating him alive too.

He bent forward and pulled at her underpants, but he forced himself to move slowly, to drag them from her with a tantalising, torturous thoroughness, his hands grazing her legs as he went. Legs that were quivering with need.

Impatient, she pushed onto her elbows, but he was standing again, his eyes running over her with such obvious hunger that her whole body flushed.

'You are perfect, Cressida.'

The sentiment was beautiful, but how it pained Tilly to hear another woman's name on his lips at this moment.

'Call me *cara*,' she said, forcing a smile to her lips. 'I like it when you do that.'

'Then it is what I will always call you…*cara*.'

Always? She liked the sound of that.

'You are sure about this?' he asked, reaching down and stroking her face.

She nodded. She was. She absolutely was.

His laugh was uneven. 'Good.'

Then he stood once more and shook his head.

'A moment.'

When he returned, it was with a foil wrapper.

'I nearly forgot,' Tilly whispered, her eyes wide.

'You and me both.' He opened it and sheathed himself, then brought his body over hers. 'I have wanted you from the first moment I saw you,' he said seriously. 'You have a power over me…'

Her heart squeezed in her chest.

It was the same for her.

Except it was a lie.

*Everything she was turned out to be a lie.*

He'd been burned by a lover in the past, and the last thing Tilly wanted was for that betrayal to colour what they were. Because her name didn't matter, did it?

She shook her head and reached for him. Of course it didn't. This wasn't a lie. What her name was didn't matter—nor what he thought it to be. This thing between them had nothing to do with a name. It was inevitable and it was *them*. Him…her. Their bones, blood, hearts and souls.

His weight was heaven. His body was warmth. He kissed her—gently at first, and then with desperation as his manhood moved towards her, nudging her entrance slowly, gently, cautiously.

Waiting was agony; her body was on fire and only he could douse the flames. She arched her back, lifting herself higher, inviting him wordlessly inside her, and he groaned as he thrust deep, stretching her muscles, plunging to the core of her being.

She cried out in ecstasy, throwing her head back and banging it on the timber wall. He reached up, concern on his features, but she laughed.

'*Maldestra…*' he whispered, and the word ran over her skin.

She didn't know what it meant, and she had no time to ask. He gripped her hips and pulled her lower on the bed, then thrust into her again, sending her body into a spasm of awareness that travelled through her.

A low murmuring was filling the room; it was *her*. Tilly was crying out, over and over and over, indecipherable words, simply needing to express what was happening to her. She had never felt more amazing or more afraid. It was almost too much pleasure.

He brought his mouth to hers and his tongue lashed her in time with his body, so that her soul had no chance to recover. She was trembling, digging her nails into his back and even then failing to stay on earth. She was floating high above it. Then she was flying, soaring to heaven, her body barely holding together as release from sexual tension radiated from her.

Her voice was a loud cry and her hands pummelled his back. She gripped onto him for dear life, but nothing could stop the wave. It carried her until she was limp and breathless, but the pleasure didn't stop. He moved harder, shifting her with him, moving his mouth to her breast, rolling her nipple in the warmth of his mouth, and she sobbed at how good it felt. Her nerves were already over-sensitised.

He drove into her harder now, and she knew a second wave was coming. She could feel it building, as loud as the thunder outside. She tilted her head back and he kissed her neck, grating his teeth over the exposed flesh. She caught his mouth, tasting him, kissing him with all her passion and all her truth. Kissing away the lies she'd told him, making sure he understood.

This—this was who she was. This was real.

She wrapped her legs around him and he thrust deeper. She cried out, and the second her world began to shake he chased after her, linking his fingers through hers and lifting them above her head as their bodies ascended to the heavens together.

It wasn't sex. It wasn't making love. It was something else entirely. An experience unique to the two of them and to that moment.

She held him inside her, her legs tight around his waist, her hands pinned by him, their bodies in utter unison. Complete agreement.

His chest was moving with the force of his breathing. He brought his head closer, pressing his forehead against hers.

'Worth the wait,' he said, and smiled, his eyes so full of feeling when they met hers that a new wave of guilt lashed her.

'The wait was pretty excruciating,' she whispered.

'For both of us.'

He shifted, and she felt him move inside her, sparking new recognition and desire.

She expelled a shaking breath. 'Yesterday...' she murmured, hiding her eyes from his.

He brought his mouth to hers and kissed the corner of her lips. 'Yes?'

'You...you said you didn't want me.'

He shook his head. 'I didn't want you like that. I didn't want to be just another man who'd taken advantage of you.'

Tilly crashed her eyes shut, still hiding herself from him. The lie of who she was had begun to eat at her gut, but he mistook her gesture as one of embarrassment.

'I don't care who you were with before me,' he said seriously. 'I hate the idea of you being out of control drunk and asking men to sleep with you. I hate the idea that a lot of men probably give in to you.' He stroked her cheek. 'But that's not me. It's not us. And what's happening between us is all that I'm interested in.'

Her heart turned over at the words that meant so much to her.

She resolutely ignored the other words—the suppositions that had no reference to *her*, Matilda Morgan. The assumptions that should be laid at Cressida's feet, but not at hers.

'You were angry outside.'

His laugh was a deep rumble. *'Si.'*

'Why?'

'Because, *carina maldestra*, I do not like seeing you hurt. Wet. Cold. Or in any danger. It is the first time I have looked at a woman and wanted to...'

'What?' she asked, pushing at his shoulder, needing to hear the conclusion of the sentence.

'Keep her from harm,' he admitted with a self-deprecating smile.

Her stomach squeezed. She tried not to read too much into the admission, but how could she not? She smiled up at him, and her voice was weakened by emotion when she said, 'You don't need to protect me.'

His laugh was rueful. 'No. I am starting to realise that *you* are not the one in danger here.'

# CHAPTER NINE

'IT'S NOT CALMING DOWN,' she said, leaning forward, scanning the sky.

He stood behind her, his arms wrapped around her waist, bunching the sheet she'd donned toga-style at her middle.

'No.' He dropped his lips to her neck, kissing her softly.

She spun in the circle of his arms, her smile radiant. Her hair was wild around her face and her eyes were a glorious green. Her neck was pink from his stubble. He leaned down and kissed her mouth gently, smiling against her lips.

'I used to be terrified of storms,' she confided, dipping her fingers into the elasticised waist of his boxer shorts, revelling in the sensation of his smooth buttocks, almost unable to comprehend that she was free to touch him so intimately.

'They can be frightening.'

'Yes. Though I think I'll always have a special liking for them after this.' Her grin was shy. She reached up and cupped his cheeks, staring at him, trying to see if there was any regret in her heart or on his face.

There was none.

'I should go and check on the generator,' he said, with obvious reluctance.

'Really?'

He nodded, stepping away from her. 'Really. It should be on by now. There could be more of a problem than I anticipated.'

'But you'll get soaked again.'

'And I know just how to get warm and dry,' he pointed out, turning towards the front door.

Tilly watched him walk out with a sigh, but as he reached

the door she called after him. 'Rio? Where are those plans?
I might as well have a look at them.'

His face clouded with something she didn't comprehend,
but his nod was curt.

'Of course.'

He moved back into the cabin, disappearing into his bedroom. Curious, she padded closer to the door and peered in.
There was a desk against the wall, with a large drawer. He
pulled out some old pages, and a yellowed piece of paper
smaller than the rest which, she saw as he brought it closer,
showed hand sketches. The others looked as if they'd been
professionally put together.

His eyes held hers as he handed them over, his jaw set.

She didn't notice. 'Thanks.'

He spun and left the cabin while Tilly moved into the
kitchen. A cursory inspection showed the bench was clean,
with the exception of a couple of crumbs from the toast he'd
presumably made that morning. She wiped it with a cloth
anyway, and then placed the drawings down.

It took her several minutes to comprehend what had
been drawn, to orientate herself to the angle of the plans
and imagine the buildings that the architect had envisaged.

They were brilliant.

Instead of a large-scale hotel, several cabins had been
drawn—some with one bedroom, others with several, allowing for families or groups. The architect had marked
an area of the beach to be roped off for activities. On the
other side of the island the architect had sketched in a ten-
storey building with a pool that ran right to the sand of the
beach. And there was the cable car over the volcano, with
a restaurant perched right on top, so diners could peek in
as they ate.

The door slamming heralded Rio's return.

'These are incredible,' she called, flicking to the next
one, which showed the elevations for the buildings.

He made a grunt of agreement and she turned to face him.

'You're wet,' she said, the words breathy.

'Yes.' His eyes glittered when they met hers. He lifted a finger and pulled it through the air, beckoning her towards him.

She didn't hesitate.

He pushed at the sheet, discarding it easily, and lifted her to sit on the edge of the kitchen bench. Her legs were naked and he moved between them, moving his mouth over hers. She pushed at his jeans, loosening them, and he stepped out of them. Naked and so close to her. She edged forward, wanting him again already, *needing* him.

His hands pulled at her legs and she lay back on the bench, her voice a hoarse cry as he took possession of her, running his hands down her front, teasing her skin, delighting her breasts.

He took her as though his life—and hers—depended on it. He gripped her hips, holding her as he pushed deep into her core, and then his hand moved to the entrance of her womanhood. His fingers brushed against her as he moved and her body shook and trembled with the potency of need.

She exploded just as the lights flicked back to life and everything was bright again. She wrapped her legs around him and he came with her, chasing her, whispering to her in his own tongue, imprinting himself on her for evermore.

She lay there, staring at the ceiling, her mind slow, her eyes heavy with spent desire, her pulse racing. She stared and waited for her breathing to return to normal.

He pressed a finger against her lips and she looked up at him, a smile on her face. 'The power's back.'

He nodded. 'Apparently.'

She pushed herself up to sit, but didn't relinquish the grip her legs had around his waist. She curled her arms around his neck, tangling her fingers into the hair at his nape. His lips sought hers and they were gentle, sweet, curious.

She breathed in deeply, smelling him, tasting him. Loving him.

'These plans are amazing.' She pulled away just enough to see his face. 'Have you looked at them properly?'

Again his jaw clenched, and this time she did notice.

It wasn't until an hour later, after they'd showered and changed into dry clothes, that she began to suspect why.

'Rio?' she called, her head bent over the yellow page with the sketches. 'This is a house,' she murmured. 'Not a hotel.'

He was reading the book she'd bought him, and the sight did all sorts of funny things to her equilibrium.

'Yes. It was an option that was being considered, apparently.'

'A beautiful house,' she said wistfully, turning it over to view the floor plan that was on the back. 'Though quite the change from this little cabin,' she quipped, for the house was three storeys with tremendous glass windows overlooking the ocean.

He was watching her, as if he sensed that she was about to discover something. Something he had guarded carefully all his life.

'Rio?' She frowned as her eye caught the corner of the plan. 'What was your mother's name?'

He was quiet, so she lifted her gaze to him. 'It was Rosa, wasn't it?'

She looked at another page and saw the same name printed neatly in the corner.

*Rosa Mastrangelo*

'Your mother did these plans.' She moved away from the bench and crossed to him, sitting on his lap so that she could wrap an arm around his neck and hold him. Instinctively she knew that this changed things. That she'd found something that would be hard for him to talk about.

'And you were left this island.' She stroked his cheek, lost in thought. 'By your father...'

His expression gave little away; it made it impossible for her to forget that this was who he was, first and foremost. A successful tycoon who could control his emotions easily—who'd made a fortune in his ability to do just that.

'Am I right?'

Only the pulsing in the thick column of his neck as he swallowed showed that her supposition was correct.

'A month ago,' he said, by way of confirmation.

His expression was a firm mask, emotionless and resonating with strength. But she knew him too well to buy it. He was hurting. This strong, powerful man was in pain and she wanted to fix it.

She shifted, straddling him so that she could stare straight into his eyes. 'Tell me.'

His face shifted. A small shake of his head, a twist of his mouth. 'There is not much to tell. As a rule, *cara*, I do not speak of him. Ever.'

'I feel like you and I are people who would break rules together,' she said with a small smile. 'Who was he?'

His expression was contained. Still, she understood his struggle.

'You don't trust me?' she prompted quietly, padding her thumb over his cheek.

'The strange thing is that I do.' His lips quirked into a downward twist as he studied her thoughtfully. 'For the first time in my life I *want* to confide in someone about this.'

Warmth spread through her. She waited, enjoying her closeness to him as he searched for words.

'My father was Piero Varelli.' He looked at her, waiting for comprehension to dawn.

He saw the moment recognition lit her eyes. 'The shipping guy?'

'Ships.' He jerked his head in a small nod. 'Planes. *Si.*'

Outrage fizzed in her gut. 'You're saying your father was a *multi-millionaire*...'

'A billionaire,' he corrected.

'And he let you and your mother...?'

His smile was without humour. 'You see, perhaps, why I do not have time for him.'

'Oh, yes,' she agreed with true anger. 'But I don't understand. How could he refuse to help you?'

He expelled a harsh sigh. 'He was married when he met my mother.' The words rang with bitterness. 'He tricked her into loving him because it suited him—or perhaps he thought he loved her. But he didn't. Not enough to tell her the truth—to tell her he was married.'

With an enormous effort she kept her own guilt far from her mind. There would be a time to reckon with her choices and the consequences of them. She didn't want to face it yet. But already remorse was washing over her, no matter how she tried to keep it at bay. She was lying to him. She was lying to him just as his father had lied to his mother.

Only this was different. Wasn't it?

'And she didn't know?'

'She was young and in love. My father was rich and charismatic. She'd never known anyone like him. It was not difficult for her to lose her heart.' His eyes met hers. 'Right here, on this island. She spent some time here with him, touring it just as you have been.'

The notion of history repeating itself filled her with a strange sense of wariness.

'And she got pregnant?'

'Right. And that's when he offered to pay for an abortion.' His face shimmered with determination.

'Your mother must have been so upset.'

'I'm sure she was. But she focussed on making a life for us.'

'I don't understand why he didn't pay child support. And I don't understand why your mother let him get away with that,' she said quietly.

His eyes were hard in his handsome face. 'I think she knew she could have. But she was proud. *So* proud. He made it obvious he didn't want her—or me—and she was not going to beg.'

'I'm sorry, Rio.'

He brushed away the apology, shifting a little and reminding Tilly of their powerful attraction.

'He got in contact with me about five years ago, trying to "connect", as he called it.'

Indignation rushed through her. 'How dare he?' she said fiercely. 'After all that time! And what you'd been through! What did you tell him?'

His laugh was short. 'Exactly that. His explanation helped me understand, I suppose, though ultimately it just proved how selfish he was.'

'What did he say? How did he explain it?'

His eyes clouded and he shook his head.

She dipped her head forward and kissed him, letting her mouth tell him what was in her heart and soul.

'What did he say?' she murmured, keeping her face close to his.

'That he was married. And, yes, he loved his wife—very much, he said.' Rio's scathing tone showed how little he believed that. 'Carina—that's her name—and he were high school sweethearts. They had been trying to conceive a child for ten years. He told me that it took its toll on their marriage. That he met my mother and was captivated by her.'

Tilly was quiet, but inside she was raging against this

selfish man who'd conned Rio's mother into an affair. 'And she didn't know he was married,' Tilly clarified.

'No. Not until she told him about me. That's when he told her that he and Carina had been trying for a baby. News of my mother's pregnancy would have been devastating for her.' His smile was flat. 'My mother actually felt sorry for Carina. Can you believe it?'

'Yes,' Tilly said honestly. 'I can tell what kind of woman your mother was, and I imagine her heart would have been easily touched.'

His eyes flashed with unknown emotion as they met Tilly's. 'He told my mother that he would never acknowledge me. That he would never speak to her again. So *she* was left devastated instead of his wife,' he said softly.

'How awful.' She frowned. 'You said he contacted you a few years ago?'

He made a noise of agreement. 'Eventually they adopted. A boy. Then, six years ago, their son died. And a year after that he left Carina. Or she left him. I do not know. Only that he suddenly felt a compulsion to meet with me, his biological son.' His expression was harsh.

Tears, unwanted and hot, stung Tilly's eyes. 'You must have been—'

'Furious?' he interrupted. 'I was. But by then I had established myself. I had a fortune behind me, and I had learned to live without my mother. And, obviously, my father. What did I need from him? A man who had given my mother only heartache?'

His bitterness touched Tilly deep in her heart. She understood it, and yet it was impossible not to grieve for both Rio *and* Piero.

'I could not look at him without seeing my mother's pain. The way she'd been when she was ill. Weakened by cancer and chemotherapy, pale and hollowed out, as if all the living had been scooped from inside her. I wanted nothing

to do with him. *Nothing*. And I told him so. I particularly
did not want him to have the satisfaction of claiming me
as his prodigal son.'

His eyes were loaded with enmity.

'How did their son die?' she murmured softly.

'An accident. Drink-driving.'

'He was hit?'

'He was the drunk. He collided with a tree. Thankfully
it was only him who died.'

How awful for Rio—to have discovered his father and
also a brother he might have known and loved if only things
had been different.

'When you met with your father, did you feel anything?'

'No.'

'Nothing?'

'*Niente.*'

'And yet,' she said softly, cautiously, 'she loved him.
And he is in you.'

She tapped a finger against his heart, her lips pressing
against his gently.

His rebuke was swift and determined. 'I am who I am
because of my mother. Not him.'

She ran her fingers over his cheek. 'And he died a month
ago?' she murmured.

At this, Rio's face briefly flashed with an emotion she
didn't comprehend. Regret? Sorrow?

'And he left me Prim'amore.'

She expelled a soft breath. 'I suppose he felt it was the
least he could do.'

'I don't know. I think he was a stubborn, selfish man
who wanted to make sure I faced this.' His eyes glittered.
'Because it suited him that I should.'

Tilly stroked his cheek. 'His wife must have been devastated when he died and she found out about you.'

'She still doesn't know,' he said, with a flicker of something in his eyes.

'But...he left you Prim'amore.'

'And a lot of money I will never touch.' It was a dark admission.

'But surely when she saw his will...?'

'They were divorced,' he reminded her gently. 'She did not go to his funeral.'

'Did you?'

Something like disappointment marked his face. '*Si.*' And then, as though he needed to defend the action, he said angrily, 'I know my mother would have wished it. It felt like I was closing the chapter on them.'

Her heart squeezed with anguish. 'I'm so sorry for you, Rio.'

'I do not want the link between that bastard and me to become known. Not now. Nothing would be served by it being made public. I certainly see no benefit in hurting Carina's feelings.'

'That's why you're hurrying to sell the island. Why you're handling it yourself,' she said, remembering the way his face had been so adamant when she'd first stepped off the boat. '*No agents,*' he'd said, as though the very idea was anathema to him.

'You know what the press is like.' His eyes met hers, grey to green. 'You, of all people, understand about their intrusion into things that do not concern them. I want a quick, private sale. Only three people in the world know about this—you, me and your father.'

And Cressida, Tilly thought with a sudden warning feeling of panic. And whoever *she* had mentioned it to in passing. Adrenalin spiked inside her. The real heiress was hardly discreet, and she would have no reason to suspect that Rio needed his link to Prim'amore kept secret.

'I've been here a month,' he said, the words darkened

by memories. 'I came to the island after my father died, intending only to stay a day or two.'

'And yet you've been here a month?' she asked with interest.

Because he felt close to his mother here. Because he was saying goodbye—to his father, yes, but to the father he might have had, should have had. He was making his peace with a bitter resentment that would eat him alive if he let it.

He shrugged his broad shoulders, tilting his head back to see her more clearly. 'I want to sell this island and as quickly as possible. Having anything from him feels like a betrayal.'

Tilly nodded, but inside she wasn't sure she agreed with him. 'This island is…' She bit down on her lip, trying to find words for the strange idea that was forming inside her. 'It's like it's a *part* of you,' she said, with the tilt of her head that Rio had learned indicated she was deep in thought. 'They fell in love here; you were conceived here.'

His grunt showed how little he thought that mattered. 'This island is too little, too late. It is a reminder of what a weak, pathetic man my father really was.' His brows drew together. 'And yet my mother loved him. She loved him all her life. Even at the end he was all she talked of when she faded in and out of consciousness.'

Sadness swamped them.

When Rio spoke next, it was as if from a long way away. 'When my mother used to tell me about him, about how they'd met, it was like she'd been hit by a truck. *Gravità*, she called it. Gravity. Like he was earth and she was floating in the heavens and *bam!* She met him and fell…crashed. Burned, as it happened.'

His smile was tight, and it gave way to a rueful grimace.

'I never understood that. How could she meet a married man and fall in love with him? How could she ignore common sense?'

'She didn't know about Carina,' Tilly answered softly. 'So far as she believed she'd simply fallen in love with a man.'

'How could she love a lie? That's what it was. It was all fake.'

Tilly swallowed, but panic made her blood flash hot and cold. 'Not to her.'

'No, not to her. But the whole idea of that kind of feeling is foreign to me.' He shifted, his fingers tangling in the hem of her dress, pushing it so that he could connect with her bare thighs. 'It *was*, anyway.'

'Oh?' *Bang, bang, bang*—her heart slammed hard against her ribcage.

'Mmm…' His hands pushed higher, gripping her legs right at the top, his fingers stroking the sensitive flesh of her inner thighs. 'Until I met you I thought love at first sight was a lie invented by Hollywood.'

Her breath caught in her throat as her entire world shifted into blinding focus. Had he just said he loved her? That he was falling in love with her? Hadn't she been feeling that since she'd first met him? Or had she misunderstood?

Doubt was quick to follow hope, but love was unmistakable and ever-present.

*'Cara…'* He spoke with gravelled determination. 'When I decide I want something, I go after it. Do you know how long it took me to realise I wanted you?'

She shook her head, not trusting her voice to speak.

'Minutes. When you fell into the ocean and laughed about it. You were beautiful. The most beautiful woman I'd ever seen. But it was more than that. You were humble.'

Happiness and her future hovered in front of her, like a butterfly with mesmerising wings. But no vision could wipe out the awful truth.

She'd fallen in love with him, too. But she'd lied to him. And once he knew would he forgive her?

She already knew the answer to that. She'd heard the way he'd spoken of Marina, his ex. But she'd lied about being pregnant with his baby—surely a greater betrayal than this?

A throb of resentment shifted inside her. She wanted to be honest with him, but what then? Could she tell him and be sure Cressida would never find out? And what if Cressida learned the truth? Tilly had already given the money to her brother; the lie was bought and paid for.

'The first time I have ever told a woman I love her and I get silence.'

She laughed, a husky sound, as the present sucked her back towards perfection. 'I didn't expect it.'

'Nor did I. Nothing about this is expected.'


'Look. It's clearing.'

Tilly yawned, her head pressed against his shoulder. He stroked her hair absentmindedly, his gaze settled on the wall opposite. It was not late, but a day in the darkened cabin, distracted by so much emotion, had left Tilly tired. The storm was finally abating, though, and a hint of sunshine crested through the window.

He shifted abruptly, placing her head against a pillow. 'Stay here.'

It was a command she didn't care to disobey. Her body was languid and floppy after being pleasured by him again and again. Her heart was full to overflowing with his suggestion of love.

She let her eyes drift closed, but didn't sleep. How could she? There was a constant shuffling of things, and the regular slamming of the door to keep her awake.

She listened, though, with a smile playing about her lips. A smile that was wilfully ignoring the prickly path that lay before her.

She wasn't who he thought she was. And if she revealed the truth to him how would he react?

Her heart turned over, and briefly a frown crossed her features. Imagining life outside the island had become impossible. She had joked, on her first day on Prim'amore, that it was as though they were the only two people on earth. Yet that was how she felt after a few days alone with Rio.

The pressures that had brought this to be—worries about her brother, compassion for Cressida—all came to nought when she was with Rio. Could they not just remain on the island for ever? Pretending the outside world did not exist? With a few trips to Capri to secure essentials?

Life would go on; the world would spin. And she would spin with Rio.

Her heart.

Her soul.

Her other.

'I'm ready.'

She blinked, opened her eyes, yawning as she focussed on him.

'For what?'

'Come.'

She followed him towards the door of the cabin and down the steps. The sand was cold and wet beneath her bare feet, but she didn't care. She wanted to look up at him, but a glow in the distance called to her.

Several candles were set out in the sand, and in the middle a makeshift bed.

'You did this?'

He linked his fingers through hers and lifted her hand to his lips, then pulled her towards the blanket.

They walked slowly, breathing in the scent of fresh air in the wake of the passing storm. It was on the horizon now—a dark cloud dissipating into the sea.

'You *must* have mixed feelings about selling the island?'

He squeezed her fingers, perhaps to acknowledge that he'd heard the question, and then focussed his gaze out to sea. 'No.'

'Even though it's where they fell in love?' she murmured, saddened to imagine him selling it and that link being lost for ever.

'Their love broke her.'

'*Cancer* broke her,' she corrected pragmatically, wrapping an arm around his waist as they walked.

'I know that.' He expelled an angry breath, then cleared his throat. 'When she was dying, at the end, she spoke of him almost more than she spoke to me. He was so heavy in her mind and heart. I couldn't ever forgive him for that.'

His smile was tight.

'He cheated on his wife. Mistake number one. Never cheat; never lie. He left my mother pregnant and alone, and never once checked to see that we were comfortable. And we weren't.'

He cleared his throat again. They were almost at the blanket and he slowed a little.

'I was twenty when I made my first million. If she'd managed to live a few more years I could have given her comfort and security…'

Tilly's stomach churned. 'I think… I think she wanted you to be happy and smart and brave, and you are. I think you were the greatest gift in her life.'

His smile was perfunctory. He nodded towards the carpet and she moved to sit on it, but her eyes stayed glued to his face.

'I really am sorry for what you've gone through.'

He shrugged. 'I do not think your childhood has been a walk in the park either,' he said pragmatically.

She thought of Cressida, and then she thought of Art, and it confused her. Art adored Cressida. Tilly knew he did. But he didn't understand her. And Cressida was not the kind of daughter the businessman knew how to work with. She was beautiful, and she was smart, but she was smart with people and things—not numbers and contracts.

Cressida Wyndham was never going to step into Art's shoes and start running the family business. She didn't want to. She wanted to live her own life and to live a darned good life, too, with all the luxuries that most people could only dream of.

But that wasn't exactly Cressida's fault. She was a product of her upbringing.

Speaking to Rio, and reflecting on Cressida, could only make Tilly recognise her luck in having been born into the Morgan family. Sure, Jack was a bit anxiety-inducing—especially with his recent interest in gambling—but essentially things for the Morgans were simple. They loved each other and they were there for each other.

That was family for Tilly.

'I don't think I have any right to complain,' she said softly, settling herself onto the rug and staring out at the ocean.

It was angry and churning, and the sun was a fluorescent orange as it tunnelled through the woolly clouds.

'Why not?'

Tilly put herself in Cressida's shoes, but they were pinching now—leaving blisters she knew she didn't want to deal with.

'Because I had everything growing up.' She smiled at him as he sat beside her, glad when he put an arm around her shoulders and pulled her close. 'My family life is idyllic compared to yours,' she said seriously. 'No offence.'

He stroked her hair. 'None taken.'

She turned to face him, feeling safe and complete in the circle of his arms. 'Why did you do this?'

His eyes linked to hers before flicking back to the

storm-ravaged ocean. 'I have never known a woman like you before.'

She saved that little admission for revelling in later.

'Most of the women I have slept with have been good for only one purpose.'

Jealousy was a fever inside her. 'I see,' she responded crisply.

'I have not wanted to know what moved their hearts and minds.' He ran his fingers over her shoulder, sending goose-bumps of fire and ice through her soul. 'With you, I want to know everything and I want to see everything. The sun setting after a storm like this? I want to share it with *you* and only you. I want to feel your thoughts as we watch it together. *Cara*, I do not know I could ever watch a sunset without knowing you would see it with me.'

# CHAPTER TEN

THE SOUND OF a motor broke through their solitude. Tilly spun in the water, her eyes scanning the horizon, a frown nudging across her face when she saw a boat coming close to shore. It took her a moment to recognise it as the speedboat that had first brought her to the island, almost a week earlier.

'Rafaelo,' Rio murmured beside her, standing in the water and striding towards the shore.

He was more beautiful than any person had a right to be. Broad-shouldered, strong, tanned. She stared after him as he emerged from the crystalline ocean, droplets running down his back, and her stomach swooned, as if she was on a rollercoaster that had gained speed and was heading into its deep descent.

She watched as Rio moved to the boat and stood, one hand on his hip, his chest shamelessly ridged, his expression relaxed as he spoke to the old man. He threw his head back and laughed, then pointed towards Tilly and laughed again.

They were too far away for her to hear what they were discussing, but when Rafaelo pointed at the generator she got the gist.

The engine revved again and then Rafaelo was leaving, waving at Tilly as he passed, and Rio was returning to Tilly, cutting easily through the water with his strong legs.

Her heart flipped.

She didn't want to leave him.

*Ever.*

Yet that was an inevitability.

Unless…

Unconsciously, she frowned as possibilities and thoughts

ran through her mind. Unless she could find a way to tell
him the truth. She would need to speak to Cressida first—
to promise Cressida it wouldn't go any further. And then
she'd need to be sure Rio would understand why she'd gone
along with the charade. She'd need him to know she hadn't
ever intended to deceive him.

'Rafaelo wanted to see how the island had fared in the
storm.' Rio wrapped his arms around Tilly under the water
and she curled her legs around his midsection, enjoying
the feeling of being close to him underwater. 'He's going
to pick up some supplies from Capri and drop back later
today.'

She made a sound of agreement, but it rankled.

His laugh showed that he understood. 'You are pouting.'

Tilly made an effort to straighten her expression. 'I am
not.'

'He won't stay long,' Rio promised, kissing the side of
her mouth.

Was she *that* transparent?

'Does he live on Capri?' she asked, purely to move conversation away from how selfishly she was guarding her
time with Rio.

'Yes. He's looked after the island for a long time.'

'Did he know your dad?'

He dipped his head forward. 'And my mother, it turns
out,' Rio murmured.

'Really?'

'He is the same age as her. When my mother came to
stay on the island he came and laid down a lot of the tracks,
helped her find the volcano. He comes and tinkers every
month or so—it's been a long time since my father came
to the island and the cabin needs attention. The generator... The bike...'

'How does he feel about you selling it?'

His laugh was unexpected.

She angled her face towards his. 'What? Why is that funny?'

'It just hadn't occurred to me to ask him for his emotional assessment of my real estate choices.'

She felt heat darken her cheeks. 'You don't think it's reasonable?'

'You think if he is upset I should keep it?'

She turned to face the island. The white sand, the green trees, the blue sky behind it and the cabin that had been the place of *her* Prim'amore.

'I think your father would feel pretty aggrieved if I backed out now,' he said. 'Making his daughter my lover and then reneging on a deal that is almost locked in.'

A shiver danced along her spine. There was something in the way he spoke that said so much more than the words alone. It created the impression of a future. A future with Art, Tilly and Rio. A future that was impossible to envisage. No, that wasn't true. She could see it—she just couldn't imagine reaching out and grasping it. It was like trying to catch rain in your hands.

This wouldn't work. It could never be more than this week. Unless she could somehow work something out with Cressida. And even then…? What if Rio didn't forgive her?

'You didn't *make* me your lover,' she pointed out, surprised at how normal her voice sounded when her heart was shattering just a little. 'It was definitely mutual.'

She was distracted, so when he kissed her it felt like their first kiss—except so much better. Because he loved her, and she loved him, and their kiss was full of that.

'I am addicted to you,' he growled against her neck, flicking his tongue against the sensitive skin that covered her racing pulse.

'That's mutual, too.'

* * *

The ocean was lapping quietly, the sun was warm overhead, the air smelt like salt and Rio was beside her—still working, but beside her. And she needed him there.

Tilly's eyes were heavy—and no wonder. Sleep had been snatched between making love to Rio—and they'd done that a lot. Her body was sore all over, but deliciously so. Every movement reminded her of how he'd claimed her, of how she had moved over him, taking him deep inside her. She stretched a little, sighing and letting her eyes drift shut as sleep began to press down on her.

Rio's hand on her hair was perfect. Gentle, reassuring. Loving.

Her smile widened. She felt like the cat who'd got the cream. Future be damned; in this perfect moment she was going to enjoy it.

She was almost asleep when the purring of a boat's engine penetrated her haze of pleasure.

'Rafaelo…' he murmured.

She pushed up onto her elbows in time to see the older man push an anchor overboard.

'Stay here,' Rio said, and the words were a command she found incredibly sexy, even when a part of her knew she should be offended at being ordered around.

She opened her mouth to say something, but he brought his body over hers and she was reminded of how much she wanted him—needed him—and how incredible he felt on top of her. Her throat was parched, her mind blank.

'You look too perfect. I want to see you like this always.' He kissed her quickly, and then stood with an athleticism she couldn't help but admire.

'We're going to go and check for damage. Shouldn't be more than an hour.'

'An hour?' She pouted again and he laughed.

'Half an hour,' he amended, winking and then turning towards the ocean and jogging the rest of the way to the boat.

She watched, not bothering to hide her interest, as he took a cardboard box from the boat and began to walk towards the cabin.

She stood reluctantly, tiredness still fogging her, but a plan giving urgency to her movements.

'Mind if I check my email?' she called towards him, striding away on a trajectory that would lead her to the cabin too.

They arrived at the deck together.

'No. I will dial it in for you now.'

'I can manage,' she said, and he arched a brow.

'Without electrocuting yourself?'

'Hey!' She punched his arm playfully.

He grinned, pulling the door open and holding it with his foot so she could precede him into the house.

'What's in the box?' she asked, peeking over the top as he walked behind her.

'Groceries. Batteries. Candles. And newspapers.'

'Ready for a siege?'

'Or another blackout,' he pointed out.

He placed the box on the kitchen bench, then moved to his laptop. He opened it up and logged into the phone's signal, then straightened.

She looked so beautiful—so different from the images he'd seen of her in the press. In those pictures she was always made up to within an inch of her life, her body bared for the world to see. Here, she was stunning, but in a completely natural way, her hair shimmering, her eyes enormous, her skin fresh.

He kissed the tip of her nose. 'I won't be long.'

She watched him walk towards the door.

When he reached it, he turned to face her. *'Cara?'*

She waited, her breath held, for him to speak.

'Don't go tomorrow.'

Another command. One her heart and soul wanted her to obey.

'I'm sorry?' she whispered, not sure if it was an apology or a question.

'Don't go. Not yet.'

She bit down on her lower lip and tears built at the back of her eyes, threatening to spill down her cheeks.

'Rafaelo's waiting,' she said in response, the words moist.

He nodded—a curt tilt of his head. '*Si, lo so.* And yet we need to discuss this.'

'We will. But not now.'

Not until she'd emailed Cressida.

He seemed to take that as acquiescence. The smile he flashed her as he walked out through the door was filled with a confidence that bordered on arrogance.

And it made her heart swell even more.

She made herself a coffee—or a kip in a cup, as she liked to think of it—and then moved to his laptop. Even that made her smile, at how much it reminded her of him. She ran her fingertips over the case of the screen, her pulse tingling. She sipped her coffee and loaded up a browser.

Her inbox was full—little one-liners from her mother, a chatty email from Jack that filled her with hope that he was sounding more like himself again, and a few from Art, asking where to locate various files or emails.

She dealt with the business ones first, apologising for having been out of contact, then she opened up her Facebook profile. It was a time-waster she couldn't afford. She'd peruse her friends' holiday photos and new baby pictures another time. When she was back in England. When this was over and reality was intruding.

She clicked on to Cressida's profile, marvelling as always at how similar-looking they were, and opened up a new message to her.

Hey, I hope you're having a good time. Something's happened here and…

And what? *I can't keep your secret? The secret you paid me thirty thousand pounds for?* She groaned and deleted the sentence, staring at the blinking cursor.

She wasn't afraid of Cressida. Not at all. But Matilda Morgan was honourable and loyal, and she'd promised Cressida that she would do this.

Was it Cressida's fault that Matilda had fallen head over heels in love with Rio Mastrangelo?

Hi, Cressida. It's Tilly.

Crap. That was even worse. She'd know who was messaging her! Matilda deleted it, then took a big gulp of coffee.

Cressida, we need to speak.

She loitered over the 'send' button for a moment and then hit it before she could second-guess what she was doing. She bit down on her lip, and had gone back to her emails when a 'ping' noise indicated that she'd received a new message.

Her breath held, she clicked back into Facebook and saw a little green circle beside Cressida's name. She opened the message up, her nerves firing in every direction as Cressida began to type. The little dots moved frantically and Tilly waited with impatient panic.

Finally words appeared, and Tilly leaned close to the screen as she read them.

Hey, babes! What's up? Hope you're having a bloody ball. I know I am. You are such a superstar for doing this for me! I owe you. xxxxxxxx

Tilly couldn't help the smile that pulled at her lips. Cressida was extravagant with praise and censure. She was one hundred and ten per cent sure of how she felt at all times.

Tilly ran her fingertip over the space bar as she tried to find words. Eventually she typed her reply, testing the water with a small white lie.

Don't thank me yet. I think Rio suspects something.

The response was immediate.

You're not serious?

Tilly expelled a breath and began to type again.

Yes. Did you know he was going to be the one showing me around? For a whole week?

There was a pause and Tilly suspected Cressida was doing her own word-searching, looking for a way to explain why she hadn't been upfront about that.

Now that you mention it, I think Daddy did say that might be the case. Something about not wanting people to know he was selling the island.

Tilly ground her teeth together.

A heads-up would have been nice. We're sharing a tiny cabin…

Cressida sent a little laughing face emoji which made Tilly roll her eyes.

It's not funny.

Tilly's response was another emoji and then:

LOL! Sorry. Just imagining Miss Prim & Proper spending a week on a gorgeous island with that spectacular piece of man. What a wasted opportunity. Maybe I should have gone instead...

Tilly expelled an angry breath.

Actually... she began to write, thinking through a way to tell Cressida the truth that wouldn't result in gossip spreading like wildfire.

'Urghhhh!' she shouted into the cabin.

It was useless. She was caught between a rock and a hard place. If she told Cressida that she'd fallen in love with Rio, Cressida might tell the world—and Tilly didn't want that.

Although... Realisation fired inside her. Cressida was as bound by silence as Tilly was. How could Cressida spread the news about Tilly and Rio without owning up to her own part in the scheme, thereby admitting to her deception?

The thing is, I like him.

Tilly sent the message, instinctively disliking the lukewarm sentiment.

And I want to see him again.

There was a pause. A long silence.

No.

Tilly read the single-word response with indignation.

What do you mean, 'no'?

The dots began to move and Tilly waited, gnawing on her lower lip and fidgeting with her fingers in her lap.

Part of our deal is that you don't tell anyone. That's what I pay you for. What good is it having a doppelgänger if I can't trust you?

Tilly squeezed her eyes shut. Thirty thousand pounds. The money she'd given Jack to save his life. Or at least his kneecaps.

Can we find a way around this? Tilly responded, her heart pounding, her eyes wet.

What do you suggest? If you tell him, he'll tell Dad. And that's not our deal.

Tilly swiped at her eyes, pushing the tears away.

I'm going to see him again.

Silence.
Tilly stared at the computer, but no dots were moving. Finally, Cressida began to type.

If you tell Rio, I'll tell Dad. And not just about this. About all the jobs you've done for me. I'm sure he'd be fascinated to hear how his golden-girl PA has been lying to him for years.

Tilly's cheeks flushed pink.

Come on, Cressida. I'm not trying to ruin anything for you—I think Rio would keep this to himself.

Tilly waited, her body radiating with silent tension.

It's your decision. Don't forget to send my 30k back if you tell him, though.

The words were black and white, and Tilly saw them through a veil of stars.

A memory of Jack's face, so grateful, so relieved when she'd given him the cheque, flashed before her.

What a mess.

I have to go. Just remember, Tilly, you've got as much to lose in this as I do.

Cressida's little green dot disappeared, signalling that she'd logged off. Tilly still stared at the screen, though, re-reading their conversation with a falling feeling.

She had to tell Rio.

Surely she could get a bank loan for that amount, and repay Cressida? Still, loyalty strained at her heart. It was hardly Cressida's fault that Tilly had fallen in love with Rio. Cressida had every right to expect Tilly to uphold their agreement. Sure, she'd reacted like a cornered cat, but Tilly could hardly blame her.

With a grunt of annoyance she clicked out of Facebook, and out of her emails, and shut the lid on the laptop. Her coffee cup was empty but she was still tired.

Not from sleep-deprivation now so much as mental exhaustion. She'd turned the problem over again and again and there was still no answer. Nothing.

Except that she had to tell Rio. Somehow she had to make him understand that it had been innocent. She hadn't set out to deceive him, and she didn't want to deceive him for a moment longer.

He was gone longer than the appointed half-hour, though. An hour went by, then another thirty minutes, and she was contemplating going to look for him when he appeared at the doorway. He was covered in sweat and dirt and she'd never wanted him more.

'Hi.'

Sadness bubbled through her. Despair, too. But nothing mattered more than being honest with him.

'Hi,' he responded.

'Everything okay?' she asked warily.

'A few fallen trees, rocks—nothing major. The path is blocked halfway up, so no more volcano visits for you.' His eyes narrowed. 'You look pale.'

'I'm just tired,' she lied, forcing an over-bright smile to her face.

He studied her thoughtfully and then shrugged, as though her answer satisfied him. After all, they hadn't got a lot of sleep the night before.

'I'm starving. I could eat a horse.' He pulled the fridge door open and peered inside.

Tilly moved behind him. 'Rio?'

He lifted out the platter they'd picked at the night before, still full of olives, cheese, grapes and *grissini*.

'*Si, cara?*'

'I need to talk to you about something.'

He placed the platter between them, peeling off the plastic wrap, his eyes probing hers. 'Go on.'

'I...'

*I'm not who you think. I've been lying to you. I'm not Cressida Wyndham. You know nothing about me.*

She groaned inwardly, her mouth unable to form the words she needed to say.

'I have to go back as planned.' She cleared her throat,

and spun away from him, so that he wouldn't detect the grief in her features.

She stared out of the large window, but her eyes saw nothing. Nothing. A bleakness, an emptiness, was settling in around her.

His arms around her waist were delirium and despair.

'Then I will come with you,' he said, the words husky.

It was a promise that she wrapped in her hands and held close to her heart for a moment.

But only a moment, because reality made that impossible. How could she risk seeing him again? It wouldn't take long, back in London, for him to realise that she was not Cressida, and then the secret would be out anyway.

Her smile was weak.

He spun her in his arms and kissed her, first on her mouth and then on her temples. He kissed her as though he understood that she was broken in that moment, as though he wanted to glue her back together.

'*Ti amo,*' he said gently, lifting her up and cradling her against his chest, carrying her until they reached his bed, where he laid her down with the same reverence with which he'd kissed her.

His mouth took hers and his hands reached under her dress. His fingers hooked into the waistband of her underwear and slowly he glided them down her legs, his palms teasing her flesh as he removed the scrap of fabric and dropped them to the floor.

'Whatever it is that worries you, I will fix it.' He crouched at her feet and kissed her ankle, rolling his tongue over the round bone before dragging it higher, flicking just behind her knee, and higher still to the sensitive flesh of her inner thighs.

She groaned when his tongue connected with her womanhood, teasing her and driving all thought from her mind.

His fingers dug into her thighs as he parted her legs, giving him access to her core.

She trembled.

The power of emotion and need he stirred washed over her and she was both powerless and empowered. It was an ancient act—one that they had made uniquely their own. She tilted her hips and he kissed higher, trailing a line to her belly button, his fingers wrapping into the fabric of her dress, pushing it up with him.

He was gone then, and she groaned, her body unable to exist without his nearness, his touch, his attention. He pushed out of his shorts, and then he was back. She almost cried with relief. His mouth sought her once more, his tongue whispering against her folds. She felt her blood pressure was about to burst.

'Rio!' she cried out, rocking on the bed as orgasm broke around her. She tangled her hands in his hair, pulling at it, fire and flame ravaging her. A sheen of sweat glossed her pale flesh.

'I *never* want to stop this,' she murmured, not even aware of what she was saying.

'We won't,' he agreed, and his hands were parting her legs so that he could enter her, take her, make her his.

And she *was* his. Completely.

From the second he thrust into her she knew she would find a way to solve this—without hurting Cressida, without betraying her promises, and without losing Rio. There was some kind of magic out there *somewhere*. She just had to uncover it.

His hands were roughened by demand as they moved over her body, pushing at the dress until they found her breasts and cupped them. He groaned as he massaged their weight, his fingers teasing her sensitive nerves while he drove into her.

She was lost at sea. She arched her back and lifted her

legs, and he dropped a hand, catching her thigh and holding it, holding her leg where it was, high in the air. He nipped at her calf with his teeth and she groaned.

It was sensual torment. She was a willing prisoner and would be for ever.

Pressure built; it was a dam about to burst. She could not contain it. She didn't want to. She caught hold of his shoulders as it broke and he was on top of the water, riding the wave with her, his body moving in unison with hers, pleasure dousing them together.

Their panting filled the room, and finally pleasure. Release. Relief.

She wrapped her arms around him and brushed her cheek to his.

She belonged here. With Rio.

Tilly couldn't have said how much time passed. Knew only that they lay together, bodies entwined, sweat mingling, needs satiated—for the moment—until he spoke.

'I was gone too long,' he said with a rueful grin. 'I was ready to punch Rafaelo when he suggested we tour yet another path.'

Her smile was wide on her face, her lips pink, her cheeks stained from desire. 'You're forgiven.'

He laughed. 'I'm glad.' He pressed a kiss against her forehead. 'Want to come and see the caves?'

'Caves?' she murmured, her eyes showing confusion.

'I said we'd get back to them, remember?'

She did—of course. She just hadn't thought of them since. She nodded. She would find a way to tell him the truth, and in the meantime what harm could come from enjoying every minute they had left on the island?

'Sounds perfect.'

And it was.

The caves were every bit as beautiful as she'd imagined.

Swimming in them with Rio was something she would always remember—something to cherish. But her nerves were stretching to breaking point. Every joke they shared, every kiss, hug, touch, made her more conscious of the fact that she needed to tell him the truth.

He looked at her as though she was the most perfect specimen on earth. And even as she wondered why she couldn't find the words, she knew.

She didn't want him to stop.

She didn't want him to see her flaws.

And when he learned the truth, he would. It would change things. Would he even want to be with her once he knew who she was and why she'd lied?

She was breaking his cardinal rule and it was breaking her heart.

She fell asleep with the secret in her heart and Rio's arm around her. She fell asleep with no answers and very little hope.

# CHAPTER ELEVEN

'Why do we not spend some time on Arketà next?' he murmured, flipping the pages of a newspaper, his eyes resting on hers.

Tilly's pulse trembled like a guitar string being plucked. 'Your island?'

'My *other* island,' he said with a teasing smile.

'I told you—I have to get back,' she said, dropping her eyes to the table to shield her uncertainty from him.

'So? Next weekend, then.'

She shook her head, consternation drawing her brows together. 'I have something on,' she mumbled.

'What is it?'

'Just a thing.'

His expression was pleasant, but she could see the ice-like determination in his eyes. He was assessing her, as though she were a problem he needed to solve.

'Training for a mission to Mars?' he said with mock seriousness. 'Adopting a guide dog? Running in the marathon?'

Her smile was cursory. 'Just a thing. It's not a big deal.'

'So cancel it.' He shrugged, his eyes still hard and unyielding. 'I will have my plane collect you.'

'Your *plane*?' she said, and the chasm between them seemed to grow. 'You'll have your plane come and get me and take me to your island? Your *other* island?'

He was as rich as Croesus. And she was not. She was nothing like he thought. In the normal course of events they would never have crossed paths, and they'd never have become lovers. He was sleeping with Cressida, not Matilda.

Sharp spikes of feeling stabbed at her heart.

Cressida was the kind of woman he made a habit of dating. Cressida with her expensive jewellery and haute couture and luxury handbags and Bugatti Veyron and Cartier account.

Cressida with her VIP entry to any party around the world, with her private jet to match his, her penchant for rich, gorgeous men.

'Except for Marina, have you ever been in a serious relationship?' she asked jerkily, her eyes not meeting his.

He put the newspaper down on the table, his expression impatient. 'I have dated. Why do you ask?'

'I just…' She shook her head. 'Am I your type?'

He shook his head. 'I don't know if I have such a thing as a "type",' he said finally.

'But, I mean, you usually date women like me, right? Women who have trust funds and move in the same circles as you?'

'As *us*,' he said, with no idea of how the slight correction hurt. 'And, yes. *Naturalmente.*'

'Why *naturalmente*?'

He expelled a breath. 'What is this about, Cressida?'

'I'm just trying to understand you better,' she hedged quietly.

'I have never had a serious relationship,' he said through compressed lips. 'I have dated many women…'

'And by that you mean slept with?'

He dipped his head in acknowledgement. 'I date, yes, but primarily these relationships are about sex. For me and for them. I do not lie about my intentions, if this is what worries you.'

'No.' She shook her head, her throat thick and scratchy. She knew quite definitively where he came down on the whole honesty issue. 'Have you ever dated—slept with— someone who *didn't* have millions of pounds?'

He laughed, then, apparently finding the question ridiculous. 'I do not ask to inspect their bank statements at the door to my bedroom.'

Her cheeks flushed. 'I just mean someone *normal*.'

'I know what you mean, yet I do not understand why you're asking me this now.'

She forced a smile to her face. 'I'm just trying to understand you, that's all.'

He picked up the paper again, flicking a page abruptly. 'I do not find it easy to trust. Marina taught me well,' he said finally. 'I do not want to sleep with women who might have ulterior motives.'

She sucked in an indignant breath, shocked to imagine him ever thinking that of her. 'Just the ones you're using for sex?' she snapped back.

His confusion was obvious. 'Why are you so angry about this? I have casual sex with women, and yes, generally they're moneyed. So what? What does it matter?'

'It matters,' she said finally.

'Fine.' He closed the paper again. 'If you want to discuss our sex lives, let's come back to yours. You exercise no judgement in the men you take to your bed. Is that any better than *my* approach?'

Fury whipped through her. She scraped her chair back and glared at him—but, damn it, the tears that had been stinging her eyes for days fell from her lashes.

He narrowed his gaze, his expression shifting.

He swore darkly in his own language, staring at Tilly as she battled tears, and felt like a first-class moron.

She had been looking for reassurance that she was special, and instead he'd made her feel like the last in a long line of wealthy lovers. And then he'd basically called her a tart into the mix.

'How dare you?'

She was so beautiful, even when tears were staining her cheeks, sending little wobbles of moisture down her face.

She dashed them away, and her chest heaved with the effort of breathing.

'You are not like the women I've been with. I have told you this. Money, background—none of this matters to me with you. It is *you* I have fallen in love with, Cressida. You. Cressida Wyndham. The last woman on earth I would have thought I had anything in common with, and you have dug your way into my heart.'

She sobbed again, her tears falling faster now.

He couldn't understand it. 'Please, do not cry,' he said softly. 'I don't want to argue.'

She sniffed, but nodded.

The future she had held such hopes for was looking almost impossible to grab.

He turned his attention back to the paper and pretended to read. Something was worrying her. Something he didn't understand and certainly couldn't help her with unless she chose to speak to him. She was on edge—like a cat on hot tin.

He turned the page again—and froze as his beautiful lover appeared before him, her head bent, dark sunglasses covering her eyes, and her hand held by a man with scruffy blond hair and a ring through his nose.

'Would you care to tell me how you can be in two places at once?' he heard himself ask, the question calm despite the volcanic lava hammering him from the inside out.

Across the table, Tilly froze too. Her eyes met his with a tangle of confusion and then slowly dropped to the newspaper.

Even upside down she could read the headline.

*HEIRESS WEDS LOVER!*
*SECRET CEREMONY!*
*DETAILS HERE!*

Her stomach swooped and she gripped the table for strength.

Her eyes were enormous in her face as he lifted the page and she skimmed the first bold paragraph.

Shock and a thousand questions slammed into her. The press were always printing outrageous stories about the somewhat outlandish heiress. Surely this was just another? It couldn't be true.

Her eyes dropped to Cressida's hand; an enormous diamond ring glinted from her finger.

She'd married *him*? Ewan Rieu-Bailee, the man she'd been tangled with earlier in the summer?

Rumours weren't fact, and yet the picture was pretty damning.

As was the look Rio had for Tilly.

She darted a tongue out, moistening her lips. 'That's not me.'

'Obviously,' he said sarcastically, still staring at her.

It was a look that spoke volumes. It said everything she had been shouting at herself. Confusion, disapproval, anger, mistrust.

'She married him…'

Tilly thought back to their conversation. *'I have a wedding to go to. And Daddy would never approve.'*

Her own wedding?

Her heart turned over as she thought of Art Wyndham and how furious he'd be. And Tilly had unwittingly played a part in the whole thing! She would never knowingly hurt her boss—she adored him. And yet she'd been a crucial instrument in allowing Cressida to skive off and get married, with the whole world none the wiser.

'Oh, God,' she groaned, squeezing her eyes shut, no longer able to meet the full force of his interrogating glare. 'I had no idea.'

'You are not Cressida Wyndham.'

Though he hadn't spoken them particularly loudly, the words reverberated through the small cabin with the force of furious bullets.

'Who are you?'

'I...' She stared at the picture and the world collapsed around her.

'Who *are* you?' Now he shouted, his temper impossible to contain. He scraped his chair back so that he was standing, staring at her as if she'd sprouted four heads.

Tilly was shaking, her whole body quivering. She propped herself on the table, needing strength and support.

'Who the hell *are* you?'

'I'm... I'm the same person you fell in love with. My name is different, that's all.'

'You have been lying to me. You have been in my bed, in my arms, and I know nothing about you.'

'You know *everything* about me,' she whispered, reaching out and curling her fingers around his forearm. 'I'm not Cressida, but I'm still me.'

'And who is *that*?' he demanded, his eyes narrowed, his expression grim.

'I'm...'

Nausea was a wave and she was surfing it unrelentingly, occasionally dipping beneath the surface to the point when she thought she might vomit.

'My name is Tilly. Matilda. I work for Art Wyndham.'

His eyes, so grey when he was in a state of passion, almost blue when he laughed, were dark now, like a bleak, storm-ravaged night.

'Did Art set this up? What possible purpose could he have for sending you here?'

'No,' she whispered, her pulse thready as she denied the older man's involvement in this.

But Rio was jumping two steps ahead. 'Was he hoping

I'd drop the price if you asked it of me? That the inducement of you in my bed would be some kind of a bargaining chip?'

'No—no!' She shook her head violently, repulsed by even the suggestion. 'He doesn't know. It's… Cressida asked me…we're so alike, you see.'

He stared down at the picture. The woman had long red hair like Cressida—no, like Matilda. Pale skin, and, yes, a wide mouth. But there were differences too. A thousand of them. Though perhaps not to the untrained eye. It was simply that he was the world expert in all things Cressida—no, *Matilda*.

'You lied to me.'

She nodded. That was undeniable, something she would always regret. But that didn't mean she couldn't make him understand her reasoning.

'I… I didn't even know you when I agreed to do this.'

His lips twisted in a cruel smile. 'You know me now, though, and still you have been lying to me. Why?'

She opened her mouth and closed it again, her eyes shifting to the paper. She stared at Cressida, and the sense of having been betrayed filled the room. Not just for Rio, but for Tilly, too.

Cressida had used her.

Tilly had provided cover for Cressida to do something Tilly would never knowingly have been involved in. Her marriage to this man was a disaster. He'd already cheated on Cressida publicly, joked about getting her addicted to drugs… He was bad news. And now he was Mr Cressida Wyndham.

'Well, Matilda?' asked Rio, and the sound of her name on his lips did something odd to her heart.

It squeezed as though a band was being tightened around it. She had dreamed of him saying her name! But not like this. Not with derisive anger and disgust.

She no longer felt bound by secrecy. Cressida's news was in the papers; there was nothing left to protect.

Except herself.

The idea that she'd taken money so that Cressida could scamper off and marry a man no one in their right mind would approve of made Tilly feel dirty and mercenary. Rio was already looking at her as though she were filth on his shoe; how would he react if he knew she'd been paid? That this was a business deal for her, first and foremost—a chance to profit from a genetic twist of fate that had made her and Cressida twins that weren't related?

After so many lies, surely honesty had to be the way forward. She needed to trust him enough to tell him the truth. He'd said he loved her. That meant that he loved *all* of her. What was in a name?

'Who I am doesn't change what we are.' She moved to him with urgency and pressed her hands to his broad, strong chest. 'I lied about my name.' Her words were hoarse with urgency. 'Nothing else. *Nothing* else.'

Her fingers splayed wide and then his mouth was crushing down on hers with ferocious intensity. His hands pushed at her shoulders, tangling in her hair, and her heart skidded in her chest with a kind of relief she'd never imagined.

It was going to be okay.

This made sense.

She kissed him back and her fingers sought flesh, pulling at his shirt and lifting it so she could run her fingers over his ridged abdomen.

His hands dragged over her sides and she ground her hips against him, needing him, needing to remind him of what they shared. It was a primal imperative, a certainty that she wouldn't allow him to forget.

Her mouth clashed with his in a fierce meshing of teeth, tongues and lips, angry and desperate. His mouth was demanding and she met his demands, explaining in that kiss that she was still the woman he loved.

He swore into her mouth—a guttural expression of his anger and darkness as he lifted her, hooked her legs around his hips and pushed her back against the wall. His weight held her captive.

She groaned and tasted salt. Sweat? No, tears. *Her* tears.

'I love you,' she promised him through her kisses and her tears, and he pulled away, his hands lifting her from the wall and carrying her through the cabin to his bedroom. The bedroom she'd woken in that morning, feeling that all was right in the world.

His expression was a hard mask of disbelief. He laid her down on the bed—not gently, but not roughly either, just matter-of-factly. Tilly had the sense that he was as focussed on her as he would be a competitor in the boardroom. There was determination in the steel glint of his eyes as he brought his mouth back to hers, as though he was weighing her strengths and weaknesses and developing a plan.

But, for Tilly, this was what she needed. He was angry, and she understood that, but still he wanted her—because he knew, deep down, that there was rightness in what they were. Was he angry at himself for wanting her even now?

He pushed out of his shorts and relief speared through her.

It would be okay. It couldn't *not* be.

His body was heavy on hers and his tongue insistent as it lashed hers. Her body responded in ways she couldn't control. Fires were spinning through her and she had no control to stop what was happening; she had no control over anything. She was at his whim and at his mercy, his for the taking for ever and ever. Did he realise that she was his? Utterly and always?

'I love you,' she said again, and the words were tumbling out of her. She needed him to understand. 'I didn't come here to lie to you. I didn't even know you'd be here.'

His expression showed impatience. Was he listening? Did he hear her? His fingers pulled at her panties and she stared up at him, then reached for his face, cupping his cheeks, holding him still.

'Look at me,' she said, with a voice that trembled and a heart that was hammering wildly. 'Look at me and tell me you don't know me,' she implored, her eyes scanning his face, willing him to remember what they were.

His grunt was impossible to interpret, but the pressing of his arousal at her core was everything she needed. She sobbed with dark desire—when they made love she would feel better. *He* would feel better. This just made sense.

'You want me?' he asked through gritted teeth, his hands trapping her wrists and pinning them out to her sides.

Tilly's face was covered in tears, her cheeks pink, her hair in disarray. There were scratches on her from his stubble; she was marked. She was his. But he needed her to say it. He needed her to surrender completely to him. Even then, would it be enough? To overlook her betrayal and manipulations?

'Yes,' she moaned, writhing, hot beneath him.

His smile held no humour; it was a twist of his lips. If Tilly had seen it she would have described it as cruel. But her eyes were shut. She was waiting for him to give her everything she needed, to remember that he loved her.

He thrust inside her and she cried out as relief exploded like fireworks in her blood.

'Yes!' she shouted again.

'Do you love me?' he demanded, pulling out.

His desertion was a physical ache low in her abdomen. She lifted her hips, trying to find him, to welcome him back but a muscle jerked in his cheek.

'You said you love me.'

'I do,' she groaned, her eyes clashing with his, begging him, silently communicating the truth of her heart.

He shook his head. 'I don't believe you.'

And he thrust into her again.

Her grief and shock were quickly pushed sideways by the desire that was rocking her. But they were there still, in the back of her mind, like little bombs of reality she couldn't detonate just yet.

She didn't realise that she was saying it over and over again. *'I love you, I love you, I love you…'* like an incantation that would wrap him up in the magic they'd created.

He swore in his own language and his mouth dropped to hers. He kissed the words angrily into her being, silencing her finally, leaving only the sound of their heavy breathing and the cracking whip of desire in the room.

Misery was there, on the edge of everything, but it couldn't stave off the pleasure that was climbing to a fever-pitch inside her, taking control of her body nerve by nerve until finally she catapulted over, sobbing and moaning as the crescendo of physical joy broke over her. He chased her, his body releasing itself in a guttural cry, his hands around her wrists loosening to push his body weight off her as soon as he'd exploded, so that he could look at her, rocked by the final throes of desire.

He stared at her with an intensity that she might have believed to be love if it hadn't instantly struck her heart cold.

'I will remember you like this,' he said bleakly, and before the last vestiges of pleasure had ebbed from her he was gone, pulling himself up to stand, turning his back on her. His shoulders moved with the rise and fall of his breathing.

Tilly stared at him and those little disastrous truths exploded now—terrors that filled her with pain. 'How can you doubt this?' she asked quietly, wiping her cheeks and noticing absentmindedly that his fingers had left red marks on the pale flesh of her wrists. They were fading already and she resented that. She didn't want to lose any physical markers of what they'd shared.

His laugh rang in the room like an accusation. 'I doubt *everything*!'

'You love me and I hurt you,' she said quietly.

'*Love* you? I don't even *know* you, Cressi— Damn it! Matilda. You are every bit as bad as Marina. No, you are worse! I actually loved you, and you allowed me to…to bare my soul to you even knowing how dishonest you were being.'

She winced and he spun to face her, his expression fury personified.

'You weren't supposed to be here,' she said, pushing up onto her elbows, her eyes imploring him to hear what she was saying. 'By the time I'd fallen in love with you and we were…*this*, it was too late.'

'Too late?' He jerked his head back as though she'd struck him. 'How many times could you have told me the truth?'

'I wanted to,' she whispered. 'But it wasn't my secret.'

He shook his head, his expression a mix of anger and mistrust. His hair was tousled and loose over his forehead. 'What we just did—*that* is the only truth we have shared this week.'

Her orgasm was still subsiding, her mind was fogged, and it took her a moment to hear his words and to make any kind of sense of them.

'Sex,' he supplied with dark determination.

A shiver ran the length of her spine.

'Don't say that,' she whispered. 'It's been so much more than just a physical thing. Think of every moment we've shared and tell me that it's been a lie.'

'Easily.' His smile was grim. 'It has been a lie. I thought you were someone else. Everything I thought about you was based on misinformation.'

'No!' She shook her head, but he continued.

'We've had sexual attraction and desire—incredible chemistry. But that's not something I can't get more of. And with someone who *won't* be dishonest with every word she breathes.'

Her breath hurt. The very idea of his supplanting her in his bed nauseated her.

'Rio,' she said softly, but the word was drenched in the tears that were streaming down her cheeks. 'I wanted to tell you. *So* many times. But I promised Cressida and...' She thought guiltily of the enormous sum Cressida had paid her. How could he forgive her? 'I *had* to honour that.'

'If you say so.'

His detachment hurt far more than the anger. It was so angry.

'Can you be ready in an hour?'

'For what?' Her skirt was ruched around her hips, and her hair was a bird's nest that spoke of passion and need.

'To get back to reality,' he said crisply. 'I want you off this damned island and out of my life.'

'Rafaelo will take you to Sorrento. My helicopter there will take you to Naples, where my jet is fuelled and waiting.'

'Rio...'

She stared at him, the change in his demeanour impossible to reconcile with the man she'd woken up beside. He'd showered after they'd made love. Only it hadn't been making love. Not for him. It had been making a point.

She swallowed, the taste of acid burning her throat. 'Please let me explain.'

He stood at the table, his hands gripping the back of a chair. His knuckles glowed white with tension.

'Do you think any explanation will fix this?'

She squeezed her eyes shut and nodded.

*'Veramente?'* he demanded. 'I know nothing about you,

Matilda Morgan who works for Art Wyndham, but you know *everything* about me. Things I have never spoken to another soul I have told you this week. You *know* me. Surely you know I could never forgive this deception?'

'I didn't set out to deceive you,' she said quickly.

'What does that matter? The result is the same, whether you planned it or not. And you chose to deceive me even when you knew what we were becoming.' He shook his head. 'What I *thought* we were becoming,' he corrected with cruel derision in his words.

She sucked in a deep breath. She *had* to make him understand.

'I have a brother,' she said firmly, her eyes holding his even as the withering uninterest in his made her gut churn. 'Jack. He's my twin. We've always been close. And he got into trouble recently.'

She paused here. She had made a habit of concealing Jack's failings from the world out of a need to protect him. But even that had to be sacrificed for any hope with Rio.

'Do not misunderstand me. I do not *wish* to know you,' he said coldly. 'Rather, I know all I need to know about you.'

'Please,' she said thickly. 'Let me tell you this.'

He flicked a lazy glance at his watch. 'Rafaelo will be here any minute. You have until he arrives.'

Urgency made her speak faster, louder. 'Jack owed money to some guys—bad guys—and at the same time Cressida asked me to come here and pretend to be her. She would pay me to come here as her.' She darted her tongue out and licked her lower lip. 'I was very worried about Jack, and then all of a sudden there was this perfect solution.'

Her eyes met his and then darted away, scared by the Arctic hatred she saw there.

'Why would you think this a solution? Impersonating someone is not easy.'

'I've done it before,' she muttered, staring at the floor. 'Not ever for as long as this. It started with a party she didn't want to go to, and then there was a film premiere. Sometimes she's asked me to leave a restaurant before her so that the press think she's gone.'

'And she *pays* you for this?'

Tilly nodded. 'But that's not why I do it.'

His laugh was a scoff. 'I see. I presume you do it because you get some kind of psychopathic kick out of lying to people?'

She shook her head. 'I feel sorry for her,' Tilly whispered the words. 'She's not a bad person, Rio. Just selfish and spoiled. But she…she deserves better than the treatment she gets in the press.'

He made a noise of disagreement.

'You weren't meant to be here. I thought I'd meet an estate agent, get a tour of the island and then…'

The words dwindled away as embarrassment over her naivety swallowed her.

'And then what? Take payment for the deception? Fix your brother's problems? Go back to your life, having lied to your boss?' He shook his head. 'None of this is making you look any better to me.'

She nodded, her throat raw. 'I didn't know she was going to get married. I would never have taken part in this if I had.'

He didn't respond, and for a second she hoped that maybe she was getting through to him. But one look at his features, set in a mask of stone, and she was absolutely sure that she'd lost him for good.

'How much?' he asked with a thick accusation.

She didn't pretend to misunderstand. 'Thirty thousand pounds.'

His eyes swooped closed on the information as he digested it. She had no idea what he was thinking. In the distance she heard the unmistakable sound of the speedboat and panic slammed into her.

'I love you,' she said quietly, with complete honesty.

His eyes snapped open. 'Another lie,' he ground out. 'Where is your bag?'

'Not a lie,' she insisted, walking around the table and putting a hand on his arm.

He stared at it as though she was wiping butter all over him. His gaze met hers with challenge.

'I don't want to leave you,' she said thickly. 'Let me stay.'

His eyes flashed with a dark emotion she couldn't understand.

'You want to stay?' he murmured.

Hope soared inside her. She nodded.

'You can stay, *cara*. But you should know that all I will ever want you for is sex. It is the only part of this that I believe you weren't faking. I'll even throw thirty thousand pounds into the mix if that makes you feel more comfortable.'

It took several aching seconds for the implication of his words to sink in.

Never in his life had he seen such visceral pain cross the features of someone's face. No matter how furious he was with her, how much he loathed her in that moment, seeing his words hit their target left him with a hollow feeling in his chest. All the colour had drained from her flesh and tears had sprung to her eyes.

When she lifted a hand to slap his cheek he made no effort to stop her.

It seemed like the perfect end to what they had been.

'I'll take that as a no,' he said, the words blank of any emotion.

'Take it as a go to hell.'

# CHAPTER TWELVE

THE ELEVATOR WAS SLOW.

Or perhaps Rio was just impatient.

Not that he conveyed a hint of emotion.

His eyes were like steel as they stared straight ahead, his expression set.

Would she be surprised to see him?

His smile was tight and humourless. He had deliberately avoided making an appointment so that he didn't tip her off. When he saw Matilda Morgan again he wanted it to be with the edge of surprise.

He flicked a glance at his wristwatch, noting the time with dispassionate interest. He'd chosen to arrive in the late afternoon, knowing the chances of Tilly still being away from her desk at lunch were slight.

The metallic doors of the lift pinged open and he strode out of the lift with no concept of the heads that lifted as passed. Speculative glances, some recognition, a lot of interest.

A bank of three receptionists sat in the centre of the tiled foyer. He paused in front of one of them, employing a banal, non-committal smile. 'Art Wyndham.'

The woman curled her manicured fingers over the felt end of her telephone headset. 'Is Mr Wyndham expecting you, sir?'

'No.' He smiled again, and saw the effect it had on her. 'But he won't want to miss me.'

The woman stared at him for a moment too long and then returned her attention to the computer screen.

She checked a diary and then went to press a button

on the phone, but Rio shook his head. 'I'd prefer to surprise him.'

'Oh…'

Perhaps the receptionist should have employed more care, but she was face to face with Rio Mastrangelo and any powers of thought and reason had deserted her.

She nodded. 'You'll need to go up one more level. His PA's desk is just outside the lift. She'll direct you.'

*'Grazie.'* He spun on his heel, stalking back to the lift and pressing the 'up' button. It appeared immediately, of course. That was how things generally worked for Rio.

The ride up took seconds.

He stood, a study in nonchalance, and waited for the doors.

They slid open silently and his eyes immediately moved to the desk. As promised, it was directly in front of the elevator, though halfway across the floor. A woman's head was bent. A dark head.

He frowned. Had she changed her hair? Disappointment fired in his gut. Her hair had been spectacular.

Time seemed to stand still as Tilly's head lifted and he waited for her eyes to meet his.

He frowned.

She was not Matilda.

He recovered quickly. He'd come to see Art, not Matilda. What did it matter that she wasn't at her desk?

'Is Art free?' he asked, his tone clipped, his words impatient.

'Oh….um…' She stared down at her desk and then reached for her phone, dropping it once before shaking her head and lifting it to her ear.

'Mr Wyndham?' she said, and then bit down on her lip shamefacedly as she pressed a button. 'Mr Wyndham?' she tried again. 'There's a man here to see you.'

The woman was quiet for a moment, nodding, and then she lifted her eyes to Rio's face. 'What's your name?'

Rio's lips curled in a small smile of disapproval. This woman wouldn't have lasted two hours in *his* employ. 'Rio Mastrangelo,' he offered.

She'd obviously heard of him. 'Oh! *Oh!* It's Mr Mastrangelo, sir!' Another pause. 'Right away.'

She put the phone down and smiled brightly. 'His office is the second door on the right.'

Confident that the usual form would have been for her to lead him there, and to offer refreshment, Rio nodded in a terse acknowledgement and strode across the floor.

'Rio!' Art pulled the door inwards, sending a bemused look down the hallway at his PA. 'Come in.'

Rio stepped into the office, barely noting the luxurious surrounds.

'You'll have to forgive the temp. Nice enough girl, but what she knows about administration you could fit on the back of a postcard.'

Art waved a hand at the comfortable leather sofas near the enormous windows that painted an expansive view of the Thames.

Rio sat, crossing one ankle over his knee.

'I had to fire my assistant,' Art grumbled. 'Though, having spent the last four weeks getting intimately acquainted with the dregs of every temp agency in the city, I almost wish I hadn't.'

Rio didn't want to analyse the emotional response he was having to this discovery. 'You fired Matilda?'

Art narrowed his eyes, putting two and two together with less efficiency than Rio would have liked.

'That's right,' he murmured. 'You met her. Or rather you met her in the guise of my daughter.' He spat out the summation with deep condemnation. 'Sorry about that. Of course I had no idea what they were up to.'

'Of course.' Rio nodded, his mind poring over this fact. 'When?'

Art looked confused. 'When, what?'

'When did you fire her?'

'As soon as she got back. I can't believe she helped Cressida marry that useless waste-of-space *artist*.' He shouted the last word as if it were the worst thing a man could be. 'Anyway, that's not your concern. What can I do you for?'

The pounding wouldn't stop. The pounding in her head and then, making it worse, the pounding at the door.

'I'm coming,' she called, wincing as the words shredded her raw throat.

She grabbed a tissue as she passed the nightstand and blew her nose, then discarded the white paper on the floor. She pushed her hair back from her face, tangling her fingers in knots. When had she last showered? Days ago, she thought with a frown, hating the idea of standing upright for any period of time.

A sneeze burst from her and it was like being slapped over the head with a hammer. She pulled the door inwards and the sneeze was quickly followed by a second, then a third, so that she was disorientated when she blinked her eyes open.

It was early evening, and the sky was dark. Surely that explained why she wasn't seeing properly?

Confusion followed disorientation. Was she hallucinating? Or was Rio Mastrangelo really standing on her front doorstep looking better than anyone had a right to?

Gone was the coarse hair that had covered his chin and upper lip in a mask of stubble. He had shaved, and his hair was neat—not a hint of Island Rio remained in evidence. But it was him, all right, nonchalant and sexy in a slate-grey suit with a crisp white shirt open at the collar to reveal the thick column of his neck. A neck she had loved to kiss and bite and taste.

She swallowed and looked away quickly. Stars burst at her temple too fast. Her eyes had been sore for days.

'What are you doing here?'

'*Dio*. You look like death warmed up.'

She groaned inwardly, keeping her fingers gripping tightly to the door. He was right. She hadn't just been skipping showers, but meals and hair-washing, and she was pretty sure she'd spilled some coffee down the front of her cream shirt, leaving a tell-tale trail of caramel staining.

Still, that was no business of his. He hadn't even walked her to the door of the cabin when Rafaelo had knocked. She'd walked away from him, head held high, and she stood before him now with her shoulders squared. 'Did you come to insult me a little more?'

'Have you been crying?' he asked with incredulity.

As if she hadn't had every *reason* to cry! The first two weeks back from Prim'amore had been strewn with tears. Not just tears over losing Rio, but tears over the injustice of losing her job and the friendship with Art that she had foolishly believed mattered as much to the older man as it had to her.

'No.' She sneezed emphatically, her head spinning with the jerk of movement, and he took advantage of her distraction to move closer, lifting a hand to the door.

'What are you doing?' she demanded, the words thick with congestion.

He frowned. 'You are ill?'

'I have a cold.' She kept her hand on the door even as he went to move it inwards.

'A cold?' he repeated, his frown deepening.

She coughed. 'Yes. You know—sneezing. Coughing. Sore throat.' As if to emphasise her point, she sneezed again.

'It's summer.'

Her eyes narrowed. 'So?'

He expelled a deep breath. 'Then get inside and sit down before you fall down.'

Tilly feared his prediction was not an unlikely one. Her head was woozy and thick, her body shivering. 'I will—as soon as you go.'

He took the final step so he was level with her—though he towered over her, in point of fact, his strong body so close she could feel his warmth and smell his spicy fragrance. His nearness was intoxicating and overpowering, and her already ravaged senses weren't up to fending off the kick of desire that surged inside her.

It surprised her.

It was wholly unwanted.

And it weakened her too, so that when he pushed at the door again it gave easily.

She didn't resist. She did move back, though, putting distance between herself and Rio.

He stepped into her home, his eyes glittering in his handsome face as they bored into her for a long moment and then moved down the hallway, studying the pictures on her walls and the arrangements of tulips that were wilting now, their water emitting a faintly rancid odour. Or at least she imagined it was, judging by from the brown sludge outline on the glass vase. Her nose was too blocked to fully appreciate it.

Strangely, though, Rio tickled every one of her senses, even though she was barely functioning.

'What are you doing here?' she asked, focussing on a point over his shoulder. Surreptitiously she pressed her back against the wall, needing the support to stay upright.

A muscle jerked in his jaw. 'Where is your bedroom?'

Stricken, she shook her head. 'What? You can't be serious?'

He looked at her as though she'd taken leave of her senses. 'As hard as I find it to resist you,' he said with a hint of droll amusement, 'you look like you are about to faint. Go and sleep. I will make you tea.'

'Tea,' she repeated, confusion making her eyes crinkle.

'Go. Lie down.'

'No. Rio, I'm… I do need to…to rest. But please,' she said with a quiet stoicism that came from the heart, 'don't make me tea.'

She lifted a hand, because she couldn't not touch him, and pressed her fingers into his chest. Electricity arced between them, but this time it burned her. It wasn't just an arc of desire; it was an explosion.

She dropped her hand away quickly and swallowed. 'I don't know why you're here, but I want you to go away again.'

The words rang with palpable grief.

'Go to sleep,' he said with a small nod.

She sighed, reaching for the wall for support. He was going to go. Whatever had brought him to her home, it wasn't important enough for him to fight for it.

'Goodbye,' she said, and it was only as she reached her bedroom that she realised he had said nothing back.

It was early in the morning when she woke. Not yet dawn, the sky was just yielding its black finality to the hint of daylight, negotiating the terms of their treaty with leaden grey and pale pink.

She sat up without sneezing or grabbing her head for the first time in over a week. She lifted a hand to her hair, pulling it over her shoulder in one big tangle of red. She ran her fingers over its length. It was a tangled bird's nest, and for the first time since getting sick she found the idea of washing it didn't leave her feeling exhausted.

She coughed. It didn't feel as though her throat had been slashed with razor blades.

But it wasn't until she'd started the shower running and stripped her three-day-old outfit from her body that she remembered Rio's visit the evening before. Had it been a dream? What reason could he have had for coming to see her in real life? Their business was over. More than over.

It was broken beyond repair.

Had she dreamed his visit? Lord knew she'd had enough dreams of Rio Mastrangelo for that theory to be utterly plausible. She looked down at her fingertips, trying to remember the sensation of touching him. She'd pressed her hand against his chest.

And she frowned.

He'd been clean-shaven. It was easier to imagine him as the formidable tycoon when he looked like that, instead of the island version of himself.

She lathered her hair and rinsed it, then conditioned it and soaped her whole body, propping her back against the tiles when a wave of tiredness returned.

This cold had been dogging her steps for well over a week. At first she'd thought it was just exhaustion, but then her ears had begun to ache, her throat to sting, her eyes to scratch, and finally she'd succumbed to the sickness. In some ways it had been a relief. A physical justification for her pervasive sense of misery.

It had allowed to her to climb wearily into bed.

To stay there.

To hide under her duvet and let the world roll past, carrying on without her contribution.

Strength was in her now, though. She'd slept solidly, as though seeing Rio had given her some kind of closure.

Closure? *As if.*

Her heart twisted with a pain she was becoming used to. She flicked the water off and grabbed a towel, wrapping it around her body and then aggressively drying her hair. She felt much better, but there was still an exhaustion within her that came from having not eaten properly in days.

She didn't bother to dress. Instead she cinched her silk robe around her waist and pulled the door inwards, padding down the hall. The scent of decaying flowers assailed her and, as she'd suspected, it was disgusting. She curled her fingers around the vase, lifting it and carrying it with her to the kitchen.

As she cut through her small, cheery lounge, with its white fabric sofa and colourful throw cushions, its view of her small courtyard, she froze.

Rio sat amongst the cushions on her sofa, his body still, in a seated position, his head bent over the coffee table. He wore the same clothes as he had the day before, though at some point in the night he'd discarded his coat. It hung on one of the chairs that were perched at the window.

She was so shocked she almost dropped the vase.

'What are you doing here?' she demanded, even as her body screamed at her to go to him, to close the distance and straddle him.

Her body begged her to give in to her craving but her mind was rejecting that idea wholesale.

He didn't want her.

*'You can stay, cara. Stay. But you should know that all I will ever want you for is sex. It is the only part of us that I believe you weren't faking. I'd even throw thirty thousand pounds into the mix if that made you feel more comfortable.'*

He turned to look at her, his eyes probing hers before dropping, performing a cursory inspection of her figure.

'I asked what you're doing here,' she said through gritted teeth.

He stood then, skirting around the sofa and crossing to stand right in front of her. He reached out, and for one thrilling, confusing second she thought he was going to hug her. But instead his hands took the vase from her.

'Before you drop it on your feet,' he explained with a tight smile.

She didn't return the smile. 'Rio.' It was a warning. Though it was only one word, it showed how close she was to breaking point. It was both a plea and a closed door.

He compressed his lips; they were a line in his handsome face. More handsome now that she could see the hard angles of his cheeks, the cleft of his chin. She swallowed convulsively and looked away. Morning sun dappled the windows.

He turned and stalked towards the kitchen. Confused enough to be curious, she followed. He held the gloopy flowers around their stems as he tipped the water down the sink, then lifted them out and dropped them into the bin.

There were two coffee cups at the side of the sink and a plate that held crumbs. He'd eaten? Toast?

He was looking at her, and it was a look that penetrated her soul.

When he spoke, the words were quiet and husky with emotion. 'You look better.'

She took it as an assessment of her health rather than as a compliment. Her skin was pale, her eyes red-rimmed, her hair still wet. 'Thanks.'

His mouth twisted.

'This is you?'

He pointed to the fridge and one of the many photos she had taped across its bland white front.

Her eyes slid sideways, taking in the old family photo he'd pointed to. It had been taken around the time she and Jack had finished secondary school. She'd been in a full-blown *Sex and the City* phase and was wearing a fabric flower hooked into her shirt that even Carrie Bradshaw would have called excessive, with lace pink and white petals. Her parents sat as their bookends, proud smiles on their faces.

'Yeah.'

'Your brother?'

'My twin.'

He nodded, filing the information away. 'You don't look alike.'

'No.' She reached up a hand to her hair, tugging at its damp red length. 'He got Dad's colouring; I got Mum's.'

Rio was in her kitchen, and the strange thing was she felt an overwhelming sense that he belonged. It was unnerving in the extreme.

He turned away, reaching for two more cups and hooking one under the coffee machine spout. He fed a pod into the top and pressed the button. The noise was reminiscent of his machine on Prim'amore.

It sent shivers down her spine.

Fragments of the last time they'd seen each other were like sharp glass, cutting through her equilibrium. The way he'd refused to listen to her, refused to let her even try to explain. The way he'd seen only the worst in her actions.

Time away from him had dragged anger towards bewilderment. How *dared* he think he'd loved her when he'd found it so easy to turn his back and walk away? No, push her away even as she'd been begging to stay.

'What are you doing here?' She spoke with a steely determination that replicated his the last time they'd spoken.

'I went to see Wyndham last night. You weren't there.'

Mortification at having lost her job—and having this man discover the fact—caused her stomach to flip. She lowered her gaze, but couldn't hide the bright red that bloomed in her cheeks.

'He fired you.'

Her eyes flared wide; but what was the point in lying?

Spurred on to the defensive, she snapped sarcastically, 'Did he? I hadn't realised.'

A muscle jerked in Rio's cheek. Her eyes dropped to it of their own accord.

'I do not think he can fire you because you took a week off work.'

'That's not why—'

'There are laws to protect employees,' he said quietly, overriding her explanation.

She nodded, moving around him, skirting him at a safe distance, lifting the coffee cup out from the machine. He might be a guest in her home—albeit an uninvited one—but she was desperate for food and energy. She lifted the cup and inhaled its delicious scent gratefully.

'I know that. But...' She lifted her slender shoulders, unconscious of the way her robe gaped a little at the chest. 'I like him too much to fight it. I couldn't work for him now anyway. Not knowing what I'd helped orchestrate.'

Rio's eyes were watchful. 'Correct me if I'm wrong, but you had no idea Cressida was going to get married.'

'It doesn't matter.' She bit down on her lip and forced herself to meet his gaze. It would be over soon. 'I let her pay me to impersonate her. I lied to Art—a man I care for and admire beyond words. I lied to you, Rio. To *you*, the man I loved. And I'm lying to my parents now—it would kill them if they knew I'd been frogmarched out of the building by Security. That I'd been fired.'

Mortification crept along her skin at the surreal indignity she'd suffered. Strangely, she saw a corresponding anger in his expression. Had he come here to enjoy her failure? To show her how deserving she was of such humiliation?

'In any event,' she said quietly, 'none of that is your concern.'

He lifted his lip in a small flicker of a smile.

'Isn't it?'

His eyes were drawn to her face as if by an invisible magnet. He stared at her for so long that she shifted self-consciously, moving away from the coffee machine to the other side of the kitchen. She propped herself against the door, pretending fascination with the rim of her coffee cup.

'I didn't have your address,' he said quietly.

The sentence was strange. Discordant.

'The fact you're here disputes that,' she pointed out, sipping her coffee so fast she burned her throat a little.

He ignored the comment. 'Nor did I have your phone number. When you left the island—'

'After you *ordered* me to leave,' she felt obliged to remind him.

'I seem to remember giving you the option to remain,' he said, and the words were heavy with an emotion she couldn't identify. Anger? Annoyance? Irritation?

'As your paid lover?' she muttered, her stomach squeezing painfully at the recollection.

To her embarrassment, more tears drenched her eyes. She dug the nails of one hand into her palm, refusing to let them fall. Refusing to let him see her sadness.

'I was very angry,' he said, but it was not an apology and she noticed that.

'I know.'

She sipped her coffee and then turned away, walking with her spine straight and shoulders squared to the lounge. She sat on one of the dining chairs, though mistakenly chose the one with his jacket on it, so a very faint hint of *him* reached her, making her crave him so badly she felt as if she'd been punched low in the abdomen.

She cradled her coffee, taking warmth from it.

'I had thought love to be a construct, and then I met you and I lost myself completely. Discovering that it had all been an act of pretence for you…' He pulled a face. 'My pride was hurt. I lashed out.'

She swallowed. 'You had every right to be angry,' she murmured softly. 'I never thought I would meet *you*. I certainly didn't plan to…to feel like that. I wanted not to. I wanted to be able to ignore it.'

'Neither of us could ignore it,' he said with grim honesty.

'It doesn't matter now.' Her mouth lifted in what she seemed to remember was a smile. It felt incredibly strange on her face: heavy and tight.

'It matters to me,' he said, the lines of his body rigid. 'I came here today to apologise, Matilda.'

She closed her eyes. Her name—her real name—on his lips was heaven. But the knowledge that all this was coming to an end was an answering degree of agony.

'What for?'

'Take your pick,' he said, with a rueful smile that was belied by the self-disgust in his eyes. 'Suggesting you prostitute yourself to me. Telling you that all we'd shared was sex. Forcing you off my island even when every bone in my body wanted me to beg you to stay.'

Her eyes lifted to his, clashing with their grey depths in confusion.

He moved towards her now, and finally crouched at her feet. 'For telling you I loved you and then proving myself unworthy of your love in every way.'

He didn't touch her, but he was close, and just having him near her was sending goosebumps over her flesh.

'For leaving you to face all this alone, when I should have been standing beside you? For showing that I didn't support you even after I'd promised you with every kiss and every moment that I would?'

Her heart was racing but it was agony, each beat like a tiny blade pressing into her ribs. She felt it scratch and her breath burned in her lungs.

'You were angry,' she said again. 'But you need to know

that the woman you met on the island…the one you said you loved…that was me. All I lied about was my name.'

He nodded. 'I know that.'

She froze. The three words brought her an exquisite sense of confusion. *He knew that?* What did that mean?

'I think I knew it even as I was telling you to go.'

He lifted a hand and rubbed it over her knee, as though he could scarcely believe it possible.

'I went to Prim'amore to deal with my own demons. I thought I had. But then there was so much anger—anger about my mother, my father, their choices and their lives— and I took it out on you. That was wrong of me.'

She flashed her eyes to his, but looked back at her coffee instantly.

His voice was insistent. 'Because *you*, Matilda Morgan, are the love of my life, and you deserved so much better than that. I should have stood shoulder to shoulder with you, listened to you and told you that I didn't care. That nothing you could do would change the facts. That I'd fallen in love with a coffee-addicted, clumsy, teetotal book-lover, and that I wanted to love her for ever. I want to love *you* for ever.' He cleared his throat. 'I will anyway, regardless of what you say. But, *cara*, I beg you to let me love you.' He groaned. 'Give me another chance to love you as you deserve.'

The words didn't make sense.

Nothing about this did.

She shook her head, her eyes huge in her face.

Was she hallucinating? Heaven knew she'd been sick enough and Rio-obsessed enough to be imagining this.

'I had no way of contacting you,' he admitted, the words gravelly. 'And I fought with myself for a long time. I stayed on the island and told myself again and again that I was glad you were gone. But every night I would reach for you, needing you.'

'That's just sex,' she intoned flatly, her heart thumping achingly. 'Like you said.'

'No,' he denied quickly, as though his life depended on her understanding. 'It was never just sex. I've done that. I know the difference.'

Great—just what she needed. A reminder of his virility and the way he'd indulged it with other women.

'I told myself I'd come to London to see Art, but really I should have known it was all about you. I wasn't sure you'd want to speak to me after the things I'd said and the way I'd behaved. I had a whole plan worked out, to make it impossible for you to ignore me, but then you weren't there.'

'What plan?' she asked, lifting her coffee to her lips and sipping it slowly while her mind worked even more slowly.

'To surprise you at your desk. To tell you I was meeting with Art to let him know that I can never sell Prim'amore after what it has come to mean to me. That I plan to build the house my mother designed and live in it with the woman I love. That I want to wake up every morning to the sound of you making coffee and turning the pages of your book. That I want to swim through the caves with you by my side, that I will build you your very own stairway into the volcano so that you can swim in its depths any time you wish. That the island is our home—that I believe it was our home from that very first night.'

A sob bubbled inside her chest and she dug her nails into her palms again, trying to quell it.

'But you weren't there, and when I heard you had been fired I felt guilt and despair in measures I have never known. I didn't protect you. I left you to face the firing squad.'

'It wasn't your job to protect me,' she said with stoic determination.

'No, but it is my privilege to *want* to,' he corrected quietly. 'I had arrogantly assumed you would be there, waiting for me to make my grand gesture and sweep you off your feet.'

'I would have quit if he hadn't fired me,' she said with a small shake of her head. 'I betrayed him.'

'You were trying to do a favour for Cressida,' he pointed out. 'You weren't to know she was using you so that she could marry that dropkick.'

Tilly swallowed. 'Anyway,' she said softly, her heart and mind fogged from all that he'd said, unsure how to proceed, 'it's done.'

'How is your brother?' he asked.

She started, shifting her eyes to his. 'I… He's okay,' she said, though she was guilty there too, for she had been so caught up with her own sadness that she'd barely checked in with Jack.

'Matilda?' he said, and she pulled a face.

'Tilly, please. The only time I'm called Matilda is when my parents are really, really angry with me.'

His smile flickered but it was reserved; uncertainty sat heavily around his shoulders. 'Tilly,' he said, the word low and deep.

Her nerves clenched.

'I was angry with you, and yet I am so lucky. I get to fall in love with you not once, but twice.'

She looked at him in confusion.

'The woman I met on the island, whom I loved instantly and completely—the woman who opened her heart to me and buried herself deep in mine. And now you and everything about you I don't yet know. Who are your family? What are your dreams? I want to know, and I want to love all of you. Will you let me?'

She let out a small sound. A sob? A laugh? She couldn't have determined, but it was accompanied by a watery smile and a nod of her head.

'I didn't want to lie to you,' she whispered. 'As soon as

I knew how serious we were I wanted to tell you, but there was the money and… It all happened so fast.'

'I know this,' he said, stroking her hair. 'Tilly, I am sorry you lost your job. And if it's any consolation I believe Art would welcome you back with a flowery speech that would even outdo me.' He grinned.

She smiled. 'His is not an easy office to run.'

'I can imagine.' Rio nodded. 'But, as you are not working now, perhaps you would consider coming with me. Now. Tonight.'

'Coming with you where?'

His smile spread across his face like butter on warm toast. 'Into our future, *mi amore.*'

'You never told me how Art took the news?' Tilly murmured, her eyes trained on the water, looking for the first sign of Prim'amore.

He squeezed her hand and she looked up at him, her heart tripping over itself with its spasming response to the love in his eyes.

'I softened the blow a bit.'

She lifted a brow, waiting for him to continue.

'Arketà,' he explained. 'Why do I need *two* islands?'

Her smile was broad. 'You sold him your island?'

'I have it on good authority that two is excessive.' He grinned. 'It is a much better buy for him. It already has infrastructure and it is an easier commute to the mainland.'

'That was kind of you,' she said, but embarrassment at the unceremonious way she'd been dumped from her job still made her cringe.

Rio understood. 'When you are ready, we will visit him together. He was wrong to fire you, and even more wrong to blame you for his daughter's duplicity. I believe he is aware of that, and regrets his actions.'

She shrugged, her eyes turning back to the water, seek-

ing the island. 'I worked for him a long time. I really came
to care for him. It's strange to think that he blamed me…
And yet without me it would have been a lot more difficult
for Cressida to run off and get married.'

'Do you think that would have stopped her?'

Tilly lifted her eyes to his, her expression thoughtful.
'No,' she said finally, shaking her head. 'When Cressida
wants something, nothing will stand in her way.'

'Speaking of weddings…' He changed the subject subtly.
'I thought we could marry on the island. But, on reflection,
this presents two problems.'

She jerked her head to his, her eyes showing that she
didn't completely understand. 'Marry?'

'Our wedding,' he said with a nod, as though it were a
foregone conclusion.

She laughed. In the two days since he'd arrived at her
apartment they'd barely been separated. But she was pretty
sure she hadn't missed a discussion about getting married.

'Did I sleep through a proposal?'

He blinked rapidly. 'I told you, didn't I? That I want to
love you for ever?'

She laughed. 'Yes.'

'What did you think that meant?'

'I… That you love me?' she replied with a shake of her
head.

'I said I would love you for ever, and I asked you to let
me love you,' he said, his lips twitching at the corners. 'Is
that not a proposal and an acceptance?'

She tilted her head to the side. 'I don't recall a bended
knee.'

'I do,' he grinned. 'I was crouched at your feet, wasn't I?'

She slapped a hand to her forehead, her cheeks hurting
from smiling so widely. And behind his shoulder she saw
the tip of the volcano crest above the ocean, and then, rapidly, the island.

Rafaelo turned the boat sharply, pushing it around into the cove that housed the cabin.

She let her eyes drift back to Rio's face and saw he was watching her.

'We'll see,' she said with another laugh, too enthralled by being back at the island to give the conversation her full attention.

As the boat slowed into the shallows Rio stood, moving to the back and pressing a button to let the anchor down. It made a mechanised noise as it began to drop, and then Rio leaped from the boat, landing with confident ease in the shallows of the ocean.

He lifted a hand up to Tilly, and she looked at it for a brief moment before jumping overboard, happily landing on her feet before dropping into the water, grinning from ear to ear as the water wrapped her, fully clothed, in its depths.

When she stood, he was looking at her as though she lost her mind—and he loved it. 'You are utterly unique,' he said with a shake of his head.

On the boat, Rafaelo cackled softly. Tilly winked at him and then jumped up, pushing at Rio's chest until he fell backwards into the water.

He laughed as he splashed to the ground. 'Why do I think life with you is going to leave very few dull moments?'

'If any,' she agreed with a nod.

He stood, shaking his head and reaching down to scoop her up. And she let him carry her out of the water towards the beach. He deposited her wet feet on the sand and then paced back to the boat, taking their two small bags and carrying them easily towards her.

She watched him, her heart soaring. Behind him the sun was dipping down, and everything was right in the world.

'Let me stow these inside,' he said.

She nodded, tears of happiness clogging her throat. She waved at Rafaelo as he turned the boat back out to sea and found a path just to the left of the sun's golden trail.

When Rio returned, it was with an ice-cold bottle of champagne and two glasses.

'After last time?' she said with a rueful smile.

'A small glass,' he said. 'I feel like celebrating.'

'And what are we celebrating?' she asked rhetorically, because fate and destiny had conspired to bring them every good thing in life.

He crouched down, so that he could better pop the champagne cork, but before he'd taken the foil from the top he reached for her hand.

'I think you missed my proposal earlier. So let me ask you now, Matilda Morgan, if you will marry me? Marry me anywhere, any time, but be my wife for always. I want to save you from falling into volcanoes for the rest of our days.'

She turned to look down at him and saw, for the first time, that he was holding a small velvet box. And it was saturated. Her cheeks flushed as she realised he must have had it with him when she'd ploughed him into the ocean.

'Oh...' She blinked, almost blinded by the solitaire diamond. It was surrounded by a circlet of green stones.

'Like your eyes.'

The words were a love song all on their own. She felt the rhythm and verse move over her and her heart danced.

'I love it,' she promised.

'Will you wear it, Tilly? Knowing that you wear it as a sign that I belong to you and you belong to me?'

She nodded, not trusting herself to speak.

'Will you marry me? In front of our family and friends?'

She nodded again, her eyes sparkling. 'Only if you marry me back.'

His laugh filled her soul with happiness. 'I will.'

* * *

And so it was that, two months to the day after leaving the island in such a state of despair, Tilly stood before her family, her friends, and even the Wyndhams, and promised to have and to hold Rio Mastrangelo for all her life.

She didn't see them, of course. Though two hundred guests had joined them on the island, and were standing on the beach sipping champagne and adoring the obviously in love couple, Tilly saw only Rio.

She saw him as he was—the handsome billionaire who had devoted his skills to preserving buildings and objects of interest. She saw him as he had been—the boy with too much worry on his shoulders, who had loved and felt loved by one person on earth, the person who had spent years saying a slow, painful farewell to her only child. She saw him as he would be—her life partner, her lover and, yes, the father of her children.

A smile curled her lips as she thought of the tiny life shielded in her belly.

But that was her secret. A gift she would give him later, when they were all alone.

Night fell and the guests remained. A blanket of stars shone overhead, and as Tilly pressed her body close to Rio's and he wrapped his arms around her, holding her to him, a shooting star passed directly above the party, serenading it with wishes from heaven.

Tilly blinked up at her husband and smiled.

Their future was brighter than a thousand shooting stars.

* * * * *

# WE'RE HAVING A
# MAKEOVER...

We'll still be bringing you the very
best in romance from authors you
love...all with a fabulous new look!

Look out for our stylish new logo, too

## MILLS & BOON

COMING JANUARY 2018

# MILLS & BOON®

# MODERN™

**POWER, PASSION AND IRRESISTIBLE TEMPTATION**

# MILLS & BOON®

## *EXCLUSIVE EXTRACT*

Leonidas Betancur was presumed dead after a plane crash, and he cannot recall the vows he made to his bride Susannah four years ago. But once tracked down, his memories resurface – and he's ready to collect his belated wedding night! Susannah wants Leonidas to reclaim his empire and free her of his legacy. But dangerously attractive Leonidas steals her innocence with a touch… And the consequences of their passion will bind them together for ever!

*Read on for a sneak preview of Caitlin Crews' next story*
### A BABY TO BIND HIS BRIDE
One Night With Consequences

There was a discreet knock on the paneled door and the doctor stepped back into the room.

"Congratulations, *madame*, *monsieur*," the doctor said, nodding at each of them in turn while Susannah's breath caught in her throat. "The test is positive. You are indeed pregnant, as you suspected."

She barely noticed when Leonidas escorted the doctor from the room. He could have been gone for hours. When he returned he shut the door behind him, enclosing them in the salon that had seemed spacious before, and that was when Susannah walked stiffly around the settee to sit on it.

His dark, tawny gaze had changed, she noticed. It had gone molten. He still held himself still, though she could tell the difference in that, too. It was as if an electrical current ran through him now, charging the air all around him even while his mouth remained in an unsmiling line.

And he looked at her as if she was naked. Stripped. Flesh and bone with nothing left to hide.

"Is it so bad, then?" he asked in a mild sort of tone she didn't believe at all.

Susannah's chest was so heavy, and she couldn't tell if it was the crushing weight of misery or something far more dangerous. She held her belly with one hand as if it was already sticking out. As if the baby might start kicking at any second.

"The Betancur family is a cage," she told him, or the parquet floor beneath the area rug that stretched out in front of the fireplace, and it cost her to speak so precisely. So matter-of-factly. "I don't want to live in a cage. There must be options."

"I am not a cage," Leonidas said with quiet certainty. "The Betancur name has drawbacks, it is true, and most of them were at that gala tonight. But it is also not a cage. On the contrary. I own enough of the world that it is for all intents and purposes yours now. Literally."

"I don't want the world." She didn't realize she'd shot to her feet until she was taking a step toward him, very much as if she thought she might take a swing at him next. As if she'd dare. "I don't need you. I don't *want* you. I want to be free."

He took her face in his hands, holding her fast, and this close his eyes were a storm. Ink dark with gold like lightning, and she felt the buzz of it. Everywhere.

"This is as close as you're going to get, little one," he told her, the sound of that same madness in his gaze, his voice.

And then he claimed her mouth with his.

# YOU LOVE ROMANCE?

# WE LOVE ROMANCE!

For exclusive extracts, competitions
and special offers, find us online: